CARA'S LAND

ELVI RHODES
Cara's Land

BANTAM PRESS

LONDON · NEW YORK · TORONTO · SYDNEY · AUCKLAND

TRANSWORLD PUBLISHERS LTD
61–63 Uxbridge Road, London W5 5SA

TRANSWORLD PUBLISHERS (AUSTRALIA) PTY LTD
15–23 Helles Avenue, Moorebank, NSW 2170

TRANSWORLD PUBLISHERS (NZ) LTD
Cnr Moselle and Waipareira Aves,
Henderson, Auckland

Published 1991 by Bantam Press
a division of Transworld Publishers Ltd
Copyright © Elvi Rhodes 1991

A catalogue record for this book
is available from the British Library.

ISBN 0–593–02100–2

Typeset in Plantin by
Falcon Typographic Art Ltd, Edinburgh & London.
Printed in Great Britain by
Mackays of Chatham, PLC, Chatham, Kent.

To the memory of Harry, and the happy times, over many years, we have spent together in the Yorkshire Dales

Acknowledgements

My sincere thanks to Robert and Dorothy Close, of Kettlewell, who farmed in Wharfedale at the time in which this book was set. They gave me freely of their time, their memories, and their scrapbooks, and I am enormously grateful to them.

I also wish to thank Martin Leake, farmer in Yorkshire, who courteously and patiently answered my many questions.

Any errors there may be on farming matters are mine, not those of Rob, Dorothy or Martin.

ONE

Cara, beautiful in her wedding dress, her green eyes shining, tendrils of vibrantly red, unruly hair escaping from the veil which was now thrown back from her smiling face, moved hand-in-hand with her new husband amongst the guests in her parents' home. Joy filled her, delight curved her lips. It was true what people said. It *was* the happiest day of her life, of her entire life. But there were even happier days to come. She knew that with certainty, and squeezed Edward's hand to convey her feelings.

'When can we leave?' he asked.

Edward had not wanted all this. He had gone through it before with his first marriage.

'Let's just go off, get married,' he'd said.

'No!' Cara had objected. 'It's my first time. I hope my only time! I mean to make the most of it.'

'All right, Puss!' He'd given in gracefully. 'You shall have it exactly as you want it.'

And so they had, the whole works.

'We can't leave just yet,' she said now. 'You know we have to . . .'

She broke off in mid-sentence to shake hands with Miss Aitchison, her father's secretary. 'Thank you *so* much for the lovely tray, Miss Aitchison! We shall use it often.'

They might or they might not. When their short honeymoon was over Edward would take her to live at Beckwith Farm, in Arendale. It had never even been questioned that they would live in the old farmhouse with his parents. It was a large place, with room enough and to spare for all of them. Edward had been born there, and his father and grandfather before him. The Hendrys had been in Arendale since the early years of the eighteenth century, longer than any family now

9

farming there. Generations of Hendry wives had added to the contents of the house until, Cara was sure, not so much as an extra teaspoon was needed, let alone a large tray with a picture of York Minster.

'I'm glad you like it, Cara – or I suppose I should call you Mrs Hendry now that you're a married lady!' Miss Aitchison blushed deeply. Weddings did that to her. She hoped the speeches wouldn't be too embarrassing.

'As you've called me Cara since I was a little girl, I don't see why you should change,' Cara said.

Mrs Hendry, she thought. No longer Cara Dunning. Mrs Edward Hendry. I'm a married lady! She touched the slender gold ring on her finger. It had their initials and the date engraved on the inside – 31 August 1946. A sign to the world. But the seal on their marriage was still to come. With this ring I thee wed; with my body I thee worship. And she did, and she would. It was after tonight that she would feel truly married. She had no fears about it, only longings.

She would not be nervous then, as she had been this morning in church. Although the words of the service, the hymns, the presence of their friends and relatives had been wonderful and moving, standing before the altar, when she made her vows, her voice had sounded like a stranger's. But that part was over and as soon as they could they would escape from this reception which her parents had so lovingly laid on for her. Moving away from Miss Aitchison she whispered to Edward.

'I'm as anxious to leave as you are, dearest, but we shall have to stay for the meal, and for the speeches. The minute the speeches are over I'll go upstairs and change.'

'I hope your father doesn't go on and on,' Edward said.

'I hope your cousin Derek doesn't either! In my experience the best man is far more long-winded than the father!'

It was easier for the best man, Cara thought. All he had to do was to thank the right people and crack a few jokes. He wasn't emotionally involved, not losing a daughter and gaining a son-in-law he didn't particularly want.

'Didn't particularly want' was a gross understatement. Her father heartily disliked the thought of Edward as a son-in-law. The announcement of her engagement to a man her parents hadn't even met had caused a storm. Her father, never one to mince his words, had been furiously angry, deeply hurt.

'You must be out of your mind!' he'd thundered.

'Dad, if you'd only *meet* Edward . . . !'

'I neither want nor need to meet him,' he'd cried. 'You've told me all I need to know and I don't have to see him to know he's totally unsuitable! He's fifteen years older than you are, he's been married before, *and* he has two children. What's more, he's dragging you off to the depths of the country, which is not where you belong.'

'He's *not* dragging me, Father! I'm going of my own free will, and most happily,' Cara said.

'I knew no good would come of it when you went into the Women's Land Army,' Arnold Dunning went on. 'That wasn't what I wanted for you.'

'Oh I know!' Cara said. 'You wanted me to go into the Forces, rise rapidly to some high rank, and then when peace came you wanted me to be the headmistress of some important girls' school!'

'And why not? You had it in you. It would have been a damned sight better than what you're proposing now!'

'But Dad,' she'd tried hard to be patient, 'all that was what *you* wanted for me: none of it was what I wanted.'

On and on the battle had raged; on and on they'd argued, neither giving an inch. Arnold had found other objections to Edward.

'How can I hand my daughter over to a man who's a *pacifist*?' He spat the word out as if it was poison. 'A man who refused to take up arms for his King and country!'

'Doesn't it count that even though Edward was a conscientious objector he volunteered for an ambulance unit and served three years overseas?' Cara asked passionately. 'And have you thought that as a farmer he needn't have left home at all?'

'And you are *not* handing me over,' she'd added. 'I am not a parcel. I'm marrying Edward of my own free will, and because I love him!'

Beth Dunning stood on the sidelines watching her husband and daughter fight. Nothing she could say would make the slightest difference. It wasn't the first fight they'd ever had, not by a long chalk, but it was the most serious. In some ways they were so alike; red of hair and hot of temper, both obstinate as mules.

And yet, at bottom, they adored each other, she thought. Cara was always closer to her father than she was to me. But the truth was that in Arnold's eyes a prince of the realm on a shining white charger, hung about with bags of yellow gold, wouldn't be too good for Cara.

And so throughout their engagement, during which time Cara had not given an inch, Arnold had found excuses not to meet Edward until, less than two weeks ago, Cara had persuaded her father. Threatened, more like!

'If you won't meet him, then we won't get married in Akersfield. We'll just go off and do it in Shepton Registry Office. And you can come or not, as you please!'

She was calling his bluff, and she knew it. She'd be heartbroken if her father wasn't at her wedding.

11

'No daughter of mine is going to have a hole-and-corner wedding in a registry office!' he'd thundered.

'The choice is yours, Dad,' Cara said quietly. She knew she'd won. The next weekend Edward had come to Akersfield to meet her parents. The atmosphere around her father had been cool, but reasonably polite. Edward and her mother had taken to each other at once.

All the same, her father had behaved beautifully today, as she had known he would. He would never let her down. Nor would he reveal his feelings in front of all these people. He was too proud for that.

He was standing now over by the door, where her mother, an anxious smile on her face, was attempting to tell him something to which he wasn't paying the least attention. Arnold Dunning was a tall man, well built, and holding himself so straight, shoulders back, chin raised, that he seemed to add extra inches to his six feet. His hair was greying at the sides and receding a bit at the front, giving him an even nobler brow. But it doesn't make him look any older, Cara thought with a rush of affection as she observed him. Simply more distinguished. Beth Dunning, nothing over five feet, had to tilt her head back to speak to him.

Cara moved to where Edward's parents, Edith and Tom Hendry, were sitting. She wondered if they had been dismayed at the thought of their son's marriage. They *could* say she was too young, only twenty, and a town girl at that. But if they had objected they hadn't shown it. Also, they knew her. She'd worked on Beckwith Farm for the best part of two years, while Edward was overseas.

'You must have had to leave Arendale very early this morning,' she said to them.

'We did,' Tom Hendry replied. 'But farmers are used to getting up early, as you well know. I must say, love, you're looking very bonny! Very bonny indeed!'

Cara beamed with pleasure. Her new father-in-law was a taciturn man. His few words were the equivalent of a full-length speech from anyone else.

'You are that,' Mrs Hendry agreed. 'And it was a nice service. Do you know,' she added, 'I've never been as far as Akersfield before! I did once go to Leeds, but that was some time ago.'

The hired waitress came into the room bearing a tray of drinks. She was followed close behind by Grace, Mrs Dunning's twice-weekly help with the rough, now almost unrecognizably kitted out in a black dress and a frilly white apron and cap, and suitably burdened with a similar tray.

'Easy to see your father has a wine merchant amongst the bank's customers,' Edward said, joining Cara.

'Yes. We'd not have this much sherry otherwise,' Cara agreed. 'But it's all quite legitimate. There's no black market deal involved. Dad wouldn't stand for that, as you well know.'

Edward did know. His new father-in-law was as upright as a judge, patriotic to the core, upholding every edict and instruction issued by authority. He had probably enjoyed the entire war, Edward thought, and been only sorry that he was just too old to serve in the army. Which is why he doesn't like me, he reckoned. It sticks in his craw that he, with his row of medals, his Military Cross for bravery, must have me for a son-in-law.

Moreover, though in the nature of things often under fire, Edward had come through it all without so much as a scratch, while Arnold, in the first lot, had been gassed twice and collected a nasty leg wound which still niggled at him whenever the weather turned frosty.

Arnold Dunning now raised a hand and cleared his throat in a purposeful manner. It was quite enough to silence the chatter and bring everyone to attention.

'I trust each one of you has a full glass,' he said, 'because we're about to drink a few toasts!'

He would have liked to have proposed all the toasts himself, made any necessary speeches. It was, after all, his daughter's wedding. She was the important one and no-one knew her worth better than he did. But good manners would prevent him declaring what was in his heart, so he might as well do the right thing and let the best man have his say.

'When we've paid tribute where it's merited and honour where it's due,' he announced, 'my lady wife says you'll find refreshments in the dining room. Help yourselves. There's plenty for all!'

'Thanks to friends, relatives and neighbours!' Beth interrupted bravely.

'Indeed! Quite so! I was coming to that,' Arnold said. 'We shall not forget those who have shared their rations and surrendered their points for this occasion!'

In Dunning's rich baritone, Edward thought, it sounded like the last great sacrifice.

And I shan't forget Mr Thwaite, who let me have a dozen bottles of this quite passable sherry, Arnold thought later, drinking a toast. Not that it could be allowed to influence the matter of his overdraft.

The buffet was a triumph of generosity and ingenuity over shortages and adversity. Edward's mother had supplied and cooked a piece of ham which Beth Dunning, with the sharpest knife, had sliced paper-thin. This, flanked by the contents of two tins of Spam, equally wafer-like, drew cries of greedy amazement.

13

The mother of a young baby had contributed a whole bottle of orange juice issued by the clinic.

'It's a pleasure, really,' she said. 'The kid hates it. Sicks it up all over himself whenever I give it him!'

It had made a very nice orange jelly, by the side of which stood a cut-glass jug, brimful of real custard; palest yellow, smooth as silk, the eggs for which were once again by courtesy of Beckwith Farm.

'You know that my sister in Australia sent the fruit for the wedding cake?' Grace said with every glass of sherry she handed out. 'Though only the one layer is real, o' course. The rest is cardboard under the icing! What a lark!'

The other cakes on the table were real enough, though regrettably mostly fatless sponges, of which everyone was sick to death.

'Still, I have to admit, it all looks very nice,' Beth's Aunt Mabel remarked grudgingly to her niece. 'You've done a good job. Naturally I'd prefer a sit-down "do" myself. Feet under the table. They do say the Copper Kettle does quite a nice wedding breakfast for three shillings a head, and it saves you the washing-up into the bargain.'

Beth sighed. Doubtless there was an Aunt Mabel in every family, and they were at their awful best at functions.

'I know, Auntie,' she said. 'I've heard. Lettuce sandwiches, tinned pineapple and fairy cakes! Anyway, Cara wanted the reception at home and that's exactly what we've given her. It's not been easy but people have been generous. It's amazing how folks will always chip in for a wedding.'

Not you though, she thought. Not so much as an ounce of margarine.

'They'll do even more for a funeral tea,' Aunt Mabel said cheerfully. 'A sort of last tribute, I suppose.'

'Look, why don't you and Uncle Joe take your plates and sit at that little table?' Beth suggested. 'I'll bring you both a cup of tea.'

'Nay love,' Uncle Joe said when his niece brought the tea. 'Do you not have owt stronger? And I don't mean sherry. A fancy drink, that. Only fit for ladies.'

'Taste your tea,' Beth told him.

He gave her a suspicious look, then as he sipped and tasted the whisky, his face broke into a smile.

'That's better, love! Now that's what I call a cup of tea! I shall have a second cup of this brew.'

'Not if you don't keep quiet, you won't!' Beth warned him. 'I can't serve this to every Tom, Dick and Harry!'

14

'I hope you've not doctored my tea,' Aunt Mabel sniffed suspiciously at her cup. 'As you well know, I joined the Band of Hope as a slip of a girl, signed the pledge; since when not a drop has passed my lips!'

'I do know,' Beth said. 'Yours is quite safe to drink.'

'It's amazing how you've managed to cram everyone in,' Aunt Mabel remarked, looking around.

'What do you mean "cram"?' Beth demanded. 'It's a fair-sized house, we've got three good rooms on the ground floor, all in use. I don't see that anyone's crammed.'

'Now don't flare up,' Aunt Mabel said. 'It's not a bit like you, our Beth. I expect you're nervy, all this on your plate and losing Cara into the bargain.'

'I am not losing Cara,' Beth said patiently. 'Arendale isn't the other side of the world. It's no more than thirty miles from Akersfield.'

'And the train runs to Grassington,' Cara said, joining them. 'Only nine miles from Beckwith Farm, so I shan't exactly be marooned! And Edward has promised not to keep me in chains!'

Aunt Mabel sniffed. 'We'll see! Well I must say, you look very bonny. You've got a nice figure – a bit thin perhaps – and it's a nice dress, though I thought you might have worn your mother's. I expect she still has it and it would have saved coupons. She was a pretty bride, your mother.'

'I know. I've seen the photographs,' Cara said. 'But Mother was married in the twenties, with a dress up to her knees. I couldn't have worn that! Still, I'm glad you like this.'

'The bride' she reckoned the *Akersfield Record* would say, under a photograph of herself and Edward, taken as they came out of the church into the fitful sunshine, 'wore a white satin dress with a circlet of white rosebuds over an embroidered veil. She carried a bouquet of white carnations and roses. The bridesmaids, Miss Susan Hendry and Miss Laura Dunning, wore ice-blue satin and carried pink carnations. The hymns were "Love Divine" and "Lead us Heavenly Father, Lead us".'

It would not say where the happy couple would spend their honeymoon because Edward had told no-one, not even his bride.

'It's a bit easier now that the petrol ration has gone up,' he'd said. 'It won't take us as far as I'd like, but in any case we've only got three days.'

'I must have a word with Laura and Susan,' Cara said to her mother. 'And then get changed. Weren't they lovely bridesmaids?'

She found Laura in the breakfast room, looking out of the window, intently studying the garden as if she was seeing it for the first time. She was such a still, quiet little figure, standing there.

15

'All alone?' Cara queried. 'I thought your fellow bridesmaid might have been with you.'

It was a stupid thing to say. It had been clear from their first meeting that Laura and Susan disliked each other. Apart from the fact that they were more or less the same age, all they would ever have in common, and only for a few short hours, were their identical bridesmaids' outfits.

'I don't know where she is,' Laura said, not moving. 'Did you want her?'

'I wanted you first.'

Cara went to her sister, put her hands on her shoulders and turned her around so that they faced each other. Laura's grey eyes were too bright, Cara drew her close, then felt the dampness on her wedding dress as her sister's tears began to fall.

'Oh honey, please don't cry!' she begged. 'I'm so happy, I can't bear to think of you not being!'

'I'm sorry! I wasn't going to cry. I'd made up my mind not to. But oh, I'm going to miss you so much!' Sobs shook her as Cara held her close, her arms tight around her sister's thin little body.

'I know, love. And don't think I won't miss you. But we'll still see each other a lot. As soon as we get back from the honeymoon you can come and visit us for a weekend, and you can spend all your school holidays at Beckwith if you want to. So please cheer up – for my sake, pet!'

'I'm sorry. I will. And you won't let Susan stop me coming to see you, will you?'

'Not a chance!' Cara assured her.

'Shall I be allowed to play the piano at Beckwith?'

'Of course. We'll have it tuned especially. Hearing you play is one of the things I shall miss most.'

Laura had been playing the piano since she was five – seven years now. Music was in her blood and no-one knew from where her considerable talent came, though Aunt Mabel sometimes quoted a distant cousin on their mother's side who had played the trombone in a brass band – 'He were a wizard at double-tongueing,' she said. Otherwise, Laura was one on her own.

Laura had always been one on her own. She was born, after her mother's protracted and agonizing labour, with her right foot twisted back to front. Also, early on, she developed a tendency to chest infections. Years of treatment and massage and hospital visits, of her leg in an iron and her feet in special boots, had improved things to the extent that now only the boots, and a limp, remained. Her chest infections were long outgrown. But her infirmities had caused her to be thought of as delicate, to be treated as a bit of an invalid.

16

After twelve years it was difficult for her family to throw off the attitude.

'You were a splendid bridesmaid, love,' Cara said. 'Thank you very much.'

'Thank you for the boots,' Laura said. 'They felt good.'

So that her sister's special footwear, clumsy-looking and always made in black leather, shouldn't spoil her outfit, Cara had with some difficulty had a pair of boots fashioned in white leather. They were almost inconspicuous beneath the hem of her satin dress, though nothing could quite disguise her limp.

'They looked good,' Cara agreed. 'And now I must find Susan and say thank you to her before we leave.'

'I expect you'll find her near the food,' Laura said with a touch of acid.

Cara laughed at the malice. It was better than tears.

The dining room was indeed where she did find her stepdaughter. Stepdaughter, she thought suddenly! Great heavens, I'm a step-mother! Susan was gleaning what she could from a now depleted table. Her plate held a curious mixture of Spam, jelly, iced buns and lettuce leaves. Her young brother David was standing close by.

'Still hungry?' Cara enquired.

'There's not a lot to eat,' Susan complained.

'I thought we did very well, considering,' Cara said mildly. She was determined not to be drawn into an argument; not today.

'So did I,' David said. 'I'm full to busting!'

'Oh well, we all know you can eat *anything*!' Susan's voice was filled with the scorn of an elder sister for a six-year-old brother. 'Anyway, at really fashionable weddings they have the reception in a restaurant, or even in an hotel!'

'That's what my great-aunt Mabel said,' Cara observed pleasantly. 'Have you met Aunt Mabel? You'd probably get on well together.'

Susan pouted. She hadn't met any of them and she didn't want to. She couldn't see why there was all this fuss, or even why her father had to get married at all. It had been more or less all right when Cara was a land-girl, working on the farm, but she should have left at once when Daddy came home from the war. She wasn't needed any longer. And if she imagined she was going to take the place of their mother she had another thought coming!

Anger rose in her, and anger always made her hungry. She began to pile her plate higher than ever.

'I'm going to get changed now,' Cara said. 'Do you want to help me? It's the bridesmaid's privilege.'

'No thank you,' Susan said through a mouthful. 'When will Daddy be coming back?'

'We shall both be back on Tuesday. We're needed on the farm.'

'That's why Grandpa and Grandma Hendry say we have to leave for home soon,' David said. 'You can't leave the animals for too long with only Johann to look after them.'

Cara smiled at him. He was a lovely little boy, and already every inch a farmer. She would have no difficulty in loving him, and she believed he loved her. She would just have to work harder with Susan. Her stepdaughter was only twelve, still a child, and a child who had had a hard time.

In the event, it was her mother who followed Cara shortly after she had gone upstairs to change. She found her staring out of the window.

'I've looked at this same view ever since I can remember,' Cara said.

Beth came and stood beside her daughter. 'I know,' she agreed. 'When your head hardly reached above the windowsill I used to lift you on to a chair so you could see better. Do you remember?'

'Clearly! Yet you wouldn't think it was a view to interest a child, would you? Not a lot of activity.'

The house stood on hilly ground about two miles from Akersfield town centre, at a point where the town, with its houses, shops, offices and mills, began to give way to the country. From the front the view was of blackened stone buildings with their smoking chimneys, incongruously interspersed, in the fashion of the West Riding, with emerald green fields. But from Cara's room the whole aspect was different.

At the edge of the garden the land plunged down into the valley, where the beck and the canal ran side by side. It then climbed up again to where, at the distant top of the far hillside, the moors began. Along the floor of the valley the railway ran, steam from the trains etching itself against the landscape until it re-formed into a white cloud where the line curved towards the hill and the train, with a shrill warning whistle, entered the tunnel.

'It was the trains I used to watch,' Cara said. 'I used to make up stories about where all the people were going, and what happened to them when they were plunged into the tunnel. I wasn't sure they ever came out again.'

She would miss all this, but she would exchange it for the greater grandeur of Arendale. And there she would share her view with Edward. There could be no regrets about that.

'Now I really must change,' she said.

'I'll help you,' Beth offered. Cara took one last look at herself in the long wardrobe mirror. Yes, it was a beautiful dress.

'I'll see that it's carefully packed for you to collect at a later date,' Beth promised. 'Perhaps you'll decide to have it dyed, use it for an evening dress? It's good material. It should dye well.'

'I doubt evening dresses will feature much in my life,' Cara said, laughing. 'Hardly a garment to milk the cows in!'

'Oh I don't know! Not the cows, of course, but there'll surely be a Farmers' Ball from time to time, now that the war's over?'

'Well, at least I won't be wearing my Land Army clothes,' Cara said. 'They *were* terrible, if you like! Thick breeches, those awful socks and that heavy sweater. I tell you, when we went to the occasional "do" in Faverwell or Shepton, and there were ATS or WAAFs there in their smart uniforms, we felt like hiding under the table. We also used to wonder if we smelled of manure! Anyway, I'm going to find Dad now, before we leave.'

'In spite of everything he says, you're still the light of his life,' Beth said.

Clara nodded.

'I know. And I love him dearly. As I do you, Mother, though I don't always show it.'

'I know that too!'

'It's been a lovely wedding,' Cara said. 'I'm so grateful.'

'Oh, love, it's the least we could do!' Beth said. 'I'm glad all went well.'

Cara put on the suit she had chosen for her going-away outfit; a skirt of fine, West Riding worsted in small checks of green and mauve and grey, the colours soft, and blending with each other like colours in the landscape. Her blouse was pale lilac and her jacket grey. She had been lucky enough to find a narrow-brimmed hat whose colour picked up the mauve in her skirt.

'You look lovely,' Beth said. 'The colours set off your hair far better than more obvious ones might.'

And her eyes, too, Beth thought. She gets those from me. Her hair and her height from Arnold, but at least her eyes from me; eyes which seemed to change colour from green to brown, according to the owner's mood. Now her daughter's eyes were bright and clear and very green.

Cara put her arms around her mother and the two women held each other close, and kissed.

'And now I'll find Dad,' Cara said.

He was at the foot of the stairs, standing for a moment on his own, no-one around. He looked curiously lonely. Cara ran down the stairs and flung herself into his arms.

'Oh Dad, I do love you! I'm going to miss you so much!'

'I'll miss you,' he said. He found it hard to speak.

'Dad, you do like Edward, now that you've got to know him a bit? You do, don't you?'

19

'I daresay.' He wasn't giving himself away. 'Anyway, I can see you do, and I can see he thinks a bit about you.'

'And you'll come and see us at Beckwith?'

'When I can,' he said. 'Don't forget I work for a living.'

Edward appeared from the sitting room and joined them.

'The car's at the door,' he said. 'We ought to be going.'

Arnold Dunning looked at him sternly.

'Now think on you look after my daughter! She's very precious to me and her mother. So you take good care of her. You'll have me to answer to if you don't.'

'I will!' Edward promised.

The car at the door was Edward's old Morris, which had seen better days, though now it had been cleaned and polished within an inch of its life.

They got in, and Edward started the car. Cara turned to give a last wave to the guests who had come out of the house and were standing around. It was her father she looked for, and there he was, ramrod straight, a head above the rest. He met her eyes and she saw the sadness in his and for a swift moment felt guilty at her happiness. Then he smiled and waved.

As he watched them drive away Arnold felt the tears pricking at his eyes. Swiftly, he turned and went into the house.

Edward drove north-east, taking the Harrogate road and then towards York and beyond.

'Where are we going? Do tell me!' Cara said.

'Why can't you wait until we get there?' Edward teased. 'But if you must know, there's an hotel on the North York moors, on the way to Whitby. You'll like it there.'

'Have you been there before?'

'Once.'

Had he been with Nancy, Cara wondered? But surely he wouldn't take her where he had been with his first wife? She had never met Nancy, who had been killed in an air raid when she'd gone to visit her parents in Sheffield, leaving the two small children behind in Arendale. Edward, tending the wounded in the Western Desert, had been given short compassionate leave, and it was only a day or two after his return to the war that Cara had come to Beckwith Farm as a land girl. Not until just before he was demobbed had she met Edward in the flesh, though she had often looked at his photograph on the sideboard, admired the good-looking face with its regular features, high cheekbones, grey eyes.

He had never talked about Nancy, but sometimes others did. She seemed to have been popular in the dale.

'I know you'll like it there,' Edward repeated.

Cara put her hand over his on the steering wheel, leaned her head against his shoulder.

'Of course I shall, my love. I shall like it anywhere, just as long as you're with me!'

TWO

It was late afternoon when they reached the hotel. It sprawled along the crest of the hill, an old house, many-gabled, curiously shaped, as if succeeding generations had added whatever took their fancy, a wing here, a chimney or two there. Yet the whole was harmonious, welded together beneath the vast expanse of Virginia creeper which covered the walls to the eaves. The red and bronze leaves, caught in the low sun, looked as though they might at any moment burst into flame. The long drive to the house climbed to the main door. Edward drew up.

'There you are!' he said. '"Chimneys"!'

'Well-named,' Cara smiled. 'I like the look of it. Are we expected?'

'Of course,' Edward assured her. 'I booked weeks ago! Around the time you were fussing about your dress!'

At the reception desk she watched while he signed the register, Mr and Mrs Edward Hendry, and felt a glow of pleasure.

An elderly porter, looking far too frail for the job, gathered up their cases with surprising ease and led the way to their room.

'Oh, this is lovely!' Cara exclaimed. 'Isn't it a lovely room, Edward?'

Flowered curtains hung at the low window. Kneeling on the broad window seat, Edward standing beside her, she looked with pleasure on the view, to where the immaculate green lawns and tidy shrubs of the hotel grounds gave way, not far beyond, to the vigour of the moors, resplendent in the royal purple of the heather in full bloom.

'It's wonderful!' she said. Then she turned away from the view to take in the rest of the room.

The furniture was old, with the patina of age and countless polishings, the wardrobe massive, the dressing table many-mirrored; but dominating everything else was the wide four-postered bed. Cara

22

caught her breath at the sight of it, and felt a *frisson* of fear. Will it be all right? she asked herself. Shall I be what he wants? Her new husband was a man sexually experienced. Though he never talked about it, she believed his first marriage had been a happy one, but she would come to him as a virgin, inexperienced. Until now she had trusted and assumed that the depth of her feelings and the strength of her desires would suffice, but would they?

Her feelings *were* strong. Of late she had sometimes ached with desire, with the longing to lie with Edward and take his body to hers. Suddenly, she wanted him desperately, as she was sure he must her. And now at last there were no barriers between them, neither time nor place nor legalities. They would draw the curtains, shut out the daylight and the world with it, and be in each other's arms. Trembling with longing, she put down her handbag on the dressing table and turned to him.

'Oh Edward! Oh, my love!'

He held out his arms and she ran into them. He kissed her lovingly and then, surprisingly, drew away a little. It was only a little and she might have imagined it, but . . . In a matter-of-fact voice he said:

'I expect we could both do with a cup of tea. Shall we go downstairs and find some?'

Ah, but he was teasing her! He couldn't be serious. But when he quite gently disengaged himself from her embrace she looked at him, and knew he wasn't. He meant it.

Her sharp disappointment was tinged with embarrassment at her own forwardness. What a fool she was, and how nearly she betrayed herself. Edward was conventional, she already knew that, but was he also more romantic than she had given him credit for? Perhaps he wanted everything to be exactly right; the time, the place, the ambience. And perhaps five o'clock in the afternoon, in broad daylight, both of them in their outdoor clothes, was not exactly the thing. In fact, she realized, she was still wearing her hat!

Her laugh covered her disappointment.

'A cup of tea would be lovely. And a scone or something. In spite of all that spread I had very little to eat.'

Downstairs the buzz of conversation guided them to the lounge. It was crowded with late holidaymakers, but Edward found a small table in a corner, and ordered tea.

'I hadn't expected it to be so busy,' he said, frowning.

'It's because it's the first year after the war,' Cara said. 'Everyone wants to take a holiday, to shed responsibilities, be cosseted.'

'While you are taking on new ones, my dear!'

'I'm happy about them,' Cara assured him.

'Thank you, my love,' Edward said. 'And now if we don't take too long over tea we'll have time for a walk before the sun goes.'

'A walk?'

'Yes. I'll be glad to stretch my legs, breathe some fresh air, won't you?'

'Yes. Oh yes, of course. If that's what you want,' Cara said bleakly.

When they'd drained the last drop from the teapot Edward said, 'Run upstairs and get yourself a coat. It might turn chilly. But don't be long or we'll miss the best of the day.'

In their room she looked at the bed, ran her hand along the cover. Why hadn't Edward come upstairs with her? Why did he want to go for a walk when they could be here together? Or was it she who was wrong to feel like this? Was she not normal, was she too eager? She had only her instincts to guide her and perhaps they were not to be trusted.

She flung herself on the bed, face down, buried in the softness of the quilt. She was perilously near to tears. Then she jumped to her feet and smoothed down the quilt. She was certainly not going to cry on her honeymoon. She snatched her coat from the wardrobe and ran out of the room.

Leaving the hotel, Edward tucked her arm through his and held her close as they walked briskly along the cliff path. The wind there was sharp from the east, the North Sea steel-grey and choppy. Cara shivered.

'Darling, you're cold!' Edward said. 'Never mind. The walk will soon warm you up!'

They walked until the sun went low in the sky, until the cliffs and the curve of the headland were darkly silhouetted against the sky, all colour gone. Far below them the waves crashed and thudded against the rocks with rhythmic, menacing sounds. By the time they were back at the hotel, dinner had started.

'I hadn't realized how late it was,' Edward admitted. 'Well, we needn't change.'

'But I must tidy myself!' Cara protested. 'I'm all windblown!'

'You look fine to me,' Edward said with appreciation. The wind had brought colour into her cheeks and tousled her curly hair into a frame around her face. 'Go and titivate yourself if you must, and be down in the bar in ten minutes. We'll have a quick drink before we eat.'

When she joined Edward in the bar he was caught up in conversation with a man and his wife.

'Mr and Mrs Plummer!' Edward said.

'So this is the little lady we've been hearing about?' Mr Plummer was a little fat man, all geniality.

Surely Edward can't have told complete strangers we're on our honeymoon? Cara thought. Her look asked the question.

'I was just saying you were fond of walking,' Edward explained.

'I see!' Am I? she thought.

'Not for me,' Mrs Plummer said. 'My corns won't stand it. Hadn't we better go into dinner, Oswald? There'll be no choice left.'

They ate at their separate tables, but afterwards it seemed natural that the four of them should drift together in the lounge. At least it seemed natural to the others. Cara was deeply disappointed. The Plummers – he ran a small clothing factory in Leeds – would have been a boring couple at any time. Surely even Edward must feel that? The conversation, more of a monologue from Mr Plummer with occasional interruptions from his wife, at last began to slow down, hopefully to a stop. Then Mr Plummer, a sudden gleam in his eye, said, 'How about a game of billiards, old chap?'

'Fine!' Edward agreed, though without enthusiasm.

'I didn't know you liked billiards,' Cara said quickly.

'Well if you must, Oswald. But don't stay up too late,' Mrs Plummer. warned. 'I know what you're like when you start playing billiards.'

When the men had gone she turned to Cara.

'I shall give them an hour and then I shall go up. I advise you to do the same. You know what men are!'

I don't, Cara thought. That's the trouble, I don't. But surely on our wedding night . . .? Did Mrs Plummer guess they were on honeymoon? Had she given it away by not knowing that Edward played billiards? She didn't want the woman to be sorry for her.

At the end of an hour Mrs Plummer rolled up her knitting, stowed it in her tapestry bag, and rose.

'Well that's it, my dear! I've got to have my beauty sleep or I'll be fit for nothing in the morning. So good night.'

What do I do now, Cara asked herself. Shall I find Edward and drag him away? She decided she would. She couldn't go on sitting here, and almost certainly he'd be glad to be rescued. She found the billiard room, thick with smoke, thronged with men, not a woman in sight, and braved her way in. Edward was at a table, his face furrowed with concentration. She stood aside quietly until he had played his shot and then went up to him.

'Edward, I wondered . . .'

'Not now, love. I shan't be long.'

He called her love, but his tone wasn't loving. She had done the wrong thing, venturing into this holy of holies.

'You go on up,' he added.

'Aren't you . . .?'

'I shan't be long!' he said, his eyes on the arrangement of the balls on the green baize.

Cara marched instantly out of the billiard room with short, sharp steps, her heels stabbing the parquet floor. She had been dismissed, and in no uncertain manner. How dare he order her about like that? I will *not* go up to the room, she thought furiously. I will *not* do as I'm told. I am *not* a child and I won't be treated like one! On the contrary, she would go straight back to the lounge and she would order a brandy. A double brandy.

'I'm afraid I can only serve you a small one,' the waiter said, his voice icy with disapproval. 'There's a shortage.'

She took too large a sip. It burned her throat and she choked on it, coughing until the tears came to her eyes, aware that people were looking at her. Why could nothing go right? She left the rest of the brandy and hurried upstairs.

She ran a bath, defying the rule by more than half filling the tub instead of sticking to the permitted five inches. There she lay and soaked until, gradually, the hot water soothed her, body and mind. Afterwards, when she had dried herself, she looked at her naked body in the long wardrobe mirror, studying it critically. What would Edward think of her? Would he think her breasts were too small? But they were shapely, weren't they, so perhaps it wouldn't matter? And her waist was trim, her thighs long and smooth, her skin clear. But was she desirable?

'Of course you are!' she told her image. As Aunt Mabel hadn't hesitated to say, she was a bit on the thin side, but she had all the essentials, and in the right places. So snap out of it, she ordered herself. Stop being so stupid!

She stuck out her tongue at her reflection, then turned away and put on her new peach satin nightdress, on which she had squandered money and coupons as if there were no tomorrow. Well in a way, there wasn't. Tonight was what mattered.

She lay to one side in the large bed, her arms flung out over the space where Edward so soon would lie beside her. Her body was alive with longing.

'Oh I do so love you, my darling husband!' She said the words out loud, as if he were there to hear them.

She thought back to the day she had first set eyes on Edward, not his photograph, which stood on the sideboard in his absence from home, but Edward in the flesh. He had been on his final leave before demobilization and his father had gone to Shepton to collect him from the station. She had been diffident about her presence on such a family occasion and had said as much to Mrs Hendry.

'Don't worry, love,' Mrs Hendry said. 'Edward won't mind.'

He had looked so smart in his uniform: tall, dark and handsome like all the best heroes. She realized soon afterwards that she had fallen in love with him the minute he had stepped through the door, and never for a moment since then had she felt differently. He was all she'd ever wanted: he had aroused feelings and desires in her which were new, and as she got to know him she had discovered that he was kind, considerate, gentle – and often funny.

It had taken him a little longer to fall in love with her.

'All of two days!' he'd said when she asked him about it.

He'd been demobilized in September. She should, by rights, have left the farm then, since she had come out of the Land Army.

'Please stay on a bit,' he'd begged. 'I can do with your help until I get back into the swing of things.'

She'd stayed through tupping time, working side by side with him. Then somehow, because Tom Hendry hadn't been well in the winter, she'd remained through Christmas and on until lambing time.

'I couldn't manage without you now!' Edward told her.

Lambing time was the crown of the year at Beckwith: busy, absorbing; filled with many satisfactions and some sorrows. The flock was a large one and soon the meadows closest to the house were filled with small white lambs, and with the heart-touching sound of their bleating, and the deeper calls of the ewes when their lambs strayed. Cara worked with Edward every day, and often through the chilly nights.

'Lambs are like human babies,' Edward said. 'They frequently choose to be born in the middle of the night, no matter how inconvenient!'

She'd marvelled at the tenderness of this big, strong man with the frail new-born lambs; at his care and concern for the ewes. She had watched him help a ewe with an awkward birth of twins, and had been impressed by his skill and patience.

'I do believe all these sheep are individuals to you!' she'd teased.

He'd looked at her, astonished.

'Of course they are! They're all quite different from each other, just like people; and just like people, I know them by sight.'

'"I know my sheep and am known of mine"?'

'Of course. A sheep farmer understands that.'

It was during one of the most difficult nights during lambing time that he'd proposed to her. In the cold middle hours of the night a ewe had died after giving birth to her lamb – a weak, puny little thing – and another ewe had borne a stillborn lamb. Edward had held the orphaned lamb tenderly in his arms before handing it to Cara.

'We must get back to the house quickly,' he said. 'Keep it warm at all costs.'

She knew the routine, it was nothing new. They would wrap the lamb in a warm blanket, feed it from a bottle, and keep it near the heat of the kitchen fire, perhaps even on top of the oven, until it recovered.

27

While she was tending the lamb Edward disappeared. When he came back his face was pale.

'What's wrong?' Cara asked.

'Nothing. It's just that I don't like doing it.'

He had been skinning the stillborn lamb and would put the skin over the orphaned one and present it to the ewe which had lost her own. Because it was wearing the skin of her own lamb, and smelt the same, she would with luck think it was hers.

'If she takes to it, then she'll have a lamb and this little chap will have a mother,' Edward said. 'But often as I've done it, the job always saddens me until I see the ewe accept the lamb, see her begin to suckle it.'

Eventually he'd told her to go to bed.

'I'll be here until Johann comes down from the field,' he said. 'You get some sleep.'

'I shall miss all this,' Cara had said as she stood there. 'When I go back to Akersfield, I mean.'

He'd looked at her long and steadily; it was a look which rooted her to the spot.

'If you marry me,' Edward said, 'you needn't ever miss it. You needn't ever go away again. And I love you, Cara. Will you marry me?'

'Yes,' she said quietly. 'Oh yes, I will! And I love you too, with all my heart!'

The summer, though they were as busy as ever on the farm, had gone too slowly. Every minute she had been looking forward to being married, and now she was. This night, as she lay in bed waiting for Edward to come, was less than five months since that other night, but it seemed like a lifetime, a lifetime of joyful longing.

And I'm still longing, she thought. Where is he? Why isn't he here with me, lying beside me? She picked up her watch from the bedside table and consulted it yet again. Eleven o'clock!

She became tearful, then angry – and then fearful. What had happened? Had Edward been taken ill? Should she dress again and go down to find him?

But when he came into the bedroom ten minutes later, treading quietly, but clearly fit and in one piece, her anxiety quickly turned to swift, flaring anger, well laced with humiliation.

How could he treat her like this? Clearly he didn't love her, he didn't care tuppence for her! Damn the man. She closed her eyes and breathed deeply, pretending to be asleep.

Edward stood quite still by the bed. She was strongly aware of his presence, and in the end she couldn't keep up the pretence. Opening her eyes she met his, full of contrition, as he looked down at her.

'I'm sorry, love!' he said. 'Are you very cross with me? I'm sorry I was so long. I won that game so we had to have another to let him get his own back. It went on a bit. You should have gone to sleep. I'd have understood.'

Cara sat bolt upright. That was the last straw! Edward observed her clenched fists, her angry eyes.

'Gone to sleep? GONE TO SLEEP!' she yelled in fury. 'On my wedding night? On my honeymoon? I may not know much, Edward Hendry, but I do know it isn't usual for the bride to go to sleep alone on her wedding night! I may be ignorant but at least I know that much!'

Beside herself with anger, she beat at his body with her fists. He grabbed her by the wrists and for a while she struggled, but he was too strong for her.

'Calm down, sweetheart! I've said I'm sorry and I truly am. Give me two minutes and I'll be in bed.'

'Two minutes or two hours!' she shouted. 'It's all the same to me! See if I care!'

He undressed in seconds and, switching out the light, was quickly beside her. So this was the moment she had dreamed about? She had thought, fool that she was, that on this night he would leave the light on, that he would then gaze at her, long and lovingly, marvelling at every inch of her body, while divesting her of her beautiful nightdress.

You've been reading too many romantic novels, she told herself. Real life is obviously different. So far, there had been as much romance as when the farm animals mated.

But when he turned her towards him, when he caressed her, everything was suddenly different. When his hands touched her breasts she was flooded and swamped and drowned in sensations she had never known existed.

'Oh Edward,' she murmured. 'I do love you so much!'

'And I love you,' he said. 'Do you forgive me?'

She forgave him everything. She could hardly believe what was happening to her. All she knew was that she wanted more – and more and more. If he heard her sharp cry of pain at his penetration he gave no sign of it. She didn't mind the pain, she welcomed it and it was quickly gone. She wanted what was happening now to go on for ever, never to stop until the world ended, and they with it.

Then with a surge and a frenzy from Edward it was over. She was still riding on her cloud, a cloud of ecstatic longing, of desire for something not yet known, though surely there, rushing to meet her. But Edward had left her. The Edward that she knew and wanted, though he lay beside her in the bed, had gone away.

'Edward,' she coaxed, 'Edward, please come back!'

He was lying on his back, his body was stiff and motionless, and though it was too dark in the room to see his features she felt sure he was staring at the ceiling.

'Go to sleep!' His voice was quiet, his tone flat.

She couldn't believe this.

'Why . . .?' she began. Why are you suddenly like this? she wanted to ask. What's gone wrong? What have I done? But there was something in his voice which had stopped her.

'I'm sorry if I hurt you,' he said.

'Hurt me? It doesn't matter if you did. It's just that . . .'

He turned on his side, faced towards her, took her hand in his, like a child asking forgiveness.

'I'm sorry,' he said. 'Try to sleep.'

She couldn't sleep. For what seemed like hours she lay awake. She felt alone, deserted; no anger now, only cold misery, and a longing to understand. She stared into the darkness until eventually her eyes adjusted and she could see every object in the unfamiliar room. Like a cat, she thought. She made out the wardrobe, the armchair, the broad white mount of a watercolour on the opposite wall.

At first she lay in the curve of Edward's body, so that they were like two spoons in a drawer. Warmth radiated from him, but it was the warmth of his sleeping body, she thought, not the warmth of his heart and his love which was what she craved. Does he love me? Why has he married me? she asked herself. Is it me he wants, me for myself, Cara Dunning, and now for better or worse Cara Hendry? Or does he want help on the farm, a mother for his children?

Then she chided herself. Of course he loved her. And he was a gentle, caring man. She knew that side of him well enough. This was something totally new, totally out of character.

But it was the first night, the very first night of their marriage. Did it matter, in the end, that things had gone wrong this time? Why should it be perfect? People said honeymoons could be awful, that they were hardly ever like married life. Because she hadn't known what to expect, she'd expected too much: that was the long and the short of it.

Thus she tried to convince herself, but failed. After all, part of the reason why she expected things to go well was because Edward, surely, knew about women, and love. An ice-cold thought came into her mind. Perhaps he still loved his first wife, so cruelly taken from him? Was that it? Round and around the thoughts raced in her head, blacker than the night.

'Oh Edward, I love you!'

She said the words out loud. He stirred, and for a moment she thought he would waken, then he would take her in his arms and everything would be all right between them; but he turned on to his other side, away from her, and was immediately asleep again.

Towards morning the fatigue of the previous day, the wedding, the journey, the awful boredom of those people from Leeds, caught up with her and she fell into an exhausted sleep.

When the day came she wakened slowly, turning to touch Edward, but he was not there. Then she heard him singing in the bathroom, sounding unbelievably cheerful. She stifled her first faint feeling of resentment and caught something of his mood. It was a new day. Everything would be all right. What a fool she had been to lie awake worrying! She got out of bed and drew back the curtains, letting in the sun. When Edward emerged from the bathroom she smiled at him.

'You sound cheerful, love!' she said.

'Why not? It's a beautiful day out there.'

'Kiss me,' Cara demanded. 'Tell me you love me!'

'You know I love you,' Edward said, kissing her. 'But you'll have to hurry or we'll be late for breakfast. I would have wakened you earlier but you were sound asleep. So come on, love, jump to it!'

Later, Cara thought, we'll talk. We have all day, and most of tomorrow. There'll be plenty of opportunities. They would be totally open with each other, she would explain her feelings and ask him about his.

Going into the dining room she waved happily at the Plummers, sitting at a table close to their own.

'A lovely morning!' Mr Plummer called out.

'Beautiful!' Cara agreed.

Half an hour later she was sorry she had been the least bit friendly. The Plummers stopped on their way out of the dining room. Mr Plummer spoke.

'We've been saying, the wife and me, we'd like to take you two for a run in the car. Edward said he was a bit short on petrol for side trips, but we're not without a gallon or two!' He winked, and rubbed the side of his nose.

'I'm not sure . . .'

Mr Plummer ignored Cara's interruption.

'We thought we'd go to Scarborough. You've been there, of course?'

'As a matter of fact, no,' Edward replied.

'You don't say? Well then, now's your chance,' Mr Plummer said. 'We'll have a right good time, the four of us!' He turned to his wife. 'What do you say, Marion love?'

'A good idea,' she agreed. 'Certainly!'

Cara waited for Edward to refuse the invitation, as surely he would, but he didn't, or he wasn't quick enough.

'Then that's settled. Splendid!' Mr Plummer said quickly, slapping Edward on the back. 'On parade in the lobby in fifteen minutes sharp!'

'How could you?' Cara said as the Plummers left the dining room. 'Oh Edward, how could you agree?'

'I didn't,' Edward said. 'He jumped in too quickly!'

'But Edward, it's going to be ghastly! They're so boring. And I wanted to be with you today.'

'You will be with me, love,' Edward said. 'You'll be with me every minute.'

'That's not what I mean and you know it!' Cara protested. 'I want just you, no-one else. In fact, I won't go! I refuse.'

She jumped up from the table and hurried out of the room. In the bedroom she slammed the door behind her. Seconds later Edward was with her. She stood with her back to him, staring out of the window at a landscape unaccountably blurred.

'I'm sorry, love!' Edward said. 'I didn't realize it would make you so unhappy. I'll go and find them right away and tell them we can't go.'

'Would you really do that?' She looked at him doubtfully.

'Of course. If you're so against it.'

Why am I making such a mountain of it? she thought. Why am I being so awkward? She felt ashamed.

'If you're quite sure you *would*, then you needn't,' she said.

Edward blinked at her inexplicable logic.

'We'll go,' Cara decided. 'I suppose it might be all right.'

'Are you certain?'

'Yes. *And* I'll be on my best behaviour. Come on, we're due on parade!'

The outing started badly in that Cara was firmly shown into the back seat of the car with Mrs Plummer, it being taken for granted that the men would sit together in the front. But that was not ill-intentioned. Cara recognized it as typical West Riding segregation, the men together, the women likewise. It would have been unfriendly for any of them to have sat with their own spouse and unthinkable to have sat with each other's.

Mrs Plummer knitted furiously all the way, only occasionally looking up to view the passing scenery.

'I knitted like mad all through the war,' she explained. 'I can't seem to stop now the war's over. Lucky I've got grandchildren!'

From knitting, the conversation moved, via dressmaking, sewing, washing and ironing to the inevitable subjects of food and rationing. Mrs Plummer was a deep mine of recipes for delicious dishes requiring no fat, no sugar, and very little else – though grated carrot featured prominently.

'Though they do say too much of that can turn you yellow,' she admitted. 'And what do you do with yourself, love?'

What indeed, Cara wondered. How can I put herding sheep, milking cows, raking hay and muck-spreading against that catalogue of womanly virtues?

'Oh, this and that!' she said. 'You know.'

Mrs Plummer was content to leave it at that because she was off on the subject of her grandchildren, which occupied her happily until Scarborough was reached.

Edward, Cara noted with some amusement, was doing no better in the front seat, where Mr Plummer was regaling him with the trials of the wholesale clothing business.

'You farmers don't know you're born!' he said jovially. 'Plenty of food, no labour problems.'

Edward would not dream of telling the man that for farmers matters were far from easy; also he was not long returned from his quite gruelling part in the war, Cara thought.

In Scarborough, Mr Plummer drove immediately to the Grand Hotel.

'Still the best meal there is in these parts,' he said. 'They work miracles, considering they can't charge more than five bob a head. And the treat's on me! Me and Marion are glad of your company. We like getting to know people, don't we, Mother?'

'Oh yes,' his wife agreed. 'It's nice to hear about other people's lives.'

In the afternoon they walked along the cliffs, in a stiff breeze which whipped up the sea and threatened to take Cara's hat. On the way back, at Mr Plummer's insistence, they stopped at a stall to eat plates of crab.

'Delicious!' he pronounced. 'You only get shellfish like this at the seaside. Fresh from the briny!'

The journey back to Chimneys was a replica of the outward journey, except that Mrs Plummer proffered copious details of the feeding and teething difficulties of her newest grandchild and Mr Plummer berated those who had overturned the Government by voting against Churchill. 'After all Winnie's done for us!' he said angrily.

It wanted less than an hour to dinner by the time they were back at the hotel and in their own room again.

'Well, that's over!' Cara said thankfully. 'Why don't we call room service and have a quiet drink on our own before we go down to dinner? I've had just about enough of being sociable for one day. But was I good?'

'You were very good, love. I must admit it was a bit boring. I hadn't imagined . . .'

33

What he hadn't imagined was never revealed. In mid-sentence he broke off, turned ghastly pale and rushed to the bathroom, where he was violently sick. It was several minutes before he emerged, ashen-faced, his skin beaded with sweat.

'Oh Edward! Edward, whatever is it?' Cara cried. 'You look terrible! Oh my poor darling!'

'I feel terrible,' he said faintly. 'I've never felt so awful in my life!'

The words had hardly left his lips before he dashed to the bathroom and was sick again.

'I must get a doctor,' Cara said quickly. 'I'll phone Reception at once!' She was alarmed, not only by Edward's appearance, but by the violence and suddenness of his illness.

The doctor was there within the half-hour.

'Something you've eaten,' he said in a calm voice. 'What have you had?'

'We lunched at the Grand in Scarborough,' Edward said. 'I can't imagine . . .'

'The crab!' Cara interrupted. 'It must have been the crab. We all ate crab from a stall.'

'Ah! Then that's the likely culprit!' the doctor said.

'But four of us had it,' Cara said. 'Only my husband is ill – at least as far as I know.'

'Quite likely. Quite likely he's the only one allergic to it. I'll give him something which will help a bit, but it'll take a few hours for it to work out of his system.'

'*You* must go down to dinner,' Edward said weakly when the doctor had gone. The very word 'dinner' made him feel worse.

'I wouldn't dream of it,' Cara assured him. 'I'll have a sandwich sent up. But I'd better phone the Plummers, see if they're all right.'

Mrs Plummer was fine, but her husband, it appeared, was under the weather.

'Can't keep anything down,' Mrs Plummer said. 'Luckily there was a doctor about to leave the hotel, so he popped in.'

'It must be the one Edward saw.'

'I expect so. I dare say they'll both be all right by morning. Oswald had better be. We have to be in Leeds before midday. Trust the men to go under! Weaker vessels!'

By the time Cara's sandwich arrived Edward had fallen into a sleep. It was almost dark now so, not wishing to disturb him by switching on the light, she tried to read her book by the gleam of her bedside torch. Everyone carried a torch. It was a habit picked up in the war years and difficult to break.

From time to time she broke off her reading to look at her husband. Dear Edward! He was so handsome. She stroked his face, traced his strongly-curved lips with her finger, and kissed him lightly. He didn't stir.

When the telephone rang she answered it quickly.

'Mine's fallen asleep,' Mrs Plummer said. 'If yours has done likewise why don't you come down and have a coffee?'

'I'm not sure . . .' Cara began.

But he did look quite sound asleep. There was nothing she could do for him. Her book was boring.

'Very well,' she agreed.

'I mustn't be long,' she said, joining Mrs Plummer. 'I wouldn't like Edward to waken and find me gone.'

'They'll probably both of them sleep like logs until morning!' Mrs Plummer said.

Cara felt near to despair. Her honeymoon! The first night had been a disaster and now the second and last night he wouldn't even know she was there! She sniffed, trying to keep back the tears.

Mrs Plummer looked at her keenly. 'Why, my dear, I do believe you're crying! You mustn't take on so! It's nothing serious. Your hubby'll be as right as rain tomorrow!'

'Tomorrow is too late!'

'Too late? What do you mean?'

'Oh Mrs Plummer!' Cara could hold herself in no longer. 'Oh Mrs Plummer, it's so awful! We're on our honeymoon – and everything's going wrong! Everything!'

'On your honeymoon?' Mrs Plummer's voice was rich with astonishment. 'Oh, love, I had no idea! Why, we wouldn't have taken your time today if I'd known that! Why didn't you say? I thought . . . well, I thought your husband . . .' She came to a lame stop.

'Edward has been married before,' Cara said. 'So it isn't his first honeymoon. But it is mine. Oh, I did so want it to be perfect!'

'They seldom are,' Mrs Plummer said. 'Married life is much better than honeymoons. You'll see! It'll all be all right once you're home.'

'I do hope so,' Cara said, blowing her nose. 'I think I'd better finish my coffee and get back to Edward, just in case he wakens.'

He didn't waken. Mrs Plummer was right about that; he slept like a log. Cara lay close to him, then finally fell asleep. When Edward wakened in the morning he was still pale and queasy.

'I can't face breakfast,' he said. 'You go down on your own.'

'I don't want any,' Cara told him. Nor did she want to meet Mrs Plummer again. 'Why don't we get off home? Would you like me to drive?'

It was a pleasant drive, the roads were quiet. In Harrogate Edward insisted, for Cara's sake, that they should stop for coffee, though he scarcely touched his.

'I'm sorry I've spoilt things,' he said when they were on the road again. 'I mean yesterday, and then being ill. You were quite right, we should never have gone with them.'

'It doesn't matter,' Cara said. And it didn't, except that events had robbed them of the chance to put right what had gone wrong on their first night. He hadn't mentioned that. 'I'm just sorry you felt so wretched,' she added. 'And you still look pale.'

'I'll be all right by the time we're back at Beckwith,' he promised.

It was probably true. Beckwith meant everything to him, she'd recognized that from the first. And not only Beckwith, but Arendale itself. It was Edward's world. And from now on it will be mine, she thought, and I shall learn to love it as he does. That wouldn't be difficult.

She drove through Shepton, as busy as ever, the market stalls encroaching on to the main street so that two cars could hardly pass, and climbed the hill out of the town. The road, running for much of the time parallel to the river Wharfe, was almost deserted. Cara put her foot down and drove at speed until they reached the turn-off for Arendale.

'You go too fast!' Edward chided her.

'I like to drive fast. At least when the roads are empty. But I won't speed through the dale.'

It would hardly be possible. The road was narrow and twisting, the surface frequently broken, and left unrepaired for years because of the war. At first they kept close to the little river. The Aren here was sparkling and fast-flowing, impatient to join the broader Wharfe, but in a mile or so it calmed down, became still and dark and turned away from the road to hide itself behind trees on the far side of the meadow, as if it had secrets to keep. Perhaps it had, for around here kingfishers nested and small animals hollowed out homes in the banks. Beyond the river great limestone crags, shining white in the sun, rose to the sky.

'They say eagles used to nest in those crags,' Edward said. 'It must have been a long time ago. I never knew anyone who'd seen one.'

Even longer ago, Norsemen had dwelt in these western dales. Traces of them were everywhere, in the names of the farms and hamlets, in the everyday speech of dalesfolk, some of whom, with their fair skins, their red hair and their height, still looked like Vikings.

'How did the Vikings get here?' Cara asked. 'In their beautiful ships, how did they reach Arendale?'

'They sailed around the coast of Scotland, settled for a while in Ireland, then invaded England from the west.'

'You can't blame them for staying here,' Cara said. 'It's so beautiful!'

She had known some of the Yorkshire dales since she was fourteen years old. At the Whitsun holiday a teacher had brought a group of pupils out of the smoke and grime of Akersfield to breathe some country air. It was always good to get away from Akersfield and since then she had been often. But until she came as a land girl she had not known Arendale. Few people did. It was smaller, narrower, more remote than the other dales. At the far end the road petered out and the dale closed in on itself. There were not many farms – Beckwith was the oldest – and few inhabitants.

'I should quite like to have been born in the country,' Cara said.

'Well you've got the next best thing,' Edward pointed out. 'You live here.'

For the rest of my life, she thought. Our children will be born here. Did she want children? She wasn't sure, and there was no hurry. In the meantime there were her stepchildren. The thought of Susan filled her anew with anxiety and she was thankful that in a few days' time her stepdaughter would go back to school. She was a weekly boarder in Shepton.

She slowed the car down further as Beckwith Farm came into view. The house was long and low, with the farm buildings clustered around it and the main barn built on to the end of the farmhouse. There were a few flat meadows to the front and sides of the buildings, but at the back the land rose immediately and steeply, protecting the house from the north.

She drew into the side of the lane and stopped the car.

'Why have you stopped?' Edward asked.

'I wanted to look at Beckwith. It looks as though it's stood there for ever.'

'Well, it's been there a fair time,' Edward agreed.

'And now it's my home,' Cara said.

She started up the car again and drove forward.

THREE

David Hendry climbed down from the window seat and ran into the kitchen to his grandmother.

'They're here, Grandma! They're here! I've seen the car. It stopped up the lane and then started again.'

Edith Hendry dried her hands on the roller towel, slowly and deliberately, trying to prolong the simple action. She was as nervous as a cat about meeting Cara as her new daughter-in-law, even though she'd known her for almost two years as a worker on the farm. And they'd got on well enough then, she reminded herself.

'Come on, Grandma!' David said impatiently. 'We must be outside to meet them!'

'I'll not be a minute,' Mrs Hendry said.

She gave a quick glance in the mirror over the sideboard. You'll never be a beauty, Edith Hendry, she told herself. You're too short and too plump – though your skin's not that bad. That bit of you has worn well! In fact her skin was smooth as silk and almost unlined. She dealt with a stray wisp of grey hair and pushed her hairpins firmly into place. She still wore a bun on the top of her head, which made her look rather like a nicely-rounded cottage loaf.

She took the hand David held out to her. By the time Edward and Cara turned into the farmyard she and David were there to greet them. The second the car stopped, David rushed around to the passenger side, opened the car door and flung himself on to his father. Edward got out of the car, lifted his son shoulder high and hugged him.

'How are you, old chap?'

'Fine!' David said.

Mrs Hendry waited. She was an undemonstrative woman, never one for kissing, not even her own son – but this was, after all, something

38

of an occasion. When Cara got out of the car Mrs Hendry stepped forward with open arms and embraced her new daughter-in-law. It was a quick, shy hug, no lingering, and it might seldom happen again, but she wanted to give the girl a proper welcome.

'We didn't expect you so soon,' she said. She had a soft voice, an unhurried way of speaking.

'We would have been later but Edward wasn't too well, so we decided to leave straight after breakfast,' Cara said. She had been surprised and gratified by Mrs Hendry's embrace.

Mrs Hendry gave her son a quick look. His health had often made her anxious, though her husband said she worried unnecessarily, the lad was as right as rain. But she had borne Edward, after several miscarriages, when she was well into her thirties and had begun to think she would never be blessed with a family, and as a baby he had not been strong. More than once she had thought she would lose him. Well, she no longer thought that way, but in thirty-six years she hadn't outgrown the swift stabs of apprehension.

'What is it then?' she asked.

'Only a stomach upset,' Edward assured her. He took the cases from the car, handing the smaller one to David who was keeping close to him. 'Something I ate,' he said. 'Almost certainly crab. But I'm all right now, Ma.'

She thought he looked a bit peaky but she wouldn't say so. Edward didn't like being fussed. 'You never were one for shellfish,' she observed. 'What about that time in Morecambe when you ate shrimps? You were as sick as a dog!'

'You mean when I was about six?' Edward asked, laughing. 'I'd clean forgotten that!'

'I'm glad you came back early,' David said. 'And Cara too,' he added, smiling at her.

That the occasion was a special one was shown by the fact that Mrs Hendry led the way to the front door, rather than the kitchen door at the side of the house, which was the way everyone came and went. Cara didn't recall ever having entered by the front before. Over the lintel a date was deeply carved into the stone. 1703. She wondered how many Hendry brides had entered through this doorway since then. She turned to Edward.

'Aren't you supposed to carry me over the threshold?'

He pulled a face.

'In my state of health?'

Nevertheless he put down the case he was carrying, whipped her up into his arms, and carried her in.

He set her on her feet in the large hall. Its walls were dark, panelled with ancient oak, its floor stone-flagged, as was the whole of the ground floor. Rooms led off to the right and the left, known respectively as 'the parlour' and 'the best parlour', and there, Turkey-red carpet was laid over the flags. The parlours were seldom used: on Christmas Day perhaps, in the afternoon, and after a family funeral, but the arrival of a new bride was not of that order of importance.

Though they had entered ceremoniously by the front, it was to the door at the back of the hall, which led to the kitchen, that they unhesitatingly made their way. The kitchen was huge. Here tabbed rugs in sober colours, presumably made from the cast-off clothing of earlier generations of Hendrys, lay on the stone floor. The room was dominated by the huge black iron cooking range, with a bright fire in the grate even on this late summer's day. Pots, pans, ladles, and a ham, hung from hooks in the beamed ceiling, and on the rack, oatcakes were hanging to dry.

This was the hub of the house. Everything went on here: the cosseting of weakly or orphaned lambs, the hated filling-in of government forms, sewing, rug-making, ironing, quarrelling and making up again, the entering of milk yields, the ordering of cattle cake – and above all, family meals.

'The kettle's on the boil,' Mrs Hendry said. 'I'll have you a hot drink in a minute.'

'Where's Susan?' Edward asked.

His mother busied herself with the kettle and the teapot, her face hidden.

'She's cycled over to Faverwell to see Freda Marshall.' No need to say that Susan had flounced out of the house after declaring she wasn't going to be there to welcome that woman.

'I thought she'd have been here,' Edward said.

Mrs Hendry brought the teapot to the table, poured milk into cups – the best cups, Cara noted. The Indian Tree ones, which seldom left the parlour sideboard.

'Well, you know what girls of that age are like,' Mrs Hendry said. 'They live in each other's pockets!'

It wasn't true of Susan, and both she and Edward knew it. Susan didn't make friends of her own age and this sudden courting of Freda Marshall, though the two girls had known each other since babyhood, was quite out of character.

'And where's Dad?' Edward asked.

That was easier to answer.

'He's in Top Field. But he'll be down for his dinner. He's never been known to miss that!'

'I know what he'll be at in Top Field,' Edward said. 'He'll be inspecting the lambs.'

They had had a reasonably good crop in the spring and now that they were almost six months old it was time to sell them.

'He wants to increase the flock – and for that matter so do I. But we need the money to buy winter feed.'

There would be weeks, possibly months in this part of the country, when the grass would be buried deep under snow.

'We'll choose a few ewes to keep for breeding,' Edward said. 'But not many. We can't afford to.'

There were also six human mouths to feed, plus Johann Eisl, the prisoner of war who had been assigned to them from the camp near Shepton. There were Italian as well as German prisoners in the area and you had to admit that they'd been useful on the farms. They were hard workers. All the same, in Edward's opinion it was time they were sent home, but it was seemingly a slow business. Strangely enough, Johann said he didn't want to go home.

'I am very happy here,' he said whenever the subject was mentioned. He had seldom been happier in his life.

'I'll go and join Dad,' Edward said. 'Give him a hand.'

'Are you sure you're fit enough?' Cara asked.

'Of course I am. It'll do me good. Anyway, I know what Dad is. He'll want to keep far too many ewes and this year it's not possible.'

'It's always "Not this year",' Mrs Hendry said. 'Always "We might do better next year". You'll get used to that, Cara.'

'I suppose I am used to it,' Cara said. 'I've been here full cycle and more. I can appreciate the difficulties.'

But the difference is, you didn't have the responsibility before, Mrs Hendry thought. You were paid a wage – two pounds six shillings for a week's work, plus overtime at weekends. Now you'll share the responsibility with the rest of us, you'll work all the hours God sends, and you'll be lucky to get a bit of pocket money at the end of it!

'It doesn't make sense, does it?' she said. 'The Hendrys have been farming here for generations and as far as sheep farmers go they're top notch, but when it comes to hard cash there's never a penny to spare.'

She refilled the teapot, poured out seconds of tea.

'Perhaps there never was,' she added. 'Of course the war didn't help. Short of this, short of that, all the time wondering how you were going to feed the animals. And then the Government making us grow oats on land which has never grown crops and isn't suitable. Anyone in their right mind knows we can't ripen crops in this dale! There isn't long enough sunlight. Would you believe, Cara, the summer before you came we used to move them around on a cart, to catch the sun? Well, they've come to their senses about that, but we still have dozens of forms to fill in. Time-wasting, I call it!'

'I'll get you a soap box, Ma! You can stand in Shepton market,' Edward said mildly.

It was the longest speech Cara had ever heard Mrs Hendry make, nor was she usually given to grumbling. She took things placidly, as they came. Then sure enough her mother-in-law laughed.

'Oh well, what can't be cured must be endured! There's many worse, I dare say.'

Edward drained his cup and put it down.

'I'll be off then,' he said.

'I'll go with you,' Cara offered quickly.

She knew what was in his mind. He wanted to walk on his land, to feel it springing under his feet even after only three days away. He'd told her once that when he was in the war, at a moment of deep homesickness in the Western Desert, he'd vowed that if ever he was lucky enough to see Arendale again, he would never leave it.

'No need, love. You stay with Ma. I'll not be long.'

But she wanted to walk with him, their first time together over what was *their* land, or one day would be.

'Can I go with you, Dad?' David asked eagerly.

'All right then.'

They were both out of the door before Cara could protest. Through the window she watched them walk along the lane, the tall man striding out, the small boy trying to keep up with him. They turned through the gateway on the left and began the sharp climb to Top Field. Edward moved with the steady rhythm of a man who had trod this hilly landscape all his life, not appearing to hurry, yet covering the ground quickly. David skipped and jumped to keep abreast. Soon they were no more than two specks on the hillside, and then nothing. Cara turned away from the window.

'The farm always was Edward's life,' Mrs Hendry observed. 'David takes after him. He'll be a proper farmer when his turn comes. When Edward was in the army his letters were all of the farm, asking what was happening, telling his dad what he ought to be doing.'

'It was always his first love,' she was about to say – and stopped herself. This lass would expect to be his first love now, and quite right – but farmers were a race apart when it came to relationships. If there was a tussle between the awkward birthing of a lamb, or a field of hay to be cut, or a sick cow to see to, the wife couldn't win. She wondered if Cara knew that.

She reckoned Cara was a nice enough girl, but would she make a farmer's wife, even though she'd worked hard as a land girl? Edith wished she was a bit older, had more age on her back. She was not yet twenty-one and because of the war she'd not really had her fling. Moreover she was a town girl, *and* she was beautiful. Who could tell whether, when the newness had worn off, she'd find life at Beckwith too tame? Had she realized how tied up Edward was in the life of the farm? In spite of the fact that he'd travelled to far places in the war, her son was a real stay-at-home. Would that suit his young wife?

All these questions Mrs Hendry asked herself, and not for the first time, as she carefully dried the cups and washed out the teapot. She didn't want to see her son's life turned upside down again. Well, only time would tell.

'The farm is his life,' she repeated.

'I expect it will be mine from now on, and I hope to be a part of his,' Cara said.

'Of course you will, love,' Mrs Hendry said. 'It's just his way, and you can't change men's ways. His father was the same, and his father before him, as I remember it.'

'Perhaps I'll go and unpack,' Cara said. 'Then I'll help you with the dinner.'

Before her marriage Cara had occupied a small room over the stables. It had been comfortable enough and adequately furnished, but now she would share Edward's room.

'I'll give you a hand with the cases,' Mrs Hendry said, leading the way.

Edward's room was large, with deep mullioned windows on two sides, facing south towards the river and east down the dale.

'It's all ready for you,' Mrs Hendry said. 'I gave it a real good spring-clean last week when you were staying in Akersfield with your ma and pa. But if there's anything you don't like, well then you must change it. Get it to your own taste. And think on, love, if you and Edward want to be by yourselves, well there's always the parlour, *and* the best parlour.'

Cara was touched by that. She knew just what a concession it was.

'Thank you, Mrs Hendry,' she said. 'As for this room, it looks fine to me.'

It was pleasant and welcoming. For a brief moment she wondered how much of it had been chosen by Edward's first wife.

'Nay, you mustn't call me Mrs Hendry,' her mother-in-law protested.

'I'm sorry. It's just that I always have.'

'Well, it's different now. You're family.'

'So what shall I call you?' Cara asked.

'The children call me Gran – but I'm not your gran, am I? You can call me Ma, or Edith, if you prefer it. It's my name after all. And now I'll leave you and get on with the dinner. They'll expect it on the table the minute they get in.'

Mrs Hendry was leaving the bedroom when Cara called her back.

43

'Mrs . . . oh dear, there I go again! You see, sometimes I call my own mother Ma. Why don't I call you Mother Hendry? Would that be all right?'

'It's a bit of a mouthful,' Mrs Hendry said. 'But if it suits you, it suits me.'

'Good! Well what I wanted to say was that I'm very happy to be here, to be part of the family. Really I am!'

Mrs Hendry flushed with pleasure.

'Me and Dad are happy to have you. This is your home now and you must feel free in it. And as well as having you for a daughter-in-law I'm looking forward to you being a mother to the children. They need a mother. No matter how hard a grandma tries, it's not the same.'

Nor is a stepmother, Cara thought. And I don't know how to be a mother. I don't know a thing about it. She had not yet learned to be a wife, which was first and foremost what she wanted to be.

'I'm not sure that *they* will be looking forward to it,' she said. 'David might be, but I have my doubts about Susan.'

Mrs Hendry sighed.

'Susan isn't easy, I'll grant you that. You see, she's old enough to remember her mother, which David isn't. He was barely two when Nancy was killed. Susan missed her mother badly, but David found comfort in me. Any road, I'm sure you'll make a go of it, love!' She sounded more cheerful than she felt. 'The best way with Susan is to stand no nonsense – and don't let Edward spoil her.'

How can I stop him? Cara thought when Mrs Hendry had gone. I've no right to. Oh well, she would do her best and it would no doubt work itself out.

She unpacked her suitcase, and the other bags which her in-laws had brought up from Akersfield after the wedding. She found ample room for her things in the huge oak wardrobe in which Edward's clothes already hung. Cara was surprised by how few he had: a couple of suits, extra trousers, a tweed jacket. Her father, until coupons had put a stop to it, had ordered a new suit every year from his Akersfield tailor, whether he needed it or not. He was always smart, always elegant. She had been proud to be seen with him. She wondered when she would persuade him to come to Beckwith.

She arranged her brushes and hand mirror and her precious bottle of 4711 cologne on the dressing table. On a convenient nail on the wall she hung her framed message from the Queen:

'By this personal message I wish to express to you, Cara Dunning, my appreciation of your loyal and devoted service as a member of the Women's Land Army . . .'

It seemed no less personal because every member had one. She was pleased with it.

Her underwear and other small items she disposed of in the drawers of the dressing table and tall chest. Her mother-in-law had clearly been at work on the drawers; they were newly lined with pretty flowered wallpaper.

When she had found a place for everything she looked around the room with satisfaction. Really, there was no reminder, anywhere, that another woman had once shared this room, and she had been silly to think otherwise. Except the bed, she thought swiftly – and then immediately put the idea from her. She had never before felt jealousy of Nancy – how could she? Nancy had had Edward and her children for so short a time. I have him for the rest of our lives, she thought. She was not going to allow doubts and apprehensions to spoil things. The simple act of claiming her own space in the room had made her feel better and she was thankful for that.

Before leaving the bedroom she paused for no more than a second, and touched the bed lightly. Then she went downstairs to join her mother-in-law in the kitchen.

'I love *this* room!' she said, looking around.

'Of course in the old days we'd have had a dozen hams and sides of bacon hanging up there,' Mrs Hendry said. 'Not like now!'

'Everything feels so permanent,' Cara said.

'I suppose it should,' Mrs Hendry said. 'It's been used by so many generations of Hendry women and I doubt if any of them have made many changes. I certainly haven't. A farmer's wife is too busy to start moving the furniture around! I know I always have been.'

'Well, I'll be glad to help you,' Cara offered. 'When I'm not busy outside. I shall have to see what Edward wants me to do, what regular jobs he has for me, I mean.' She hoped she'd work a great deal on the farm, rather than being relegated to the house, though probably Edward would see that as improving her lot, not as relegation.

'I'll not say no to a bit of help,' Mrs Hendry said. 'I'm nearing seventy and it doesn't come any easier with age. Of course I don't do as much as I used to. At one time, before the war that is, I made the butter and the cheese and sold them in Shepton market, along with the eggs and the oatcakes. Regular as clockwork, every Saturday morning. I did a good trade, but I gave it all up when rationing came in. The game wasn't worth the candle. Then later on I had the childer to look after, and Edward away and all.'

'What can I do now?' Cara asked.

'You could lay the table. They'll be here in a few minutes and everything's ready. I've made a rabbit pie. Thank God for rabbits, I say, though normally we don't like them. They foul the land and encourage poachers. And a rice pudding to follow. At least we don't have to bother with milk rationing like they do in the towns. However does your poor mother manage?'

'Not easily,' Cara admitted. 'Especially as Dad likes his puddings. I was going to ask you, Mother Hendry, when do you think I might invite them to Beckwith – my mother and dad and Laura?'

'Good heavens, any time you like!' Mrs Hendry said. 'It's your home now.'

'I thought I'd like to ask them as soon as next week's sheep sales are over. The only thing is, Edward said we might be cutting a second crop of hay then, on the low meadow, if the weather keeps up.'

'I'm not so sure we'll get a second crop, but it *is* important,' Mrs Hendry agreed. 'It makes all the difference to the winter feeding. But if so be as we are hard at it, I dare say your family could help. We can always use extra hands at such times.'

Can I see my father bringing in the hay? Cara wondered. But why not – except that he'll tell Edward how to do it more efficiently!

'I'll see what Edward thinks,' she said. 'Shall I lay a place for Susan?'

'I wish I knew,' Mrs Hendry said. 'Who knows when she'll show up?'

Cara was not sure whether she wished her stepdaughter would come home soon, so that the meeting between them could be over, or stay as long as possible, postponing the encounter. She was pretty sure it would be an encounter.

As punctually as if they had all been drawn there by a magnet, Edward, David, Tom Hendry and Johann came into the kitchen. They queued to wash their hands at the sink then sat at the table.

'Now lass,' Tom Hendry said to Cara. 'How are you then? You're looking fair bonny!'

'Thank you, Tom. I'm fine,' Cara said. She had always called him Tom. 'How are you?'

'Middling,' he admitted, pulling up his chair to the table.

'Rabbit pie,' he observed. 'They say there's a fellow catching a hundred rabbits a day up Pen-y-ghent. Sells them to the market.'

David looked up from his dinner.

'You can tell the weather from the rabbits,' he said.

'Tell the weather? How?' his grandmother asked.

'If they eat a lot of grass in the afternoon it's going to be a wet evening.'

Tom smiled at his grandson.

'The lad's right! My father told me that when I were knee-high to a grasshopper!'

The rest of the meal was eaten in comparative silence, but Cara was used to that. As a family the Hendrys didn't hold with interrupting the serious business of eating with idle chatter.

Johann was silent throughout, partly, Cara supposed, because he had very little English. He ate like a man who knew what it was to go hungry, devouring every morsel, scraping his plate, and never refusing a second helping. At the end of any meal he never failed to thank Mrs Hendry for providing it.

'A bit more pudding, Johann?' she said now.

'May I have the dish to scrape, Grandma?' David asked. 'I like the brown sticky bits best of all.'

Edward finished his meal quickly and rose from the table.

'Johann, there's a bit of wall needs seeing to in Top Field. I noticed it this morning. If it's not done we'll have the lambs jumping over. Near the gate on the left – and you could look at the gate at the same time. It needs strengthening.'

Johann was the jack of all trades on the farm. He had been hired out to them as someone who knew a little about farming, but when faced with the actual jobs proved to know nothing at all. In Austria, his native country, his trade had been woodcarving. He had carved figures which sold in the shops in Salzburg, but he had never set foot on a farm. All the prisoners wanted to work on the farms, and claimed expertise which more often than not they didn't have. Such work released them from the boredom of the camp and, in most cases, they were much better fed.

Tom Hendry had been fit to send Johann packing when he learned the truth, but in the end he'd agreed to give the man a trial. Johann had proved adaptable, quick to learn and hardworking. He was also quiet and self-effacing, which Tom liked.

'I'm going down to Low Pasture,' Edward said. 'If Susan phones, tell her to set off from Faverwell in time to get home before dark.'

'You'll not fetch her in the car?' his mother asked.

'No. She can walk. I'm too busy.'

'She'll not like that,' Mrs Hendry observed.

It was four miles from Faverwell, nor was it like Edward not to fetch Susan even when petrol was short. He must be pretty mad at her for not being at home when they arrived.

'I'll fetch her,' Cara offered.

'I'm counting on you to help me fill in some returns,' Edward said.

'And so I will. But it won't take me long to fetch Susan.' I might even notch up a good mark with the young lady, Cara thought.

Perhaps the same thought occurred to Edward.

'Very well,' he agreed. 'If you don't mind.'

He had just left the yard when the phone rang. Cara answered it. It was Susan.

'I'd like to speak to my father,' Susan said.

'I'm sorry, he's gone. Can I help?'

'Put Grandma on.' It was a brusque command.

Cara handed the telephone to Mrs Hendry, who listened, then said, 'Your dad's too busy. Cara's coming to fetch you.'

'I don't want her,' Susan said. She shouted down the phone and Mrs Hendry reddened. The young monkey had done that on purpose, knowing full well that Cara could hear.

'Take it or leave it,' she said tersely.

'I'd rather walk,' Susan replied.

'If you're staying to supper there you'd better leave in good time,' her grandmother advised. 'If you're not home before dark you'll be in trouble with your dad.'

There was a quick click as Susan rang off. Mrs Hendry turned to Cara.

'Try not to mind her, love. She'll come round. After all, you've got on all right with her up to now, and you will again.'

'I never had much to do with her,' Cara said. 'She was at school during the week and a lot of the weekends I was in Akersfield. Our paths didn't cross that often.' But when they did, she thought, when she was around in the school holidays we seemed to manage all right.

'It's not me Susan dislikes,' Cara went on. 'It's the situation. She doesn't want me in the family.'

'Well she's got you, hasn't she?' Mrs Hendry said. 'And since the rest of us are pleased to have you she'll have to learn to like it.'

'We'll see. Shall I go and fetch her later on, in spite of what she says?'

'No,' Mrs Hendry said. 'Let her walk. She can walk some of her temper off!'

Towards teatime it began to rain, suddenly, heavily.

'When it rains in Arendale there's no half measures about it,' Mrs Hendry said. 'It's coming down like stair rods!'

Edward came back to the house, followed by his dog, which shook itself vigorously and showered everyone else.

'Did Susan phone?' he asked.

'Yes,' Cara said. 'You hadn't been gone long.'

'What time are you collecting her?'

'I'm not. I'm not her choice of chauffeur. She said she'd walk.'

'Did she indeed!' Edward said grimly.

Without another word he left the house, got into the car and set off down the dale.

Forty minutes later he was back again, Susan with him. She marched into the house, head high, mouth closed in a thin, straight line, went through the kitchen like a sharp north wind and up the stairs to her room, slamming every door behind her.

Mrs Hendry and Cara stared at Edward, waiting for an explanation.

'She's mad at me because I made her leave the Marshalls there and then,' he said. 'Says I showed her up in front of her friends.'

'Why did you fetch her?' his mother asked. 'Why didn't you let her walk?'

'In this rain? In a summer dress?'

'A drop of rain might have cooled her temper!' Mrs Hendry remarked tartly.

It's my fault, Cara thought. None of this would have happened if I hadn't been here. But she didn't intend to let it pass. She would give Susan a little time to simmer down and then she'd go up and have it out with her. Her stomach lurched at the thought, but it had to be done.

An hour later she knocked on Susan's door.

'It's me. May I come in?' she called out.

'Go away!'

Cara could tell by the thickness of Susan's voice that she had been crying.

'I won't go away, Susan. You and I have to talk. Please unlock the door!'

She turned the knob as she spoke. To her surprise the door wasn't locked. She opened it and went in, and stood in the doorway.

Susan, who had been lying on the bed, jumped to her feet.

'How dare you come into my room! Get out!'

'I will quite soon,' Cara said. 'But not just yet. We have to talk, Susan. We can't go on like this. I know you resent me and I understand . . .'

'You don't understand anything!' Susan interrupted. Her voice shook with passion. 'If you did you wouldn't be here. You'd be where you belong, in Akersfield.'

Cara sat down on the nearest chair. She had to sit, her legs were trembling. For a moment she couldn't find her voice.

In the silence she looked at the wall, straight at a photograph of Edward and Nancy on their wedding day, the pair of them radiant with happiness. She looked away, only to find herself staring at the photograph on Susan's dressing table. It was a studio photograph, in a silver frame, of Nancy. Her blond hair fell like heavy silk to her shoulders – that's where Susan gets her corn-gold mane, Cara thought. Her features were small and even; her blue eyes, large and lustrous, were alight with invitation. Scrawled across the photograph were the words 'Eddy, With all my love, Nancy'.

49

Cara found her voice.

'Your mother was a beautiful woman,' she said steadily. 'She looks nice. I'm not surprised you miss her.'

'Of course she was beautiful!' Susan said scornfully. 'She was the most beautiful woman you ever saw. I don't suppose Daddy told you that?'

'No he didn't. I know almost nothing about your mother,' Cara admitted. 'But I should like to hear.'

'She was beautiful and clever and lively. Daddy adored her. She gave *him* that photograph when he was going off to the war. He was going to throw it away afterwards because he couldn't bear to look at it, but I made him give it to me.'

Cara was aware that Susan was watching her, waiting for her reaction. She *wants* to hurt me, she thought, but I won't let her.

'I understand how you must have felt when she died,' she said quietly. 'Your father, too.'

'Stop saying you understand!' Susan cried. 'You don't at all. And she didn't just die, she was killed. And when Daddy was sent home on leave he was so upset I thought he might die, too! It was horrible! So how could he marry *you*? How could he forget *her*? I never shall! Never!'

'I'm sure your father hasn't forgotten,' Cara said. Her heart felt like a stone. She understood now why Edward never mentioned his first wife. He couldn't bear to.

'Life has to go on,' she said. 'We have to make fresh starts. I dare say your father wants companionship again.'

That's what he wants of me, she thought miserably. Companionship.

'Well, he doesn't love you,' Susan said defiantly. 'When Mummy died he told Gran he'd never love any woman again. Ask her if you don't believe me!'

'He does love me,' Cara said. She knew she was trying to convince herself as well as her stepdaughter. 'He *does* love me, but perhaps not in the same way. There's more than one kind of love. And I love your father very much, and I would love you if you'd let me.'

'I don't want it,' Susan said harshly. 'No-one can be like Mummy. No-one can take her place. Daddy knows that as well as I do.'

Cara looked at Susan's white face, at her eyes brimming with tears which she was too proud to shed, and felt desperately sorry for her. We're in the same boat, she thought, Susan and me. Both of us wanting all of Edward's love, both of us having to share: she with me, me, it seems, with Nancy.

'I don't want to take your mother's place,' she assured Susan. 'I want my own place. Is that so bad?'

Suddenly, she could take no more.

'I'll leave you now,' she said. 'But any time you want to be friends, I'll be ready.'

When she went to bed with Edward that night she was not surprised that he made no demands of her, clearly didn't want to make love.

'I'm jolly tired,' he said. 'I expect you are too.'

He had married her to take Nancy's place and that, it seemed, she couldn't do. Not for him, not for his children.

FOUR

Every day this week it had been almost dark, no more light to work by, before the men came in for supper. Now they were seated at the table enjoying cold ham and pickles, fresh-baked bread spread with rich golden butter which Mrs Hendry still made herself.

'There's apple pie and a bit of cheese to follow,' Mrs Hendry said. 'Get that lot down you and you'll not come to much harm!'

She had also made the cheese; white and creamy, but with a tang, made to the recipe she had learned as a girl in Wensleydale.

'I'm not sure you're allowed to make cheese if you're not registered for it, Ma,' Edward teased, cutting himself a generous piece. 'I think there's a regulation against it.'

'Oh, there's sure to be,' Mrs Hendry agreed. 'There's a regulation against everything. But I personally haven't set eyes on it and I don't intend to. What the eye doesn't see the heart doesn't grieve over.'

'And ignorance of the law is no excuse. I wonder if you'd be sent to prison,' Edward mused.

'Well if I am, you'll go with me, since you're eating it!'

She turned to her grandson.

'A bit for you, David? I reckon you've worked as hard as the men today.'

'No thank you, Gran,' David said.

He yawned widely. It had been good up on the fells with his father and grandfather, and Ruby and Bess, the dogs. He'd enjoyed every minute of it, felt like a real farmer, but now he was tired. He was sorry the holidays were almost over. Next week he'd have to go back to school.

'I think you should go to bed, love,' Cara said.

'I haven't shut the hens up yet,' David told her. It was his responsibility, every evening, to see that they were safely cooped for the night.

'I'll do it for you this once,' Cara offered. It had been too long a day for a six year old, but David was so keen.

'Go on up,' she said. 'I'll come and tuck you in presently.'

'Isn't it time you went to bed, Susan?' Edward asked his daughter. 'You're not looking quite the thing.'

'I'm not the least bit tired,' Susan said. 'And I'm not a small child, even if I'm treated like one.'

They were the first words she had uttered throughout the meal. And no wonder she's not tired, Cara thought, she's done nothing but moon about all day. Still, they had had no further confrontations, she and Susan, though Cara wasn't certain whether the vow of silence her stepdaughter seemed to have taken wasn't worse. If they couldn't communicate they'd get nowhere.

'Will *you* come and tuck me in?' Susan asked her father. Her tone was sweetly persuasive.

'I thought you were too grown-up,' Edward said. 'Isn't that what you were just saying?'

Poor girl, she doesn't know *what* stage she's at, Cara thought. One minute she's too old, the next she's younger than David. But Edward can't see that. She felt sorry for her.

'Not if *you* do it, Daddy!' Susan said pointedly.

'All right. But get to bed soon. I shan't be long myself.'

'You look tired,' Cara said.

But it was her father-in-law who looked ready to drop. It was also too long a day for a man turned seventy, even though he was used to it.

They'd been sorting out the sheep which would go to Shepton market for next week's sales. There were the surplus lambs from this year's crop, fat lambs for the butcher, store lambs to be fattened up on lowland farms. And then there were the older ewes which had produced five lots of lambs and were now to be sold to lowland farmers.

'I'm allus sorry to see the old ewes go,' Tom said. 'It's like parting wi' friends. But they'll have an easier life where they're going, happen lamb for another two or three years.'

'It's been a busy day,' Edward said. 'The difficulty is sorting out which ewe lambs to keep for breeding. They can't be put to the ram until November next year, so it's a bit of a gamble. Always is. But we've got to keep enough to replace the old ewes we're selling, and a few more to increase the flock.'

'I think we've got it about right,' Tom Hendry said.

'I reckon we should buy another ram or two in the October sales,'

Edward suggested. 'There's last year's ewes ready to be served come tupping time.'

Tupping time was when the rams, usually called 'tups', were set free among the ewes for mating.

'I didn't realize until I came to work here that you chose tupping time as carefully as the date for a favourite daughter's wedding,' Cara said.

'It's more important,' Edward said. He turned to Susan. 'I hope you'll remember that when your turn comes to wed, young lady!'

'Don't worry, Daddy, I am *never* going to get married,' Susan said emphatically. 'And if I did,' she added, 'it would *never* be to a farmer!'

'Hoity-toity miss!' Mrs Hendry said. 'You could do a lot worse!'

In Arendale, tupping time was usually around the second week in November, chosen so that the new lambs would be born in April when the fresh green grass was coming through. The grass was all-important.

'So are you going to give this lot a bloom dip?' Mrs Hendry enquired. The sheep had been dipped earlier in the summer, against ticks and suchlike, but the bloom dipping was simply to make them look better when they were offered for sale.

'It's a daft business, that,' Tom Hendry said. 'We know, and the buyer knows, that they've been dipped just to prettify 'em.'

'Nevertheless, we get a better price, or sell them quicker, if they look good,' Edward said. 'We thought we'd start it on Friday.'

Mrs Hendry put down the dish she was holding and looked at her son in consternation.

'Nay, Edward love, I don't like that! I don't like Friday!'

'Why not, Ma?' Edward asked – as if he didn't know!

'It's bad luck, that's why. Never start anything new on a Friday. There isn't a farmer's wife in the dales wouldn't say the same. You know that as well as I do!'

'Nothing but superstition, Ma,' Edward said.

'Call it what you like,' she said. 'But don't do it. Why, we'd never even start haymaking on a Friday, even if the weather was set fair and the grass was right. Not on a Friday!'

'Well we can't start sooner and we can't afford to wait longer,' Edward said obstinately.

'Then don't blame me if something happens,' his mother said angrily.

'I won't, Ma,' Edward promised.

'I'm off to bed,' Tom Hendry said suddenly. 'I'm all in!'

His wife looked at him critically.

'You look it,' she admitted. 'You're too old to work like you do. You're a fool to yourself, Tom Hendry! Edward, why do you let him?'

Edward shrugged.

'You tell me how to stop him and I'll do it,' he said. 'He's as obstinate as a mule!'

'Good night all,' Tom said, getting up from the table. 'You can chew me over when I've gone, but if you don't mind I'll not stay to hear it!'

There was a knock at the door and Johann entered. He never came in without first knocking and, with fine tact, he never presumed to eat this last meal of the day with the family.

'You've finished the milking?' Mrs Hendry queried, then thought what a daft question that was. Of course he had or he wouldn't have presented himself.

'Yes thank you, Mrs Hendry,' he said. 'Primrose was . . .' He struggled to find the English word he wanted. '. . . difficult . . . again. She is naughty, that one!'

'She is,' Cara agreed. 'She tries it on with me sometimes!'

Mrs Hendry handed Johann a tray set with his supper.

'There you go,' she said. 'Good night.'

'Good night, Mrs Hendry.'

With the utmost courtesy he bade each of them in turn a formal good night before taking the tray to the privacy of his quarters, a lean-to affair at the far end of the barn. There, when he had eaten his supper, he took up a piece of wood he had found in the copse by the river and began to carve it into yet another small animal. His animals were ranged around the room. He wished he had someone to whom he could give them.

While he whittled away he listened to the music of a Mozart quintet on an ancient wind-up gramophone which Mrs Hendry had found for him in the attic. She had found the records too: military marches, the Indian Love Lyrics, and a song called 'Asleep in the Deep' sung by Dame Clara Butt in a voice which would have served as a foghorn to any ship at sea.

It was the Mozart he listened to most. It reminded him of his homeland, his beautiful land of mountains and lakes. Yet he didn't want to go back there. His parents had been taken and shot and he had no other relatives, so what would he go back to except unhappy memories? His daily prayer was that he would be allowed to stay here.

As Cara emerged from the house with Edward, who always did a round of the buildings to check on the livestock before going to his own bed, the strains of Mozart on the worn record drifted across the farmyard.

'Poor old Johann,' she said, tucking her arm through Edward's. 'I really must get him another record or two when I go into Shepton. If only he could sell some of his carvings he could buy records.'

'None of which would sound up to much on that old gramophone,' Edward said.

When everything had been seen to and Edward was satisfied, Cara said, 'Let's take a walk, just a short one. It's such a lovely evening and a walk will relax you!'

And perhaps it will make you feel more in the mood to make love to me, she thought.

They walked down the lane and climbed over the stile to the footpath which led down to the river. The day's warmth still lingered on the air, mingled with the scents of a variety of grasses. Everything was highlighted by the full moon, but with a silver light, gentler than that of the sun.

'I love the smell of the grass at night,' Cara said.

'Which reminds me,' Edward replied. 'I've taken another look at Low Meadow. We won't be able to cut the grass the week after next, as I'd hoped. It won't be ready. Perhaps it won't be at all and we'll have to give up the idea. Pity!'

Must he always think about farming? Cara asked herself. The night was so beautiful.

At the river bridge they stopped, and leaned over the stone parapet, peering into the dark water which lapped and gurgled and ran as if there were no difference between night and day. In the daytime you could watch the trout here, but not now, she thought, until suddenly one was caught in a shaft of moonlight before it darted under the shadow of the bridge.

They stood there in silence until Cara said: 'Do you really love me, Edward?'

He looked at her in astonishment. 'Of course I do! You know I do.'

'Sometimes I don't know. Oh Edward, I do want to be a good wife! I want us to be happy.'

'Who's complaining?' he asked. 'I'm not.'

'I know I might be different from Nancy . . .' she began.

At the mention of his first wife's name she felt his whole body stiffen.

'I'm sorry . . .' she said hesitantly.

'If you want to please me you won't mention her name,' he interrupted harshly. 'Is it too much to ask?'

'Of course not. It's just that sometimes I feel . . . shut out.'

'You're talking rubbish,' he said. 'You're my wife, aren't you? I chose you, didn't I? You're being fanciful.'

If there had been tenderness in his voice the words would have reassured her, but there was none. She had angered him, and now he had angered her. She withdrew her arm from his and began to walk quickly.

'Let's get back home,' Edward said. 'It's turning cold.'

It *was* turning cold, Cara thought. A sneaky wind had sprung up from nowhere. She started to shiver.

Edward made love to her that night, but once more it was, to her, as if he did it in protest against some appetite which drove him. Like a secret drinker. He seemed hardly aware of *her* part in this, let alone of her needs. Afterwards, when she would have questioned him, he was already asleep, or appeared to be.

Cara's nerves jangled with unfulfilled longings. What am I to do? she asked herself. True, they had been married less than a fortnight, but if he had no appetite for her now, in the first flush of their marriage, when would he have? But appetite, she reminded herself, he did have; an appetite which he satisfied as quickly as possible, like a hungry man, needing to be filled but tasting nothing. If she were to conceive a child in these circumstances she would hardly believe that any part of it was hers.

Much later she fell asleep, having resolved nothing except that she would not invite her family to Beckwith just yet. They were too perceptive, especially her mother. She would know almost at once that all wasn't well, and for now Cara wished to keep what she felt as her failure, to herself. All the same, she longed to see them. Perhaps she would go to Akersfield. If they were not going to cut Low Meadow there would be a lull in the work of the farm.

On the following Monday David returned to school for the start of the new term.

'I'll take you into Faverwell,' Cara offered at breakfast. 'In any case there are one or two things I want to buy there.'

'You can pick up the tea and sugar rations,' Mrs Hendry said. 'And ask Winnie Sykes if she's got that elastic in yet. I've been waiting a month of Sundays for it.'

'What do you want elastic for, Gran?' David enquired.

'What do you think, lad!' she laughed. 'Let's just say if I don't get it things could be very awkward. Now here's your sandwiches, love, and an apple and a piece of parkin. Think on you eat them all at dinnertime.'

The school at Faverwell, by far the biggest village in the area, was the only one in the dale. It catered for children up to eleven years old. They were drawn from Faverwell itself, and from neighbouring dales within a radius of about five miles.

'Will Miss Pratt still be there?' David asked.

'Of course, love!' his grandmother assured him.

Miss Amy Pratt taught the whole school, thirty children in all. In the early days of the war, when the evacuees had flocked from the West Riding (most of them to return, bored to tears, within six months), the numbers had risen to more than fifty and Miss Sedgwick had had to be brought out of retirement to help teach again.

'Can we buy some sweets?' David asked Cara as they drove towards Faverwell.

'I don't think you have any sweetie points left,' Cara said, then seeing the child's face fall added, 'but I think I have a few. We'll see!'

She parked the car and, as it was the beginning of a new school year, went in with David to speak to his teacher, who at this moment was surrounded by parents and children.

'Good morning, Miss Pratt,' she said when it was her turn. 'David has had a lovely holiday, as no doubt he'll tell you. I hope you have.'

'Thank you. I've been to Bridlington. Very bracing. And may I wish you much happiness, Mrs Hendry. I haven't seen you since you were married.'

'I haven't been into Faverwell,' Cara said. 'I've come to collect the rations.'

'They say there's some elastic at the shop,' Miss Pratt whispered.

They chatted for another minute or two – there was never any hurry in Faverwell – before Cara left, and almost immediately returned.

'I forgot to tell you, Mrs Stansfield will give David a lift home as far as Aren bank, and he'll walk from there. If it turns out wet I'll come to meet him. Good luck, Miss Pratt.'

Rather you than me with thirty children, she thought.

In the village store she collected the rations and after a conversation conducted in low voices, was handed a small parcel.

'A yard for you and the same for Mrs Hendry,' the shopkeeper said. 'I reckon it's just about come in time, the elastic. Another month and half the knickers in Faverwell would be at half mast!'

There were two other shops in Faverwell, a cobblers, which had been there as long as anyone could remember, and a gift shop which had opened a year or two before the war to cater for the visitors who came there in the summer, and had somehow kept going, though mostly now with second-hand goods. Cara visited this shop whenever she was in Faverwell. Now she had the idea that she might buy some small gift for Susan to take back to school. The two of them were on no better terms, but she wasn't going to fail for want of trying.

'Hello, Miss Wilding,' she said. 'May I look around?'

'Of course, love! Are you looking for something special?'

'Yes,' Cara said. 'But I won't know what it is until I see it.'

Really she had no idea. She rummaged around, hoping for inspiration, discarding brooches and beads and belts. She wanted nothing too intimate, nothing which Susan might feel obliged to wear in front of anyone else. She had almost gone through the contents of the little shop, almost given up the idea altogether, when she found what she wanted. It was a small book, about six inches by four inches and almost an inch thick. The covers were marbled paper and the spine was of red leather, tooled in gold. Most exciting of all, the book had a small gilt clasp with a lock and key. At first she feared it might be a volume of poems, not at all what Susan would want, but when she opened it she was delighted to find that the pages were entirely blank. It was a journal, waiting to be written in. Quite perfect, she thought.

'How much is this?' she asked.

'You can have it for half a crown,' Miss Wilding said. 'It came in with some second-hand things from Leeds only a few days ago. All quality stuff. It's pretty, isn't it?'

'Yes,' Cara agreed. 'I think it will do very well.'

When she arrived back at Beckwith, Susan was not there, but it didn't matter. She'd rather not hand the gift to her directly. She planned to leave it on Susan's dressing table, and this she did, saying nothing to anyone, simply writing on the wrapping paper, 'Best wishes for a happy term, Cara'.

'Was the lad all right?' Mrs Hendry enquired.

'He seemed fine,' Cara said. 'He likes school, and obviously he gets on well with Miss Pratt. Will it be convenient if I go into Shepton tomorrow when they go to the sale?' It was also the day Susan was due back at school.

'Nay lass,' Mrs Hendry protested, 'you don't have to ask my permission! You're a free spirit. You can come and go as you like!'

'Is there anything you want from the market, or the shops?'

'I'll make a list,' Mrs Hendry said. 'Though most of the things on it you won't find. Whatever happened to pomegranates, I wonder?'

'Where's Susan?' Cara asked.

'She went off with Johann. Funny how she gets on with him, even when she's at cross purposes with the rest of us.'

Johann, Cara knew, was examining the walls and repairing them where necessary. When Cara first set foot in the Dales it was the dry-stone walls which had caught her eye before anything else. Miles and miles of them, dark grey in the rain, silver white in the sun, they climbed everywhere: across the land, in horizontal or diagonal lines, up the steep fells until they disappeared from view, dividing the green fields into random shapes of no particular pattern or symmetry, except that they always looked right. No-one seemed to know how long the walls had been there. Four hundred years, some said. Others said longer, said the monks had started them in the thirteenth century.

Johann was the latest in a long line of men who had built these walls and kept them in repair. Not that *he* could build one. That was a job for a craftsman, and there were few of them about now.

On Tuesday morning it was all go. The sheep had to be driven into the cattle wagon which would take them to the market in Shepton, then quickly after that Edward, his father, Susan and Cara followed in the car, the men to attend the sales, Susan to be taken to school, Cara to do a bit of everything.

Mrs Hendry came out to wave them off.

'I'll see you home again on Friday, love,' she said to Susan. 'Think on you work hard at school!'

'I shall be thankful when I'm old enough to leave,' Susan said. 'School is boring!'

'That'll not be for a while yet,' her grandmother said. 'In the meantime you must work hard and be a credit to your dad.'

Cara got into the back of the car with her father-in-law, and almost immediately leaned back and closed her eyes. She had been up before daylight, helping Johann with the milking, as she often did. It was the job she liked most on the farm. She enjoyed the quiet gloom of the shippon, the sweet smell of hay, and the cows themselves, gentle creatures except for the sometimes awkward Primrose. But even Primrose had been docile this morning, no kicking the bucket over!

In Shepton Edward delivered Susan to her school while Cara stayed with Tom. She was sure she'd not be welcome to accompany Edward. Susan would want her father to herself, which was reasonable enough.

Nothing had been said of the gift of the journal. Cara had hoped that Susan might thank her, however briefly. But it didn't matter, she'd received it. I just hope she likes it, Cara thought, even if she can't bring herself to say so.

She had been to the sales just once before and looked forward to repeating the experience, hoping she might understand a little more of the proceedings than she had then. There were what looked like the same farmers leaning over the same fences examining the same sheep. The noise was certainly as she remembered it. Everyone talking, one minute everything so casual, the next minute the auctioneer quick-firing his spiel in a language she hadn't understood the first time and didn't now. And over everything there was the constant plaintive baaing of sheep and lambs. The air was thick with it.

'I have a long way to go before I can buy and sell sheep like you can,' she said to Edward when he joined them.

Tom wandered off to find his cronies.

'I can't see you doing it just yet, love,' Edward agreed. 'Anyway, you don't have to.'

'Oh, but I want to learn. I want to learn everything. And one thing two years as a land girl has taught me is that I don't know it all. There are so many sides to farming.'

'No need for you to know it all,' Edward repeated.

'Aren't there any women farmers?' Cara asked.

'Not many I know of. There's one or two women own farms but they employ men to do the men's jobs.'

'And the market isn't a man's job?'

'Look around,' Edward said. 'How many women do you see?'

'Quite a number, actually.'

'Yes, well they're mostly farmers' wives. They'll not hang around here long. They'll be off to sample the delights of Shepton – shops, cafés and the like.'

'I'd like to stay here a while yet,' Cara said. 'I won't be a nuisance.'

'Of course you won't, love! Anyway I want to introduce my new wife to as many people as possible!' He squeezed her arm as he spoke. How was it, she wondered, that he was so loving in the daytime and a different man in bed? It was as if he changed into someone else.

He was in a good humour this morning, in his element here. Every few minutes, it seemed, men came up to him, sometimes just to greet him, often to ask advice. He introduced Cara to more farmers and farmers' wives than she would ever remember.

'Be sure you get him to bring you to the Farmers' Ball,' one said. 'And promise you'll give me the first dance!'

'I don't doubt you'd be a big success there,' Edward said dryly when the man had gone. 'Myself, I'm not much of a one for dancing!'

'Nevertheless I hope you'll take me,' Cara told him. 'It sounds like fun.'

'I'm keeping an eye out for Ralph Benson,' Edward said. 'He farms over in Nidderdale. I thought it would be a good place for overwintering. It's a deal milder than Arendale and there's ling grows there. The sheep can feed on that a bit in the winter.'

Every winter most farmers in the more remote dales sent at least a portion of their flock to spend the winter where the weather was less severe. They would be taken down in December and brought back before lambing time.

'How many can we send?' Cara asked.

'It depends on what we can afford,' Edward said.

Tom joined them again.

'What, you still here?' he asked Cara. 'Isn't this dull stuff for a lass?'

'Not a bit,' Cara assured him. 'But I am going to tear myself away because there's shopping to be done.'

'Just as long as you're back when it's time to go home again,' Tom said.

'You can depend on that. I'd not like to walk all the way back to Beckwith.'

'No? Well I mind the time – I was young then of course – when we'd drive the sheep from Beckwith to Shepton. We'd turn them into a field to rest overnight while we stayed at the Cow and Calf and then drive them on next morning. Two days it took us, and now it takes less than two hours!'

He spied another friend and wandered off again.

Cara was about to leave Edward, to go down into the town, when yet another man came up and spoke to Edward. Her husband, she noticed, had little to say to him, leaving the other man to make the running. Edward doesn't like him, she thought – and studied the man, wondering why.

He didn't look like a farmer, yet he looked a countryman. There was nothing of the city about him. He was as tall as Edward, swarthy-skinned, with hair as black and shining as coal, and longer than the fashion called for, so that it curled over his collar and in the back of his neck. He was clean-shaven yet, even so early in the day, with a blue-black stubble. His eyes were as near black as made no difference; alert, searching, slightly mocking as he spoke to Edward. There was something raffish about his person, from his tight-fitting breeches to his fancy waistcoat and the patterned scarf knotted around his neck.

No, she thought, definitely not a farmer. But what?

'I hope you're going to introduce me to your new wife?' the man said. The words were for Edward but the smile which accompanied them was entirely for Cara.

'This is Kit Marsden. My wife.'

Cara sensed the reluctance in Edward. Marsden held out his hand and took hers in a strong grip, at the same time giving the faintest possible bow. He had something foreign about him.

'And do you have a name other than Mrs Edward Hendry?' he enquired. His voice was grave but his eyes were laughing.

'Cara,' she said.

'A beautiful name,' he declared. 'Very fitting!'

'My wife was just leaving,' Edward said pointedly.

'I have some errands in Shepton,' Cara explained.

She enjoyed her leisurely shopping in Shepton, though there wasn't much to buy. She joined a long queue for oranges which she was allowed on David's ration book, and even the queueing didn't, for once, seem tedious. Perhaps it was that the weather was unusually warm and sunny for September, an Indian summer; perhaps it was the fact that she savoured her few hours of freedom and solitude. Whatever the reason, she felt a sense of well-being which had not been hers since before her marriage. It was a day on which she could only feel that everything was going to turn out right.

She ate in a small café, shepherd's pie, and tinned fruit to follow; not nearly as good a meal as she would have had at Beckwith, but she enjoyed every bite. Afterwards, walking up the High Street, she paused to look at the posters outside the Elysian cinema.

David Niven! David Niven! She adored David Niven.

'How about having nine pennyworth?'

She jumped at the voice, and spun around to face its owner.

'Oh, Mr Marsden! You startled me!'

'You were deep in worship of David Niven,' he said. 'So how about it?'

'How about what?'

'The ninepennies – with David Niven and me!'

'Thank you,' Cara said. 'I couldn't possibly, much as I like David Niven.'

'So I'm the stumbling block! Now why?'

'I hardly know you,' Cara replied stiffly.

'But you *do* know me,' he said. 'No less a man than your husband introduced us.'

And now I understand why Edward was reluctant, she thought. The cool cheek of him!

'I'm on my way to rejoin my husband,' she said. 'So if you'll excuse me . . .'

'Ah well,' he said. 'The ninepennies would have been more fun, and I don't like being turned down for a flock of sheep – but perhaps another time?'

'Good afternoon, Mr Marsden,' Cara said, walking briskly away.

When she rejoined Edward he had sold his lambs at a reasonable price and he and his father were ready for home. Cara said nothing of her further encounter with Kit Marsden, but as they drove along she asked:

'What does Mr Marsden do?'

'Marsden? He's a horse-dealer. A bit of a shady character, and a womanizer. I don't like the fellow but he's the best judge of horseflesh for miles around.'

'He looks a bit foreign,' she said,

'They say his mother was a gypsy.'

'That would explain it,' Cara said. 'Did you have a good dinner? Where did you go?'

'The Bull. Not bad.'

After that there was silence until they reached Beckwith.

Mrs Hendry had a substantial tea ready for them. She couldn't believe that they had had anything at all nourishing in Shepton. As soon as it was over the two men went out and Cara was left in the kitchen with her mother-in-law, who demanded a full report of the day's events. Cara gave her all the details, except for the encounter with Marsden, which was really of no interest, not even any longer to herself.

'And what have you been doing?' Cara asked.

'This and that. I cleaned Susan's room. That was a mess, if you like! And look what I found!'

She went to the waste-paper basket, took something out and handed it to Cara.

It was the journal – but not the journal as Cara had left it. Now the beautiful cover was half torn off, the leather spine was ripped, the clasp broken away and the pages torn.

Cara held it in her hands, staring at it, unbelieving. She felt sick to the stomach. How much strength had it taken to reduce it to this state? The strength of hate, she thought! The strength of hate! The day which had gone so well turned sour, bitter. Unhappiness engulfed her like a wave.

'It's such a pretty thing,' Mrs Hendry said. She was poking the fire, her back to Cara. 'I've never seen it before. I wonder where she got it?'

'*I* gave it to her.'

Cara's words were startling enough, but it was the tone of her voice which caused Edith Hendry to turn quickly. She was shocked by what she saw. Her daughter-in-law was deathly pale, looking as if she would faint. There was horror on her face as she stared at the mutilated book, yet held on to it as if she couldn't let it go.

'Whatever is it, love?'

'I gave it to her,' Cara said. 'Not exactly gave it to her. I left it on her dressing table with a note. It was a present, something to take back to school.'

Mrs Hendry, speechless for the moment, stared at Cara. Then:

'The wicked, wicked girl!' she cried. 'For this she's *got* to be punished. Just wait until her father comes in!'

'No! Please don't tell Edward! I don't want him to know! Oh, Mother Hendry, why does she hate me so? And why doesn't Edward love me?'

Cara had never meant to say those last words. They were out before she knew it. But now that they were out there was no stopping. The rest poured from her, while her mother-in-law listened.

64

'I'm sure Edward does love you,' Mrs Hendry said at last. She sounded hesitant, and to Cara her words didn't ring true.

'As for that little minx . . .' Mrs Hendry began.

'He doesn't,' Cara said miserably. 'I know he doesn't. Oh Mother Hendry, I can't help it that I'm not Nancy! Edward shouldn't have married me if he can't forget Nancy. I can't be anyone but me!'

'I was worried about him marrying you,' Mrs Hendry acknowledged. 'Me and Tom both were – not because we didn't like you, but because we knew his feelings about Nancy.'

'What am I to do?' It was a cry of anguish.

Mrs Hendry took a deep breath, made a resolve.

'Well first of all, love, you're going to drink a cup of hot tea with some brandy in it. And while you're drinking it I'm going to tell you about Nancy. Edward should have, but since he hasn't, and whether he likes it or not, I shall!'

FIVE

'Now love, I'm going to tell you a few home truths,' Mrs Hendry said.

'Oh, Mother Hendry, I don't know if I can bear home truths,' Cara protested. 'When did home truths ever make pleasant hearing?'

'You can bear it!' Mrs Hendry said. 'You're strong, I could tell that from the first. And I reckon what I have to say will help you, otherwise I'd keep my mouth shut. Of course by rights this should fall to Edward, but for reasons best known to himself it seems he's said nothing. So I will. Whether he'll thank me for it is another matter, but right's right!'

She poured the tea, handed a cup to Cara, then seated herself in the armchair, leaning her head against the sheepskin which was draped over the back for extra comfort.

'Please believe me, Mother Hendry,' Cara said, 'I do love Edward. I want our marriage to be a success.'

'I know, lass. I've got eyes in my head. And I love my son, you know. I want his happiness and I reckon you're the one to give it to him. So get that tea down you and listen.'

Cara put the mangled remains of the notebook on the table and looked at the cup of tea. She knew she could not drink it. It would choke her. This wasn't an occasion to be soothed by tea.

'Edward met Nancy in Morecambe,' Mrs Hendry began. 'He'd gone for a few days' holiday, once the hay harvest was in, with a lad from Faverwell. Edward hadn't had a lot to do with lasses, being an only child and allus busy on the farm – so when he met this one he fell for her like a ton of bricks. And for a shy lad he lost no time. Before you could turn round they'd wed, and pretty soon after that she was pregnant.'

'She wasn't a local girl, was she?'

'Oh no! She came from Sheffield. Her father was a manager in a foundry. I don't think she'd ever set foot on a farm before, didn't know a Swaledale sheep from a Shorthorn cow. But no matter; our Edward was besotted.'

Do I want to hear this, Cara wondered?

'I must say that she tried her best,' Mrs Hendry continued. 'She was willing enough, but it was all new to her and sometimes you could see she was homesick.

'Edward thought the sun shone on her. And when she had Susan he was over the moon. You'd think no-one had ever had a bairn before!'

Cara felt a sharp pang of envy. Yes, a woman who had given a man children would always have some claim on his love – but she hadn't had the chance, not yet.

'Then in the first summer of the war,' Mrs Hendry said, 'David was born. It had been a bit of a surprise to us that there was six years between them, but there you are. And the little lad was, oh, so welcome! After that, though, Nancy seemed to change. At least me and Tom thought so, but I don't think Edward noticed. He was still that stuck on her, though they'd been married seven years then. We thought she was – well, a bit restless. We put it down to living here. Arendale is a bit out of the way for a city lass. Then when Edward announced he was going to join the war she took it so calmly. I'd go so far as to say she seemed relieved. It puzzled us. I was worried she'd go back to Sheffield to her parents once Edward had gone, take the children with her. I dreaded that. But no, she didn't. She stayed on.

'Of course she was very anxious about her mother and dad. They had some bad times in Sheffield, you know. She used to go and see them whenever she could, but for safety's sake she didn't take the children. She'd leave them with me. On this particular occasion she said did we mind if she went to Sheffield for a week or two. Her mother wasn't well. And of course I didn't mind. But then the awful thing happened.'

She faltered, bit her lip. Cara leaned forward and covered her mother-in-law's hand with her own.

'Leave it for now if it distresses you.'

'Nay lass, I must go on,' Mrs Hendry said. 'I shan't ever forget it, not to my dying day. She'd been gone ten days when we got word from her parents that she'd been killed in an air raid.'

'How terrible!' Cara said. 'Poor Nancy! Poor Edward.'

Mrs Hendry nodded.

'Yes, it was shocking. But there was more to come. Edward was in the Western Desert, and because of the children he was given compassionate leave. But when he came home he was a changed man. I saw it the minute he walked through the door. The pain in him was terrible. You'd have thought he'd had a sword run through him.'

There was pain in her own voice as she spoke, as if she was living it all again.

'It must have been dreadful.'

Mrs Hendry took a sip of tea, shook her head.

'It was, love, but not in the way you might think. Naturally I put it down to the shock of Nancy's death, but I was wrong.'

'Then what . . .?'

'He'd had a letter. It turned out he'd received it just a day before she was killed.

'He handed me the letter. He didn't speak a word, just handed me the sheet of paper. I hardly liked to look at it – well, I expected it was a love letter, private like. But oh no! Oh dear me, no!

'You see Nancy hadn't really been going to visit her parents in Sheffield. She'd been going to see this other man. This letter was to tell Edward she was leaving him, *and* the children, for good. The affair had been going on a long time, even before Edward had gone overseas, and she was deeply in love with the man. Those were her very words, "deeply in love". She'd been seeing him every time she went there, and now she was going to live with him. She was very sorry and all that, but she was sure Edward would understand, and he'd agree to a divorce.'

'Poor Edward,' Cara said. 'Oh, poor Edward!'

'He got the letter when he was fighting in the desert, a thousand miles from home. I found that hard to forgive. As for me and the children – when would we have known? The first thing we knew was word from her mother to say Nancy had been killed. It was in a dance hall, a direct hit. I expect the man was killed with her but that we'll never know.'

She couldn't go on. The memories were too much for her. She got up and went and poked the fire, fiddled with the oven dampers, as if getting the right draught to heat the oven was all that mattered.

'It was good that the children had you,' Cara prompted gently.

Mrs Hendry went back to her chair.

'It was that. And we were thankful to be there for Edward. Oh, I know it's a common enough story. It happened many times during the war; but what happens to other people doesn't ease your lot.'

'And Edward took it badly?'

'Very badly indeed. You see, he'd worshipped Nancy. She was the whole world to him, and he'd had no reason to think she didn't feel the same way. He never suspected anything, nor did we for that matter. He'd have trusted her to the ends of the earth and back again. Now he wouldn't allow himself another second to mourn her death.

'"I never want to hear her name again!"

'Those were his exact words as I handed him back the letter, and he said them like he was slamming a door, pulling down a shutter, and his voice so bitter. And that was all he said and all he ever would say on the matter. Not another syllable. If Nancy's name was spoken he would leave the room.'

'That must have made it hard for Susan,' Cara said.

'It did that. She cried a lot for her mother. She adored her and still does because she's never learned the truth. I hope she never has to.' Mrs Hendry looked anxiously at Cara.

'She won't from me,' Cara assured her. 'How much *did* the children know?'

'Only that their mother had been killed. What good would it have done to know that she'd abandoned them?'

'Perhaps Nancy would have come back,' Cara said.

'I doubt it. And I'm telling you this, love, because I think you have the right to know. It's wrong that you should think yourself not able to live up to Nancy.'

'Thank you. I appreciate it. But I wish Edward had told me.'

'He should have. In a way,' Mrs Hendry went on, 'I was almost glad when Edward had to go back to his Unit. I could deal more easily with the children. He was as bitter as gall. So when he came home at the end of the war and met you, and took to you like he did, me and Tom didn't know what to think. And then there was the fact that you were another city girl. But he seemed genuinely fond of you and I do believe he is, love. I really do.'

'Fond is a different word,' Cara said. 'Fond doesn't sound like the passion he had for Nancy.'

'Maybe not,' Mrs Hendry conceded. 'But happen it's better; steadier, not so wild. Lasting.'

But what if that's not what I want? Cara asked herself. And it isn't, or at least it's not enough. *I* want passion; *I* want to be the only woman in the world for Edward.

'Was she very beautiful?' Cara was driven against her will to ask the question. 'I've seen her photograph. She looks beautiful.'

'She was,' Mrs Hendry admitted. 'Oh, no more so than you, love – but in a different way. She was very fair, a bit delicate-looking.'

'And he still can't get her out of his mind,' Cara said. In spite of what Nancy had done to him he couldn't stop loving her.

'If he can't,' Mrs Hendry said, 'it's not for love. They say love is very near to hate, and in his case I think it is. He hates Nancy. It's the hate he can't let go.'

At her mother-in-law's words relief surged through Cara, relief that she needn't battle against another love, a stronger love. Then almost instantly she was ashamed. How could she be pleased that Edward now hated his former wife? And in any case, hate could be as strong as love, even more insistent. It is Edward's hate for Nancy which is robbing me of his love, she thought.

'But it's me he's punishing!' she cried. 'He's punishing me for something Nancy did!'

Every time he turned away and wouldn't make love to her, he was rejecting Nancy. Every time he *did* make love – selfish, brief, inconsiderate love – he was punishing Nancy. But I'm not Nancy, Cara thought. I'm *me*! But does he, at such times, even know that?

'I'm not Nancy!' she said out loud. 'I am *not* Nancy!'

'And thank the Lord for that,' Mrs Hendry said. 'You're as different as chalk from cheese!'

'So where does this leave me? I don't know!'

'I thought . . . if I told you, if you could understand, it might help you both.'

Cara shook her head. She was filled with doubt. 'It's not so simple. I can't even decide whether I should tell Edward what I know. How would I do that?'

'Well love, only you can answer that. But it's my belief that if it's the right thing to do, then the opportunity will come. "Knock and it will be opened to you"!'

Halfway through Mrs Hendry's last sentence Edward came into the kitchen, followed by his dog, Ruby.

'I brought the cattle down, as I was coming,' he said. 'Your turn for milking, Cara.'

He looked from one to the other.

'Is everything all right? Has Ma been preaching you a sermon, love?' He smiled at Cara as he asked the question.

'Not at all.'

While waiting for his mother to pour his tea he saw the mangled notebook on the table and picked it up, idly curious.

'Hello, what's this? I haven't seen this before?'

'It's mine!' Cara said quickly. 'Just something I was throwing away.'

She didn't want to discuss it. Having listened to her mother-in-law, one thing was certain. She was filled with compassion for her step-daughter. She wanted no more trouble for her. In spite of what the girl had done, she would have liked to have taken her in her arms and hugged her.

'Throwing it away?' Edward said. 'Why? What happened to it?'

Mrs Hendry spoke up suddenly.

70

'It isn't Cara's. She gave it to Susan, for a present.'

'Please!' Cara interrupted.

'No love, it's right he should know!'

'Come on,' Edward said. 'Out with it. What's the mystery? And if you gave it to Susan what's it doing here in this state?'

'I bought it in Faverwell,' Cara said reluctantly. 'I thought it would make a nice present for Susan to take back to school. I left it on her dressing table with a note.'

'And I saw it in the waste-paper basket, after you'd all left this morning,' Mrs Hendry said. 'Either Cara or me was bound to find it there.'

'You found it like *this*?'

'Exactly like that,' Mrs Hendry said. 'It's a wicked shame!'

'Please,' Cara begged. 'Let's forget it! I don't want to hear any more about it.'

'Forget it?' Edward shouted. His face was white with rage. Cara had never seen him so angry. 'I shall do no such thing! How could she do this to you? She'll be punished – and severely. If she were a bit younger I'd give her a good tanning!'

'Oh no you wouldn't,' Mrs Hendry said. 'When did you ever lift a hand to her, however much she provoked you?'

'Well, she's gone too far this time. It's as well for her she won't be home until Friday!'

'Please, Edward!' Cara said. 'I know it's annoying . . .'

'Annoying? It's a damned sight more than that! It's downright deliberate insolence and it's got to be punished.'

'Edward, please listen to me! One way and another there's been enough punishment. It's time it all ended.'

There was something in Cara's tone which made Mrs Hendry get up from her chair and move towards the door.

'I've got some jobs to see to in the dairy,' she said.

'What do you mean?' Edward asked Cara. 'I don't understand you.'

'I'll make it plain,' Cara said. But she didn't want to, not here and now. It was neither the time nor the place she'd have chosen – if she'd chosen to speak at all. She was already regretting having taken her stance, but it was too late now.

'Do you ever talk to Susan about Nancy?' she asked.

'I've asked you not to mention that name,' Edward said harshly.

'I know you have. And I'm sorry, but I think Nancy has to be talked about, for my sake as well as Susan's.'

'Your sake? What has she do with you?'

'A lot that's important. I think you know!'

He stepped towards her and grasped her by the wrist.

'Has my mother been talking to you? Is that what it's about? Tell me the truth, she has, hasn't she?'

'I've no intention of telling you other than the truth.' Cara's voice was cold. 'Unlike you, I'm not trying to hide anything. Whatever your mother said, she said it because she thought it was necessary, and so do I. Oh Edward, my love,' she said, relenting, because she couldn't do otherwise at the sight of his troubled face, 'why didn't you tell me? I'd have understood things much better!'

He let go her wrist.

'I didn't want you to know anything about it. I wanted everything to start afresh between you and me. I didn't want to burden you with the past.'

'Burden me? Oh Edward, it isn't a burden! It's *sharing*. In my book that's what marriage is – sharing the past, as well as the present and the future. How can we be real partners if we close off parts of ourselves from each other?'

'It needn't have had anything to do with you,' he persisted.

'But it did, and it has. Nancy has come between us already.'

'If you're thinking of Susan, I'll sort that out . . .' Edward began.

'I'm not thinking of Susan, not at this moment. I'm thinking of you and me,' Cara said. 'You can't love me as I long for you to love me – and I think perhaps as you want to – because Nancy comes between us. Every time you make love to me she comes between us!'

He sank into the chair his mother had recently vacated. He covered his eyes with his hand, as if he couldn't bear to see her or be seen. Swiftly, Cara knelt on the floor in front of him and took both his hands in hers, forcing him to look at her. From her place in the corner Ruby came and lay with her head across his feet.

'You know that's true, don't you?' Cara said gently.

He sat in silence.

'Please answer me!'

'Yes,' he said. 'I know. I didn't at first. I knew things were wrong. I knew I was treating you badly, but I didn't know why, not at first.'

'And now that you do, it can change,' Cara said. 'But only if you stop hating. If you go on hating Nancy, you'll go on hurting me. She'll always be between us. You've clung to those feelings so long, but now you'll have to let them go.'

'The last thing in the world I want is to hurt you,' Edward said. 'Oh Cara, I do love you! Truly!'

'I know you do,' she said. 'And I love you. More than ever, if that were possible. And I didn't mean to say all this now. I meant to wait for a better time, when we were *really* alone. David will be in any minute.'

'I promise you we'll talk about it later,' Edward said.

'There's one other thing,' Cara said. 'I have to say something about Susan.'

'Leave it to me to deal with Susan,' Edward said. 'I won't allow her to treat you like this.'

'No! You misunderstand me, love.' Cara was emphatic. 'I don't want you to punish Susan. You've been doing that for years.'

'I've hardly ever punished her!' Edward protested. 'You heard what my mother said. It might have been better if I had.'

'Your mother said you'd never raised a hand to her, but you've punished her all right. You've punished her by not letting her talk about her mother. Don't you see? Her mother, who was perfection, was killed – and the other person she loves most in life, her father, refuses to discuss it. By never mentioning Nancy you act as if she never existed, and that's more than Susan can bear.'

'It was difficult,' Edward said.

'Even more difficult for Susan. And I'm sure Susan will never accept *me* until you acknowledge her mother.'

'What sort of a mother was she?' Edward demanded bitterly. 'She deserted her children!'

'You wouldn't want Susan to know that?'

'Of course not! I'm not a monster.'

'Well, whatever else Nancy did, she gained Susan's love – and you're shutting out everything that Susan remembers of her mother. I'm sure you should talk to her, Edward. Oh, not all at once, no dramatic scene. But gradually, just little things, to show that you also remember. There were good times with Nancy. You could help Susan by remembering those.'

Whatever Edward might have replied was prevented by the appearance of David, who marched purposefully into the kitchen. He was followed by his grandfather and by Bess, Tom's rough-haired collie dog.

'Dad, when can I have my own dog?' David demanded. It wasn't the first time he'd asked the question, and got no for an answer, but it was worth trying again.

Cara observed with tenderness the visible effort Edward made to pull himself together and answer his son.

'Not yet awhile – as you well know. You can't have your dog until you're old enough to look after it properly, spend time with it, train it.'

'Not that a good dog takes a lot of training,' Tom chipped in. 'The best ones seem born to herd sheep. You can see it in 'em when they're puppies in the litter. It's bred in 'em!'

'Will Bess or Ruby have puppies?' David enquired hopefully. 'I could have one of those.'

'They're a bit past it,' Edward said. 'Bess certainly is. But don't fret, you shall have a puppy all in good time. Until then you must make do with Bess and Ruby.'

'But they always stick with you and Grandpa,' David complained.

'Of course they do!' Tom said. 'It's a shepherd's best friend, a dog is. *And* his best worker. The dog's worth any bit of farm machinery you can name, and better than any two men! You couldn't farm sheep without dogs. These fells wouldn't be worth tuppence an acre without the dogs.'

'Then I'll *have* to have one,' David persisted. 'I'm going to be a sheep farmer the minute I leave school!'

'I'd better see to the milking,' Cara said.

She was glad to go into the shippon. It was cool and dim and the atmosphere – the combination of the sweet smell of the hay, the gentle movements of the cows, the physical satisfaction of milking – always had its own healing quality. If she had to choose a favourite place on the farm, it would be the shippon; and the cows were her favourite animals.

They kept only eight cows now at Beckwith, though there were stalls for more, and before the war when the farm produced butter, cheese and cream for Shepton market, every stall had been filled. All the cows were milkers: finer and more angular at the front, with broad hindquarters and a shape suitable for calf-bearing. Beef cattle in Arendale, the farmers agreed, were a sure and certain way of losing money. They couldn't be fattened up enough. Like most of the cows in the dale, Beckwith's were Dairy Shorthorns; roan, red, and white cattle, bred right from their beginnings in the northern counties. One or two farmers had experimented with Friesians, but Edward wouldn't.

'They've got uncertain temperaments, Friesians,' he said. 'As for Jerseys, they're no good on these uplands, it's too cold for them to breed. Shorthorns are definitely the best.'

Following Beckwith's long tradition, every cow in the herd had a flower name: Primrose, Hyacinth, Rosie and the like. But apart from all being Shorthorns and having similar names, each cow was totally different from the rest, not only in looks, but even more in temperament.

'And if we had eighty cows,' Tom Hendry was fond of saying, 'they'd still all be different!'

Cara knew, as she now prepared to milk them, that some would stand placidly and yield their milk freely, others would be harder. If Primrose was in a black mood she would like as not kick the bucket over. Daisy would give the milk which would produce the sweetest butter, although, Mrs Hendry said, it was slow to churn,

74

while Hyacinth's milk churned quickly, though the butter was not so flavoursome.

Not much butter was made now. Almost all the milk was collected and taken for sale in the West Riding towns.

Cara placed her stool on the right of the first cow. It was one of the things Tom had had to tell her in that first week at Beckwith, when she'd been as green as grass. 'Otherwise you'll run into trouble,' he'd said. Then she began to milk; gentle but firm strokes, smooth and rhythmical, her head pressed against the side of the cow. The swish of the milk into the pail was like music.

'Do you realize, Marigold,' she said – she always talked to the cows – 'that your milk might be going to my little sister in Akersfield?'

Marigold's only reply was a swish of her tail, but she gave freely, holding nothing back. If Cara had a favourite cow it was Marigold.

'You're in better condition than you were, old girl,' Cara told her.

Rations for the animals in the early part of the summer had been lower than ever, with farmers buying anything they could lay their hands on to supplement the feed.

'A lot of it's rubbish,' Tom Hendry had said. 'Not fit for any beast.' But things were a bit easier now.

Cara's thoughts turned to Edward, remembering in detail what they had said to each other earlier. Would matters be better now that the air had been cleared between them, now that there were no secrets? Surely they must be? Of Susan she hadn't much hope. That would be a long haul.

When she and Edward made love that night it was different, better than she had ever known it. She sensed that the struggle was still there for Edward. She could tell from the tenseness in his body that there were moments when he had to fight the feelings that had for so long been ingrained in him. But he didn't turn away from her; she no longer felt she was being punished for someone else. They were tender with each other, loving and supportive,

When it was over and she was lying in Edward's arms, she said:

'My darling, I don't ever want you to think that this is all that matters to me, or even that it matters most. It doesn't. It's the everyday living which counts. I know that.'

'This will come right, love,' Edward said. 'I know it isn't perfect, but can you be patient? All we need is a little time.'

'It will come right because there aren't any barriers between us now,' Cara said. 'As for time – we have all the time in the world!'

I am content, she thought. Our married life has truly begun, and every day it will get better. In the circle of Edward's arm she fell into a dreamless sleep.

★

75

On Friday afternoon Susan came home from school; by train, then bus, as far as Faverwell, where Edward picked her up in the car. David, who finished school earlier, had been given a lift home by the parents of his best friend, and was already out on the fell with his grandfather. Usually, Edward would have taken Cara to Faverwell to give her the opportunity to shop, but on this occasion he made no such offer, nor did Cara ask it of him. If he intended to bring up the matter of the torn journal she didn't want to be present. She had already decided that she would say nothing more about it.

When Susan marched into the house it was clear that something had been said. Her cheeks were two vivid spots of colour and her eyes were too bright. She greeted her grandmother briefly, ignored Cara entirely, and made straight for her room.

Edward, his face like a thundercloud, followed close behind her and sharply called her back.

'You know what I told you!' he snapped. 'You are to apologize!'

'Please . . . !' Cara began.

'No,' Edward said. 'She knows what she has to do!'

Susan faced her father, fists clenched, head high, her whole body stiff with rebellion.

'I won't do it! I don't see why I should apologize!'

'Then you can go to your room and stay there,' Edward ordered.

'Gladly!' Susan cried.

'You've not heard the end of this!' Edward shouted after her.

'Oh, Edward love,' Cara said when Susan had made her noisy exit, 'why?'

'Because I won't have her treating you so,' he said hotly.

'But this way won't stop her! Don't you see that? She'll hate me more than ever.'

'I don't want to interfere,' Mrs Hendry broke in. 'And I don't like to see Susan get away with it any more than you do, but I think Cara could be right.'

'Then what am I supposed to do?' Edward asked testily. 'Am I to let my daughter ride roughshod over my wife? Is that it?'

'Why don't you go in to her,' Cara pleaded. 'Why don't you start building bridges? Someone has to, and the real trouble is between you and Susan. I'm just the scapegoat. Why don't you do as we discussed the other day – let her know that you love her, and talk to her about her mother. Just a little, only a little to begin with. Go gently.'

'"A soft answer turneth away wrath",' Mrs Hendry said.

Edward looked from his wife to his mother.

'Either of you would do this better than me.'

'Only you *can* do it,' Cara told him. 'And you must leave me out of it entirely.'

76

'Very well.' He was decidedly reluctant. 'Though I'm not entirely convinced and I don't know how I'll begin.'

'Tell her you love her,' Cara repeated.

He was a long time in Susan's room. Mrs Hendry and Cara went quietly about their chores. Though neither admitted it, they were listening for sounds – sounds of battle – and none came.

When Edward rejoined them, looking white and tired, they both abruptly stopped what they were doing and looked at him, their faces full of questions.

'I don't know!' he said, shaking his head. 'I did the best I could, but I don't know. She cried.'

Cara went up to him and put her hand on his arm.

'Perhaps that's good,' she said. 'I've never seen Susan cry.'

SIX

'When are you going to invite your ma and pa to Beckwith?' Mrs Hendry asked Cara.

'And Laura!' David added through a mouthful of apple pudding.

They were all at the table, just about finishing the midday dinner. As it was Saturday, Susan was also present. She gave her brother a dirty look. She had no wish to see anyone from Akersfield, and least of all Laura Dunning. That awful wedding had been quite enough, thank you!

'I'd like to invite them,' Cara admitted.

There was no longer any reason why she shouldn't do so. The rift between herself and Edward, which she'd been afraid her mother's keen perception wouldn't miss, no longer existed, if indeed it had ever been a rift. A 'distance' would have described it better, and now there was none. They were close, even though there were times when Edward found it hard going, when he couldn't excise his hatred of Nancy from his mind. He didn't say anything, but Cara could always tell.

As for waiting until she and Susan were on better terms, that could be a long, long wait. Anyone with half an eye could see Susan's antagonism towards her. It was in every action, every glance, though not in her words because she hardly ever spoke to Cara. It was, however, more subtle than it had been, so that neither her father nor her grandmother could find concrete reasons these days for reprimanding her.

What she did increasingly was to hold conversations with her father from which Cara was carefully and deliberately excluded. Thanks to Edward's efforts, Susan's relationship with her father had improved, so it was difficult to object to this. But she knew what she was doing. Everyone knew, and no-one could do a thing about it. If Cara attempted to join in such a conversation, Susan would find a valid excuse for leaving the room.

'When would be convenient?' Cara asked. She looked to Edward. 'When would suit you, love?'

'Sooner rather than later. From now on it's going to get busier every day.'

It was mid-October. Tupping wouldn't start until the second week in November but already the rams needed to be looked at often. Autumn was mating time for the sheep and as the days grew shorter the rams grew restless. This was the time of the year when they'd pick fights with each other, or unaccountably go lame. Anything to be awkward.

'If the tups aren't watched they'll like as not try jumping the wall, if the mood takes 'em,' Tom Hendry said. 'Owt to get at the ewes, but it's too soon.'

'Would next weekend be all right for a visit?' Cara asked her mother-in-law.

'Of course!' Mrs Hendry said. 'And you must invite them to stay overnight.'

'Lovely,' Cara said, smiling. 'I'll telephone Ma, suggest they come Saturday morning until Sunday afternoon.'

'That would be wonderful!' Beth Dunning said when Cara phoned her later that day. 'We've missed you. It seems a long time.'

'We'll catch up with everything on Saturday,' Cara promised.

'Dad's usually at the bank on Saturday mornings,' Beth reminded Cara. 'But what's the point of being the manager if you can't take half a day off?'

Mrs Hendry found the prospect of three visitors a good reason for cleaning the house from top to bottom, washing the curtains and cushion covers, and working out what menus she could from the food available.

'They'll bring their rations,' Cara said. 'Tea, sugar, that sort of thing.' Everyone did.

'They must do nothing of the kind!' Mrs Hendry protested. 'Things have come to a pretty pass if we can't feed a few visitors! It's disgraceful!'

'Anyway, they'll fare better at Beckwith than they do in Akersfield,' Cara said. 'I'm sure of that.'

It was true. There'd be eggs and cream, a chicken – or at least a boiling fowl; a bit of bacon, a piece of pork. Bread was rationed, but that hadn't hit Beckwith yet. Mrs Hendry had laid in a good store of flour whenever she could and was still able to bake her own.

'Yes,' she said. 'I shall feed them up, poor things!'

'Where will Laura sleep?' Cara asked. There was no problem about her mother and father, there was a spare double room.

'She can double up with Susan,' Mrs Hendry said. Then she caught sight of Cara's face. 'Well, happen not! It'd be best if David slept in our room – I can make him up a camp bed – then Laura can have David's room. He won't mind, nor will me and Tom.'

'It's very good of you,' Cara said. 'And there's another favour I'd like to ask. Would you mind if I had the piano tuned? You haven't heard Laura play and I'd like you to.'

'I'd like it,' Mrs Hendry said. 'The piano tuner lives over at Hawes. Nathan Briggs. Get in touch with him and see if he can come this week.'

He came, an elderly man who pushed his bicycle up the steep hills which divided the dales and sailed as swift as a bird on the downhill slopes, his coat tails flying in the wind, the tools of his trade jangling in his saddle bag. Not since she had come to live at Beckwith had anything been as evocative of Cara's Akersfield home as the sounds of the piano being tuned. It had been a regular sound there. Even the deliberate discords were music to her ears. When the tuning was done Briggs went into a spirited rendering of a Sousa march before coming into the kitchen to take a cup of tea and a piece of jam pasty.

'Yon's a good instrument,' he said. 'You should look after it better. That parlour's a bit damp. You should light a fire more often.'

'Coal's rationed,' Mrs Hendry said.

'Peat isn't,' Nathan Briggs replied. 'You only have to dig it out of the ground.'

'Oh, we do that,' Mrs Hendry assured him. It was one of Johann's regular jobs.

On Saturday morning, in Akersfield, the Dunnings were getting ready for their visit to Beckwith Farm, Beth Dunning patiently waiting for her turn at the dressing-table mirror which was, for the moment, entirely taken up by her husband. He had already brushed his hair meticulously, making sure that every hair which sprang from his ruler-straight parting lay in the right direction, sighing at the amount of grey at his temples. He was now, his wife's embroidery scissors carefully poised, delicately trimming his moustache.

He stopped suddenly and looked hard at his reflection.

'I'm not at all sure about it!' he said.

'Not sure about what, dear? Please do hurry, Arnold. You've been hogging the mirror for ages!'

'My moustache.' He peered more closely and snipped away a millimetre of hair. 'It's showing more grey than my hair.'

'Well, there's not much you can do about that,' his wife said sensibly. 'Not unless you intend to dye it!'

'Dye it? Don't be ridiculous, Beth!' He was affronted at the suggestion. 'I just wondered . . . well . . . should I shave it off?'

He covered his moustache with his hand, narrowed his eyes and gazed critically at his image, trying to imagine himself with a clean-shaven face. Hitherto he always felt that his moustache lent him a certain distinction, gave him something of a military bearing. Now he wasn't sure.

'Shave off your moustache? Oh Arnold, whatever next? You wouldn't be yourself without it. Why, I've never seen you without a moustache!' Beth sounded horrified.

He lowered his hand, smoothed down the appendage. Perhaps she was right. It was an old friend. It had adorned his face throughout two world wars and the twenty-odd years in between. And if it was not so bright a red as it once had been, well, a few grey hairs could be quite distinguished.

'Do hurry, love,' Beth said. 'You're worse than a young girl going to a ball!'

What nonsense women talked, Arnold thought. There was nothing wrong in wanting to look his best when visiting his daughter. He was wearing what he thought of as his country clothes, though as a matter of fact he seldom ventured into the country. Grey flannels, a discreetly checked sports jacket, a plain green tie and brown brogues which gleamed like ripe chestnuts. Best take his gaberdine mac, though. It always rained in the country. That and his tweed hat should see him through. He could not possibly take his black umbrella on a country walk.

Satisfied with what he saw, he moved away from the mirror.

'Come along!' he said briskly, five minutes later. 'It's time we were off. What's Laura doing? Prettying herself up, I've no doubt!'

Laura emerged from her bedroom and followed her mother and father to the car. Yes, she did look pretty, Beth thought.

'You've got colour in your cheeks this morning,' she remarked. 'It must be the excitement.'

'It *is* exciting,' Laura said. 'And I'm longing to see Cara!'

But underneath the excitement she was apprehensive, even a little afraid, though she liked the Hendry family, all except that pig, Susan. Laura admitted to herself that she was a little bit afraid of almost everything. The only time she was totally confident was when she was seated at the piano, playing. Nothing and no-one could touch her then.

'Lucky you'd saved some petrol coupons,' Beth said to her husband.

81

'Not lucky, dear. Provident,' he corrected.

'Of course, love. As a good bank manager should be!'

He looked at her suspiciously. It was sometimes difficult to pin down Beth's exact meaning, though now her tone of voice was calm and measured.

'I'm not sure that a good bank manager should be away from his desk on a Saturday morning,' he said. 'It doesn't set a good example.'

Beth let out a peal of laughter.

'Oh Arnold, how often have you done it? Hardly ever! It can't matter all that much.'

'You may laugh,' he said, 'but in business you've got to keep a tight rein. You wouldn't know that. Things can only too easily get slack, standards fall. Where would we all be then?'

There was, for instance, the matter of Saturday morning dress in the bank. Head Office had decreed that the staff could wear informal attire on Saturday mornings: jacket and flannels much as he was wearing now, though never in a thousand years would he set foot in the bank dressed like this. It was the thin end of the wedge. It was up to him to set the example for others to follow.

'Never mind, dear,' his wife said. 'You can lick them all back into shape on Monday morning.'

The traffic was light, and though as a matter of principle Arnold never drove at more than thirty miles an hour, they quickly left the smoke of Akersfield behind them. That was one of the good things about Akersfield, you could get out of it quickly. 'You can be up on the moors in twenty minutes!' its inhabitants boasted.

It was strange, Arnold thought some time later as he slowed down to a crawl to get through Shepton, that they had never actually visited Beckwith Farm. When Cara had worked there before her marriage she'd come home whenever she could, at weekends. In the short period between getting herself engaged and marrying, either time or petrol seemed to be in short supply. If he hadn't wanted to see his daughter so badly, he wouldn't be making this visit now. In his heart, he wasn't at home in the country. Nor could he fathom how any daughter of his could be, either.

Half an hour later, short of Faverwell, he turned left into Arendale. There was no need of a map; Cara's instructions had been quite explicit.

'Isn't this beautiful?' Beth demanded as they drove along the side of the river. 'Isn't it gorgeous?'

She took in the green of the fells, which climbed to the bright sky, the fast-running little river, the russets and browns and yellows of the autumn-tinged trees on its banks, and gave a deep sigh of pleasure.

'It'll be very cold in winter,' Arnold said.

'Of course it will,' Beth said shortly. 'But it's not winter! It's October, and it's like a summer's day. An Indian summer! Who wants to think about winter?'

And when winter came, she thought, these hills would be covered in pristine white, like clean sheets on the bed, while in Akersfield the smoke of the mills and the trampling of hundreds of feet would change the snow to blackish-grey sludge underfoot. Best not thought about.

'It's a long way from civilization, but yes,' Arnold conceded. 'I suppose it does look quite nice. I shall go for a good walk after dinner, climb to the top of the fell. After all, it's what we came for – a breath of good country air!'

Beth contradicted him. 'No it's not! We came to see Cara!'

'I know that,' Arnold said testily. 'I haven't the slightest doubt that Cara will want to come with me.'

And I haven't the slightest doubt that you'll monopolize her, Beth thought. Her husband knew very well that someone would have to stay down with Laura. A long walk, let alone a climb, was impossible for her. Not that she usually minded staying with Laura. She loved her younger daughter dearly, but she had so looked forward to spending hours with Cara, hearing everything there was to hear, learning about her daughter's new life.

'Do you suppose all these sheep belong to Edward?' Laura asked.

'Very likely,' Beth said. 'Or will one day, if they're Beckwith sheep. For now they belong to his parents.'

'I like Mr Hendry,' Laura said. 'He was very funny at the wedding. I liked him best of anybody.'

'Did you really?' her father said. His voice was non-committal. Privately he thought Tom Hendry was a bit of a country bumpkin. Honest as the day, of course; heart of gold, no doubt; but no polish. Not that any of this family into which Cara had chosen to marry had much polish. Still, if she was happy . . . He brought his thoughts to a doubtful close.

Nearing what must be Beckwith Farm he was agreeably surprised by the size and style of the house.

'Oh, isn't it lovely?' Beth enthused. 'What a setting!'

Arnold felt bound to agree.

'Very nice. Very nice indeed!'

When they drove into the farmyard Cara was out there to meet them. Arnold's heart lifted at the sight of her, as it had since, at less than a year old, she'd called his name and taken her first, unsteady steps with her arms held out towards him. Her parents-in-law and David were close behind, but there was no sign of Edward.

'Oh Ma! Oh Dad! It's so lovely to see you! And Laura!'

Cara embraced them in turn. She hadn't realized until this moment just how much she'd missed her family.

Arnold shook hands formally with Mr and Mrs Hendry and patted David on the head. As he followed his hosts to the house he noted with distaste the mud which had already splashed his beautiful shining shoes.

'Edward will be here in just a few minutes,' Cara told them. 'He had to go down to Low Pasture. In fact I thought you might have passed him on the way.'

'We didn't see him,' Beth said. 'We didn't see a soul all the way up the dale. So peaceful!'

They trooped into the house by the kitchen door but Mrs Hendry immediately led the way to the parlour.

'Now make yourselves at home,' she said. 'Dinner won't be more than a half-hour and Tom is going to pour you a nice glass of sherry, aren't you, Tom?'

'Aye, if that's what suits,' Tom agreed. He turned to Arnold. 'We've a nice drop of ale if you'd rather sup that.'

'I'd be happy with sherry,' Arnold said. 'If you don't mind.'

'Oh I don't mind,' Tom said agreeably. 'A little of what you fancy does you good!' He turned to Laura. 'And what about you, young lady? What do you fancy, then? Your wish is my command.'

Laura turned to her mother.

'May I have sherry?'

'A small one, then,' Beth agreed.

Within minutes Edward came in and joined them.

'I'm sorry I wasn't here to greet you. There's always something needs seeing to on a farm.' He turned to Cara. 'Susan not back yet?'

'No.'

'Susan cycled into Faverwell,' David explained.

'She'll be back in time for her dinner,' Mrs Hendry said. 'My granddaughter's not one to miss a meal. And speaking of that, when I've drunk your health I'll take my sherry into the kitchen if you'll excuse me, else there won't be a meal!'

When his mother left the room Edward followed her.

'Did Susan know what time she had to be back?' he asked.

'Since she's had her Saturday dinner at the same time for most of her life, I reckon she knows all right.'

'Well if she's not here, we start without her,' Edward said sharply. 'I'll not keep guests waiting.'

'And I'll not keep my Yorkshire pudding waiting neither!' his mother said firmly.

'Why did she go to Faverwell, anyway?'

'She didn't say. I put it down to cussedness,' Mrs Hendry replied.

In the event, Susan slid into her place at the table at the exact moment the Yorkshire pudding, crisp, brown, well-risen and as light as a cloud, was being taken out of the oven. She gave a brief, cold 'Hello' which covered everyone. After that, during the course of the meal, she spoke only to her father. He answered in monosyllables and from the set of his mouth and the hardness of his eyes Cara, if not everyone else, knew he was angry.

Susan's sullen silence, though no-one could fail to notice it, did nothing to dampen anyone else's spirits. Talk flowed freely around the table. Encouraged by Tom Hendry, even Laura contributed her small share.

After the meal, when the Dunnings had returned to the parlour, when Susan had taken herself off without a word to her room, and Cara and Edward were alone for a minute, he said:

'I won't have it! I'm going to give her a piece of my mind!'

Cara put a restraining hand on his arm.

'Not now, love! It would make it worse for everyone, and that's what she wants. We both know she's behaving like this to punish me; but I promise you if she's rude, either in word or deed, to any of my family from now until the minute they leave, then this time, the moment they've gone she'll hear from me!'

'And me!' Edward threatened.

'Then let's ignore it for now and decide what we'd like to do this afternoon.'

'I'd quite set my mind on walking to the top of the fell,' Arnold said when asked a few minutes later. 'A breath of fresh air. A bit of exercise after that excellent meal!'

It *had* been a good meal. People in the country didn't know they were born, he thought.

Tom Hendry looked doubtful.

'You'll have to take care,' he said. 'It's quite certain to come in misty on the tops later this afternoon.'

'Oh, a bit of fog won't put me off!' Arnold said with confidence. 'We get our share of fogs in Akersfield, you know. Real pea-soupers!'

'This is different,' Tom warned. 'When the mist comes down it comes quickly, covers everything. It's like being in the clouds and neither man nor beast can beat it. Even the dogs don't go on the tops when there's mist.'

'Tom's right, Dad,' Cara said. 'It's dangerous. You can lose your way in minutes, and there are pot-holes up there which go nobody knows how deep into the ground; and steep scree, as slippery as glass.'

'So does that mean you're not going with me, love?' Arnold challenged her.

'Of course I'll come,' Cara said. 'But we'd better get off soon, and I shall insist we turn back if there's the slightest hint of mist.'

'Perhaps you'd like me to show you round the farm, Mrs Dunning?' Mrs Hendry suggested. 'And we could walk down to the river. It's not far.'

'I'll come with you,' David offered. 'Shall I ask Susan?'

'Do that,' his grandmother said.

He was back in two minutes.

'She's got homework to do.'

He was making that up, just to be polite. What she'd really said was, 'With that lot? Never!'

'I expect you've plenty to do on the farm, Edward,' Arnold said hopefully. He wanted his daughter to himself and he didn't much care who knew it.

'Yes,' Edward said. 'There's always something. Tell me which way you're going, Cara love, and I'll come up to meet you later on.'

'We'll go up by Broad Field and keep to this side of the brook,' Cara said. 'Come along then, Dad! Let's see what you're made of!'

'Oh, I'll show you that,' Arnold promised. 'You're talking to a man who thought nothing of a twenty-five-mile route march, *and* with a full pack!'

But how long ago? Cara asked herself. All of thirty years. Her father was fifty-two and the most he took in the way of exercise was a leisurely round of golf. Poor old Dad, she thought.

Arnold strode out briskly with her across the first level meadow, but once beyond that the land began to rise, not gradually, not gently, but suddenly and steeply. Cara slowed down her speed to match her father's.

'So tell me how you're getting on?' Arnold asked, trying not to sound as breathless as he felt.

'Very well indeed,' Cara said. 'I love it here. I'm glad you could come to see what it's like.'

He grunted. It was all he had breath for. Not only was the way steep, but underfoot the going was rough. There was a track of sorts, narrow and stony, but as they climbed even that gave out. Now the grass, cropped close by the sheep, was slippery; scattered with limestone boulders and riddled with rabbit holes. Arnold kept his eyes on his feet. It was easier that way. A step at a time and before you knew where you were you'd be at the top.

Cara kept up a one-sided conversation. She could see her father had no breath to spare for speech, but she also knew he wasn't a man to give in easily.

It was a rabbit, running across almost over his feet, which caused Arnold to look up. What he saw in that brief moment was the incredibly steep fellside in front of him, rising, it seemed, to touch the sky, to infinity. He stopped, turned around and looked back – and realized with a shock that they'd come no more than halfway. But at least he could use the pause to get some breath back.

'Are you all right, Dad?' Cara asked. His face was flushed and beads of sweat stood out damply on his brow.

'Of course, love. I'm just stopping to look at the view. "What is this life if, full of care, we have no time to stand and stare?" I learnt that at school.'

'So did I. Do you want to carry on or have you had enough?'

'Had enough, love? Certainly not!'

He tried to take a deep breath – surely the air was getting thinner – and set off again. Of course, he thought as he slipped on the grass, I'm wearing the wrong shoes! That's why it's so difficult!

Cara stopped and gazed earnestly towards where the top of the fell would be if it hadn't gone out of sight again over yet another rise.

'Is that mist up there, Dad? What do you think?'

Arnold lifted his head and looked hopefully. It would be irresponsible to carry on if there really was mist. After all, he was not alone. He had his daughter to think of. Not that he could see the mist as yet, but Cara could, and she knew about these things.

'I think it might be. I think it just might be!'

'Well really, Dad, I hate to disappoint you, and I know you want to go to the top, but Edward was quite right, it could be dangerous. And he'd be very cross with me if I acted foolishly.'

'And I wouldn't want you in any danger, love,' Arnold said firmly.

'Then if you think we'd be wiser to turn back, why don't we sit down here for a bit first? I'd be glad of a short rest.'

'If it's what you want, love,' Arnold said.

They sat on a large flat limestone slab by the side of the narrow brook which tumbled over the rocks down the hillside to join the river. For a moment they sat enjoying the view down the dale, neither of them speaking. Then:

'Are you really happy here, Cara love?' Arnold asked. She heard the anxiety in his voice.

'Oh Dad, I'm blissfully happy! Don't I look it?'

'I suppose you do.' He acknowledged the fact with some reluctance. 'You know your happiness is what I want. It's very important to me.'

'More than me being headmistress of a famous school?' Cara teased.

'We all have ambitions for our children,' Arnold said. 'If we care about them, that is. But it's not my ambition that counts, it's what you want.'

'Everything I want is here in Arendale,' Cara said. 'Just as long as you and Ma, and Laura, visit me from time to time.'

'You know we'll do that, love.'

'Edward is the best of husbands,' Cara said gently. 'We're happy together.'

'But not with Susan,' Arnold said. 'I can see you've got a tough job there.'

'She's had a hard time, much too hard for a child. She'll come round, sooner or later.' Her words were more optimistic than her thoughts.

'Well, as long as you've chosen the right thing,' Arnold said.

She leaned across and touched his hand.

'Oh I have, Dad! I'm sure of it!'

They sat quietly for a few seconds more, then Cara saw Edward in the distance, climbing the slope towards them, Bess at his heels. As he reached them, and before he could speak, Cara quickly said:

'It's coming in misty on the top. Dad thought it was wise not to go further up.'

'Oh!' Edward said. 'Oh yes. Quite right!'

They set off back. When they reached the farm Cara looked up and to her pleasure observed a white mist obscuring the top of the fells. Arnold saw it with even greater relief.

'Just in time!' he said. 'Just in time!'

'And I'm in time for the milking,' Cara said. 'Do you want to come with me, Dad?'

'I think your mother and Laura might enjoy that,' he said. 'I mustn't monopolize you.'

'Perhaps you'd like to look at a few things with me,' Edward suggested. 'I'd be glad to show you round.'

'Lead on!' Arnold said.

He expressed a polite interest in everything Edward showed him, but it was not until his son-in-law began to talk about the running of the farm, the rules and regulations laid on them by the Government, the economics, the profit and loss, that Arnold's enthusiasm was really aroused. These were the kind of matters he understood.

'Well I must say,' he remarked as they made their way back to the house, 'there's more to all this than meets the eye! Now if ever I can be of any help, in the way of banking, let's say, you have only to ask.' He felt a new respect for Edward.

After supper Mrs Hendry ushered everyone into the parlour. It was growing dark now and through the window the fells were dense black against a sky which had faded to slate blue.

'We'll draw the curtains,' Mrs Hendry decreed. 'Susan, give a hand! It'll be more cosy, and really the nights can get quite chilly at this time of the year.'

She drew the heavy crimson plush curtains at the windows then poked the fire into a blaze. She had set a match to it during the afternoon, so the room was no longer chilly.

Cara sat on a deep window seat, Laura beside her. Everyone chatted happily, except Susan, who sat alone, not looking up from the magazine she was reading. She wouldn't have been in the room at all if her father hadn't quietly but firmly insisted, but if they thought she was going to be sociable they were mistaken. No-one could make her talk when she didn't want to.

'Now Laura,' Mrs Hendry said after a while, 'how about giving us a tune? I've never heard you play and by all accounts you're first class!'

'Please do,' Cara whispered to her sister.

'Cara's had the piano specially tuned,' Mrs Hendry said.

'If you really want me to,' Laura agreed. It would be easier to play the piano than to talk.

'There's music in the stool,' Mrs Hendry said.

'I'll play something from memory, if that's all right,' Laura said. She would choose something everyone knew, she thought – and began with Mendelssohn's 'Spring Song'.

Cara watched Susan almost immediately close her magazine and creep out of the room. It was a unmannerly thing to do, but they were as well off without her.

Laura brought the Mendelssohn to a close and began to play 'Für Elise', quietly, delicately. No-one spoke, everyone was intent on listening. She is really talented, Cara thought. Dad *must* allow her to make a career of it.

The Beethoven had hardly begun, only the first few bars played, when the deafening sound of the Saturday night Variety Orchestra, from the wireless in the kitchen which must have been turned on at the top of its volume, flooded the house. Everyone in the parlour flinched at the noise, except Laura, who went on playing. Presumably Susan had turned the volume so loud by mistake, Cara thought – even Susan couldn't be so rude – and waited for it to be turned down. But when it continued at full spate, the orchestra giving way to two loud-voiced comedians whose every word could be heard, she jumped to her feet and rushed out of the parlour.

In the kitchen she found Susan sitting in the armchair, reading her magazine.

'TURN IT OFF!' Cara yelled.

'I'm listening,' Susan said in a cool voice. 'I prefer this, if it's all the same to you.'

'TURN IT OFF!' Cara shouted again.

89

'I won't,' Susan replied. 'I've a right to listen to what I want in my own home. This was my home long before it was yours.'

'Well it's mine now! You might as well believe that because it's not going to change! You are the rudest, most selfish person I've ever met in my life!'

Cara was beside herself with rage. She could no longer think about or care what this row must sound like to her family, who in the parlour couldn't fail to hear it all. At the back of her mind she was aware that Laura had stopped playing.

'No-one asked you to come! No-one wants you,' Susan said. 'Not even Daddy wants you!'

They were screaming at each other, with the wireless still on at full pitch. In the bedlam, Cara didn't realize that Edward had come into the room until he brushed past her, making for the radio. She caught hold of his arm and pulled him back.

'No!' she shouted. 'Not you! Make *her* turn it off!'

'Turn it off at once!' Edward commanded his daughter. 'At once!'

Susan rose from her chair, walked over to the wireless and turned it off.

'For you, Daddy,' she said sweetly.

It was Edward who was in a rage now.

'Get out!' he shouted. 'Get to your room and get to bed!'

'Gladly!' Susan agreed.

'But don't think this is the end of it,' Edward said. 'I'll deal with you when our visitors have gone. Don't think you'll get away with it this time.'

When Susan had left the room Cara sat in the nearest chair. She was trembling from head to foot. She felt sick. She should never have let herself go like that.

Edward pulled her up from the chair and held her close.

'I'm sorry, love! I'm really sorry. And you know it's not true what she says. You know I want you, more than anything or anyone in the world.'

'I know, love,' Cara said. 'If I didn't think that I wouldn't stay a minute. I'd go straight back to Akersfield with the others. But I just wish I knew how to make her like me even a little bit!'

'We're not going to let this spoil our weekend, love, or even the rest of the evening,' Edward said. 'Come back and join the others.'

Arm in arm, they went back into the parlour.

'If you can excuse my very rude daughter, I'll be grateful to you,' Edward said. 'She's at an awkward age. Cara has the patience of a saint with her, but sometimes it's just too much!'

'Girls can be very difficult,' Beth Dunning declared cheerfully. 'Don't I know it! I've got two!'

Cara smiled at her mother. She had said the right thing, broken the embarrassment.

'I reckon I'll pour everyone a drink,' Tom Hendry said. He turned to Laura. 'That was lovely stuff you played, lass, but now can you play us some nice songs? Something we can all join in and sing. I like a good sing-song!'

'Certainly,' Laura said. 'What would you like?'

'Owt we can sing to,' Tom said. '"White Cliffs of Dover". "Tipperary". You might like to look through the stuff in the stool.'

Arnold Dunning left his seat and went upstairs to the bathroom. At first, because the staircase was dark, he didn't see Susan sitting there on the top step, nor did she see him. Her knees were drawn up to her chin and her head rested on them, her hair covering her face. She was sobbing as if her heart would break.

'Nay lass!' It was a measure of Arnold's astonishment that he used the dialect expression of concern.

'Nay lass, whatever is it? Don't take on so!'

He bent down and touched her shoulder. This was the girl who caused his daughter so much anguish, and by rights he shouldn't be wasting his sympathy on her, but just now she was nothing more than a deeply unhappy child. For a moment he felt towards her as he might have done to one of his own daughters when they were younger, and something had gone wrong.

'I'm so unhappy!'

Her head was bent and tears choked her voice, muffling the words.

'Everybody's hateful and they all hate me!'

'Now I don't believe that, a pretty girl like you!' Arnold said.

'It's true!'

They had started singing in the parlour. The sound of their voices came strongly up the stairs.

'Now why don't you come down and join in?' he said persuasively. 'How about it, then? Singing makes anybody feel better.'

She lifted her head and looked at him. For a brief moment he saw indecision in her eyes. Then she said:

'No. I'm a bit tired. I think I'll go to bed. But thank you all the same.'

'As you wish, love,' he said.

'You won't tell anyone, will you?'

'Not a word!'

When he went downstairs again Cara and Laura were sorting through the music. He said nothing to anyone of what had happened.

'I'm sorry you were upset, Laura,' Cara said. 'I didn't want that to happen.'

'I wasn't,' Laura said. 'The others were, I could tell, but funnily enough I wasn't. I feel differently when I'm playing. I just decided I wasn't going to let her upset me, so I didn't.'

'Laura! I've never heard you talk like that before!' Cara looked at her sister in astonishment.

'I know. It just came over me. I wished I was playing something really loud so I could have bashed it out!'

'Well there's quite a lot here you can bash out,' Cara said. 'That and the singing should make a rare old din!'

It was a din which went on, to the pleasure of those taking part, for hours, until the clock struck midnight and David had long been asleep in the armchair. The sound rose through the ceiling to Susan's room, but she had fallen asleep, the tears still wet on her face.

SEVEN

Susan did not appear at breakfast next morning, though it was Cara's private opinion that she had sneaked down early and smuggled food back to her room. No-one remarked on her absence; what was more natural than a girl rising late on a Sunday morning?

It was dinnertime before she showed herself. Beth Dunning smiled at her across the table and was met with a blank stare. The moment the meal was over Susan left the house, went to the shed for her bicycle, and took off down the dale. An hour later the Dunnings left for home.

'Thank you very much indeed,' Beth said to Mrs Hendry. 'It's been really lovely. We've all enjoyed it, haven't we, Laura?'

'Very much,' Laura agreed.

'I've been glad to see Cara so settled,' Beth added.

'Indeed. And thank you for your hospitality,' Arnold said. He could say that with truth. He'd quite enjoyed himself. He'd have liked to have seen Susan again, but it was fairly plain she didn't want to show her face.

Mrs Hendry suddenly threw her hands in the air, gave a shriek, and ran back into the house. Two minutes later she reappeared carrying two bags.

'I almost forgot!' she said. 'I'd put a few things up for you. Help out the rations. I hope you don't mind?'

What she had packed was a dozen fresh eggs, a large pat of butter, a jar of cream, a new-baked loaf, some slices of ham and half a dozen oatcakes.

'Why, that's lovely of you!' Beth said. 'What a feast!' Arnold would disapprove, of course, though he'd help to eat the spoils.

'Best say nothing,' Mrs Hendry cautioned. 'Edward's always telling me I'll end up in prison!'

'Well, that went off very nicely,' Cara said a minute or two later as she stood in the lane with Edward, watching until the car was out of sight.

'Most of it,' Edward agreed. 'We still have something to settle, and the minute that girl gets back from wherever she's sneaked off to it's going to be settled. We'll face her together.'

'No, Edward!' Cara's reply was swift and sharp. 'This is between me and Susan.'

Edward shook his head.

'When she offends you, she offends me. She's got to learn that.'

'She already knows,' Cara said. 'She knows the whole situation. Coming to terms with it is another matter.'

'She's got to,' Edward declared. 'I'll not stand much more of this.'

'Even so, I'd rather tackle her on my own,' Cara insisted. 'You've begun to build up a better relationship with Susan, even if I haven't. There's no need to harm that. Anyway, don't you think two of us on to one child is a bit too much?'

'In this case, no,' Edward said. 'But have it your own way, love. And promise you won't go soft on her.'

'Oh, I won't,' Cara assured him. 'She'll not get away with anything this time!'

When Susan returned, well after teatime, Cara was alone in the kitchen, the table spread with paperwork which she had put aside during her family's visit. Edward and his father had gone to inspect the sheep, taking David with them, and Mrs Hendry was busy in the dairy. Susan, looking neither to right nor left, strode across the kitchen, making straight for the door which led to the stairs and her room. As she went past the table Cara caught her by the arm and pulled her back.

'Not so fast, Susan! I have something to say to you!'

'I don't want to hear it,' Susan said. 'Let me go at once!' She tried to shake off her stepmother but Cara held firm.

'I daresay not, but you're going to!'

None too gently, she backed Susan towards a chair and pushed her down on to it, then stood immediately in front of her. Afterwards she wondered why Susan hadn't just walked away. It could only be because she had been taken by surprise.

'I'm glad we have the place to ourselves,' Cara said. 'But if anyone comes in it won't save you. I intend to have my say.' In fact she was trembling, her stomach was churning; she just hoped it didn't show, that her voice wouldn't give her away.

'You can't make me listen!' Susan was all defiance. She lolled in the chair, her legs stretched out, her jaw thrust forward, her eyes hard with anger.

'You will if you know what's good for you. What I have to say won't take long. First of all, let me remind you, Susan, that I'm here to stay. I belong at Beckwith as much as you do. Nothing you can do or say will drive me away. It might be what you hope for, but it's not going to happen.'

'Too bad,' Susan drawled. 'Can I go now?'

The words, and the girl's whole tone, were rude and pert, but never, Cara thought, had she looked so young, so vulnerable. All the hardness in her at this moment couldn't hide the childish roundness of her face, the immaturity of her mouth. For a moment she wanted to put her arms around Susan and comfort her. But something in the girl's face stopped her. She steeled herself to continue, whipping up her courage by raising her voice until in the end she was shouting.

'No you can't go. I haven't finished. The next thing is – and you'd better listen hard – I don't care any longer what you think about me but I will not – repeat *NOT* – countenance you being rude to anyone I ask to Beckwith, relative or friend. Nor will I allow you to get away with being rude to me in front of others. I've had enough. Do you understand?'

'I heard you. I should think the whole of Arendale heard you!'

'I suppose it's too much to expect an apology for last night's performance? You embarrassed everyone.'

'Much too much,' Susan agreed. 'Is that the end of the lecture? May I go?'

Cara stepped aside. Susan walked past her and left the room. Cara sat down quickly in the chair Susan had vacated. Suddenly there was no strength left in her legs.

I told a lie, she thought. I said I didn't care what she thought about me. It's not true. I do care. I care very much. What can I do?

On Monday morning Susan returned to school, and because her father was too busy on the farm to do so, Cara had to drive her to Shepton. From the back of the car – Susan had refused to sit beside her in the front – Cara felt the waves of hatred swirling around her head.

I hate her, Susan thought. Why did she ever have to come to Beckwith? How could Daddy marry her? What if she has a disgusting baby? Why did Mummy have to die?

She also hated school, only one degree less than home. There was nowhere in the world she wanted to be. The minute she was old enough, she vowed, she would find somewhere. Anywhere.

A week later the weather broke. The Indian summer was over and the fell tops of Arendale were hidden in the rain which poured down relentlessly, day after day, from grey skies.

'It's coming down like stair rods!' Mrs Hendry said, peering out of the window. 'Not a sign of a break. Not enough blue in the sky to make a sailor collar, let alone a pair of sailor's trousers!'

She sounded worried, Cara thought. It wasn't like her mother-in-law, who tended to take things as they came, especially weather. A lifetime in the dales had brought every imaginable kind of weather, and a lot of it bad. Dry in the spring when you needed the rain, wet the minute the hay was cut. It was the farmer's constant adversary.

'Anyway, there's nowt to be done about it,' Mrs Hendry observed.

She came away from the window and returned to her work. She was making oatcakes. She had prepared a large bowlful of batter, mixing oats with milk and a little yeast, and now she poured a ladleful, making a pool, on to the hot bakestone, spreading it out in the traditional oval shape until it was the right thickness, then skilfully flipping it over to cook the other side.

In exactly the same way women had made oatcakes in this dale for hundreds of years. Sometimes she gave a thought to all the women who must have used this old bakestone before her, but usually she concentrated on the job in hand. You had to judge just the right moment to lift the limp oatcakes from the bakestone and hang them on the rack to dry. It didn't leave much time for daydreaming.

'You look worried, Mother Hendry,' Cara said.

'I am a bit,' Mrs Hendry admitted.

'Well it can't be oatcakes,' Cara said.

'No, it's Tom,' Mrs Hendry said. 'I don't like him out in this weather. He's been wet through four times this week and he's got a cold on him. He's not as young as he was. Colds settle on his chest. Get a chill this time of year and it can stay with you till next spring.'

'Yes, the men have been wet through too often,' Cara agreed. Every day the kitchen had been hung with garments set to dry. Right now the clothes horse was draped with them, gently steaming in the heat of the kitchen.

'Can't you persuade Pop not to go up on the fell?' she asked. 'Couldn't Edward and Johann manage it between them?'

'Tom wouldn't hear of it,' her mother-in-law said. 'He thinks the farm would come to a standstill without him. He doesn't give Edward credit for being as good a farmer as he is. And of course it's nigh on tupping time. He'll certainly be needed then.'

'All the more reason he should take care now,' Cara observed.

'Try telling him!' Mrs Hendry said gloomily.

She hung the last oatcake on the rack, scraped the bakestone clean, took the batter bowl to the sink to wash it.

'That's them done for another week,' she said. 'I wish I could deal with that husband of mine as easy as I can oatcakes!'

As expected, the men came in an hour later, wet through. It wasn't that they didn't wear protective clothing, but nothing was proof against the torrential rain combined with the strong wind blowing from the north-west. It blew into every nook and cranny, driving the rain before it.

'Get those wet clothes off you, Tom Hendry!' his wife said sternly. 'And just hark at you coughing! You've got a real chill on you, that's for sure.'

'What are you going on about, woman?' Tom demanded. He stood inside the kitchen doorway, the rain running off him to make a pool on the flagstones. 'I've been wet a hundred times. It doesn't signify.'

'That cough signifies!' his wife retorted. 'Get your wet things off at once. You'll get no dinner else.'

'In fact,' Tom said a little later when, now wearing dry clothes, he sat at the table, 'in fact, I'm not all that hungry!'

Breaking off her serving of the meat pudding, his wife stared at him. So did Edward and Cara.

'Now I *know* you're not right,' she said. 'When have you ever not wanted your dinner? Well then, if you can't eat, you don't go up on those fells this afternoon. And that's telling you straight!'

'All right! All right! No need to make a song and dance about it,' Tom said. 'Happen I will take an hour or two off.'

'You'll take more than an hour or two, or else!' Mrs Hendry threatened.

'Ma's right,' Edward said. 'And Johann and I can manage this afternoon.'

'Aye, well then, I think I'll go and lie down,' Tom said. 'Forty winks'll see me as right as rain.' He felt weary. His head burned and ached. He'd be glad to get between the sheets.

'I'll put a hot-water bottle in the bed,' his wife said. 'Drat it, what you need is some home-made lemonade, but where can a soul get a lemon these days? It's a crying shame!'

She bustled about the kitchen, muttering and grumbling in a manner quite unlike her usual self. Everyone knew that her behaviour was a measure of her worry.

'Give me one of your potions, lass,' her husband suggested. 'We all know you've got a cure for everything. But nothing too unpleasant, mind!'

She was opening cupboard doors, pulling out drawers, looking on shelves.

'Paregoric! Cinnamon. Boiled onions,' she murmured. 'Camphorated oil! Yes, that's it!'

'As long as you don't rub me wi' boiled onions and make me drink camphorated oil,' Tom said.

'Treacle and vinegar,' she went on. 'That's always good for a poorly throat. The treacle soothes and the vinegar cuts the phlegm.'

'I haven't got a sore throat,' Tom protested.

He was wasting his time. She was already spooning treacle into a pan, heating it over the fire, adding vinegar. Well it couldn't kill him, he thought. He just wished she'd get on with it so he could go to bed, lose himself in sleep.

'When you've got yourself into bed I'll give your back and chest a rub with goose grease,' Mrs Hendry said.

Tom looked at Edward and Cara, raised his eyes to heaven, then thankfully took himself off.

'I could go out with you this afternoon,' Cara said to Edward. 'There's nothing I can't put off, as long as I'm back in time for the milking.'

Edward looked doubtful.

'I don't know, love. You've never dealt with the sheep, not even when I was away.'

'It is heavy work for a lady,' Johann put in. He had been silent up to now, eating his meal while anxiously observing Tom Hendry.

'We have to examine all the tups,' Edward said. 'They can be very awkward to handle. And then we have to collect the sheep, bring them lower down so they're more easily accessible for the tups.'

'I could give a hand with that, and leave the tups to you and Johann,' Cara said. 'If I can persuade Ruby to go with me she can almost gather the sheep on her own.'

'I don't know . . .' Edward remained doubtful.

'I need to learn these things,' Cara persisted. 'Anyway, I want to, I'd enjoy it. I want to be a farmer, not just a farmer's wife.'

'There's plenty to do as a farmer's wife,' Edward said.

But we already have a farmer's wife at Beckwith, Cara thought. Much as she liked her mother-in-law, she didn't want to live in her shadow. She wanted her own space.

'What you could do, if you're keen,' Edward said, 'is to begin by coming out with me and Johann and watch how we tackle the sheep. That way you'd learn something. But why choose a foul day like this?'

'When better?' Cara asked. 'Pop's laid up. He might be out of commission for a day or two. You could be glad of my help. Anyway, I'm not made of sugar. A drop of rain won't melt me.'

Half an hour later Cara climbed the fell with the two men, keeping close to the stream which, when she had brought her family here not so long ago, had been a less-than-moderate flow, and was now a minor torrent, splashing and frothing over the rocks. The climb was difficult, with the wind in their faces and the rain still beating down;

98

also her wet-weather clothing was heavy. At the same time, there was an exhilaration not to be found in the valley, and the weather forced a challenge which could never be experienced on a calm summer's day. She felt herself part of the wildness, exulting in the fight against the elements.

'Most of the ewes have already been brought down from the tops,' Edward said, 'though there'll be one or two strays still up there. As soon as the weather clears we'll go up with the dogs and search them out. I sometimes wonder if a farmer ever has all his sheep where he wants them!'

She walked around with Edward while he sought out the rams and examined them. It was evident how restless they were, how strong and difficult to handle in their restlessness. She admired the way Edward dealt with them in spite of their resistance.

'I see what you mean,' she said. 'Would I have the physical strength to deal with them?'

'There's also a knack,' Edward acknowledged. 'Anyway, a few more days and we'll have the ewes together where we want them, then the tups marked, and we can let the tups loose.'

Each ram would be liberally marked on the chest with a brightly coloured dye which, when he mated with the ewe, would rub off on her as evidence that she had been served. The rams would not be loosed indiscriminately, but according to plan, one ram to about fifty selected ewes.

'Once they're loosed,' Edward said, 'we spend a lot of time watching the tups don't desert their own ewes and go jumping over the wall to another lot!'

It was for this reason that Johann was re-examining the walls. The least cranny, the smallest break in a wall, was an invitation to tups or ewes to stray, usually taking a friend or two with them. 'There isn't a farmer in the dales who at one time or another hasn't found sheep in his flock which don't belong to him,' Edward said. 'If we didn't mark them we might lose them for ever!'

Throughout the afternoon the rain fell.

'I really think I must go and meet David,' Cara said in the end. 'It isn't fit for him to walk, even from Dale End. The wind is so strong.'

'I think you'd better,' Edward agreed.

She went back to the house and changed into dry clothes.

'How is Tom?' she asked her mother-in-law.

'Sleeping like a baby. But he looks very flushed. If he's no different tomorrow I shall get Dr Speight to look in.'

'You'd be wise,' Cara said.

She drove to the road junction where the bus would drop David.

He was already there, sheltering in the lee of a wall and under a tree, though since the tree was almost devoid of leaves the shelter was minimal.

'I knew you'd come!' he said.

'Have you been waiting long?' Cara asked. 'I'm sorry if I'm late.'

'Only a minute or two. And you're not late. I think the bus was early. I've got a note for you.'

'A note? For me?'

'For you and Daddy. Shall I read it to you? I know what it's about.'

'In that case you might as well,' Cara said.

He unfolded the note, then spoke the words slowly and carefully, stumbling over the longer ones. He'd not long since learned to read.

'It has been suggested that parents and children from the area might like to go to the pantomime in Helsdon. It is already too late to book seats for any performance before early February. We would go by coach. Please let me know if you are interested and we will make further plans. The pantomime is *Cinderella*. Yours truly, Amy Pratt.'

'Amy Pratt is the teacher,' David added unnecessarily.

'I know.'

'I didn't know if you knew she was called Amy. Can we go? Oh do please say we can!'

'We shall have to ask your daddy,' Cara said. 'I expect he'll say yes, or at least he'll say I can take you. It's not the busiest time on the farm.'

'Miss Pratt said brothers and sisters can go,' David said. 'Do you think Susan will want to?'

'Who knows?' Cara said. 'We'll ask her at the weekend.'

The next day, after a restless night, Tom was no better. In answer to Mrs Hendry's call Dr Speight came promptly.

He was a big man, who filled the kitchen doorway where he now stood. All the years of his practice had been spent in the dales, and those of his father before him. There was hardly a child for miles around, including Susan and David, whom he hadn't brought into the world.

'So what's all this then?' he enquired.

Tom Hendry was an old friend, but it was unusual for him to require medical attention. He was, like most dalesmen, healthy and hardy.

'I thought you'd best take a look at him,' Mrs Hendry said. 'He's got a bit of fever on him, and he's had a cough for a week or two, though he'll not admit to it.'

'Now then, Tom!' Dr Speight said, following Mrs Hendry into the bedroom. 'What have you been up to?'

'Nowt!' Tom said in disgust. 'I'd not mind so much if I'd had my bit o' fun first, but I haven't! All the same, there was no need for Edith to send for you.'

'Best let me be the judge of that,' the doctor said. 'Take off your nightshirt and I'll hearken to your chest.'

For the next minute or two, with Mrs Hendry hovering anxiously near, he tapped and listened, listened and tapped.

'Put your shirt back on,' he said in the end. 'And get back under the bedclothes.'

'I said it were nowt!' Tom protested. 'It isn't, is it?'

'You've got bronchitis, Tom. Not all that bad, I've known worse cases, but it's there right enough.'

'But I can't have,' Tom contradicted him. 'We're starting tupping any day now. I can't be poorly.'

'Aye well, there it is,' Dr Speight said calmly. 'Though I don't doubt when they're loosed with the ewes the tups will know what to do without you there! They'll do what comes naturally.'

'There's a sight more to it than that,' Tom said angrily. 'As you well know!'

'Of course I do,' the doctor said. 'I also know that this year you'll have to miss it. I order you – *order*, do you hear? – to stay in bed for at least a week. Keep warm, drink plenty of fluids, and take whatever concoction Edith mixes up for you. And when I *do* allow you up, you'll not go climbing the fells for another week or two. Have I made that plain?'

'As plain as a pikestaff, Doctor,' Mrs Hendry said. 'And you can rely on me to see he does as he's told!'

Tom Hendry looked from his wife to his doctor in deep disgust.

'How shall we manage?' he demanded. 'Tell me that!'

'You've got a son,' Dr Speight pointed out. 'You've got one of those German prisoners everybody says are so good. And if you get really stuck there isn't a farmer in the dales won't help if he can.'

'If he can is about it,' Tom said. 'It's tupping time for all on 'em. They're all throng.'

'Well, you lie back and think of other things,' the doctor advised. 'Try to sleep. If you can't get to sleep, try counting sheep!'

'Very comical!' Tom said in deep disgust.

That evening Cara, Edward and Mrs Hendry sat around the table debating what was to be done, while David played on the floor with his collection of Dinky cars.

'I don't think we can look to anyone else for help,' Edward said. 'Everyone's up to their eyes!'

'In which case we'll have to share the work between us,' Cara said sensibly. 'I see no reason why I couldn't help with the tupping, Edward. It's too much for you and Johann.'

'Happen we just could get another POW,' Edward said. 'But I doubt it. They'll all have been spoken for.'

'Then let's assume we can't,' Cara said.

'If Cara's going to be up with you, I can take on the milking,' Mrs Hendry offered. 'Heaven's my witness I know how!'

'And I could bring the cows in,' David said, looking up. 'And feed the dogs and the hens, and collect the eggs.'

'Of course you could, love,' his father said. 'You'll be a great help, that's for sure.'

'I'd like to learn to milk,' David said.

'Happen I'll teach you,' his grandmother suggested. 'You're a bit young, and your hands are a mite small, but we'll see.'

'What about the paperwork?' Edward asked. 'It won't go away, more's the pity.'

'It'll just have to wait,' Cara said firmly. 'Animals come first.'

'Why couldn't Susan do a bit of that at the weekends?' Mrs Hendry asked. 'All that schooling, she could put it to some use.'

'I'd need to show her the ropes.' Cara sounded doubtful.

'Well if not that, then she can help Ma in the house,' Edward said. 'She's got to take her share.'

When the news was broken to Susan at the weekend she was not pleased, though she was concerned about her grandfather. Reluctantly, she chose to help in the house rather than be instructed in the mysteries of the paperwork by Cara.

'You could learn to milk,' David suggested. 'That's what I want to do.'

'No thank *you*!' Susan said. 'That's the last thing!' Except for the dogs, she disliked anything to do with the animals.

'Just as well,' her grandmother said tartly. 'I doubt they'd yield a drop to you. Beasts can soon tell if a person's not sympathetic.'

It was a busy weekend. Fortunately the rain had ceased, and though the weather was cold it was clear and dry.

'Tell me exactly what you want me to do,' Cara said to Edward.

'Well,' he began. 'First off could you take Ruby and see if there's any strays on top? Bring them down. We all know Ruby's a one-man dog, but I think she'll go with you.'

'I'm on my way,' Cara said.

'Don't be too long!' Edward called after her. 'We need Ruby, if not you!'

'Cheek!' Cara laughed.

It was like being on the rim of the world, she thought as, after a climb which had left her breathless, she stood on the summit and looked around her. The air was unbelievably clear for November. She could see for miles in every direction: to the west the hills which bordered Lancashire; to the north the high road over Fleet Moss which led into Wensleydale, her mother-in-law's birthplace; to the south, though not in view, lay Shepton, and beyond that the road to Akersfield. Range after range of high green hills opened out before her, and over them the pale limestone walls, in their totally random patterns, climbed to the very tops.

Not long afterwards, on the specific day Edward appointed, the rams were loosed and tupping time was under way. The daylight hours were short now, and growing shorter. Cara was on the fells with the two men for most of them, and learned to do whatever they asked of her. Tom Hendry was on his feet again but, though out of bed, he was still confined to the house. Every day of his convalescence increased his irritability.

'It's not right!' he protested. 'I ought to be up there wi' em. First tupping time I've missed i' thirty years. And I'm quite well enough.' He peered out of the window like a prisoner behind bars.

'For goodness sake man, stop blethering!' Mrs Hendry begged. 'You're *not* fit enough. You heard what Dr Speight said.'

'He's an old woman!' Tom said spitefully.

'He's no such thing! He's a very good doctor, as you well know. But you're driving me into being an old woman before my time, I can tell you that for nothing!'

She knew she was short with him, and she ought not to be, but he was recovering too slowly and this worried her. It wasn't like Tom.

Minutes later Edward and Cara came in for dinner. Johann had stayed on the fell and would come down later. For now, they didn't leave the sheep too long.

'How's it going?' Tom asked anxiously.

'Fine!' Edward said. 'Of course I won't say we don't miss you,' he added hastily. 'But Cara's a help.'

Cara was at the table, already tucking into the nourishing stew which Mrs Hendry had heaped on her plate. She was always ravenously hungry these days.

She ate her meal quickly, picked up the flask of tea and the tin which Mrs Hendry had packed with slabs of cake and a few biscuits for their teatime snack, and left the house.

'I'll not be many minutes,' Edward called.

Tom Hendry watched her through the window.

'Yon lass shouldn't be doing this. It's my job!' His voice was full of longing.

Halfway through the afternoon Cara straightened her back and looked down the hillside towards the valley. She could see the river in the distance, and their cattle in the meadow close by. Compared with the activity here, all was serene down there. Then she saw a stranger.

'Edward, there's someone coming!' she called out.

'Who? Where?'

'I don't know. A man. He's coming up the hill.'

Edward strained his eyes. The man was still a way off.

'I don't know him,' he declared. 'But it's not the time of year for a stranger to be climbing the fells.'

If Edward didn't recognize the man it went without saying that he didn't belong in the dale. Edward knew everyone. Either he or his father had grown up with most of them. Nevertheless the man climbed steadily towards them in a purposeful way. He was not idly climbing the fell, he was coming directly to see them.

Cara stood still and appraised him as he drew nearer. He was young, not more than a year or two older than herself, she judged. He was tall, blond-haired, country-dressed, but when he was almost on them she noted that his skin lacked the usual tan of the countryman. He didn't look as though he'd been out in all weathers.

The man strode the last few yards with his hand outstretched in greeting.

'Hello!' he said. 'You won't know me. I'm Grant Fawcett. Joseph Fawcett at Penghyll Farm is my uncle.'

'Pleased to meet you!' Edward said. 'Of course I know your uncle. This is my wife, Cara.'

Edward spoke pleasantly enough, but he was niggled at the interruption. Obviously the man wasn't a farmer or he'd know better than to pay social calls at tupping time.

'I know it's not a good time,' Fawcett said quickly, as if he could read Edward's thoughts. 'I came to see if I could give you any help. Uncle Joe said your father was laid up with bronchitis and maybe you could use another pair of hands.'

'That's good of you,' Edward said. 'And it's kind of your uncle. But surely he's throng with tupping time himself?'

'All but over,' Fawcett replied, smiling. He had a wide, pleasant smile which creased and lifted his whole face. 'He doesn't have nearly as many sheep as you do. From what he says, your family is the biggest owner in these parts.'

'That's true,' Edward acknowledged.

'I called at Beckwith, saw Mrs Hendry. That's how I knew where you were. So what can I do? Can I help?'

'Well,' Edward said. 'My wife has been working like a Trojan, helping out. If yours is a serious offer, she might well like to take a break.'

He turned to Cara. 'What about it, love?'

Her back ached, her hands were sore, the November afternoon was damp – but did she want to give up? Not really, she decided.

'As Edward says, it's kind of you, but honestly I'm all right!'

She looked all right, Grant Fawcett thought. Her skin glowed with health, her eyes were the greenest and brightest he had ever seen. In spite of the fact that she was dressed in breeches and a drab-coloured duffle coat, with a woolly hat on her head, she managed to look nothing like the farmer's wife he'd expected.

'Well, perhaps I can muck in generally?' he offered. 'And if I get under your feet you can send me packing.'

In fact he proved helpful. He'd been less than a month on his uncle's farm but he'd taken quickly to handling the sheep. Also he was strong.

'Of course I know next to nothing,' he admitted. 'But I'm learning.'

'I'm in the same boat, at least where sheep are concerned,' Cara told him. 'I've just jumped in at the deep end.'

'Are you visiting your uncle, then?' Edward asked.

'Oh no! Didn't I say? I'm here for good. I've come to learn the business and hopefully take over from Uncle Joe when the time comes – which I hope won't be for years yet. You know he doesn't have children.'

'I know,' Edward said.

'Will your wife like it here?' Cara enquired. 'Does she like the country?'

'If I had a wife she'd have to be a country-lover,' Fawcett said. 'But I don't have one. Now tell me what I can do next, Mr Hendry.'

'Edward.'

'And Grant.' He turned to Cara, questioning her with a look.

'Cara,' she said.

He worked with a will and was more skilled than Edward expected. When dusk fell, all too soon, Edward said, 'Thank you very much. It was good of you.'

'I'll come tomorrow,' Grant offered.

I reckon we're nearly through,' Edward said. 'A few more days and I'll put the chasers in.'

'The chasers?'

Edward grinned.

'Your uncle hasn't done that yet?'

'Well if he has, I don't know of it.'

'There's always a few ewes left over which haven't been tupped,' Edward explained. 'Towards the end we round 'em up and put a couple of tups in with 'em. Oh, not the pedigree rams! They've done their bit. Just a couple of chasers. The lambs we get from them mostly go to the butcher.'

'I live and learn,' Grant smiled.

'Me too,' Cara said. 'Will you come back and have some supper with us?'

'I'm tempted,' he said. 'But I'd better not. My aunt will be expecting me.'

As November moved into December, and towards Christmas, it was the quietest time of the year at Beckwith. There was less to do on the farm. The in-lamb ewes had been sent off to winter in Nidderdale, as arranged by Edward at the Shepton sales in the autumn.

'I'd like to send more,' he told Cara. 'This year's ewes could do with going, but it's a matter of money.'

The rest of the animals had been brought down closer to the house now. They would need supplementary feeding right through the winter when the weather made grazing impossible for much of the time, and it would be difficult to reach them on the hill. Already the snow covered the fells and the long nights were sharp with frost.

Tom Hendry had recovered, though sometimes his wife thought he looked white and tired, and at night in the chill of the bedroom he coughed. She was glad that the slowing down of work on the farm meant that he wasn't tempted to stay out of doors too long.

Johann, in his small room in this foreign country, thought about his homeland, especially the Austrian Christmases of his childhood: the Christkindl market which he would visit with his mother, the tree, the coming of the Christ-child with gifts. And every evening while he dreamed he whittled away at his wood-carving, so that on Christmas Day each member of the family received a beautifully-carved gift from him. With the exception of Cara's present, all were wild animals and birds common to Arendale: a stoat, a fox, a pheasant, a kingfisher, and for Mrs Hendry a tiny chaffinch. But Cara's present was different and everyone agreed it was superb. For Cara Johann had made a shepherd's crook, the handle of which was exquisitely carved in the shape of a ram's head.

'It's the most beautiful thing I've ever owned!' Cara said.

'You have well and truly earned it,' Johann told her.

'Yes, you've served your apprenticeship,' Edward said.

'Only a few more weeks and we shall be going to the pantomime!' David exclaimed. It was a subject he brought up constantly. 'I can hardly wait! Can you, Susan?'

'I can easily wait, silly!' she said. 'It's not the biggest thing in my world.'

She had graciously decided to accompany David and Cara to

the performance, but she was certainly not going to enthuse about it.

Once, a long time ago, just before David was born, her mother had taken her to the pantomime in Sheffield. She had never forgotten it, and never would: the glittering, many-coloured lights, the warmth, the orchestra, but most of all the young girls singing and dancing in their beautiful dresses. In her heart she had danced every step with them.

She had lied when she said to David that she could easily wait. Ever since the booking had been made she'd been counting the days.

EIGHT

For David, January 1947 dragged on interminably. The first week was not so bad: he was on holiday from school then and could go out with his father on the farm. After that, when the new term started, it was dark by the time he was home, and the evenings were long. All that mattered to him was that February should come, and the quicker the better. February would bring the pantomime.

He had never been to a pantomime before, not even to a theatre, but a few of the children at school had, and they boasted of it constantly. So, she had let it slip, had Susan, but she would tell him nothing more about it. Anyway, he knew it was going to be wonderful.

'I can't think why he's so set on it,' Tom Hendry said. 'I never went to a pantomime when I were little.'

'I did,' Cara said. 'Living in Akersfield, we went every year; either there, or to Helsdon, or sometimes to Bradford. I thought it was magic!'

'Then I expect it's you has been stuffing his head with it,' Tom grumbled. He did quite a bit of grumbling these days. He wasn't his cheery self.

'It'll do him no harm,' Mrs Hendry said. 'He doesn't get a lot of treats, and he's a good little lad.'

She herself had also had a treat. Soon after Christmas Cara had taken her into Shepton to a performance of the *Messiah* at the Methodist chapel. She'd listened to it on the wireless, of course, but that was nothing to actually being there, in the flesh, with all those wonderful singers.

'I'm in favour of treats,' she said. 'Good luck to him!'

'And to Susan,' David chipped in. 'She's going.'

'Of course!' How would that work out, his grandmother wondered?

The tops of the fells had been covered in snow since mid-December, but in January it fell on the lower slopes; not heavily, by the standards of the dales, but enough to make it possible for David to take out his sledge at the weekends.

'I made that sledge for your dad when he were a young 'un,' Tom said to David.

'I know, Grandpa. You told me.'

'And what if I did?' Tom said testily. 'Am I not allowed to say anything twice?'

'Of course, Grandpa!' David said. 'Anyway, it really is the best sledge in the dale.'

'Well, there you are then!' Tom was mollified.

He knew what was the matter with him. He was suffering from too little to do. There was still plenty of work, of course – the farm didn't come to a standstill, animals had to be tended – but the outside jobs were what he liked best, always had done. He wanted to be high on the fell with Bess, with the wind on his face and the sky seemingly not all that far above him.

It wasn't possible. For a start, the sheep were down, and what had to be done – extra feeding; seeing, when the hard frosts turned everything to ice, that there was water – seemed now to be taken care of by Edward and Johann. Sometimes he suspected there was a conspiracy to keep him indoors.

'I've a good mind to go sledging with you,' he said to David.

His wife looked up from the batter she was beating for a Yorkshire pudding.

'You'll do no such thing, Tom Hendry! Have you gone daft? You've got nicely rid of that chest and I'm going to see you don't get it again, if it's the last thing I do!'

'How will you manage that, then? Lock me in?'

'If I have to,' she said firmly. 'Sithee, if you want to make yourself useful you can take a turn at beating this batter.'

'I'll do no such thing!' Tom said indignantly. 'Cooking is woman's work! What do you take me for?'

Cara listened, but took no part in the conversation. All the same, she could imagine how Tom felt. For the time being she, too, had lost most of her outdoor jobs. She still looked after the cows, milked them twice a day, but they had been brought in from the fields now that there was no grazing for them, and were kept in the shippon all the time. There was very little she could do outside to help Edward.

Mrs Hendry was sometimes aware of her daughter-in-law's restlessness. It was a period of the year, she thought, when they all had a bit more time to observe each other. Much of the year they were too busy to notice.

'Why don't you take advantage, and go and see your folks in Akersfield?' she suggested one evening.

She was sitting with Cara, each of them working at opposite ends of a tabbed rug they were making for the kitchen. It was a regular winter job.

Cara brightened at the suggestion, stopped in the act of pushing a tab through the canvas.

'Do you think I could?'

She turned to Edward. 'What do you think, love?'

'All right if you want to,' he agreed.

'It would be nice,' she said. 'I'd only stop away one night. I'll tell you what,' she said to her mother-in-law, 'I could look out for a bit of brighter-coloured material for this rug. They sell bags of pieces in the fent shop in Akersfield.'

The rug, like most of the rugs in all the houses, was in sober shades of grey and black and navy – because it was made from old clothes cut into small pieces, and these were the usual colours of the garments. There was seldom enough brightly coloured material to make more than a small design in the centre.

'That would be grand,' Mrs Hendry said. 'Try for some bits of red and green.'

'Are you sure you don't mind me going, love?' Cara asked Edward later on, when they were getting ready for bed. She was at the dressing table in her nightdress, brushing her hair. He came over and put his hands on her shoulders, meeting her eyes in the mirror.

'I don't mind if it's what you want,' he said. 'But don't stay away long. I hate being without you.'

He stroked the back of her neck, then slowly ran his fingertips down her spine. She arched her back and leaned her head against him and he moved his hands from her back and slid them over her shoulders, and downwards to cup her breasts. A shiver of desire ran through her.

'Come to bed,' he said.

Their lovemaking had taken a new turn, improving all the time. In the weeks leading up to Christmas, when work had taken too much of their time and energy, there had been many nights when one or the other, or both of them, had been too weary to make love. All they could do then was fall asleep in each other's arms. Now it was different. They came together most nights, exulting in the strength and fierceness and delight of their intercourse.

'Why should I want to be away from you even for one night?' Cara said later, on the point of going to sleep. 'I must be mad.'

'I shall be mad for you when you return!' Edward said. 'I'm warning you!'

'Then I shall go,' she said. 'Oh Edward, tell me you love me!

110

I want it to be the last thing I hear every night before I go to sleep.'

'I love you,' he said. 'Always and for ever, for the rest of our lives!'

Three days later Cara left for Akersfield, Edward driving her as far as the station. The weather was cold, but the sky was clear and the sun bright, picking out a myriad of diamonds in the snow-covered landscape. There was snow as far as the eye could see, for the most part untrodden, though in the fields, and especially near the hedges, the surface was marked by the footprints of birds and an occasional small animal. Trees, in the valleys and in the meadows by the river, stood out blackly against the snow.

On the station platform Edward embraced Cara as the train came in sight.

'Take care of yourself,' he said.

'And you, love. I'll be back tomorrow night.'

'I'll be here to meet you.'

He watched the train out of sight, hating to see her go. Life without Cara now would be only half a life. He had fallen in love with her quickly and had thought that that was it, and had been happy in the thought. He hadn't known, then, how love could grow.

In Akersfield Cara, feeling the need to stretch her legs, chose to walk from the station to her parents' home, even though the snow was turning black and slushy underfoot. In these streets she felt totally familiar with every corner, every landmark, yet now at the same time she felt alien. All my life until the last five months I've lived here, she thought. I've walked this road, passed the library, the Co-op, Hansen's the pork butcher's, a thousand times – and now I'm a stranger. This isn't my home any longer.

Beth Dunning, watching for Cara from the window, felt a lift of the heart as she saw her daughter approach. By the time Cara reached the gateway – the ornate iron gate, as well as the railings, which had once kept dogs and small children from straying into the garden, had long ago gone to be melted down for the war effort – the front door was open and Beth was standing on the top step.

'Oh love, you look frozen!' she cried. 'Come in at once!'

'And you shouldn't be standing out here,' Cara admonished. 'You'll catch your death.'

'It's not much warmer in the house,' Beth apologized, leading the way to the sitting room. 'We're almost without coal. And they say there'll be power cuts before long if things don't improve – electricity and gas. Your dad says it's our patriotic duty to save all we can and he won't let me switch on the fire.'

So saying, she bent down and switched it on, and in a minute both bars glowed red.

'So why . . .?' Cara began.

'Oh, I take no notice when he's out at work. I'm not going to sit and shiver, not until I have to! I don't suppose they're shivering in the bank! Now you get warm and I'll go and make a cup of tea. Oh, I am glad to see you, love!'

Cara, leaving the fire, followed her mother into the kitchen, Beth talking all the time. I don't remember her talking as much as this, Cara thought.

'So how are you getting on with this fuel business?' Beth asked. 'What will you do when the power cuts come?'

'We're down on coal but we've got peat. As for power cuts, well, as you know we don't have either gas or electricity, so it won't matter.'

'Good heavens! I'd forgotten that. How awful!'

'Not at all,' Cara contradicted her. 'We shan't feel it as much as you do. Actually, they were going to bring the electricity up to Beckwith, but the war came and stopped it.'

Beth shook her head in wonder. In a way, she thought, Arnold was right. It *was* like living in the wilderness.

'Anyway, never mind all that,' Cara said. 'When will Laura be in? Is Dad coming home to dinner?'

'Dad'll be in for dinner,' Beth said. 'Sometimes I wish he wouldn't. There's a perfectly good little restaurant he could go to, save our rations. But oh no! He has to come home! Anyway, what he gets in the middle of the day he can't have in the evening!'

Her father, Cara thought, seemed much more himself than he had on his visit to Beckwith. This was his milieu. He had authority here. In his dark suit and striped tie he looked far more comfortable than he had in his country clothes.

'So you've come to town for a taste of civilization?' he said. 'Well, it's lovely to see you and I don't blame you.'

'No I haven't,' Cara said. He made Akersfield sound like the metropolis. 'I came to see you and Ma and Laura.'

'And how is Edward?' Arnold asked. 'Is he busy?'

To hear her father refer pleasantly to Edward was music to Cara's ears. There had been a time, not long past, when he could only speak of her husband in censorious, or at best grudging, tones.

'Not so busy at this time of the year, but he's well. And how are you, Dad?'

'Not bad. Not bad at all. My war wound is playing up, but then it always does at this time of the year, as you well know.'

She vividly remembered so many winters of her childhood when her father had propped up his leg on a stool while her mother tended the great weeping sore on his shin before bandaging it up again. She had been horrified yet fascinated at the sight of it.

'Why you didn't get a pension for that, I'll never know,' Beth said now, as she had every winter. 'Other men got pensions for far less.'

But her father had never complained, Cara thought. It was almost as if he'd been proud to be wounded, was proud still to bear the scars.

At ten to two precisely Arnold rose to his feet, checked the time on his watch by the time on the clock on the mantelpiece.

'Time and tide and the bank wait for no man!' he said. 'I'll have to be off.'

'See you this evening,' Cara said.

At half-past four Laura came in from school.

'Sorry I'm late,' she said breathlessly. 'I had an extra music lesson.'

'How's everything going?' Cara asked.

'Fine! Has Ma told you I might get a scholarship to Manchester?'

Cara's look questioned her mother.

'It's not certain,' Beth said defensively. 'Anyway, your dad and me aren't sure she ought to go.'

'Not go? Why ever not?' Cara was astonished. 'It would be a marvellous opportunity.'

'She'd have to board,' Beth said. 'It's too far to travel every day. I wouldn't be able to keep an eye on her, and we all know Laura's not strong.'

'Oh, Cara, do tell Ma she's wrong!' Laura exclaimed passionately. 'I'm perfectly all right, and it would be simply wonderful!'

'I do think Laura's right, Ma,' Cara said. 'And I'm sure she'd be well looked after.'

Beth sighed.

'It doesn't rest with me. There's your father to consider. Anyway, she hasn't got the scholarship yet.'

'But I will,' Laura insisted. 'I know I will.' She turned to her sister. 'Please, Cara, can't you persuade Father? He always listens to you.'

'I'll certainly try,' Cara promised.

'Can't you see this is Laura's big chance?' she said to her father after supper. Laura was in the ice-cold dining room, practising. Not even for Cara would she give up her evening practice.

'She wants to be a concert pianist,' Arnold said. 'It's not suitable. It's a rackety life for a delicate girl like Laura, travelling all over the place.'

'Listen to her now, Dad,' Cara said. 'How can you say it's not suitable? And think how proud you'd be, seeing her up there on the concert platform, bowing to the applause!'

For a second or two Arnold allowed himself the vision of his daughter acknowledging the acclaim of the crowd, and of himself, her guide and mentor, accepting the congratulations. 'Yes, she's my daughter!' 'I owe it all to my father!' she would say. Then she would take a single flower from the bouquet with which she'd been presented, and throw it down to where he sat in the front row of the stalls.

Perhaps, he thought, could it possibly be . . . that it's my younger daughter who's destined for greatness, not, as I once thought, my elder?

'I don't know,' he said gruffly, coming down to earth. 'I'll have to think about it.'

'But you will think about it?' Cara begged. 'Promise!'

'I promise.'

The next day, when the time came to leave, Cara was sad; yet as she left the house and walked away down the road, turning to wave to her mother before she went out of sight, she felt a sudden lifting of the sadness of parting, followed by an onrush of a great sense of freedom. She was on her way to where she belonged. A few hours and she would be back in Arendale; at Beckwith, with Edward. But it wasn't only Edward, or Beckwith, it was the dales themselves. It was as if they were hers, and she was theirs, and they had called out to her to come home.

Don't be so fanciful, she told herself severely.

She bought a newspaper and, settling in the corner of a compartment, waiting for the train to start, began to read. The guard had already blown his whistle when the carriage door burst open and a young man, all arms and legs, fell in.

'Made it!' he cried. Then as he fell on to the seat, 'Good heavens! It's you!'

'Hello, Grant!' Cara said. 'This is a surprise. I didn't know you ever came to Akersfield.'

'It's a pleasant surprise for me,' Grant Fawcett replied. 'Seeing you, I mean. What are you doing in Akersfield?'

'I've been visiting my family. And you? Do you have family here?'

'A friend,' he said.

A girlfriend, Cara thought. He was far too attractive to be unattached.

She had seen Grant Fawcett only once since tupping time, at church on Christmas Day. He'd been there with his uncle and aunt, and after the service, standing in the bitter cold of the churchyard, they'd all exchanged greetings.

'How are your aunt and uncle?' Cara asked now.

'Very well.'

'It was good of them to spare you when they did.'

114

In fact, Grant thought, after the first occasion he had needed no encouragement to help out at Beckwith. He had never met anyone quite like Cara Hendry. Oh, he'd seen at once that she only had eyes for her husband, though no matter, he was prepared to worship from afar. But now that he had her to himself for at least an hour – the train was a slow one, stopping at every station – he could think of nothing to say.

'How is your father-in-law?' he began.

'Much better. Not quite on top form, but much better. He's frustrated because he can't do all he wants to.'

'If I can help out at any time, I'll be pleased to,' Grant offered.

'Thank you.'

There was a pause. Cara looked out of the window; they were slowing down, approaching a station. When she turned back again it was to find Grant's serious gaze fixed on her. Caught in the act, he looked disconcerted, but when she smiled at him he relaxed. Working with him on the fell she hadn't noticed his shyness; they'd all been too busy to talk much. Now she must think of something to say to him, though really she would rather sit back and read her newspaper.

'I wonder if I might know your friend?' she hazarded. 'I've lived in Akersfield all my life, so I might well. What's his name?'

'Her name,' Grant corrected. 'I doubt you will. She doesn't belong to Akersfield. She's teaching there. Her name's Pamela Sharp.'

He didn't in the least want to talk about Pamela.

'Is she . . .?' Cara hesitated, then plunged in. 'Well, as they say in these parts, are you courting?' She laughed to show him she wasn't being too serious, or prying.

She was enchanting when she laughed, he thought. Her whole face lit up. Her eyes sparkled, her mouth stretched and curved, showing very white, even, rather small teeth, with a slight gap in the middle.

'Good heavens no! Nothing like that! She's a friend of my sister's. I'd promised to look her up, that's all.'

It was not quite all, and he should have felt guilty at his brisk dismissal of Pamela Sharp, but he didn't.

After that it was easier. Cara's laugh had warmed the atmosphere and for the rest of the journey they chatted freely. Mostly she asked him questions about his family, and told him about hers. He wouldn't have cared if they'd discussed the price of potatoes as long as they talked.

'Did you always want to be a farmer?' she asked him.

'Oh yes! I used to come up to my uncle's farm when I was a kid. It was usually holiday times, when they'd be busy with the hay or something. I think I met Edward once, but he won't remember. Anyway, my uncle always planned to take me on, and there was nothing I'd have liked more, but the war took me to

Burma – I was in the Fourteenth Army – and that was that until it was over.'

'Where do your parents live?' Cara asked.

'My parents are dead. They were both killed in an accident a few years ago. I live with my sister, but she's married now so it's not the same.'

'I'm sorry,' Cara said. 'I expect your aunt and uncle are pleased to have you.'

'I think so.'

It seemed no time at all before they were at the end of their journey.

'How are you getting back to Arendale?' Cara asked as they walked along the platform.

'My motor-bike's here,' Grant said.

Outside the station he exchanged a few words with Edward, made a polite farewell to Cara, then roared off into the night and was quickly out of sight.

'A nice young man,' Cara said.

'And nicely placed,' Edward replied. 'He'll inherit Fawcett's one day. It's a good farm.'

The rest of January passed. For Tom and Edith Hendry, like all time now, it seemed to race with the speed of a hare. For David it crawled like a snail, but at last it was the first Monday in February, the day of the pantomime visit. Edward was to take Cara and the two children to Faverwell, from where the coach would leave at eleven o'clock.

'Shouldn't it leave earlier?' David asked anxiously. He had been ready for ages. 'Supposing we don't get there in time?'

'Oh, David, please stop worrying!' Cara begged. 'Of course we'll be in time. We'll be at the theatre at least half an hour before the matinée's due to start.'

'Then shouldn't we set off for Faverwell?' David insisted. 'Don't forget we want to buy our sweets before we go on the coach.'

Tom Hendry had not only given the children a shilling each to buy sweets, he had also handed over his sweet coupons.

'I'm sure you can buy sweets at the theatre,' Cara said.

'But not the ones I want,' David said. 'I'm going to have marzipan teacakes, pear drops, and a sherbert fountain for when I get thirsty. What are you going to buy, Susan?'

'Oh, stop fussing!' Susan said. 'I haven't thought.'

All the same, she reckoned, they should get to Faverwell as soon as possible, because she wanted to grab a good seat on the coach. She was determined not to sit near Cara and David. In spite of what Mr Dunning had said – and she had quite liked Mr Dunning – she and

Cara could never be friends. As for David, he was soft. She would have been happy to sit with him, but he wasn't on her side. He wouldn't take her side against Cara. David wanted everyone to be palsy-walsy and she certainly wasn't falling for that.

'It's still snowing,' Mrs Hendry said, glancing out of the window. 'I suppose the driver won't set off if he thinks the weather's not fit?'

For a moment David felt quite sick.

'Not set off?' How could he bear that?

'Thorndike's used to snow,' Edward said. 'He's a dalesman. Anyway, it doesn't look too bad. Come on then, let's be off.'

'Now have you got everything?' Mrs Hendry fussed. 'Have you got the sandwiches and the flask?' She had insisted on packing a midday snack to be eaten in the coach, though after the performance they were going out to a restaurant meal.

'I have them,' Cara assured her. 'And the blankets in case it's cold in the coach, though I don't suppose it will be with all those bodies.'

'You're none of you well enough wrapped up!' Mrs Hendry complained. 'And what good are those flimsy shoes?'

'We want to look nice for the theatre,' Cara said for the tenth time. 'We can't really go in duffle coats and wellies!' She had felt a small thrill of pleasure, putting on her black patent court shoes. 'Anyway,' she added, 'whenever we're not in the theatre we shall be in the coach. It will drop us right at the door.'

It snowed steadily on the way to Faverwell, but in Arendale, unless it affected the welfare of the animals, you didn't let a bit of weather put you off doing what you wanted to.

The coach was waiting. The driver, Mr Thorndike, was sitting inside, out of the cold, but so far no other passengers had arrived.

'I knew we'd be too early,' Cara said. 'And we have the farthest to come. Never mind, it means we have the choice of seats. Go and get your sweets and I'll get in.'

They were in and out of the shop quickly. David joined Cara, but Susan walked past without a word and made for the back seat. Whatever she does, Cara thought, I shall let it pass. I'm not going to let anything spoil this outing.

As they left the dales behind the snow eased off, and once they were on the open road, beyond Shepton, the way was reasonably clear. A little after midday Cara, at David's request, opened up the sandwiches.

'I'll take Susan's to her,' he offered.

'We're not the only ones with food,' he said on his return. 'Almost everyone's eating.'

After they had finished it seemed only a short time before the coach wove its way around the twisting streets of Helsdon and came to a stop right outside the Palace Theatre. Cara looked at her watch.

'We've at least three-quarters of an hour before it starts,' she said. 'You see, David love, you needn't have worried!'

'When the show's over,' Mr Thorndike said as they were getting out, 'I'll have the coach right here. Don't anybody lag behind or they'll get left in Helsdon! Either that,' he added, 'or we'll not have time for that fish-and-chip tea you've been promised.'

David looked anxiously at him, and was relieved when he winked.

They had seats on the front row of the dress circle, David sitting in between Cara and his sister. It was as far away as Susan could get from Cara because the places were booked and numbered. They were huge tip-up seats of rich red plush. Cara had to hold David's down for him, and the minute he stood up to peer over the balcony at what was happening below it sprang up smartly and rapped him on the behind.

'Idiot!' Susan said. 'Anyone would think you'd never been in a theatre before!'

'Well I haven't,' he said. 'I wanted to watch the people coming in. Anyway, you haven't been all that often!'

Everything about the place was miraculous, he thought, seeing nothing of the shabbiness to which years of war had reduced it. It was not apparent to him that the crimson-flocked wallpaper was dusty and peeling. The huge lights which hung from the ceiling were, he decided, quite certainly pure gold. Then there were the little rooms close to the stage. They had curved fronts, hung with braid and tassels, and people sitting in them on gilt chairs. 'Boxes' Cara said the rooms were called. It was a strange name for something so grand.

'Are the people in them very rich?' he asked.

'Possibly,' Cara said. The little girls wore velvet cloaks, which to Cara, when she had visited the pantomime as a child, were a sure and certain sign of riches.

Though she would never show it, not in a thousand years, Susan was every bit as impressed as David. When she was grown-up and could do as she liked, she thought, she would live in a large town and go to the theatre every week. Twice a week, in fact. It wasn't really all that many years away, but from where she was now they stretched before her into eternity.

The next two hours were, for the children, spent in another world. It was a magical world of light and colour, of song and dazzling spectacle. David abandoned his seat altogether and stood leaning against the balcony rail. He joined in the hearty laughter at jokes, Cara thought, he couldn't possibly understand. Quite uninhibited, he shouted his replies to questions hurled at the audience from the stage. He booed the Ugly Sisters and sighed over Cinderella.

Cara, glancing in the near-darkness at Susan, was pleased to see that she was as enraptured as her brother. Indeed, when the time came for the audience to join in the songs it was Susan's voice which rang out, loud and true, above those around her. I never knew she could sing like that, Cara thought. Not once had she heard Susan sing at Beckwith.

When the final curtain came down on the glittering ballroom scene, David clapped until his hands were sore. Susan was beyond clapping. She was transported to a place which she wished never to leave.

'Do we have to go?' David asked, turning to Cara. 'Can't we stay and see it again?'

'Not today we can't,' Cara said, laughing. 'The coach will be waiting – and you heard what Mr Thorndike said. So now it's on to fish and chips!'

Fish and chips, Susan thought with disgust. How could her step-mother talk about fish and chips at a time like this? It just showed how insensitive she was. I shan't be able to eat a thing, she decided. Not a thing!

In fact, when the coach had delivered them at the café on the out-skirts of Helsdon, she managed to eat a very substantial meal, polishing off half of David's chips as well as her own. It was all surprisingly good: chips done to a turn in the deep lake of bubbling fat, flaky white fish in crisp golden batter; everything so hot that when you sprinkled the vinegar on, it sizzled. Some women, however, complained that they'd been given cod, though they'd ordered haddock.

'Can't tell the difference myself,' Mr Thorndike said, wiping his lips. 'Fish is fish as long as it's battered!' He had had his meal with them, a larger portion than anyone else.

When they came out of the café to board the coach it was snowing heavily, with a strong wind blowing.

'I don't like the look of this,' Mr Thorndike said as he scraped the snow from the windscreen. 'However, press on regardless!'

The coach struck chilly after the warmth of the café. Cara pulled the two rugs down from the rack and took one to Susan.

'I don't want it,' Susan said. 'You can take it back.'

'You just might,' Cara said mildly. 'I'll leave it in case.'

The further from Helsdon, the worse grew the weather. Long before they reached Shepton the snow was deep, still falling, and drifting in the strong wind. Mr Thorndike crouched over his steering wheel, peering through the windscreen, trying to make sense of the white world ahead and around.

He was truly relieved to reach Shepton, grateful to see that gangs of men were already out, attempting to clear the main street. He stopped the coach, opened his window, and called out to a man who was shovelling snow.

'What's it like ahead?'

'Bad! How far have you to go?'

'Faverwell.'

'Then rather you than me, mate,' the man said. 'It's a real blizzard. I don't know about Faverwell, but they reckon some of the villages are already cut off. The snow's drifting badly in this wind.'

'Oh well, we can but try,' Mr Thorndike said, closing his window.

He turned up the hill leading out of the town. He could hardly see a foot ahead now, which was why at first he didn't see the car. It was slewed across the road in front of him, shrouded in snow, abandoned. Its own progress had been stopped by a huge drift of snow, several feet high, which stretched the width of the road, totally blocking it.

No more than inches from the car, he braked suddenly, and the coach began to slide backwards down the hill. The women screamed, some of them jumping up from their seats.

'Sit down!' Mr Thorndike thundered.

He was managing, just, to control the slide. The depth of snow, the topmost layer too newly fallen to be iced over, helped him. There was no way forward, that was plain, nor could he turn round, but if he could manage to take it slowly he might be able to reverse down into Shepton. Thanking God he hadn't got any farther up the hill, he began the descent.

The women, some of them, were still squawking and squealing. Well, he didn't blame them, but he wasn't having it. The sweat was pouring off him with the effort of controlling the coach.

'You can just stop that, ladies!' he commanded. 'There's nothing to squawk about and it won't help. You hold on and I'll get you into Shepton safe and sound, see if I don't!'

Thank goodness he sounded better than he felt!

'Will it upset you if we sing?' Cara called out. At the sight of David's white face she knew she had to do something, though she herself felt sick with fear.

'Be music to my ears, love! You lot get on with the singing and leave me to do the driving!'

'Right!' Cara said in a loud voice. 'We're going to see how many songs we can remember from the pantomime! Come on, David. You and I will start off!'

Gradually everyone joined in. Even more gradually Mr Thorndike inched his way backwards to the bottom of the hill and into Shepton's main street. He continued to reverse until he came to the Ewe and Lamb Hotel, and there he stopped. For a second he allowed his body to go limp, and he slumped over the steering wheel; then he took a deep breath and squared his shoulders.

'Well folks, this is it!'

'What do you mean, this is it?' a woman demanded.

'I mean, Mrs Anlaby, I can't get up the hill. You saw the car across the road. You saw the snowdrift.' Trust Mrs Anlaby to be awkward! Silly old twit!

'What about the other road?' someone asked.

'That's precisely why I'm going into the Ewe and Lamb,' he said. 'To find out.'

Five minutes later he was back again.

'The other road's totally blocked a mile ahead,' he announced. 'There's no way of getting to Faverwell. No way at all! I'm sorry, but there it is!'

There was a short, stunned silence, then everyone spoke at once.

'What are we going to do?'

'My husband will be worried to death!'

'Where are we going to sleep?'

'What about the milking? Some of us have got to get back for the milking!'

And how are we going to keep warm, Cara wondered. With no heat coming from the engine, the coach was beginning to feel like an ice-house. Thanks to Mother Hendry's insistence, she had brought rugs, but many hadn't.

Mr Thorndike held up a hand for silence.

'Right! I'm going back into the Ewe and Lamb and I'm going to ask them if they'll give us shelter for the night. I don't know that they can, even if they're willing. We can but try. And I suggest one of you ladies comes with me. How about you, Mrs Hendry?'

She'd be his best bet, he reckoned. She could charm the ducks off the water.

'Very well,' Cara agreed.

She tucked the rug further around David, then left the coach with Thorndike.

The front door of the Ewe and Lamb led directly into the main bar, which, in spite of the weather, was busy. Mr Thorndike marched up to the bar counter and she followed a step behind him, not looking at the men sitting and standing around, though she was fully aware that they were staring at her. She was conscious of what a foolish figure she presented on a night like this, in her flowered dress, the velveteen coat she hadn't been able to resist wearing, her only silk stockings and her high-heeled court shoes. She could feel the snow which had fallen on her hair in the few yards between the coach and the inn door beginning to trickle down her neck.

The men in the bar had stopped their conversations, fallen silent.
'What can I do for you?' the landlord asked.

'You can offer forty beds for the night,' Thorndike said.

Before the landlord could reply, a man standing by the bar turned around.

'I can offer one bed,' he said. 'Willingly!'

His words broke the spell and everyone laughed, but Cara had recognized his voice before she looked up. There was a wide grin on the man's face. His eyes, meeting hers, were bold.

'Good evening, Mrs Hendry. Not a nice night for a lady to be out!'

She felt the colour creep up her face as he frankly surveyed her, and was angry with herself for showing her discomfiture.

It was Kit Marsden.

NINE

There was a gleam in Kit Marsden's eyes which challenged Cara. She looked at him steadily, then said, her voice as smooth as silk:

'That's extremely kind of you, Mr Marsden.'

She saw the quick flicker of surprise in his face.

'We have one lady who would certainly be pleased to take up your offer.' She turned to Thorndike. 'I was thinking of Mrs Anlaby!'

'Why yes,' Thorndike said, poker-faced. 'Grandma Anlaby! You'd be doing her a real service, Kit. She's an elderly lady, and elderly ladies appreciate a comfortable bed. I know my old mother does!'

'It's really very kind of you, Mr Marsden,' Cara repeated.

The landlord laughed outright.

'Hoist with your own petard, Kit!' he said.

'Whatever that means,' Thorndike said.

'Though on second thoughts,' Cara said, 'perhaps she'd be happier staying with the rest of us. Safety in numbers. We mustn't take it for granted that she'd want your bed.'

'*Mrs Anlaby* would be quite safe,' Marsden declared.

'Which is more than some ladies would be!' the landlord said affably.

'All that's as may be,' Thorndike said. 'You haven't given me an answer, Billy. Where can we put up thirty-nine women and children, plus me?'

'Well not here, that's for certain!' the landlord replied. 'We're not by rights a residential pub. We've only got four bedrooms. Empty, I grant you, at this time of year. But they'll not take forty, will they?'

'Oh come on!' Thorndike urged. 'Who's counting the beds? Shelter first, then a bite to eat. It's nobbut for one night. Me and a few others

123

– some of these lads here I don't doubt – will dig a way out in the morning.'

'It's freezing cold in the coach,' Cara pleaded. 'We can't stay there all night. As Mr Thorndike says, if we can just have a proper roof over our heads – even if we don't have beds . . .'

'Why come to me?' the landlord demanded of Thorndike. 'There's two or three other hotels in Shepton. Why me?'

'Because everybody in Shepton knows that Billy Thwaite will do a good turn when he can,' Thorndike said. 'Now come on, man. I know very well you're not one to turn away people in trouble. The same can't be said of every innkeeper in the town. Anyway, none of the Shepton hotels is large.'

'I haven't got the facilities,' Thwaite grumbled. But there was a softening in his voice, a note of concern, which gave Cara hope.

'Where will I put them all?' he pleaded.

'It doesn't matter,' Cara said. 'We'll sit on chairs, or lie on the floor. Anything, anywhere!'

Kit Marsden and the other men had listened in silence, but now Marsden spoke up.

'Have a heart, Billy! As the lady says, anywhere will do. And as Thorndike says, it's only for one night. We'll dig a way through in the morning.'

'They'll be hungry,' Thwaite protested. He turned to Cara.

'I'm afraid so,' she admitted. 'Especially the children. You know what children are!'

'I don't, thank God!' He spoke brusquely, feeling himself cornered.

'Come on, Billy,' Kit Marsden cajoled. 'Is this how we won the war? Where's your Dunkirk spirit?'

'I left it behind at Dunkirk,' the landlord said tersely. 'The war's over. So are *you* going to find food for forty people? Nobody has any to spare, as you well know, except you gentlemen of the black market – mentioning no names, of course!'

'I'll see to that.' Marsden spoke with cool assurance, as if it was an everyday occurrence. 'You find somewhere for them to park their bodies, I'll find the food.'

He looked around the bar, weighing up the strength, missing no-one.

'I'll need two or three of you with me to fetch and carry, and while we do that the rest of you can set off and look for blankets, pillows, shawls, any sort of bedding. And camp beds.'

'Where'll we find that lot, for goodness sake?' a man asked.

'Use your loaf, Charlie!' Marsden said. 'Knock on doors. Go to the other pubs. Threaten them. Tell them if they'll take their share of supplying the bedding, then the Ewe and Lamb will take care of the bodies for tonight.'

'Hold on! I haven't said . . . You can't . . .!'

The landlord's protest, if it was heard at all, was ignored.

'We could try the WVS,' somebody interrupted. 'Though they'll have shut up shop at this time of night.'

'Then find out where they live and knock them up!' Marsden instructed. 'Now drink up, get going, and be back here in an hour, all of you – and think on, no-one empty-handed.'

His easy-going manner had vanished. He has taken charge of the whole situation, Cara thought. Not only is he giving the orders, the rest are taking them. Yet she wasn't totally surprised. She had felt a streak of mastery – ruthlessness almost – in him when she'd met him at the sheep sales.

'An hour! You must be joking, Kit!' one of the men protested.

'I was never more serious. Come on, move fast – it'll keep you warm.'

'It's worse than being in the bloody army!' the man grumbled.

Nevertheless, they all obeyed. They drank up, turned up their coat collars, pulled on their caps and departed. Only Thorndike and Cara were left in the bar with the landlord.

'And that's my night's trade gone as well,' Thwaite said ruefully as he began to clear the dirty glasses. 'An hour and more to closing time and not a customer in sight!'

'I'm really very sorry,' Cara said. 'Could I bring the others in from the coach now?'

'Aye, you'd best do that afore they freeze to death. And no need to be sorry, lass,' he added more kindly. 'It's not your fault. It's nobody's fault. I suppose we must just make the best of it.'

'Thank you, Mr Thwaite. It's very good of you.'

'Well, you and Thorndike had best get them in and I'll put some kettles on,' Thwaite said. 'I dare say a cup of tea will be in order until Kit Marsden gets back wi' summat to eat.'

'Do you think he'll be able to do that?' Cara asked anxiously.

'Oh, I don't doubt it! You can be quite confident. If Kit Marsden says he'll do summat, then he usually does. But best not to ask how or where, eh?' He winked at her.

'I won't!' Cara promised. 'For all I care at the moment he can rob a bank!' And I'm not sure I'd put that past him, she thought.

'More to the point if he robs the Co-op,' Mr Thwaite said.

Five minutes later the members of the coach party streamed in through the door. The adults were pale, nipped and worried. The children, for whom it was an unexpected adventure to round off a

125

wonderful day, were in high spirits. Mrs Anlaby leaned heavily on Mr Thorndike's arm.

'I didn't bargain for this!' she complained. 'I'm too old for this sort of caper!'

'You would come,' her daughter pointed out. 'I said all along it might be too much for you.'

'You didn't tell me we'd be stranded!' Mrs Anlaby retorted. 'Where's the fire? I'm frozen to the marrow.'

'Sit over here, Mrs Anlaby,' Thorndike said. 'I'll get you a tot of whisky if Mr Thwaite has it to spare.'

'Whisky! Whisky! I never drink spirits!' she said, affronted.

'Medicinal,' Thorndike assured her. 'If Dr Speight was here it's exactly what he'd order you.'

'Well, in that case . . .' she agreed reluctantly. 'Though I shan't like the taste.'

'There you go then!' Mr Thwaite said, handing her a small tot. 'Scotland's finest!'

She pulled a face, spluttered over the drink, then, to the landlord's chagrin, tossed it back in one go, for all the world as if it was cough medicine.

'And now we've got to get these children out of the bar,' Thwaite said nervously. 'It's not allowed. I could lose my licence.'

'Police Constable Mockford isn't going to trouble you on a night like this,' Thorndike said. 'He's no doubt at home, toasting his toes.'

'Nevertheless, I'm not risking it.' The landlord was adamant. 'I've a clean licence so far and I'm keeping it that way. There's a room at the back where we hold functions. The children can use that, and one or two of the mothers to keep them in order. It's not very big but it'll have to do. The rest of the grown-ups can stay here in the bar. Then when the lads get back wi' some blankets we'll sort out where folks can bed down.'

Accompanied by two or three of the mothers of the younger ones, the children were shepherded into the back room.

'You two are old enough to manage without me,' Cara said to David and Susan. 'I shall stay in the bar. The landlord's making tea and he'll want some help.'

'I'm jolly hungry,' David said.

'After all that fish and chips? Well, we're hoping Mr Marsden might be back soon with some food.' Cara turned to Susan. 'Are you hungry?'

'A bit,' Susan admitted. She would like to have said 'No', but it wouldn't be true and she might miss her chance.

'Who's Mr Marsden?' David asked.

'He lives in Shepton. At least I think he does.' In fact, she didn't

126

know where he lived, or anything at all about him, nor did she want to. In spite of his present help, she didn't wholly take to him. He was too cheeky by half.

'Daddy knows him,' she said.

'He must be a kind man, to go out in the snow to get food,' David said.

'I suppose he is,' Cara admitted.

In less than an hour Kit Marsden, and two men with him, were back, carrying boxes and bags from which they unpacked their booty on to the bar tables. There was bread, margarine, sugar, tea, two bars of soap, lard, a dozen eggs, milk, biscuits, two pots of home-made jam and, unbelievably, six tins of Spam.

'Six tins of Spam!' Cara cried. 'I don't believe it! Where on earth . . .?' She stopped short, catching the landlord's warning look.

'It's a bit of a mixture,' Kit Marsden said. 'I had to take what I could, but people in Shepton are very generous when it comes to the pinch.'

'They didn't have much choice!' one of the men said. 'You bullied them something shameful!'

Kit Marsden laughed heartily.

'They'll feel all the better for it! Full of virtue!'

'We should make a start on the meal,' Cara said. 'The sooner the children have eaten, the sooner they can settle down.' She surveyed the food, then turned to the woman standing next to her.

'How do you think we should sort it out, Agnes?'

'Easy!' Kit Marsden interrupted. 'Slice the Spam – thin, mind you – fry it nice and crisp in the lard, scramble all the eggs and serve the two together. That's the easiest way to share it.'

'Very tasty!' Mr Thorndike said. 'And a slice or two of bread and jam to follow, with a pot of strong tea . . .'

'We must save enough bread for breakfast,' Cara cautioned. 'We'll need to eat before we set off for home.'

'And speaking of home,' Agnes said, 'isn't it time we tried to get through on the telephone? They'll be getting anxious before long.'

'I'd like to do that before we eat,' Cara said. 'I'd feel better if we could get in touch. I expect we all would.'

'Then I'll start on the meal,' Marsden offered. 'You two ladies can organize the telephone.'

'Don't say you can cook as well as everything else?' Agnes said. The flirtatious way in which she spoke to Marsden annoyed Cara. He needed no encouragement.

'You'd be surprised what I can do!' Marsden said.

'Let's try the telephone then,' the landlord said. 'Though it'll be a miracle if the lines aren't down.'

Miracle or not, the line to Faverwell was working. Immediately, anxious wives formed a queue to speak to husbands.

'Keep the talk short!' Mrs Anlaby commanded. 'Everyone wants a turn.'

'I hope I can get through to Beckwith,' Cara said. 'That's sure to be more difficult.'

It was with tremendous relief that, though the line was indistinct, when her turn came Edward was quickly on the line.

'We're stranded!' she told him. 'We can't move out of Shepton. At least not tonight, we can't. There's a drift as high as a house partway up the hill out of Shepton. But the men say they'll dig us out in the morning.'

'Even if you could get from Shepton, I couldn't possibly get the car down to Faverwell,' Edward said. 'You can't see the road here; the snow's higher than the walls, and drifting badly. What men are you talking about?'

'The men who were here in the Ewe and Lamb when we arrived. Kit Marsden seems to be the leading light. He's organized everything very well.'

'Kit Marsden!' Edward's voice was sharp. 'Steer clear of him, love. He's a good-for-nothing.'

'Well, at the moment I have to say he's good for everything,' Cara said. 'I don't know what we'd do without him! And the way we are, it's not possible to steer clear of anyone. We're crowded.'

'I should watch out, love,' Edward advised. 'That man usually has an ulterior motive. Take no notice of his smooth tongue.'

'I won't,' Cara promised. 'I have to go now, darling! There's a queue waiting for the telephone. All my love. I'll phone you tomorrow when we get to Faverwell. Goodness knows what time!'

'Take care of yourself, and the children,' Edward said.

As the meal was being served, though it had not been easy to find forty plates, saucers, dishes – anything to take the food – the rest of the men returned.

'You've been gone all but two hours,' Kit Marsden said sharply. 'What kept you?'

'When we sort out this lot you'll see just what kept us,' one of the men replied. 'It wasn't easy, let me tell you.'

'Never mind the sob stuff, Joe,' Marsden said. 'Let's see what you've got!'

There was an assortment of bedding: blankets, rugs, sleeping bags, a few pillows and cushions. There were shawls, two overcoats, a few towels.

'Towels! That's good,' Cara said.

'I thought of towels,' Joe said, pleased with himself. 'I reckoned

Mr Thwaite wouldn't have that many and you'd all feel better with a bit of a wash. No offence meant, of course.'

'And none taken,' Mrs Anlaby said. 'I've never gone to bed in my life without a wash down and I don't want to start now! Cleanliness is next to godliness! It was a good idea, lad.'

'Especially as Mr Marsden and his merry men brought us some soap,' Cara said.

'There's a few camp beds on the way,' Joe said. 'We couldn't carry any more, not with this lot. And by the way, I've promised everything will be returned to its rightful owners as soon as possible.'

'So it will,' Marsden agreed.

Joe nodded appreciatively in the direction of the food on the plates.

'My word, that looks good. I must say, I'm more than peckish!'

'Then you'll go home to eat,' Marsden said firmly. 'People haven't given this food to be shared out willy-nilly. We have our rations in our own homes.'

'Aye! And some of us have more than others!' Joe muttered.

If Marsden heard him he took no notice, his attention being diverted by the arrival of the camp beds.

'Those will do very well,' he said. He turned to the landlord. 'Now Billy, what about serving all these lads with a drink?'

The landlord shook his head.

'Nay, Kit, it's after hours. You know that as well as I do.' It broke his heart to turn away the trade.

'In that case we'll be off!' Marsden said. 'I reckon you ladies, and Messrs Thorndike and Thwaite, can take care of the rest. Come on lads!'

Cara was standing near the door as they filed out. Marsden was the last to leave. He turned to Cara, smiling.

'Now are you sure you won't avail yourself of my hospitality, Mrs Hendry? I could offer you something much better than Spam and scrambled egg!'

'Quite sure, thank you!' Cara said. But she was laughing.

'Then some other time!' Marsden said. 'Good night all!'

As soon as the meal was over they bedded down the children, mostly on the floor in the back room, where they curled up together for warmth and comfort, like puppies in a basket. Cara shared a small bedroom with Mrs Anlaby – though happily not a bed; that pleasure fell to Mrs Anlaby's daughter – and Agnes Carter. Cara had drawn a sleeping bag and a small lumpy cushion, and Agnes had chosen to curl up under a rug on the one armchair.

'I'm so tired, I could sleep on a clothesline!' Cara said, snuggling down, without undressing, into her sleeping bag.

129

At least I could if that wretched woman would let me, she was thinking almost an hour later. Mrs Anlaby, old, and apparently not in need of much sleep, was still talking, mostly asking questions which required answers.

'Oh Ma, do go to sleep!' her daughter begged. 'We're all worn out!'

'You've got no stamina, you young ones,' Mrs Anlaby complained – then suddenly fell asleep, which was evidenced by her snoring.

It was the only disturbance. If there was any late traffic in the street, the snow deadened its sound. Before she drifted into sleep, Cara thought of Arendale, and of Beckwith. It would be beautiful there, with an unearthly beauty. The dales were never more exquisite than under a blanket of snow. It would be silent, its silence intensified by the occasional call of an animal. But this imposed beauty and silence was also cruel. Man was imprisoned by it; powerless, almost.

She thought of her mother-in-law; of Tom – how was he? She thought of Johann in his room over the stables. The weather would hold few terrors for him. Along with a few other POWs in the area, Johann had been in the Alpine Corps in his homeland.

Lastly and longest, she thought of Edward, desperately wishing she was in his arms in their wide, warm bed. She wished she had told him her news before they'd left Beckwith. She'd been practically certain then that she was pregnant, but she'd wanted to hug it to herself for just a few hours longer, to wait for the precise, perfect moment to share it with him. Now, more than ever, though with no more evidence than her own feelings, she was sure it was so. She *was* going to have a baby. Well, the announcement would have to wait. It wasn't something she could make over the telephone in a crowded bar.

Whichever way she turned, her bones ached from contact with the hard wooden floor, but presently she began to drift. On the edge of sleep she saw a huge snowdrift, and beyond it Edward. His arms were outstretched towards her, but he couldn't reach her, nor she him. And then in front of the drift, close to where she was, Kit Marsden appeared with a wide, mocking grin on his face.

'Get out of my way!' she cried. 'I'm trying to reach Edward!' She carried her annoyance at the sight of him with her into her slumbers.

It was only just starting to grow light when she woke next morning. Daylight came late in Shepton in February. She ached all over. The sleeping bag was too thin for comfort yet surprisingly she had slept through the night, slept her fill.

She got up quietly, hoping to gain a few minutes of solitude before the others wakened. Mrs Anlaby, seen in the half light, was sleeping like a baby. So was her daughter, lying by her side. It must be strange,

Cara thought, sleeping with one's mother in adult life, yet in early childhood it was bliss. Agnes was asleep, but looked contorted and uncomfortable in the chair. We should have arranged to change places halfway through the night, Cara reproached herself. Why didn't I think of it?

At this moment, more than anything in the world she would have liked a bath: a long, hot bath, with scented soap and big towels. It was unlikely she could have one, and even if she could, she had no clean clothes to change in to. Never mind, she thought, it would be the first item on her agenda when she reached Beckwith.

Before leaving the room she pulled back the curtain a fraction and looked out. There was a fresh overnight coating of snow, indeed it was still snowing, though not as heavily as on the previous evening, and the wind was not so strong.

Downstairs, some of the other women were up and tea was flowing, hot and strong.

'This is heaven!' Cara said, accepting a cup.

'We've plenty of bread and jam, but that's about all,' someone said. 'We'll have to wait for our bacon and eggs until we get home.'

Agnes came into the kitchen.

'Never mind bacon and eggs!' she said. 'What I'd like is some clean underwear. But who'd think of taking a spare pair of knickers to the pantomime?'

'I dare say we can buy some in Shepton,' Cara said. 'I've got my clothing coupons with me and I expect most of you have.'

'Certainly,' the first woman said. 'I take my ration book and clothing coupons everywhere, just in case!'

While she was speaking, Kit Marsden entered, muffled from top to toe, with a thin layer of powdery snow on his cap and jacket. He was carrying a garden spade.

'Clothing coupons?' he queried. 'Now if any of you ladies are wanting clothing coupons . . .'

'At what cost?' Cara said sharply. Seeing him, she suddenly remembered last night's dream.

'Ah!' he said. 'Good morning, Mrs Hendry! I trust you slept well? Now cost, you say. Well, for you I'd do a special deal!'

'Thank you,' she replied. 'I have all the coupons I need.'

'Pity!' he said. 'However, what I came for was to meet the other fellows. This spade you see here is not the latest fashion accessory, it's meant for business. You'll be pleased to hear we're going to dig a way through for you.'

'Hip hip hooray!' Agnes cried. 'For that you can have a cup of tea!'

Other men arrived while he was drinking it, all carrying spades or shovels.

131

'Where's Thorndike?' Kit Marsden asked.

'Still in bed,' the landlord said. 'I'll wake him.'

'Do that,' Marsden said. 'Tell him to join us with a shovel. We'll be on the hill.'

'We'd best get the children up,' Agnes said.

'Oh, no rush love!' Marsden said. 'This little job won't be done in ten minutes. Let them sleep. Now tell me, have you enough tea there for the lads to have a cup?'

'Of course!' Agnes smiled.

'Right!' He turned to the landlord. 'And how about a little drop of something in it, Billy, to keep out the cold?'

'Well, all right,' Thwaite agreed reluctantly.

He carefully measured a tablespoonful of whisky into each cup.

'I'm not sure I'm allowed to do this,' he said unhappily.

'Oh, you'll be all right!' Marsden assured him. 'After all, you're giving it, not selling it!'

And how can I afford to give away Scotch whisky like it was tap water? the landlord asked himself.

In the two hours which followed the children were roused, washed, dressed and fed. After breakfast a few of the mothers undertook to organize them in nice quiet games in the back room.

'I don't want to play kids' games,' Susan protested.

'I quite see that,' Cara agreed. 'And you needn't. You can give a hand here. But by rights, love, you should go to school. You were expected today in any case. You only got the one day off to go to Helsdon. Weather permitting, you'd have come back here to school this morning.'

'I don't want to go to school, either,' Susan said. 'Why can't I go home when the rest of you go?'

'That might be the best idea,' Cara said. 'If the weather's likely to stay bad I think your dad would rather have you home than risk you getting stuck in Shepton again. I'll see what he says when I telephone, but for the moment I think it's best just to stay put until Mr Marsden and the others get back.'

It was another hour before the men returned. It was obvious the moment they walked in at the door of the Ewe and Lamb, Kit Marsden leading them, that something was wrong. They were wet and weary, which was to be expected, but the surprise was in their downcast looks, not a smile between them. Even Kit Marsden looked grim.

'I'm sorry, ladies,' he announced. 'It's no go! We've done our best, every man jack of us – and more besides joined us – but we can't get through. It's totally impossible. There's drifts nigh on twenty feet high, frozen solid. Nothing can shift them!'

'You've got to see it to believe it,' Thorndike said. 'Forty winters in the dales and I've never come across owt like it! There isn't a hope in hell of making a way for my coach.'

The rest of the men were silent and so, for a moment, were the women, until the latter all broke into speech at once.

'What are we going to do?'

'I've got to get home. There's the animals, and my husband's poorly.'

'Well, I can't stand another night in that chair,' Agnes said firmly. 'If someone will volunteer to come with me, I'm going to walk it!'

'Walk!' Mrs Anlaby cried. 'Are you off your head, Agnes Carter?'

'I mean it,' Agnes declared. And I don't want another night of your snoring, neither, she thought.

Kit Marsden smiled – and temporarily lightened the atmosphere.

'That's the spirit, love!' he said. 'And of course I'd be the first to volunteer to accompany you. But it's not on, sweetheart; we'd not make it. Mr Thorndike's right. You've never seen anything like it.'

'Go on! It can't be that bad!' Agnes protested.

'It is, love. It certainly is.'

'How long do you think it's going to take to dig through?' Cara asked.

Marsden shrugged.

'How long is a piece of string? A day or two at least, but if this weather continues, then it could be longer. It snows, the wind blasts across the Pennines, piles it into drifts, one drift up against another – then it freezes hard. Of course if the weather changes and there's a thaw wind . . .'

'And it shows no sign of that,' Thorndike said.

'You're right,' the landlord said. 'We've listened to the wireless. It's snow everywhere, and more to come. They say it's blocked the railways and the coal trucks can't get through. That means no heat.'

'It means worse than that,' Thorndike said. 'If coal doesn't get to the power stations it means no electricity, either! It's a bugger!'

'Mr Thorndike, wash your mouth out!' Mrs Anlaby cried.

'Sorry, missus!'

'What they *are* saying in Shepton,' Kit Marsden put in, 'is that they're going to get the POWs from the camp to dig a way through the other road, round Langley way. That's badly blocked, but it might be easier, it's not such a steep hill for a start.'

'This is diabolical!' Mrs Anlaby said.

'Don't worry, Mrs Anlaby,' Kit Marsden soothed her. 'We'll work out something. We'll hold a council of war!'

'And I suppose you'll be Churchill?' she said tartly.

'Why not?' Marsden replied. 'I quite fancy myself in that role! Anyway, look at it this way, you're all in Shepton. There's food here, and we'll find some sort of shelter. The folks in the villages are the ones in trouble. From what we heard they're well and truly cut off. They say you can't get through to Kettlewell, nor Grassington – let alone anything further up the dale.'

'We must telephone before long,' Cara said. 'Let our families know.'

Marsden agreed. 'But first let's settle a few things, then you can give them some positive news. For a start, where is everyone going to sleep for the next night or two?'

'Well, with the best will in the world, it won't be here,' the landlord said. 'Certainly a few of you can stay, and welcome, but not forty. And I don't think it's the place for the children.'

'Then first off,' Marsden said, 'have any of you got relatives or friends in Shepton who would put you up?'

It appeared that there were ten women who knew someone who might be persuaded to take them in, together with their children.

'But it's the food will be the question,' one of the ten said. 'How will they feed us on the rations?'

'Don't worry about that for the moment,' Marsden told her. 'We can sort that lot out later, talk to the food office.'

'Susan's school might take a few children,' Cara said. 'I'll ask.'

'I don't want to go to school,' Susan protested.

'I know you don't, love, but it looks as though you might have to. And if David can go with you I'd rely on you to look after him.'

'I reckon you'd do that very well, Susan,' Marsden said, smiling at her. 'You could happen look after a few more if the school will have them.'

Actually, Susan thought, it might be quite a lark. It would be different. She'd have to be excused lessons, of course. Anyway, it looked as though she had no choice about going, whatever anyone else did.

Agnes and another woman had been talking together, and now Agnes spoke up.

'I know you say it's impossible, but me and Jane here are going to walk it. I reckon people can get through where cars and coaches can't.'

'Anyway,' Jane said, 'I can't stop here. My husband's badly. I wouldn't have left him to go to the pantomime, but I'd booked and he insisted. There's the animals to attend to if nothing else. I've got ten cows to milk, twice a day.'

'If the villages are cut off,' Mrs Anlaby's daughter said, 'they'll not be able to send the milk away.'

'That makes no difference,' Jane said. 'T'poor cows will have to be milked even if we have to throw the stuff down the sink!'

There were, it appeared, other women who might have been willing to set off and walk, but for various reasons it wasn't possible. Some, like Cara, were wearing flimsy shoes which wouldn't last further than the length of Shepton High Street. Most had young children who couldn't possibly accompany them.

'So I reckon we two should set off as soon as we can,' Agnes said.

Marsden shook his head.

'I don't think you're wise, ladies. You don't know what you're letting yourselves in for. In fact I'd like to stop you, but I don't suppose I can.'

'No, Mr Marsden, you can't,' Jane replied. 'Me and Agnes have made up our minds, but thank you all the same. So if you'll all excuse us we'll put up a few jam sandwiches and be on our way.'

'And I'll give you a little flask of something to keep out the cold,' the landlord said. 'You're two very brave ladies.'

'Oh it's nothing, Mr Thwaite!' Agnes said airily. 'I haven't lived in Faverwell all my life without getting through a snowdrift or two. You're all making it sound like the North Pole!'

'It *is* like the North Pole, as you'll soon find out,' Thorndike said anxiously.

Within fifteen minutes they were away. The rest of the company stood in the window, watching them as they walked up Shepton High Street. It was still snowing.

'I reckon they'll be back,' Thorndike said. 'And the sooner the better.'

'We'll see,' Marsden said. 'And now what about everybody else?'

In the next hour Cara telephoned the school and spoke to the headmistress.

'So you see, Miss Simpson, we're in a real plight,' she said. 'Anything you could do would be appreciated.'

'Of course!' Miss Simpson said, in a brisk, headmistressy fashion. 'Well, I think we could look after, say, six children in addition to Susan and your little boy, but preferably not the very small ones, not under seven years old. We don't have the facilities.'

'That's wonderful,' Cara said. 'What about rations?'

'Oh, don't bother yourself about that!' Miss Simpson reassured her. 'We can always stretch what we've got a bit further. Clothes will be more difficult, but I'll send notes home with the day girls, ask the parents to help. So don't worry!'

'You're an angel!' Cara said gratefully. 'Anyway, it won't be for long. The POWs are going to try to clear the road around Langley way. Two nights at the most, I'd think.'

On her way back to the Ewe and Lamb Cara bought what seemed to be the last pair of Wellington boots in Shepton.

'I'll wear them right away,' she said to the assistant. 'And a pair of thick socks if you have them.' Her feet were wet through and frozen, her lovely court shoes were ruined.

With the rest of her coupons, and those of the other women marooned in the Ewe, she bought changes of underwear for all. There were now only six of them: Mrs Anlaby and her daughter, Meg and Dora Foster, Joan Dale and herself. The Women's Voluntary Service had found lodgings for everyone else. There being only six, she was allotted a bed to herself in a room shared with Joan Dale.

The next day Agnes telephoned.

'Well we're safe and sound,' she announced. 'But goodness knows how, It was midnight before we got home and there were times when we didn't think we'd make it. Tell the others from me that on no account must they attempt it. I'm deadly serious.'

It was a boring existence at the pub. There was nowhere to sit other than the ice-cold bedrooms and the bar.

'Decent women don't frequent bars,' Mrs Anlaby said.

'We're not frequenting it,' Joan Dale snapped. 'You make us sound like tarts! We've nowhere else to go and anyway it's the only room with a fire.'

Besides, the wireless was in the bar. Not that it gave them much comfort. The weather reports were unremittingly bad.

'Did you hear that most of the towns are without milk?' Mrs Anlaby's daughter asked.

'My dad will hate that,' Cara said. 'He likes milky tea, milk at bedtime, and milk pudding three times a week! Poor Dad!'

When the men came in in the evening it brightened things up a little. They played darts and dominoes and invited the women to join them. Kit Marsden was regularly there, both dinnertime and evening.

'Doesn't your wife mind you being here so much?' Cara asked.

It was as if a shutter came down over his face. She had never seen that black look before.

'I've got no-one to tie me down,' he said brusquely. 'I'm footloose and fancy free.'

'Well,' he added, 'mebbe not entirely fancy free, if you know what I mean?'

She did know.

'Whereas I,' she said, 'am happy to be tied to my husband. All I want is to get back to him.'

She picked up a dart and flung it hard at the board, to her intense surprise scoring an inner.

'Bravo!' Marsden cried.

Two more days passed, in which the POWs, it was reported, had made scarcely any impression on the snowdrifts on the Langley road.

'How much longer do you think, Billy?' Cara asked the landlord.

'Nay, who knows, lass?'

Though they were nice enough women, especially young Mrs Hendry, he wouldn't be sorry to see them go. He didn't like women in his bar, it could give it a bad name. And then there were all the lemonades and shandies, the sherries and small ports, the cups of tea and telephone calls they were charging up because they had no money. He hoped they'd do the right thing and pay him when things were back to normal.

'I'll ring my husband if I may?' Cara said. Unbelievably, the lines to Beckwith were still intact and she was able to telephone Edward twice a day.

He had told her that they were managing all right, though cut off. Johann had brought out the skis he had made in his first winter in the dales, and was getting around on those. So far, he'd said, they had lost no sheep that he knew of, but Mr Fawcett had lost forty-six, dug out from the snow, having died from packing together and suffocating.

Edward said that his mother was furiously making butter and cheese from all the milk they couldn't get away, but it still left a lot to be poured down the drain.

Today when he answered the telephone there were no preliminaries.

'Cara, I've got bad news!'

'The sheep?'

'I wish to God it were,' Edward said. 'It's Dad. He died in the night. Quite peacefully, in his sleep.'

'Oh Edward! Oh, my love! Oh, why can't I be with you! Oh, damn and blast this bloody weather!'

'I'd give the world to have you here,' Edward said. 'So would Ma. But under no circumstances are you to attempt to walk.'

'How is Ma?'

'I think, without saying anything, she's been expecting it. But she's devastated all the same.'

'The funeral?' Cara asked. 'When? How?'

'I don't know. Johann's gone off to see if he can sort something out.'

'Oh, Edward love!'

For a moment they were both silent, then Cara said: 'Shall I tell the children, or shall I wait until we get home?'

'I think tell them,' Edward said, hesitantly. 'Will you do that, love?'

'Of course!'

She went at once to the school. A sympathetic Miss Simpson left her alone with Susan and David.

'You both have to be very brave,' Cara began. 'I have sad news.'

'You mean we still can't get home?' Susan said. 'Oh really, I'm a bit sick of things here!'

Would that were all, Cara thought.

'No, my dears. It's about Grandad.'

She had expected both children to be upset, especially the tender-hearted David, but she was unprepared for the torrent of grief which poured from Susan. The child was beside herself. She put her hands over her ears as if to shut out the news.

'I can't bear it!' she cried. 'I can't bear it! Why *my* grandad?'

Great, choking sobs shook her body, took her breath.

Cara opened her arms wide and, without hesitation, Susan came into them. Cara enfolded her stepdaughter and held her close, her own tears now falling as fast as Susan's.

'There, love! Cry as hard as you like. It's good to cry. I know how much you loved your grandad.'

Susan rested her head on Cara's shoulder and remained within the circle of her arms. Cara stroked the child's head until, presently, the sobs quietened and Susan lifted her head and looked at her stepmother.

This is the first time she has ever looked at me, Cara thought, ever really looked at me. How terrible that it should be in such circumstances, but how wonderful that it should happen at last.

'Oh Cara, I do so want to go home!' Susan said.

'I know, love. So do I. And it won't be long now. The men are digging every day.'

'I want to go home too', David said in a trembling voice. 'I'm trying not to cry. I'm trying to be brave because I'm a boy – but I do want to go home.'

Cara put out an arm and enfolded him also.

'Boys can cry too,' she told him. 'So can men. I expect Daddy is crying. But never mind, before long we'll be home, we'll all be together . . .'

'Except Grandad,' Susan said.

'Except Grandad. But we'll always remember him. We'll always love him, and be glad to have had him.'

It was the end of the sixth day when the men at last cleared a road through, which would eventually join up with the road to Faverwell.

'Too late to leave tonight,' Kit Marsden said, breaking the news in the Ewe and Lamb, 'but we'll round everyone up and you'll be away in the morning.'

Later, he spoke to Cara.

138

'I'm sorry about your father-in-law. I liked and respected Tom Hendry.'

'Thank you,' Cara said. 'I think everyone did. And I want to thank you, Mr Marsden, for looking after us. I don't know what we'd have done without you.'

'Entirely my pleasure!' he said. He was grinning again.

TEN

The winter of 1947 was one which no-one who had lived through it in the dales would ever forget. It would be remembered even by those who, like David, were no more than young children at the time. As for the adults, the tales of their gargantuan struggles, their deprivations and losses, their heroic efforts to overcome it all – these tales, Cara thought, would last them for the rest of their lives. And never would anyone at Beckwith forget Tom Hendry's funeral, the coffin drawn to the church on a sledge, along a narrow path cut through high walls of frozen snow.

It was the end of February before the road to Faverwell was opened up, but for Arendale, and many of the smaller dales and villages, relief was much slower in coming. At first Johann skied to Faverwell, or took the sledge, dragging a sheet of corrugated iron to hold the supplies he managed to buy there, but very soon there was no point in making the journey. Faverwell had nothing to spare.

'We're nearly at the end of the flour,' Mrs Hendry said anxiously, peering into the bin which not long ago had seemed so full. 'We shall have to go easy on the bread.'

It was not only people who went short. The animals were severely rationed, since the sheep as well as the cattle had to be fed on what hay there was. And day after day, as new snowdrifts formed, Edward and Johann had to dig narrow passages through from the house to the farm buildings and dig down several feet to uncover the water troughs for the cattle. Sometimes – for there were more than a score of consecutive nights of hard frost – sheep were frozen to the ground and Cara learnt to help the men to free them before they died where they stood.

'The wireless said they're sending planes over from Dishforth to drop animal feed,' Edward said. 'I hope they get as far as Arendale.'

140

But as far as the sheep were concerned, there was more to come. When at long last the weather took a turn for the better, just when it seemed as if the worst was over, the sheep fell victim to what came to be known as 'snow fever', and from that they went down like ninepins. Cattle wagons went around the dales, taking away the dead animals, including the cattle which had died from starvation.

'I've not known anything like it in my lifetime,' Mrs Hendry said. 'It seems there's no end to it!'

'The question is,' Edward said, 'will what the ewes have gone through affect the lamb harvest? Thank God we were able to send a lot away!'

Now, on this April day, more than a year later, that awful winter seemed for the moment something of a dream. The sun, which tinged the white walls and the craggy outcrops of limestone with gold, had a hint of warmth in it, unusual for the time of the year.

'We shall pay for it!' Edith Hendry predicted.

She said the words out loud, though there was no-one else in the room with her. Sometimes, even now, she forgot that Tom was no longer there, and she spoke to him. At other times, even when she remembered, she still spoke to him. There were things she could say only to Tom.

Edward and Cara were invariably kind to her; she could find nothing to criticize in them. They couldn't be expected to know what went on in her mind and she gave nothing away. She felt, much of the time, like a spare part. Dethroned; with no real place to fill in the world. Her place, her purpose, over more than forty years had been as wife and helpmeet to Tom. Now that purpose was gone and too often she could not see herself as a real person outside that role.

And yet Tom himself had never seen her just as a wife and mother. I was a person in my own right to Tom, she thought. He had met her on a visit to Hawes market. He had courted her, loved her, married her. She was 'Edith' to Tom. Now she was 'Ma', or 'Mother Hendry' or 'Grandma'. On her worst days she sometimes wondered what use she was in the world, but one had to go on living.

'You will live long enough to fulfil your destiny,' she said, giving the fire a good poke. Where had she read that? It was probably true.

Then suddenly her gloomy thoughts dispersed, went like chaff before the wind, as Cara came into the kitchen carrying seven-month-old Emily. The sight of her youngest grandchild never failed to raise Edith's spirits. And even in the child's unformed features – or was it the look in her dark eyes? – she reckoned she saw something of Tom. No-one else did, though to please her they sometimes reckoned it was so.

'Good morning, Mother Hendry!' Cara said brightly.

'Good morning, love! Here, give her to me for a minute.'

She held out her arms and Cara put the baby into them.

'She's getting heavier all the time,' Cara said. She sniffed the air appreciatively. The kitchen was filled with the aroma of cooking bacon. 'I thought the men would have been back for breakfast by now.'

'Any minute now, I dare say,' Mrs Hendry said. 'Will you be starting yours?'

'I'd better,' Cara replied. 'Then I can go out and relieve one of them. Emily can go into her chair. Fasten the straps, though. She's such a little wriggler.'

'She's Grandma's little beauty,' Mrs Hendry said fondly. 'But there's no time to nurse you at the moment, sweetheart!' She put Emily in the baby chair, which had once been Edward's, and turned back to the stove.

Cara yawned. She never got enough sleep. 'How long have you been up?' she asked.

'Quite a while,' Mrs Hendry admitted. 'Long enough to get my second wind.'

'I feel ashamed,' Cara said. 'But Emily gives me such bad nights with her teething. As for Edward, it was the middle of the night when he got up and went out. After that I fell asleep.'

'No need to be ashamed,' Mrs Hendry said. 'Babies have to be attended to as well as lambs.'

'I expect Johann's been out there most of the night,' Cara said. 'I wish we could have got some extra help for the lambing. One more pair of hands would have made all the difference.'

'Aye, well, everyone's busy on the same job, not a hand to spare. If there was we'd have been given it willingly. Grant Fawcett would have been only too pleased to help out, I'm sure, but they're throng themselves, and the old man's not too well.'

'We haven't seen Grant for a while,' Cara said.

'Anyway, love, have your breakfast, then you can get out,' Mrs Hendry continued. 'I'll look after the bairn, and I'll get David up and ready for school.'

David would have given his teeth, which were anyway at the stage of falling out, to have been allowed to stay at home and assist with the lambing.

'In the summer,' he constantly complained, 'we're allowed time off school to help with the haymaking, but not now for lambing. It's daft!' He had to confine his efforts to the weekends, to which he looked forward with eagerness.

Even Susan might be persuaded to help at the weekend, though she never wished to be present at the actual birthing.

'Nasty, messy business!' she said. 'I shall *never* have a baby!'

'You'll change your mind, love,' her grandmother said.

'No I won't,' Susan contradicted. 'It's disgusting!'

But when the ewes had tidied up their lambs, that was different; and if there was a weakly lamb to be bottle-fed, she and David would quarrel for the privilege.

It was the same with Emily. Susan wanted nothing to do with the awful nappy-changing, but at other times, and especially if no-one pushed her into it, she would willingly give the baby her bottle, or wheel her in the pram along the lane. Once, coming into the room unexpectedly, Cara had discovered Susan holding the baby close, squeezing Emily's small body hard against her own. At the sight of Cara, she immediately relinquished her.

'She was crying!' she said defensively. 'Nobody was looking after her.'

'Then it was very nice of you to do so,' Cara told her.

Her relationship with Susan was less troubled, but still far from close. In a strange way, Tom Hendry's death seemed to have changed things for the better.

'I think it's because she sees you grieve for her grandfather as much as the rest of us do,' Edward said. 'It makes you seem inside the family rather than outside it. But it's not easy to know what Susan thinks.'

'Well, at least we no longer have open warfare,' Cara said. 'I'm thankful for that and I'll just hope for things to get better still.'

David would do anything involved with the lambing. No task was too small or, in his eyes, too big. And when he wasn't able to take part, when his father or Johann assisted with a difficult birth, he watched and learned. Last weekend he had been allowed to try to persuade a ewe to suckle an orphan lamb in addition to her own.

'You'll need patience,' his father said. 'As likely as not she'll be awkward at first. But once you've persuaded her to let the lamb suck, once it's got her milk inside it, it passes through the little one's body, then from the scent of the lamb's droppings she smells her milk and thinks it's her own lamb.'

'How do we know what the ewe thinks?' David asked.

His father laughed.

'I suppose we don't really. But we can see how she behaves. From then on she acts as though the lamb's her own.'

As Cara was finishing her breakfast Johann came into the house, carrying a lamb tucked inside his coat.

'This little one is in a bad way,' he said. 'It is one of twins. The other one is all right but this fellow is very weak. I don't know if we can do anything.'

The lamb was a scrap of a creature; thin, and shivering with cold, its breathing faint.

Mrs Hendry held an old piece of blanket to warm by the fire.

'Give it to me,' she said. 'If we can save it, it won't be the first, and I reckon not the last. But it does look touch and go, I must say.'

She gently chafed its small body to get the circulation going, then wrapped it in the blanket.

'I'll keep it on top of the oven,' she said. 'Warmth is what it needs, and I'll try to get some milk and a drop or two of brandy down it, poor little creature.'

'Will it be all right?' Cara asked anxiously. One thing she could never get used to on the farm was any animal dying, even when, as now, it was newly born and she hadn't had time to get to know it.

'Who knows,' her mother-in-law said. 'We'll do what we can.'

'I must go,' Cara said. 'Edward might need me. And if I can I'll persuade him to come in for some breakfast.'

'It smells good,' Johann said. His eyes were red-rimmed with fatigue.

'It is good,' Mrs Hendry said. 'Now you eat your fill and then you should go and get some sleep. You can't be awake every minute of the day and night, though Tom always said it felt like it at lambing time.'

The sheepfold to which Cara now made her way was fairly close to the house, not too high on the hillside. It had been chosen for that reason, and because it had a small barn which could be used as a shepherd's hut. Here they kept straw and hay, for the comfort of the ewes if need be, and to feed them after they had given birth. The men could also make tea here, and if two of them were on duty at the same time one of them might occasionally be able to snatch a little sleep.

'What sort of a night have you had?' Cara asked as she reached Edward.

'Not too bad. We've lost two lambs, but the ewes are all right. And a good crop of twins.'

'That's a poor little chap Johann's just brought in,' Cara said.

'Yes. I doubt he'll make it.'

'It's cold,' Cara said, shivering. She swung her arms and beat them against her body to get warm.

'It was a sight colder earlier on,' Edward said. 'Have you brought me some breakfast?'

'No. Purposely not. I want you to go in and have a proper meal. I'm sure I can keep an eye on things while you do. If I really need you, I'll blow the whistle.'

'I'd give anything for another pair of hands,' Edward said. 'It's going to be a busy day and an even busier night to follow. Why do they choose to be born at night?' He was dead tired, felt as though he hadn't slept for a week, but there was no letting up.

'Your ma's told Johann to go to bed,' Cara said.

'So he should. He's been up all night and most of the night before. I've only been out here since four o'clock!'

The air was full of the sound of ewes baaing and lambs bleating.

'It astonishes me how the lambs so quickly know the sound of their own mother out of all the others,' Cara said.

'I know,' Edward agreed. 'In some countries they put a bell around the ewe's neck, and for ever after the lamb knows the sound of that bell; though I never could work out how they could get enough different bells.'

'Do go and get some breakfast, love,' Cara pleaded. 'It's all ready.'

In fact, she knew that right through lambing time her mother-in-law would always have some sort of a hot meal ready on the stove. Whenever the men could snatch the time, there'd be food waiting for them.

'If you're sure,' Edward said.

'Quite sure.'

'Well, I'd quite like to see my baby daughter. I haven't seen her awake for the past two days. She'll be forgetting what her father looks like!'

He doted on the baby, as they all did. One of the nice things about Emily was that she seemed to arouse no jealousy in the other children. From the first moment they had seen her in the cot, with her crumpled face and her thick dark hair, she had been accepted as their sister. Cara had expected that of David, but by Susan she had been pleasantly surprised.

As soon as Edward had left, reluctantly, and with a promise to be back quickly, Cara began to walk around the sheepfold, inspecting the flock. It was what the men did throughout the whole of the lambing time, day and night. Two ewes were clearly in labour, but the likelihood was that they'd need no help from her, so she continued on her way.

The fold, and the fields immediately surrounding it, were dotted all over with sheep and lambs, all black-faced Swaledales. Even the lambs had tiny black faces, and often black patches on their legs. It was a perennial scene. Sheep, though not this particular breeed, had been in these dales for more than five thousand years. Cara doubted if either the problems or the rewards had changed much in that time. The management would have, of course: today's flocks were bigger. But the basics of tupping and lambing, of shearing and trading were very likely the same. Perhaps there were fewer weakly lambs now, and fewer of those died. She hoped so.

She finished her inspection and went back to the two ewes. One had dropped her lamb and seemed fine, but the other was clearly in trouble. The lamb, which she knew should have arrived feet first together with the head, presented only the head. She also knew what she must do, but could she do it?

She tried to get her hand into the birth canal to pull out the tiny creature's front legs, but she couldn't manage it. At first she couldn't find them, and then she couldn't grasp them. Yet she knew that, the head appearing first, if it was left unattended it would swell, and the lamb would suffocate and die.

What shall I do? she thought.

Whatever was to be done next must be done quickly. That much she could tell. The ewe was in distress.

She must get Edward.

She blew hard on her whistle to summon him, but the wind which had perversely sprung up carried away the sound on the air in the wrong direction. She would have to run back to the house for him, even though it meant leaving the ewe. If she didn't do so, the lamb would surely die.

Faster than she had ever moved in her life, she ran back to the house and burst into the kitchen. Edward was at the table. She scarcely noticed the other man with him.

'Edward, come quick! A breech birth! I can't get the legs out!'

He was on his feet before the words were out of her mouth. It was only when the other man sprang up that she saw it was Kit Marsden.

'I'll come with you,' he said.

'Ring for the vet,' Edward instructed his mother on his way out.

'I thought he was coming today, anyway,' she said. 'I'll ask him to make it quick.'

The two men ran with long strides to the sheepfold, Cara close behind.

'The far corner!' she gasped.

Edward was down on his knees beside the ewe. With the skill born of experience he freed the legs and the lamb was born.

'Hook the phlegm out of the lamb's throat,' Marsden advised.

'I know,' Edward said shortly.

He squeezed the lamb's nose and mouth to get out the fluid which was blocking its breathing.

'She's chock full of muck,' he said. 'Unless I can clear it she's a goner!'

But eventually the lamb coughed, spluttering out great globules of phlegm.

'That's good,' Marsden said. 'That's very good! Now let me blow into her mouth. It helps to clear the air passages.'

Edward sat back on his heels.

'She'll be all right,' he said.

'Oh, why didn't I stay with her in the first place?' Cara cried.

'You couldn't have done anything,' Marsden said.

'I could have fetched Edward sooner. But I was only away ten minutes, inspecting the others.'

'Don't fret, love,' Edward said. 'You did the right thing. And it's going to be all right.'

Marsden nodded agreement.

'I go along with that.'

'Thank heavens,' Cara said. The relief was unspeakable, but now she was trembling from head to foot and suddenly her legs wouldn't hold her. She sat down quickly on the ground.

'Best let the veterinary see her all the same,' Marsden said. 'I'll take over if you want to go back to the house, find out if he's coming.'

The lamb now uttered a demanding cry. Edward picked it up and examined it closely.

'Well, *she's* all right. A sturdy little thing. We'd best take her back to the house and give her a bottle. Give her ma time to recover.'

He handed the new-born lamb to Cara, then turned to Marsden.

'I'm grateful for your help.'

'Reckon I showed up at the right time,' Marsden observed.

'I'll be back very soon.'

'Shall I stay?' Cara offered.

'No need at the moment,' Edward said. 'You can see to the lamb.'

'Why *did* Kit Marsden show up?' Cara asked as they walked back. 'He's the last person I'd have expected to see.'

'He came after a job of work. It seems he'd heard on the grapevine we were shorthanded. As *he* put it, he came to give us a helping hand.'

'Well it would help, wouldn't it?' Cara said reasonably. 'You said yourself you'd give anything for another pair of hands.'

'I didn't think of Marsden.'

'He seems to know a bit about sheep,' Cara remarked. 'He's not a shepherd, is he?'

'No. But I dare say he knows a fair amount. He's half gypsy, don't forget. They know a lot about animals. He knew what to do there all right.'

'So shall you set him on?'

'I don't know. As I've told you before, I don't like the man. And I don't see why he should come all this way to get work. There's plenty nearer Shepton at this time of the year.'

'You said yourself he'd heard we needed help,' Cara pointed out.

147

'And you don't have to like him – though I can't think why you don't.' That was not quite true, she thought as soon as she'd said it. There was a pushiness, an arrogance, about the man which wouldn't go down well with Edward any more than, at first, it had with her. 'Anyway,' she added, 'he was really helpful when we were stuck in Shepton. I don't know what we'd have done without him.'

'Marsden would always be helpful to a pretty young woman,' Edward said dryly.

'Oh, it wasn't just that,' she assured him. 'He was every bit as good to Mrs Anlaby, and by no stretch of imagination could you call *her* a pretty young woman!'

'I grant you that,' Edward said, smiling. 'She's a bad-tempered, disagreeable old biddy!'

They had reached the house. Mrs Hendry looked at them anxiously as they entered.

'Well?'

'Yes, all's well,' Edward said. 'Did you get the vet?'

'He's on his way.'

'Then I'll go back. Send him up the minute he comes.'

'Are you going to take on Kit Marsden?' Mrs Hendry asked.

'I don't know. Perhaps we can manage after all.'

'Have you gone out of your mind all of a sudden?' his mother demanded. 'If you don't want help for your own sake, what about Johann, what about Cara with a teething baby, and still taking her share on the farm?'

'All right, Ma! You've said your piece,' Edward replied shortly as he left.

'And now I must make up a bottle for this little lass,' Cara said. 'But she'll not need wrapping up and putting on the oven. She's a big one. Maybe that was the trouble. So how's the other one?'

Mrs Hendry shook her head.

'Too soon to tell. I managed to get a few drops down him, so that's a start.'

The newer lamb took to the bottle with little trouble, tugging at the teat, gulping the warm milk. Then she staggered on unsteady legs as far as the hearthrug, where she flopped down and immediately went to sleep.

'And now I'll see what I can do for my own baby,' Cara said. 'She must be getting hungry.'

'She'll let you know when she is, bless her,' Mrs Hendry smiled.

In the next minute the vet arrived.

'Edward said will you go up at once,' Mrs Hendry told him. 'But come back when you've done and I'll have a cup of tea waiting.'

When he returned, he was accompanied by Edward, who looked strained.

'Troubles never come singly,' he said. 'Marsden spotted a ewe with ringwomb.'

That Cara knew about. It was a case of the cervix refusing to open, and it needed the vet to cut it to allow the lamb to be born.

'Dead lucky I came when I did,' the vet said. 'And dead lucky your man noticed it.'

Johann came into the house.

'Well, you haven't had a long sleep,' Mrs Hendry said.

'Long enough, Mrs Hendry,' Johann replied. 'And I feel better for it.'

'You've missed a bit of excitement,' she told him.

'All in a day's work,' the vet said. 'And now I must be on my way. Thanks for the tea, Mrs Hendry.'

'I've decided to set on Marsden,' Edward announced suddenly. He turned to Johann. 'It'll make life a bit easier.'

Johann looked stunned.

'You are engaging another man? Are you not satisfied with me, then? Am I not a good worker?'

What would he do, he thought, without his job? Several times since the end of the war he had been given permission to remain for yet another six months. Thousands of prisoners wanted to stay, and fortunately for some of them they were needed on the land. He knew it had also been said that they might make husbands for the army of British women who had lost husbands and sweethearts, but he did not see himself married. The prisoners were allowed to write home now as often as they wished, but he had no-one, no-one at all to write to.

And now at last he had been officially told that because he was a farm worker, and because his employer had vouched for him, he could stay permanently in England. It was all he wanted. He could not envisage a future not spent at Beckwith. It had become home to him.

Edward looked at him in astonishment.

'It's not like that at all, Johann. Of course you're a good worker and I'm more than satisfied with you. You know that. I've engaged this man only for the rest of the lambing time. After that he'll leave.'

'Oh! I thank you!' Johann said.

He was relieved beyond words, but still a small doubt crept in. What if this other man was better than him? He cannot work harder than me, he thought. No-one could work harder, but perhaps he knew all about sheep and everything else. Perhaps he had lived in these parts all his life, was not a stranger like himself.

'I will work very hard for you,' he said earnestly.

149

'You always do,' Edward said. 'Don't worry, Johann.'

'There's nothing to worry about,' Mrs Hendry reassured him. 'Your place is here.' But she had an inkling, just an inkling, of how he felt inside.

'If you're fit, we'd best get back,' Edward told Johann. 'I'll send Marsden down for a bite to eat, Ma. Then me and Johann will have ours later with you and Cara.'

Has he deliberately decided not to eat with Marsden, Cara wondered? But surely not!

'Where will he sleep?' Mrs Hendry asked.

'In the barn. He's agreeable to that,' Edward said. 'We have a camp bed somewhere.'

'Then I must get some bedding together,' Mrs Hendry said. 'And I dare say I can find an oil heater. It'll be cold at night in that barn.'

Half an hour later Kit Marsden came into the house. He walked in without knocking – but perhaps that's all right as he's going to live here for a little while, Cara thought. Nevertheless, grateful though she was to him, his familiarity irritated her.

'I've been sent back for some grub,' he said. 'My valuable help isn't needed at the moment. The boss and the Kraut have everything in hand!'

Cara stopped what she was doing and looked at him with eyes like green ice.

'*What* did you say?'

'I said the boss and the Kraut have everything in hand.' His grin was defiant.

'If you are referring to Johann, I'll thank you to use his name,' Cara said frostily. But why, she fumed, did she sound so prissy? Much better to ignore him.

Marsden shrugged.

'As you wish, my lady. Kraut is what we call 'em in Shepton.'

'Well, we don't at Beckwith,' Cara said.

Mrs Hendry dished up a heaped plate of food and put it on the table.

'My daughter-in-law's right,' she declared firmly. 'We have a lot of respect for Johann. Not all Germans are bad – and anyway, he's an Austrian.'

Marsden sat at the table and began to eat.

'This is good,' he said. 'And I'm ready for it. Anyway, he doesn't like me!'

'Now I wonder why?' Cara said sweetly.

'Can't think,' Marsden replied through a mouthful. 'I would have thought I was a fairly likeable chap, wouldn't you?'

Cara turned away. He always had an answer.

150

'The boss said I should go back to Shepton when I've eaten. Pick up my bits and pieces.'

'And your rations!' Mrs Hendry said.

'Don't bother about that, Mrs Hendry,' Marsden said agreeably. 'I'll bring my rations and more besides. And if there's any little thing you ladies would like, well, just say the word! Stockings, scented soap, hairnets, tinned fruit, ribbons for the baby?'

'I have everything I want, thank you,' Cara said stiffly.

'Well, I'll not be proud,' Mrs Hendry said. 'I'd dearly like some nice soap – lavender or carnation. And some stockings; fine lisle, size nine. Of course I'll pay you.'

'They're as good as yours,' Marsden promised. 'And now I'll be on my way.'

He had a battered old Morris van in which he rattled away, far too fast, down the dale and out of sight.

'You cut off your nose to spite your face, didn't you, love?' Mrs Hendry said to Cara.

'I know!' Cara replied ruefully. 'And I'm on my last pair of stockings. Knowing him, I'll bet he could have got nylons! But he catches me on the wrong foot.'

'I dare say he's not a bad sort really,' Mrs Hendry said.

'Oh, I know he's not,' Cara agreed.

What Marsden had said was true. Johann did not like him. From the moment Edward introduced the two men, in the sheepfold, Johann had taken instantly against Marsden. He didn't know why. Perhaps it was his own insecurity; perhaps at heart he was afraid: but he thought not. It was something instinctive. Anyway, he recognized, he must get on with him as far as he had to. They would have to work together.

Later in the day Beth Dunning telephoned from Akersfield.

'Laura was wondering if she could come up for the weekend,' she said. 'She doesn't go back until next Wednesday.'

Laura's dream – or the first part of it – had come true. She had won the scholarship with no trouble at all and, however reluctantly, Beth and Arnold had agreed to her going to music school in Manchester as a weekly boarder. She was in her element there, working hard, every day a blessing.

'She'll be very welcome,' Cara said. 'The only thing is, we're up to the eyes in lambing. I won't have much time to spare, otherwise I'd invite you and Dad as well.'

'Oh, I know!' Beth said. 'We'll come some other time. I must see my little Emily!'

'She's cut two more teeth and another is nearly through,' Cara told her proudly.

151

'Perhaps Laura can give you a hand,' Beth suggested.

'I'll pick her up at the station in Shepton on Friday afternoon,' Cara said. 'We're not badly off for petrol and I can collect Susan from school at the same time.'

But when Friday came it was a different story. Emily, after an uneasy night, awoke crying. The sound brought Cara to life, though reluctantly. She felt she had only just fallen asleep. Edward's side of the bed was empty. He would have gone out an hour or two ago, she thought, to relieve Johann or Kit Marsden.

It took no more than seconds for the nature of Emily's cries to waken Cara thoroughly. Usually when her daughter gave voice it was in no uncertain manner, but now she whimpered pathetically, for all the world like a small puppy.

Cara jumped out of bed and peered into the cot. Emily's face was flushed, her forehead hot and burning to the touch.

Without waiting to put on her dressing gown, Cara rushed down to the kitchen to her mother-in-law.

'It's Emily!' she cried. 'She's ill! She's as hot as fire.'

It was the look on Mrs Hendry's face which alerted Cara to the fact that she was standing there in her flimsy nightdress and that Johann and Kit Marsden were sitting at the breakfast table. She gave them a quick glance. Johann's head was down, his eyes fixed firmly on the food on his plate; not so Marsden. He made no bones about looking at her nor, by the smile in his narrowed eyes, showing his appreciation at the sight. She knew that he was seeing right through her nightdress, openly appraising her body. Anger and confusion swept through her and she turned and ran out of the kitchen, followed by Mrs Hendry.

'How dare he!' she fumed. 'How dare he!'

'He's a man,' Mrs Hendry said.

'If I told Edward he'd sack him on the spot!' But she wouldn't tell Edward.

Kit Marsden's behaviour was momentarily forgotten as the two women bent over the cot and regarded Emily.

'Feel her forehead,' Cara said. 'She's burning!'

'The back of her neck's a better guide,' Mrs Hendry said. 'Don't ask me why! That's what *my* mother told me. Yes, she is a bit hot, I'll grant you.'

'What shall I do?'

'Well, if she was a bit older I'd say give her a dose of Fennings Fever Cure,' Mrs Hendry said. 'But she's a mite young for that. No, we'll just keep her quiet and give her plenty of boiled water. That should do the trick.'

'Don't you think I should send for Dr Speight?'

152

'Oh, I don't think so, love.' Then, seeing Cara's anxious face, Mrs Hendry added: 'But if it would make you feel better . . .'

'I think it would.'

'Then I'll telephone him while you get dressed and come down to breakfast.'

When Cara returned to the kitchen both men were still there.

'Good morning, Mrs Edward,' Johann said, as if this was his first sight of her. He always called her Mrs Edward, never Cara.

'Good morning again!' Kit Marsden said.

He had not called her Cara since that first meeting when they'd been introduced at the sheep sale. But why should it matter, she asked herself impatiently. Almost everyone calls me Cara. I prefer it that way. The trouble was that there was always familiarity in Kit Marsden's voice, no matter what the words were. He was capable of investing the most ordinary remark with a different meaning.

'I'd have thought you'd have been back at work,' Cara said coldly.

'We should be,' Johann said, getting up to leave.

'Dr Speight will call on his rounds,' Mrs Hendry told Cara. 'Now what about you fetching the girls from Shepton this afternoon? Would you like me to phone and sort out something else?'

'No need to do that, Mrs Hendry,' Marsden said smoothly. 'I'll fetch them with pleasure. I'm due to a couple of hours break this afternoon.'

'Well then . . .' Mrs Hendry looked at Cara.

'I suppose so,' Cara said. Serve him right if Susan and Laura were at daggers drawn the whole of the way.

When Dr Speight came Emily was still feverish, but no longer whimpering.

'Is it teething?' Cara asked anxiously.

'Teething gets blamed for everything,' the doctor said. 'It's seldom the cause, especially with milk teeth. It's a natural process. No, she's just got a bit of infection, that's all.'

'Infection? Where from?' Cara demanded.

'Who knows? Out of the air. Anyway, nothing to worry about. Plenty of fluids and she'll be as right as a trivet in no time at all. You first-time mothers worry too much. When you've had your fourth you'll see things differently!'

At teatime Marsden arrived back with Susan and Laura. To Cara's surprise they were all smiling.

'Kit took us for ice-creams in Shepton,' Laura said.

'Kit would have taken us to the cinema only there wasn't time,' Susan said.

So it was 'Kit', was it? Cara felt unaccountably annoyed that he'd made an obvious hit with the girls, even though it meant they were at ease with each other. Later, when she was on her own with her sister, Laura said: 'Actually, Susan isn't all that bad! We got on quite well. And Kit's nice, isn't he?'

ELEVEN

The weekend went well. To Cara's relief, Emily recovered quickly.

'They usually do,' Mrs Hendry said. 'Soon down, soon up again: that's babies for you.'

The ewe recovered equally quickly and seemed pleased to have her lamb restored to her. As for the sickly lamb, it had grown stronger and could now stand on its own four feet and take the bottle, which Susan and Laura gave it in turn.

'It's a little miracle,' Cara said to Edward. 'When you brought it into the house I never thought it would live.'

'It had better stay indoors another day or two,' Edward judged. 'The weather's turned cold.' There was a sneaky wind and frequent showers.

'Typical April weather,' Mrs Hendry said. 'But it makes the grass grow, even if it's not kind to weakly lambs.'

But the great surprise of the weekend was not the recovery of babies and animals, but the new rapport between Laura and Susan. From the moment they arrived back at Beckwith they spent most of their time in each other's company. Sometimes they went for short walks along the lane, or down to the river, which was all that Laura could manage; more often than not they were closeted in Susan's room, emerging for meals.

'I can hardly believe it,' Cara said to Mrs Hendry. 'Not that I don't welcome it. But I'd love to know what they talk about, wouldn't you?'

What they talked about, discussed endlessly, made plans for, was their future which lay so tantalizingly before them. Both agreed fervently that it would be quite different from the present.

'What do you mean to do when you leave college?' Susan asked Laura.

Laura looked surprised. Surely it was obvious what she would do. 'I want to be a concert pianist,' she said, 'if I'm good enough.'

'And are you? Good enough, I mean.'

'My teachers say I will be,' Laura said modestly. 'If I work hard. What will you do?'

'Oh, I shall go on the stage,' Susan declared firmly. 'I'll be an actress. Shakespearian. Or a dancer. Or I'll star in musical comedy. I haven't decided which. But I shall certainly go on the stage.'

'Then in a way we both will,' Laura said. 'Though mine will be called the concert platform. But it *will* be a stage, really.'

'I shall wear glamorous clothes,' Susan said dreamily. 'My audiences will adore me! They'll demand encore after encore! If I decide on musical comedy I'll probably stop the show every night!'

'Stop the show?' Laura queried.

'Yes. When I sing my big number the audience will go wild. They'll applaud so long that I'll have to do it all over again, there and then. It's called stopping the show.'

'Oh!'

Would that happen to me? Laura wondered. When I get to the end of the first movement of the Grieg, will they demand that I do it again? She wasn't sure she'd like that.

'I shall wear long dresses all the time,' she said. 'You can, on the concert platform.'

Long dresses would hide her ugly boots, though she had already determined that when the time came her boots would be made of the finest leather and dyed the exact shade of her dress. The white wedding boots had inspired her to this.

'I can hardly wait for it to happen,' Susan said. 'If I go on the stage at sixteen – and I suppose I *just* could – it's still almost three years. How shall I endure it?' she demanded dramatically.

'It'll be even longer for me,' Laura pointed out. 'But at least I'll be doing what I like best, even when I'm training. Playing the piano, I mean. There's tons to learn.'

'Acting will come naturally to me,' Susan said with confidence.

She stood in front of the mirror, her body arched and twisted into a pose which showed the outline, just discernible, of her developing breasts. She gave her chest an extra thrust forward.

'Yes, I've definitely got bosoms!' she said with satisfaction. 'You haven't. Not yet,' she added kindly.

She raised her chin, tossed back her hair, tried to see herself in profile, which without side mirrors was next door to impossible.

'You're very pretty,' Laura said. 'I can just imagine you on the stage.'

156

'If you come to see me, I'll come to one of your concerts,' Susan promised graciously. 'We'll send each other free tickets.'

'I can't believe it all!' Cara said to her mother-in-law. 'All this sweetness and light. What can have caused it?'

'I don't know,' Mrs Hendry confessed. 'I think Kit Marsden may have worked a little bit of magic in Shepton. But best not ask, best take it and be thankful.'

On Saturday night, after supper, Laura willingly put aside her classical preferences and accompanied Susan in all the popular songs they could think of between them.

'You really have a very nice voice, Susan,' Cara said.

Mrs Hendry nodded agreement.

'She could have been a right little Vera Lynn if she'd been born a bit sooner!'

When Laura left on Sunday afternoon it was with promises to come again before too long, at Susan's invitation. Kit Marsden, who had an hour or two free, insisted on taking Laura into Shepton for her train.

'Then I'll come with you,' Susan said.

'I don't think . . .' Cara began.

Susan turned to her with a sudden look of the old hostility in her face.

'Why not?' she demanded.

'You're right,' Cara said. 'Why not indeed!'

It wasn't at all clear to her why she didn't want Susan to go with Kit Marsden, and it certainly wasn't worth fighting over.

'But remember you still have some homework to finish before you go back to school tomorrow,' she added.

Geometry, Susan thought with disgust! What earthly use would that be when she was facing the footlights?

Most of the lambs had been born now. Only those ewes which had been served by the chaser rams had yet to give birth.

'Not so many of those this year,' Edward said with satisfaction. 'It'll only need one of us to see to them, if all goes well. The other two can get on with the marking.'

'I wish I could help,' David said. It was Monday morning and he was reluctant to go to school. There was so much happening on the farm. 'I'd like to help with the marking.'

'You will one day,' Edward promised. 'You're too young yet.'

It was preferable to mark the new lambs soon after they were born, and if he'd had Marsden's help earlier, if he and Johann hadn't been working round the clock, it would have been done. One reason for marking them, the reason he'd have liked to have done them sooner, was so that he'd know each one's parentage. That could be useful to him in future breeding. The other reason was to identify them as belonging to Beckwith should they stray, or when they were at market, or in the washing and dipping when some of the farmers brought their sheep together.

'Of course,' he said now to David, 'there's no need for me or Johann personally to have identification marks. You recognize your own lambs almost from the beginning. Every shepherd does.'

'How?' David asked. He knew already, but he wanted to spin out the time. Anyway, he never grew tired of farm talk.

'Well, for a start they have different faces. Sometimes they walk differently, or stand in a different way; or they might be a slightly different colour. It's difficult to say why.'

'It's very clever,' David said.

'Not really. It's a bit like puppies in a litter. People can tell *them* apart, but they think it's strange when you can do the same with sheep.'

'Like the children in my class,' David said. 'Miss Pratt knows us all!'

'Beckwith sheep have been marked in the same way for nigh on two hundred years,' Mrs Hendry said proudly. 'Every farmer in the dales would know a Beckwith sheep if he met one.'

'You know the mark,' Edward said to David.

'A forked cut in the end of its ear and a letter "B" burned into its horn,' David told him.

He had seen a sheep being horn-burned at last year's lambing time and had shouted in horror at the sight.

'It doesn't hurt,' Edward had said. 'There aren't any nerves in the outer bit of the horn.'

'Are you sure?' David had asked.

'Quite sure, or I wouldn't do it.'

'Come on, David love,' Cara said now. 'Eat up your breakfast, then get ready for school.'

'And I must get out,' Edward said. Kit Marsden and Johann were already back on the fellside. 'Oh, and while I remember,' he said, 'I have to go to Hawes tomorrow. I wondered if you'd like to go with me, Ma?'

'I'd like that very much,' Mrs Hendry said quickly.

Hawes was her home town. She still had a cousin or two there. It would be nice to visit them.

'I shall want to leave straight after breakfast,' Edward said. 'You'll have to be ready.'

'I will be, no fear! When shall we be back?'

'We'll have a bite of dinner there and come back in the afternoon.'

158

'I'll see to the breakfasts, *and* the dinners,' Cara said. 'No need to hurry back, unless Edward has to.'

'I think by tomorrow this place can manage without me for a few hours,' Edward said.

On Tuesday morning Cara quite enjoyed having the place to herself. After breakfast Kit Marsden and Johann left within minutes of each other. From the window she could see them climbing the fell. Soon after that Edward and his mother departed.

In a state of unusual tranquillity Cara did all that had to be done. She bathed Emily, then laid her on a towel on the hearthrug and played with her. She was such a good child, and so plump and beautiful. She waved her arms and legs in the air and made a hundred different noises, delighted with the sound of her own voice; then she turned herself over and tried to move forward on all fours.

'You'll be crawling soon!' Cara told her.

There was no doubt, she thought, that Emily was a very forward child. She would do everything – crawling, standing, walking, speaking – long before the books said she was due to do so.

'You are a clever little girl,' Cara said. 'And I'd like to play with you all morning, but I'd better put you down to sleep and get on with my work.'

She picked her up and put her in her pram, then wheeled it out to the flagged area at the back of the house, where she could keep an eye on it from the kitchen window. In no time at all, in her own language, Emily talked herself to sleep.

The morning passed. Cara did her chores. The potatoes were on, and the carrots, and when she had seen to the bit of washing-up in the sink she would sit down with a book for twenty minutes before the two men came in for dinner.

A minute later – she was still at the sink, with her back to the door – Kit Marsden came into the house. There was no need to look around, she knew his step.

'You're early,' she said. 'I'm not ready.'

'Yes you are,' he said.

There was something in his voice that was not quite right. She started to turn around to look at him, but he was too quick for her. He was behind her and his arms were tight around her waist.

'Get off!' she shouted. 'Let go! How dare you!'

He laughed, while she beat at him with her fists, struggling to free herself. His face was close to hers and she knew he was going to kiss her, but when she turned her head away he suddenly let go.

'It was only a bit of fun,' he said. 'Don't be such a prude. Funny, I'd never have marked you down as a prude. You don't have that look about you.'

She pulled herself together. She was *not* going to show him that she'd been frightened, though for a moment she had. There'd been something in his voice, in his grip on her, which had been more than a bit of fun. And if I hadn't protested, she thought, if I hadn't struggled, what then? It was a thought she didn't wish to pursue.

'Nor am I,' she said. 'It's just not my idea of fun. If Edward knew he'd have you out of here at once. He'd sack you on the spot.'

'But he won't know, will he?' His words challenged her.

'If it happens again he will!'

He moved away from her and went and took his place at the table.

'I didn't mean any harm,' he said. 'It's nothing to make a fuss about. Some women might take it as a compliment.'

'Not this one!' she retorted.

Even so, he made her feel that *she* was in the wrong, that she'd made too much of the incident. She should have taken it lightly, even have laughed at him. But it irritated her that he made her feel like this.

'Now how is it,' he asked, 'that I get on well with every member of your family – even with Edward now – but not with you? Why do you dislike me?'

Do I dislike him? she asked herself. Yes, she did, but at the same time she found him attractive, and had from the first. Apart from his good looks there was a quality of excitement in him which she'd never found in anyone else. And was it really possible to be attracted to someone you didn't like? She wished he had never come to Beckwith. She almost wished she had never met him.

'Does it matter?' she answered. 'Why did you come here in the first place? You could have found work in Shepton.'

'Don't tell me you don't know,' he said. 'I came because you were here. I don't like to admit it, but I couldn't get you out of my mind.'

'How dare you speak to me like this?' she cried. 'You know I'm a happily married woman!'

'Alas, yes!' He sighed deeply, but there was laughter in his eyes. Did he take nothing seriously?

'I'd like you to leave,' Cara said. 'I'd like you to tell Edward you can't go on working for him.'

'Oh, I couldn't do that!' He sounded shocked. 'Edward's relying on me at the moment. I couldn't leave him in the lurch, now could I?'

I'll bet you've left scores of people in the lurch in your time, Cara thought.

Before she could answer, Johann walked into the kitchen, and at the same time she realized that the potatoes were boiling dry.

'Damn and blast!' she shouted.

Johann looked at her, startled. He wasn't used to hearing her swear.

160

He treated her so much like a lady that in his presence she usually behaved like one.

'I'm sorry, Johann,' she said. 'It'll be a few minutes. I'm behind-hand.'

'Then I will come back,' Johann replied. 'There is something I want from my room.'

He went out, and she watched him cross the farmyard.

'Now *there's* a man would kill me if I harmed a hair of your head!' Marsden said.

'Johann?'

'The same. It sticks out a mile.'

'Then you'd better not try it, had you?'

In ten minutes Johann was back. As Cara put his dinner in front of him she felt, for the first time ever, uncomfortable in his presence.

The three of them ate in near silence. The two men never did have anything to say to each other and now, for different reasons, Cara felt at ease with neither of them.

The moment he had finished his meal, Johann rose.

'Thank you,' he said. 'Please excuse me.'

'He'll cut his dinnertime short rather than walk back with me,' Marsden remarked when Johann had left. 'Now I wonder why *he* hates me?'

'You flatter yourself,' Cara said. 'I don't suppose he even thinks of you. He's a man who prefers to be alone, that's all.'

'Oh, he hates me all right,' Marsden said. 'As I told you, I wouldn't fancy my chances if I did wrong by you. Not that he'd ever know, of course. I'm too clever for the Kraut. Upright, honest and trustworthy he may be, but clever he is not!'

'He's a good man, a simple man,' Cara said. 'He's worth a dozen of you.'

'You could be right,' Marsden said. But he was mocking her again.

'Hadn't you better get back to work?' Cara asked coldly.

Strangely, from that day on Marsden was polite, and uncommonly quiet. Butter wouldn't melt in his mouth, Cara thought. All the same, she felt uneasy in his presence and took good care never to be alone with him.

'Do we need Marsden now that the lambing's over?' she asked Edward one day. It was almost the end of May and still he stayed on, Edward finding him jobs to do.

'I suppose we could manage without him if we had to,' Edward replied. 'But he's a useful chap. He's turned out better than I expected. I thought we'd best keep him on for the Washing. It's only a week or two off.'

161

Sheep washing, which took place in June, was dying out – but Arendale was a dale which clung to traditions. Even so, it had been agreed that this year's Washing should be the last.

'It's a shame we're letting it go,' Cara said.

'I know. But it's uneconomic. We do get a bit more from washed fleeces, but not enough to make it worthwhile,' Edward said. Also, when the sheep had been washed there was a 'rise' on the wool which made them easier to shear a little later.

The Washing had been fixed for the second Saturday in June. There was a natural pool or 'dub' on a bend in the river, where the water stopped its rushing and flowed quietly into the dub, stayed a while, then flowed gently out again to join the main stream.

'We've had a look at the dub, me and Joseph Fawcett,' Edward said. 'It'll need a bit of banking up, a few stones and sods to dam it. I'll get Marsden on to it on Friday and Fawcett will send his man.'

A Saturday had been chosen so that the children would be free from school. There were not many children in Arendale, but others would come with their families from Faverwell and around. The Washing was one of the great social occasions of the farming year. When the work was over there would be food and fun and games for everyone.

The day dawned fine.

'Thank heaven for that!' Mrs Hendry said. 'There'll be enough water splashing around without it falling from the skies!'

She had spent the last two days, with help from Cara, cooking and baking for the communal picnic which would take place once the sheep were washed. The stone shelves of the big larder were filled with dishes of pork brawn, potted beef, apple pie, currant pasty and various cakes. There was a ham hanging from the ceiling, oatcakes on the rack, cheeses and butter Mrs Hendry had made herself, and a large bowl of whipped cream in the dairy.

'You'd not think we were rationed, would you?' Mrs Hendry commented, surveying the spread with satisfaction.

'If everyone else brings the same amount, how will we ever get through it?' Cara asked.

'Oh we will, love! No bother! I've never known more than a crumb or two left for the birds after a Washing. It's hard work for the men, and then the bairns are always hungry.'

The business of Washing started early in the day. The sooner it was over, the sooner folks could get down to the fun. By nine o'clock in the morning the dogs and shepherds had rounded up the sheep so that they were to hand, ready to be thrown, one at a time, into the water. The Arendale dub was not a big one, only sizeable enough for two men to stand in the water at once, dealing with the sheep as they were thrown.

Though Cara had left Beckwith early, mainly at the insistence of David who didn't want to miss a thing, most of the farmers and farmhands were already there, and many of the women and children. Some of the women, those who were dealing with the food, would arrive later. Emily had been left with her grandmother. Susan, a late riser, was still in bed and would join the others when the spirit moved her.

Cara and David settled themselves on the short springy grass. It was dry and slippery, almost warm to the touch, after several days of sun.

Wasting no time, the men, one of them Kit Marsden, who would throw in the sheep, were ready to start, only waiting for the Washers to wade into the pool.

'Come on, then!' Marsden shouted impatiently. 'Let's get on with it. Sooner it's over, sooner we'll sup!'

The two Washers, fortified against their task with a nip of whisky, waded into the cold river water.

'I wish I could be a Washer!' David said with longing.

'Perhaps when you're tall enough,' Cara said. 'But as the water comes higher than the men's waists it would just about cover you now. Anyway, it must be jolly cold. I'd hate it myself.'

'That's because you're not a farmer,' David said.

Am I not, Cara wondered? She had hoped she was well on the way to being one, but Emily, and domestic duties, took up so much of her time. Also, now that Edward had Kit Marsden he had less need of her help.

The Washers signalled that they were ready to start. Both throwing the sheep and catching them were skilled jobs and the exact timing was important. It required two men to throw one sheep, which must fly through the air rear end first so that it landed in the water on its back, making the least possible splash for the Washers.

'I thought Kit would have been a Washer,' David said.

'He will be,' Cara said. 'These men can't do more than a couple of hours, perhaps less. He'll take a turn later.'

They fell silent for a while, watching the procedure. The Washers caught the sheep the second it fell into the water, gave it a good ducking on all sides, paid particular attention to cleaning its belly and backside, then briefly immersed its head before finally allowing it to swim to the side, leaving a trail of dirt in the water, before it was hauled out.

The instant they had let it go, another animal was thrown. There was no delay. The two pairs of men worked quickly, methodically and unceasingly, the Washers seemingly oblivious of the coldness of the water, against which they wore no special clothing.

'They're well paid,' Edward – who had joined Cara and David – remarked. 'But by God, they earn it!'

For the number of sheep to be dealt with on this day, three pairs of Washers and equal numbers of men throwing in were needed, taking it in turns. Shortly after half-past ten Marsden handed over his job to someone else and came to join Cara and the others. He passed Johann, who was next in as a Washer.

'Mind you don't get wet!' he quipped.

Johann said nothing.

By this time Susan had arrived, bringing flasks of tea and slices of gingerbread.

'I'm ready for this,' Kit Marsden said.

'Then I shall pour yours first, Kit, because you've been working the hardest,' Susan said.

'Oh no!' Marsden protested. 'Ladies first! Serve your ma first.'

'She's not . . .' Susan began – then stopped.

She's not my mother, Cara knew she was going to say. Well she wasn't, and she knew she never would be, but at least there was less hostility. A year ago Susan wouldn't have bitten back the remark. She smiled at her stepdaughter as she was handed a mug of tea.

'Thank you, love!' The words were for more than the tea.

'When do you start washing, Kit?' David wanted to know.

'Next lot. I take Johann's place. When I've drunk my tea I'll give a hand with hauling them out.'

'Can I help?' David asked eagerly.

'Best ask your dad,' Marsden said. 'It's all right by me, but I warn you, you'll get wet when they shake themselves dry.'

'I don't care. Can I go, Dad?' David asked.

'If you want to,' Edward agreed. 'Don't let him be a nuisance,' he said to Marsden.

Cara watched them go. What Marsden had said was true. All her family liked him, now even Edward. She watched him take his place at the side of the dub, begin to haul the sheep as they tried to scramble up the bank, sending them on their way, with a thwack, to the meadow where they would dry in the sun before being rounded up by their owners. The Beckwith sheep would be taken higher up the fells.

Marsden was so strong; he seemed to tackle the task effortlessly, even though he had spent the last hour or two throwing sheep. Just after midday he returned with David.

'My turn to do a bit of washing now,' he said.

He went to the water's edge, where Len Hodge from Fawcett's farm joined him. As Marsden walked away, Grant Fawcett came and joined Cara.

'I'm glad you're here,' he said. 'It's a long time since I saw you.'

'Will you sit down?' Cara said pleasantly. 'Or are you too busy?'

'Not at the moment,' he replied, dropping down beside her.

The Washers habitually went into the dub wearing their ordinary clothing, neither more nor less. It was always the way. But, it seemed, it was not Kit Marsden's way.

Standing on the bank opposite to Cara and Grant Fawcett he took off his waistcoat. Not hurrying – indeed deliberately pausing – he stripped off his shirt, and then his vest, baring himself to the waist. Then in a split second, aware that he had people's attention, he whipped off his trousers.

The gasp from the crowd as he did so changed to laughter as he revealed navy swimming shorts. For a few seconds he stood there in the sun. His skin was brown and smooth, with silky-fine dark hairs over his chest and across his powerful shoulders. His waist was narrow, his stomach flat, his legs strong and shapely. Freed from his shapeless working clothes, he was an Adonis of a man.

Before he entered the water he looked deliberately across to where Cara sat. He knew she would be watching him – and she was. His eyes met hers, and he smiled. Then he gave a salute to the appreciative crowd, and waded in.

'He's gorgeous!' Susan said dreamily. 'He's like Clark Gable. Don't you think Kit is gorgeous?' she asked Cara.

'Very nice,' Cara said steadily. 'Though I dare say *he* thinks he's gorgeous.'

'Why don't you like him?' Susan asked.

'Who said I didn't?' She wished Susan would not say these silly things in front of Grant Fawcett.

'It's written all over you. You don't approve of him because he stood there in his bathing shorts, because he's not stuffy, like everyone else around here.'

'Thank you very much, young lady!' Grant said.

'I'm sorry. I didn't mean you.'

'It's nothing to me one way or the other,' Cara told her. 'And I don't think people *are* stuffy. They seemed to enjoy the sight of him as much as you did.'

And, she thought, looking at him dispassionately, as if she were an artist and he a model, if appearances were all that mattered, yes, he was a pleasing sight. Against her will she watched him in the water, handling the sheep. He was skilled, quick and strong. Concentrating on the job in hand he looked neither to left nor right until, suddenly, as if he knew she was watching him, he looked once more across to the bank and caught her at it.

His concentration snapped and as the next animal was thrown to him he missed it and it went with a mighty splash into the dub, and under the water.

'Whoops!' Grant Fawcett said. 'Len won't like that!'

'Damn it, Marsden!' Len Hodge shouted. 'Watch what you're doing!'

'Sorry Len,' Marsden apologized.

'I'm going back to Beckwith,' Cara said quickly. 'I must see to Emily then help Grandma with the food. Will you come and help me, Susan?'

'In a minute,' Susan said. She was still watching Kit Marsden.

'I'll come and give you a hand,' Grant offered.

By half-past two the Washing was over. In the time it took the Washers to get into dry clothes, the food was laid out on white-clothed trestle tables and the beer, ginger pop and tea were ready to flow, according to taste. The meadows around were crowded with whiter-than-white sheep and some of the stones and sods which had helped to shore up the dub had been removed, so that now the water flowed through. In no time at all it would be clean enough for those who wanted a refreshing dip.

'Are you going to bathe, Kit?' Susan asked.

'Not me! I've had enough water for one day. And if you take my advice you won't either, after all you've eaten.'

'You're very rude,' Susan protested. 'I didn't eat any more than anyone else! So what *are* you going to do?'

'I'm going to lie flat on my back and have forty winks; gather my strength for the tug of war.'

The contest was to be between the men of Arendale and a team from Faverwell.

'Faverwell always beats Arendale,' David said.

'That's because up until now I haven't been pulling for Arendale,' Kit Marsden stated complacently. 'You'll see a difference this year.'

'You're so modest!' Cara said.

'I've got muscle, you see! It's what you're short of on the Arendale side.'

'We noticed! Yours, I mean,' Susan said.

'Mind your manners, miss!' her grandmother said sharply. But really, the man asked for it, displaying himself in that bold fashion. She had come up from the house in time to see him leave the water, strut around half-naked. It wasn't seemly in mixed company.

Before the tug of war there were the races: flat races, sack races, wheelbarrow races – and for the ladies, egg-and-spoon and three-legged ones. In the tug of war Kit Marsden made good his promise and pulled the Arendale side to victory, which only left the fell race.

Anyone could join in the fell race, with handicaps according to age.

166

The men must run to the top and down again, but the children went no more than halfway up, not only because their legs were shorter but because the tops could be dangerous. There were potholes there, deep shafts leading down into the earth.

'Here we go again!' Marsden said.

'So you think you'll win?' Cara asked.

'I reckon I have a chance,' he declared confidently.

Johann spoke up.

'I would not be too sure!'

Marsden looked at him in surprise. Johann never addressed him unless he had to.

'You think *you* might do it, old man?'

'We shall see,' Johann said.

When they had set off, Cara turned to her mother-in-law, smiling.

'Marsden hasn't a chance,' she said. 'He doesn't know what he's up against. Johann has been running up and down mountains all his life!'

'You sound pleased,' Mrs Hendry said.

'Do I? Perhaps I am. It won't do Marsden any harm to be taken down a peg or two.'

They watched as the contestants climbed the hill. By the halfway stage there were no more than six left in the running; the rest struggled behind. Of the leaders as they reached the top, Johann was first and Kit Marsden behind.

'There's not much in it, as far as my old eyes can tell,' Mrs Hendry said.

'Watch the downhill,' Cara said. 'It's not as easy as it looks.'

In fact, Johann was back at the base, well ahead, an easy winner who seemed almost to fly down the hillside. It was several minutes before Kit Marsden caught him up.

'I slipped,' he said. 'The ground's as slippery as glass up there.'

'Do you mean otherwise you'd have won?' Cara asked sweetly.

'No I wouldn't. I hand it to our foreign friend. I couldn't have beaten him.'

Johann was beaming with pleasure. It was not the race he cared about, as such. He had wanted more than anything in the world to beat that arrogant Yorkshireman – and now he had.

Later in the evening there was dancing, to the music of a concertina and two mouth organs.

'Madame, will you do me the honour?' Marsden said, bowing from the waist in front of Cara.

Why does he always sound so mocking, she thought. But it would be ill-mannered to refuse him. Besides, she didn't want to. She had already observed that he was a good dancer, and she loved to dance.

She wondered why he hadn't asked her earlier. It was almost the end of the day.

He held her lightly at first, then as the dance went on, closer and closer. She was thankful that it was growing dark, that they wouldn't so easily be seen.

Why don't I just break away from him, leave him standing? she asked herself. But she didn't, nor did she protest even when he held her closer still, so that she felt the whole of his body hard against hers. At one point she was sure that his lips brushed her hair, but she said nothing. Neither of them were speaking at all now.

Then the music faded and the dance ended. She knew she didn't want it to end. But that's because I love dancing, she told herself. He released her. 'Thank you, and goodbye,' he said.

She looked up at him, startled. 'Goodbye' he'd said, not 'Goodnight'. 'Goodbye?'

'I'm leaving.' His tone was abrupt.

'But I thought you were staying for the haymaking? Are you coming back for that?'

'No,' he said. 'I'm going away.'

At any time until today she would have been glad of the news. Now she was not so sure.

'Where are you going?' she asked.

He shrugged.

'Who knows? I don't!'

Edward appeared out of the darkness.

'There you are!' he said. 'Time we were off to bed. Same old early start in the morning.'

The haymaking, in July, went well. The weather stayed fine from start to finish and the last load was stacked in the barn in record time.

'I've never known a better haymaking,' Edward said with satisfaction as they were getting ready for bed on the last night.

'All told, it's been a good year,' Cara said.

Edward took her in his arms.

'Every year is a good year since I married you. Every day, every hour!'

'For me too,' Cara told him. 'Come to bed.'

The next day Edward said: 'I reckon one or two sheep have strayed right up to the top of the fell. I'm going after them.'

It was unusual that he was not back for his dinner. No matter what they were doing, everyone came in for dinner. Not that anyone was anxious, only puzzled. But when Ruby came flying down the hillside and burst into the house, barking and alone, it was a different story.

168

'He's hurt! Edward's hurt!' Cara cried. 'He's broken his leg! I'm sure he has!'

'Nay lass, I reckon he's just twisted his ankle and sent Ruby to fetch us,' Mrs Hendry said. 'It's easy done, twisting your ankle.'

'I will go at once,' Johann volunteered. 'Ruby will show me where.'

'I'm coming with you,' Cara said.

The dog ran forward and backward, constantly whimpering, impatient for them to keep up with her. Cara kept calling out, 'Edward, we're coming! We're coming!'

When they eventually found him it was a moot point whether he could ever have heard her, though she would always hope that he had. His body was just visible at the bottom of one of the shafts. A yard away from him was a sheep, one of this year's lambs, also dead.

Cara's screams went to and fro in the wind on the fell top. Whether she intended to jump or not she could never afterwards remember, but she recalled Johann's strong arms around her as he pulled her back. And somewhere at the back of her mind she heard Kit Marsden's voice. 'I slipped. The ground's as slippery as glass!'

TWELVE

The summer continued as though nothing had happened, the sun hot and yellow in a sky of cobalt blue, with clouds no more than white gauzy wisps moving idly in front of a gentle breeze. In the meadows by the river, where the hay had so recently been gathered, the stubble still shone pale gold, though soon it would be bronze, and then brown. The sheep, their fleeces thick now, awaited the shearer.

But at Beckwith it was darker than the deepest day of winter. To Cara it was as if she lived in a dense fog, the kind of fog she had known in Akersfield, thick and black with smoke and soot; fog through which no beam of light could penetrate; fog which deadened all sound and feeling.

She hated that summer: she hated its everlasting brightness and unconcern. The fog protected her like a blanket. No-one could touch the raw, sore places with which she felt her body was covered. Only Emily's innocence, because she knew nothing and cared neither for the past nor the future, only for the present, could penetrate the fog.

'She'll bring us back to life,' Mrs Hendry said, looking down at the baby crawling on the rug. 'Emily, and the animals we have to attend to will bring us back to life.'

But I don't want to be brought back to life, Cara thought. What sort of life, anyway?

'Sometimes I hate the animals,' she said. 'Sometimes I don't even want to bother with Emily.'

'I know,' Mrs Hendry said. 'I've gone through it.'

And I'm still going through it, he was my son as well as your husband, she wanted to say. She wanted to cry out the words, but she didn't. Yet they were in her voice.

170

'Oh, Mother Hendry, I know! I know!' Cara cried. 'And you're my rock! What would I do without you?'

'Or me without you, love. "Bear ye one another's burdens." That's what you and me must do.'

She opened her arms and her daughter-in-law went into them. The tears ran down the older woman's face, but Cara didn't cry. She had not yet shed a tear. She had remained dry-eyed through the nightmare journey from the fell top, when the Cave Rescue team bore Edward's body on the stretcher, through the inquest in Shepton, through the funeral in the little dale's church, when she had fixed her eyes steadily on the list of men who had left to fight at Flodden Field. How many wives became widows then, she wondered?

In the Shepton office, registering Edward's death, the professionally sympathetic clerk had entered her occupation as 'widow'. Is that now my role in life? Cara wondered bitterly. But she hadn't protested, it was too much trouble, though inside she was screaming.

Through the desperate, lonely nights since then, each one seeming the length of a week, when she had buried her face in the pillow, stretching out her arm to where Edward should be, and wasn't, she had longed for the tears which never came.

'Accidental death,' the verdict had been. 'A broken neck. You have the consolation that death was instantaneous. Your husband did not suffer.' Almost certainly Edward had slipped while trying to rescue a sheep from a ledge of rock. Well, not even that had been accomplished. All wasted.

Everyone had been enormously kind. People she hardly knew, near-strangers who had known Edward since he was a boy, called or telephoned with offers of help. She had been too dazed to know her needs, but Grant Fawcett, who walked up from his uncle's farm almost every day, and Johann, had between them sorted things out. Grant was too busy at Fawcett's to spend more than the odd hour or two on actual work, but Johann had toiled almost around the clock, seldom coming down from the fields or the fellside until the long northern evenings had closed in darkness.

Cara picked up Emily from the rug and took her to her cot in the bedroom for her mid-morning nap. When she came back into the kitchen Grant Fawcett was there.

'How are you?' he asked.

'I'm all right.'

It was the only answer she ever gave. I shall never be all right again, she thought, but who wants to know, who *really* wants to know? At least I needn't bore people.

If only she would open up, if only she'd let go, just for a minute, Grant thought. If not to me, then to anyone. He would have done

171

anything for her, given his right arm, but the wall she had built around herself seemed as real and as high as those solid limestone walls which climbed over the fells. Meanwhile he waited patiently for the first chink to appear in her self-made fortress.

He looked at her, searching her face for a sign. In a haunted, haggard way she was as beautiful as ever, but her red hair was unkempt and her green eyes were dulled and darkened. Now she turned away from him, not wishing to be involved.

'I've come to see you about the shearing,' he said. 'It'll have to be done soon. Actually, it's weeks behind. It should have been done before the haymaking.'

'I know,' Cara replied. 'But the hay was ready and the weather seemed settled.'

They needed the money from the fleeces. Money was one of the few realities which she couldn't set aside. The shortage of it stared her in the face and the money the fleeces would bring was an important part of the farm's income.

'We need the money,' she said.

'Aside from that,' Mrs Hendry put in, 'the sheep need to be clipped. Their coats are thick and heavy, this time of the year. Once they're clipped, they'll feel better.' Also, it would give the new coats a chance to grow before the colder weather came.

'There've been lots of offers of help,' Grant told them. 'I think you should take advantage of them. People *want* to help.'

In any case it was not unusual for neighbours to aid each other with the shearing. It was another occasion for a party, more music and dancing.

'Tom and Edward always helped the others where they could,' Mrs Hendry said. 'Me too for that matter. And I'm not the only farmer's wife in these parts who can shear a sheep. I don't suppose I've lost the knack, either, but I'll have to see to the food.'

'Aunt Rose said I was to tell you she'll be pleased to come,' Grant said. 'Either to shear, or give a hand with the eats – whatever suits you best.'

'I'm sorry!' Cara interrupted sharply. 'I can't stand a social occasion.'

'We understand that, love,' Mrs Hendry said. 'And no-one would expect it, I'm sure. Not the music and the dancing. But we'll have to feed people. Shearing's hard work and they'll be at it all day.'

Mention of dancing brought Kit Marsden to Cara's mind. The Washing seemed years away now, part of another life. She had expected Marsden to be one of the first with offers of help, but there had been no sign of him. She couldn't imagine that, wherever he was, he hadn't heard about Edward. News travelled far and wide around the dales. Still, no matter. She could do without him.

'If you leave the arrangements to me and Johann I reckon I could muster about a dozen shearers,' Grant said. 'The more there are, the quicker we'll get through, and be out of your way again. Will Saturday week suit?'

'One day is the same as another,' Cara replied.

'It'll suit very well,' Mrs Hendry said positively.

Susan and David would be at home. It would be good for them to have a bit of life about the place, and if a job could be found for them so much the better. They had taken their father's death badly – well, who could expect anything else, poor lambs? More than ever now, she thought, they needed a mother – but Cara was in no fit state. She felt worried and helpless about Cara. Something would have to be done, and she didn't know what.

On the evening of that day Cara sat at the kitchen table with the farm books in front of her while Mrs Hendry, in her usual armchair, busied herself with turning the heel of a pair of socks she was knitting for David. All her married life she had knitted socks, for her husband, then for Edward. Now there was only David to knit them for, but thank heaven he could do with as many as she could provide. He wore through them as if they were tissue paper.

With an impatient gesture Cara pushed the account books away from her.

'I can't do it!' she protested.

'Does it not add up?' Mrs Hendry asked. To her relief, she had never been called upon to do the books.

'Nothing adds up,' Cara said. 'Nothing makes sense any more.' Mrs Hendry heard the bitterness in Cara's voice. I've got to speak, she thought, and the sooner the better. But what to say? That was the problem. She knitted to the end of the row, then rolled up her work and put it down.

'Leave the books,' she ordered. 'Let them be. A day or two won't hurt.'

'The returns have to be in next week,' Cara said. 'I can't risk missing the subsidies, such as they are.'

'Then Susan can give you a hand at the weekend. Right now I want to talk to you.'

'Well, I'm here,' Cara answered. 'What is it you want to say?'

She hated herself for the harshness of her tone. Her mother-in-law had done nothing to deserve it, nothing at all. Yet it seems every time I open my mouth, Cara thought, that's how it comes out.

'I'm sorry,' she said. 'I don't mean to be rude. I just don't seem to be able to get things right. And by that I don't mean the accounts.'

173

'That's why we need to talk,' Mrs Hendry said. 'It's very early days, I know that, child, but a start has to be made. Difficulties won't go away by ignoring them.'

'Difficulties!' Cara exploded with indignation, thumping the table with her clenched fists. 'Difficulties? Is that what you call them? I've lost my husband, you've lost your son and your husband, the children have lost their father. You reckon the word "difficulties" describes that lot, do you?'

Mrs Hendry noticed with satisfaction that Cara's eyes, which had been dulled for so long, were bright green with anger. Well, at least it was a sign of life.

'I don't have the gift for words,' she replied. 'I'm not an educated person. I left school at twelve. But *I* know what I mean – and *you* know too.'

'All right then, what do you want to talk about?'

'Isn't it time we discussed what's going to happen – here at Beckwith, I mean? Surely it's time we worked out how we're going to manage, what we have to do, what we *can* do? I say "we", but Beckwith is yours now, Cara love. You've got to make the decisions, however painful. And I understand the pain, but things can't just drift.'

'I wish they could!' Cara was passionate. 'I'd like nothing better than to drift.'

But she had obligations; not written down, but as inescapable as if they were carved in granite. Ever since its beginnings Beckwith had been handed down from father to eldest son, in an unbroken sequence for almost two hundred years. It was the way things were and everyone knew it. It was taken for granted that the womenfolk, and any other children, would be housed and cared for. It was a system which, as far as Cara knew, had never failed, though she thought it must sometimes have caused hardship.

Now, she must take responsibility for the farm until David was of an age to do so. But if it proved impossible to keep going, if they couldn't live off it, what then? She had the power to sell it, but how could she do that to David?

'Well, you can't drift!' Mrs Hendry said sharply. She too would like to drift. She didn't want to face the future, she was mortally afraid of it. But the future would come, willy nilly, and Cara had to be galvanized into life, or what would happen to them all? But she had spoken too harshly to the poor girl and now she was contrite.

'I'm sorry,' she said.

'Don't apologize,' Cara said. 'I know what you're really trying to say, and I don't blame you. You're trying to say, how are we going to keep on Beckwith? Two women and a farmhand, with the help of

174

a little boy and a reluctant schoolgirl at weekends. Well, the answer is, I don't know.'

They were the words Mrs Hendry had dreaded hearing, yet she'd known they must come. Hadn't she, by her own attitude, just provoked them? Her insides churned at the thought of what such words might mean to her.

'Perhaps I could do a bit more,' she offered.

'Oh, Mother Hendry, how could you?' Cara said. 'Already you work like a slave. And look at Johann! He's at it all hours God sends, and for a pittance. We were always short of labour even before . . .' Her words trailed away.

'Could we not afford another man?' Mrs Hendry asked.

'It would cost four pounds ten shillings a week, without overtime,' Cara said. 'That's two hundred and thirty-four pounds a year in hard cash. Where would we find it? How can we make any more money than we do now?'

Mrs Hendry shook her head.

'Could we serve teas?' she suggested. 'People like farmhouse teas.' She was clutching at straws.

Cara actually found herself smiling.

'It would take a few thousand teas, love, at one and sixpence a head! Anyway, Beckwith is a bit far out for casual hikers. If we were in Faverwell it would be different.'

'Happen your dad would have some suggestions,' Mrs Hendry said. 'He's a business man, a bank manager.'

'I don't know. He might,' Cara said slowly. 'I'd have to go to Akersfield to see him.'

It would be an effort. Perhaps he would come to Beckwith? But deep inside herself she felt the first promptings that somehow she must begin to make an effort.

'If I went next weekend I could miss the shearing,' she said. 'I'd take Emily, of course.' She would like to miss the shearing. She dreaded meeting all those people, however well-intentioned they were.

'No!' Mrs Hendry fired the word. 'No, that won't do at all. You've got to be here, love. It's your farm and you've got to show your face. It would look very wrong if you just went off to Akersfield. No-one's going to expect a lot of you, but you've got to be here.'

'I suppose you're right,' Cara sighed.

'I am. Besides, David and Susan need you here. It's got to be a family thing, all of us together.'

'Then I'll go during the week,' Cara said, 'if you're sure you can manage. I couldn't be back in time for the milking.'

'I can manage,' Mrs Hendry said. 'And I reckon you could stay overnight. A little break would do you the world of good. Don't worry, me and Johann will sort things out between us.'

'You do realize what Dad might say?' Cara asked. 'He might say I should sell the farm. Bankers tend to see things in terms of pounds, shillings and pence.'

'Well, we'll have to see, won't we?' Mrs Hendry said. 'I hope it won't come to that, but you must do whatever's best for you and the children.' The firmness of her tone belied the sick feeling inside her.

'What would you do, love?' Cara asked.

'I'm not sure, and that's a fact. But there'd be something. Happen I'd go back to Wensleydale. Cousin Bertha would have me, I dare say.'

She would hate it. She would hate every minute of it. Cousin Bertha was all right in small doses, and no more. But now wasn't the time to say so.

'Well, perhaps it won't come to that. And in any case I don't have to do what Dad says. We won't think about it,' Cara said.

How will I not think about it? her mother-in-law wondered. How will it be out of my mind for a minute?

Two days later, with her heart like a lump of lead in her breast, she helped Cara to fix Emily in the car, and then watched them drive away down the dale. When they were out of sight, instead of going back into the house she left the farmyard, walked along the lane, turned in at the first gate and began to climb the fell.

She had looked out at this fellside every day of her life for more than forty years, but it was a while since she'd climbed it, and now the going was surprisingly hard. No more than halfway up the slope she was obliged to sit down to get her breath back. She looked around her: at the little road running through the dale, the road she'd travelled coming here as a bride; at the farmhouse; at the river, haunt of kingfishers and water voles; at the green fells which rose to meet the sky on the other side of the river, and also behind her. When she'd first come here she'd thought it was a little, shut-in dale, not really to be compared to the wideness and fertility of Wensleydale, but in no time at all its own special quality had spoken to her and now it was the fairest place on earth. How could she ever leave it?

She sat there a long time, but in the end she stood up and looked towards the fell top. She couldn't make it that far, she was too short of breath for the climb; she'd have liked to see the place where Edward had fallen, to have stood there for a minute. Instead, she began the descent back to the house.

Beth Dunning was already at the window, on the lookout, as Cara drove up the road. The second the car stopped she opened the door.

176

'Let me take Emily,' she said. 'Come along, little love! Come to Grandma, then!'

Cara picked up the small suitcase, mostly filled with Emily's needs, and followed her mother into the house. It was good, it was *so* good, to be here. For one brief moment she felt that she had left all her nightmares behind her and that somehow, here, everything would be resolved.

The feeling didn't last. How could it? The nightmares were not nightmares, they were real. The dream was the thought that somehow, in the security of her parents' home, things would come right. But that only happened when you were a child.

Beth put Emily down on the hearthrug.

'Now let me look at you,' she said to Cara.

Her heart ached as she did so. The pain in her daughter's face, the droop of her body – a face and a body which were usually brimming with life – cut her to the quick.

'You've lost a bit of weight, love.'

Her matter-of-fact tone covered her concern. Cara had always disliked what she called being fussed, and she could see from her daughter's expression that that hadn't changed.

'Are you eating enough?' Beth asked.

'I think so. Is Dad coming home to dinner?'

'Not only that,' her mother said. 'He's actually taking the afternoon off from the bank! He's been giving a lot of thought to what you said on the telephone. In fact we worry all the time about what you're going to do.'

'I only told him I wanted to talk things over,' Cara said. 'I won't necessarily do as he says.'

'When did you ever?' Beth asked dryly. 'But I'm sure he'll give you the best advice he can.'

Arnold was home at one o'clock sharp.

'Now if your ma hasn't already done so I'm going to give you a glass of sherry before we eat,' he said. 'It'll buck you up.'

After dinner Beth took Emily to visit a neighbour.

'I'll leave you two to get on with it without distractions,' she'd said. 'You can tell me everything when I get back.'

'What she *really* means,' Arnold said as his wife left the house, 'is that she wants to show off Emily to Mrs Simpson. According to your mother Emily is in every way superior to Mrs Simpson's grandchild of the same age. Which I'm sure she is,' he added.

'So what do you think I should do?' Cara asked after a while.

He pushed away the sheet of paper on which he had been scribbling figures.

'It's clear enough to me what your best course is,' Arnold said. 'I'm afraid there isn't a doubt about it, love. You should sell. The farm isn't viable without extra full-time help, and from what you've told me, there's no way you can afford that. And if you're going to sell, you shouldn't wait too long. At the moment some men still have their war-gratuity cash not spent, and there's a bit of a movement to put it into something like farming. It's a contrast to what people have been through in the war, you see. It was the same after the last war.'

'And did it work then?' Cara asked.

'For a lot of those who bought, no it didn't. They didn't have the experience. They didn't know one end of a cow from the other. But you'd be selling, not buying.'

'And what would I do? I mean afterwards, if I sold Beckwith?'

'Well, there's one or two things you could do. You'd get a decent price for Beckwith, I dare say. You could buy a little business, one you could run yourself, perhaps here in Akersfield. Or you could train as a teacher . . .'

'And become headmistress of a famous school?' Cara put in.

He smiled.

'I got over that a while ago, love. I'm just trying to be practical.'

'I know, Dad – and I'm grateful. But it would have to be something where I could look after all three children.'

'Strictly speaking, Susan and David aren't your responsibility,' Arnold reminded her. 'Though I quite understand you'd want to make yourself responsible.'

'I most certainly would!' Cara said. 'And it isn't just the children. There's Mrs Hendry, and Johann. Where would *they* be without Beckwith?'

'It's hard,' Arnold conceded. 'But there you are, love. You've been dealt a cruel blow, and now, however much you feel, you can't take the world on your shoulders.'

'If only there was something I could do without leaving Beckwith,' Cara said. 'Grandma Hendry suggested serving teas, but I'm afraid that wouldn't earn much. On the other hand . . .' She was struck by a sudden thought. 'Yes! That might work!'

'What?'

'We could take in visitors. It mightn't bring in much – and we'd have to advertise, which would cost money, but perhaps . . . I mean for weekends and holidays.'

Arnold looked doubtful.

'To make it pay you'd need more room,' he said. 'You'd really need to build on a couple of rooms. It's not easy, especially right now. Materials are short, and there's a lot of cases would have a bigger priority.'

'Of course. And where would I get the capital to build?' Cara

178

said, deflated. 'Well, there it is. Perhaps it wasn't such a bright idea after all.'

'Don't throw it out altogether,' Arnold advised. 'Consider all ideas. And I *might*, just *might*, be able to arrange a loan for you. But don't bank on it.'

'I won't,' Cara promised. 'But thanks anyway, Dad.' Apart from the idea of taking visitors, she didn't feel any further forward.

When she left Akersfield the following morning it was with two thoughts uppermost in her mind. One was that for everyone's sake she didn't want to leave Beckwith; the other was that she didn't see how she could possibly stay.

It was one of the late summer's most perfect days. As she drove back through Arendale, it was as if everything she saw – the little river, the fells, the animals, the stone barns, and not least the house, just coming into view – were saying, 'Look at me! How can you leave me? How *can* you leave me?' Never had she felt a stronger sense of belonging to this valley and these hills than now, when she could not afford to remain. And side by side with the longing, intensified by it, was a feeling of betrayal that she should turn her back on it.

'But *you* betrayed *me*! You took away my reason for being here!'

She shouted the words out loud, angrily. Sometimes, these days, she did that. There were moments when she was filled with anger against everything, even against Edward. 'Why did you leave me?' she would cry. 'Why? Why?'

Emily, in her carrycot on the back seat of the car, stirred in her sleep at the sound of her mother's voice, then settled down again.

The house drew nearer. What am I going to say to everyone? Cara asked herself. She would have liked to have turned the car around and driven away, though where to she had no idea. Instead she drew up in the farmyard and, leaving Emily fast asleep, went into the house.

She was met by the syrupy, spicy smell of baking gingerbread. It assailed her nostrils with its sweetness and strength. A big square tin of it lay cooling on the kitchen table. Its appearance, rich brown, shining sticky surface, crisp at the edges, matched its wonderful smell.

'I'm doing a bit of baking for Saturday,' Mrs Hendry said. 'Gingerbread's all the better for keeping a day or two before it's eaten.'

Cara said: 'May I have a bit? I like it when it's hot.'

'Of course, love!'

It was the first time for weeks that Cara had shown the slightest interest in food. It had to be a good sign. Did it mean that things had gone well in Akersfield?

'It turned out nicely,' she continued, cutting into the rich cake. 'If the oven's playing up it can sink in the middle.'

'I know,' Cara agreed. She took the chunk of gingerbread from

179

her mother-in-law, then instantly realized that she could not eat a crumb of it.

'Oh, Mother Hendry, why are we talking about gingerbread?' she demanded.

The two women stood facing each other across the table.

I know why I'm talking about it, Mrs Hendry thought. I'm talking about gingerbread because I can't pluck up the courage to say anything else. The questions were whirling around in her head but she was afraid to put any of them into words. After all, if Cara had had anything good to say she'd have spilled it out the minute she walked in at the door.

'We both know what we want to talk about,' Cara said. 'Let's sit down.'

'I'll put the kettle on,' Mrs Hendry said. She felt better doing something practical. Then, summoning her courage, but with her back to Cara as she fixed the kettle over the fire, she asked:

'Well then, what did your dad say? Let's hear the worst.'

'He thinks we should sell up,' Cara said quietly.

Mrs Hendry's legs turned to jelly. She felt consumed by fear, the culmination of the fear which had been in her ever since Edward's death. Last night she had hardly slept, watching for the day yet dreading what it might bring. Well, the words had been spoken at last. It was out in the open now. She abandoned all thoughts of making tea and sat down heavily in her chair.

'Oh, love, I've put that badly!' Cara cried. 'I'm sorry!' Her mother-in-law's face was chalk white. She looked as though she might faint.

'What other way is there to put it?' Mrs Hendry asked.

'The fact is, I haven't decided,' Cara said. 'I wouldn't make a decision like that, just from what Dad worked out on paper. And I certainly wouldn't decide without talking to you. I don't want to leave Beckwith any more than you do. I knew that more than ever today. Please believe me!'

'I do, love,' Mrs Hendry assured her.

'I did discuss another suggestion with Dad,' Cara said.

When she told her mother-in-law about the idea of taking visitors, the colour began to return to Mrs Hendry's face.

'I'm sure we could do that,' she said. 'I could look after the visitors and the profit could pay for the hire of another man!'

'It's not quite as simple as that,' Cara told her gently. 'There'd be expenses. If I took a loan I'd have to pay it back. Also, of course, we wouldn't be able to start until next summer. People wouldn't take holidays in the dales in winter.'

Mrs Hendry refused to be daunted. She had found a lifeline.

'Surely we could manage until then?' she pleaded. 'We could make economies.'

Cara smiled ruefully.

'I'm sure I don't know where. But we don't have to decide this minute, do we? Let's talk it over as often as we need. And let's get the shearing over, shall we? We both need a breathing space, a bit more time to think.'

'That makes sense,' Mrs Hendry agreed. 'The shearing has to be done, choose how!'

On Friday morning Grant Fawcett telephoned.

'I have to go into Shepton today,' he said. 'If it would help I could pick up Susan from school, and if David waits in Faverwell I could collect him too.'

'It would help a great deal,' Cara said. 'Thank you very much.'

Later in the day when he arrived with both children, he said:

'I'd better warn you, you're going to have a sight more people turning up for the shearing than you've bargained for. Everybody wants to help.'

'That doesn't altogether surprise me,' Mrs Hendry said. 'I'd better get baking again right away.'

'Aunt Rose said I was to tell you she'll be bringing a fair amount of stuff,' Grant went on. 'And I've taken the liberty of ordering a barrel of beer. Shearing is thirsty work.'

'I hardly know what to say,' Cara told him. 'You've done so much, I feel overwhelmed.'

'No need to say anything,' Grant replied. It wasn't the time to tell her, it was far too soon, that all this was a drop in the ocean to what he'd like to do for her, would do for her, given the chance.

'There's just one thing . . .' Cara hesitated.

'Yes?'

'How many of the helpers will want paying?'

'Let's say there isn't one who'd not be insulted if you offered, and certainly not one who'd take it,' Grant assured her.

'All the more reason why we should feed them decently,' Mrs Hendry said. She was already making a list.

'True,' Grant agreed. 'And they'll be here all day. Now I must see Johann so we can sort out who does what.'

'Can I help?' David asked eagerly.

'I reckon everyone can,' Grant replied. 'Though not everybody can clip. That's a skilled job. But the sheep have to be brought to the shearers, and sent off again when they've been done, and the fleeces have to be wrapped. There's plenty to do.'

'I could learn to clip,' David said.

'And I'm sure you will,' Grant agreed. 'But perhaps not for a year or two.'

'He'll make a proper little farmer,' Mrs Hendry said fondly.

But will he? Cara wondered. It hurt her to see the brightness of David's face and to know that she might have to deny him the future he so eagerly looked forward to.

'We'll set out the stools tonight,' Grant said. 'Whatever you can supply – though I don't doubt some people will bring their own and I'll bring some from Fawcett's. Anyway, some people prefer to stand to clip.'

'It's beginning to sound like an invasion,' Cara said. She wasn't at all sure she could cope with it, though she'd somehow have to, just as she would have to resolve the problem of her future.

Grant smiled.

'It will be. Just you wait and see!'

'What shall I do?' Susan asked.

In fact, she quite looked forward to it. Life was so horrid, full of bad things happening, and everyone in the house, except Emily, was so gloomy most of the time. She hated school, but it was almost better now than being at home. Of course she was sad, too. She missed her father terribly; she would never, ever forget him. Also – unlike David – she was old enough to wonder what would happen to them all. Though she wanted no part of them, she was aware of the difficulties.

'There'll be plenty you can do,' Mrs Hendry told her. 'If you don't want to work with the sheep you can help with the food and drinks. That'd be a right good help to me!'

'Can I serve the beer?' Susan asked.

'I don't see why not,' Cara agreed.

Cara was up early next morning, after a mostly sleepless night. When she came into the kitchen her mother-in-law was already there and the air was once more filled with the scent of baking.

'I've made a lot of potato cakes,' Mrs Hendry said. 'They'll heat up to a nice warm snack. They're filling, and they don't take up a lot of the rations.'

'Added to which they're delicious,' Cara said. 'How long have you been at it?'

'Quite a while,' Mrs Hendry admitted. She, too, had hardly slept. How could she, with so much worry on her mind? The shearing wasn't a worry; she welcomed it because it gave her something immediate to think about and to do, but everything else loomed large and dark.

Cara had hardly sipped her first cup of tea before Grant Fawcett and Johann walked into the kitchen together, and shortly afterwards a knock on the door announced the first of the shearers.

From that moment everything happened quickly. In no time at all the kitchen was chock-a-block with men, and one or two women, gossiping and drinking tea before starting work.

'How many are there?' Cara asked Grant as she refilled the kettle.

'Seventeen so far,' he said. 'But I know there are more to come. What did I tell you?' He called out, 'I don't want to rush you unduly, folks, but we should make a start soon. There's a lot to do and Mrs Hendry is more than grateful to you all for coming.'

By the time he had taken everyone to the big barn where the shearing was to take place, and sorted out what each one wanted to do, or was capable of doing, four more men and another woman had arrived, with Joseph and Rose Fawcett still to come.

It was amazing, Cara thought as later she and Susan took out trays of tea and slices of cake for the mid-morning break, how hard everyone worked and how organized they were.

Johann brought down the sheep in batches from the sheepfold, while another man, with an excited David to help him, brought the sheep one by one to the shearers, who sat or stood in a long row, clipping away at the fleeces.

'Could I go and watch the clipping, just for a minute?' David asked the man he was helping.

'Aye lad, you do that,' the man said. 'Happen you'll learn something.'

David went and stood in front of Mr Pratt, whom he knew because he was the schoolteacher's father and farmed near to Faverwell.

'Can I watch you, Mr Pratt?' he asked.

'You can, lad,' Mr Pratt replied, not looking up as with quick, precise movements he clipped at the sheep with his large shears.

'I start at the shoulder and do each side, then turn it over,' he explained. 'But we don't all do it the same way, as you'll see if you walk down the line.'

'How would I do it?' David wanted to know.

'Oh, you'd have to learn to do the tails first,' Mr Pratt said. 'The young uns allus start on the tails. But the tails are mucky.'

David observed closely as Mr Pratt clipped methodically, turned the sheep over on its back, then right way up again, until the complete fleece fell off it.

'There you are then, David! Do you reckon you'd be able to shear a sheep now?'

'It's very clever,' David said. 'My dad was very clever at shearing.'

'I know he was, lad. And I don't doubt you will be in time.' The little lad was the spit of his dad. He had the same steadfast look. A real Hendry.

'Why don't you move on to the Wrappers?' he suggested. 'Wrapping's a bit easier than clipping, though don't you tell 'em I said so! They might let you give a hand.'

'I will then,' David said. There was more hope that he'd be allowed to help the Wrappers, since the sharp shears were not involved.

He moved on, watching in silence as the Wrappers worked, observing how they took the whole fleece and folded it in a special way, taking care that the dirtiest, coarsest parts of the fleece, from the hindquarters, didn't mess up the finer, cleaner wool from the shoulders. They worked so quickly, they made it look so easy.

'Could I do that?' David asked one of the Wrappers.

'Have a try, lad!' the man said. There was a glint in his eye. 'And when you've wrapped a piece and tied it, start a pile of your own fleeces, see how you get on!'

It proved extremely difficult. The fleeces were heavy, but worse than that, they went whichever way they wanted to, as if they were still on the back of the sheep. Then he couldn't get the fleece into a tight roll. As for tying it up in the special way it had to be done, that was almost impossible! Yet the men did it so quickly, their piles of fleeces grew so fast.

After a time he gave it up, and went to give a hand with getting the shorn sheep back into the fold. That was easier.

All day the work went on, interrupted only by the refreshments which were regularly served by the women. When it grew dark in the barn Cara and Mrs Hendry brought lamps and lanterns so that the work could continue until the last sheep was sheared and the last fleece tied, ready to be collected early in the following week and taken to Bradford.

When all was done, the beer, and a more substantial meal, were served. Everyone was hungry. Although Cara had hoped for no jollifications, she found that she didn't mind, after all, when two men who had brought their accordions started to play, and almost everyone else joined in and sang.

But though she sat amongst them she couldn't sing. Her heart was too full of Edward, and of memories of the Washing which they had enjoyed together, when the same songs had been sung. Oh Edward, she cried inwardly, why did you leave me? And yet somehow he seemed close, closer than at any time since his death. He belonged here, he always would; in this dale, amongst these wonderful people who were the salt of the earth.

David came and leant against her as she sat.

'It's been a super day,' he said. 'And everybody says what a good farmer Daddy was. Do you think I'll be as good?'

For a second or two Cara didn't answer. Then she said, 'I'm sure you will, love! One day you will!'

And he would! In that moment she had made up her mind for good and for all. No matter how hard it was, she now knew she must find a way to keep them all at Beckwith. The Hendrys had been at Beckwith for more than two hundred years; they must have faced bad times as well as good. She was not going to be the one to break it up. In any case she was a Hendry herself now. It was her land.

'One day you will, David,' she repeated. 'But for now it's time you were in bed!'

'Oh please!' he begged. 'Not yet. I'm not a bit tired. It's been such a special day!'

'Yes,' she agreed. 'It's been a special day. And like you, love, I've learnt a lot. So you can stay a bit longer because I must find Grandma.' There was no reason why she should keep that good woman in suspense for one minute more.

'Oh Cara, love,' Mrs Hendry said when Cara had told her. 'I can't tell you what this means to me! It's a new lease of life. And I'll do everything I can.'

'I know you will,' Cara said. 'We'll manage somehow. I'm determined on it.'

THIRTEEN

'I think we'll put aside the idea of taking visitors,' Cara said to her mother-in-law.

'Well it's up to you, of course.' Mrs Hendry sounded doubtful. 'But I've told you I'll take on the work. I know you won't have time, with what you have to do on the farm.'

The thought of her mother-in-law adding even more work to her present load was one good reason why Cara didn't want to take the plunge. She was a woman getting on in years, whose willingness and energy were apt to outrun her strength.

'You already work too hard,' Cara told her. Sometimes towards the end of the day she'd seen Mrs Hendry looking fit to drop, though she never complained and never gave in.

'Rubbish!' Mrs Hendry said. 'I'm an old carthorse, I am. I keep on going.'

'Well, let's say I'm not really in favour of the idea anyway,' Cara said. 'For one thing it's not the time to start. We'd be at least nine months before we got our first visitors – *if* they came at all. And for another, I don't really want to borrow the money to build on a couple of rooms. How would we pay it back while we were waiting to make a profit?'

Mrs Hendry shrugged.

'It's your decision, love. But we've got one spare room, and there's the best parlour. We could take a couple of visitors.'

'Let's wait and see how we feel after the turn of the year,' Cara persisted.

They had gone over the whole thing, from thread to needle, in the last week or two. In the end, putting all practical reasons aside, Cara was left with the instinctive feeling that she just didn't want to do it.

'It's a strange thing, Grandma, but in spite of all the difficulties –
and I can see them piled up in front of me – all I really want to do
is farm,' she said. 'Somehow, just when it's hardest, I want it more
than ever I did.'

But was it strange? Didn't she want to farm, to throw herself heart
and soul and body into it, because that was where she felt closest to
Edward? On the high fells, with the sheep, she sometimes felt that
he was actually with her.

Mrs Hendry gave silent thanks that Cara wanted to do something,
anything; that she was at last beginning to emerge from that awful
apathy.

Just how she would meet the demands of the farm Cara wasn't sure,
and it was difficult to plan ahead. She talked to Johann, asking him
what he thought about it.

'I'm determined to keep things going,' she told him. 'But it might
be all hard work and not much return for some time to come. You
might do better, Johann, by going to someone else. Other farmers
would jump at you, I'm sure. They'd pay you more than I can. I
don't want to hold you back. I want to be fair to you.'

Johann had looked as near affronted as one of his nature could –
and then immediately afterwards, troubled.

'I would not want to go anywhere else,' he said urgently. 'Do I not
give you satisfaction, Mrs Hendry?'

'Oh Johann, what a thing to say! Of course you do, and much more
than satisfaction. I don't know what I'd do without you, but all the
same it's something you should think about.'

'There is no need to think about it,' he said. 'This is my home. I
am happy here. In fact I do not need so much money. You could pay
me less. What do I want with money?'

'That I couldn't do,' Cara said firmly. 'You get less than the
proper rate as it is, though I shall do something about that when
I can.'

The following day he came into the kitchen when she was alone.

'May I please speak with you?' he asked.

'Of course, Johann!' He stood in front of her, looking incredibly
nervous, clutching at a small bundle wrapped in a kerchief.

'Is anything wrong?' Had he changed his mind, had he decided,
after all, to move on? Her heart sank at the thought.

'Nothing is wrong. It is just that . . .' he hesitated. 'Well, because
I do not have the need to spend money I have saved a little. I would
like you to have it, to help towards the farm.'

With a quick movement he dropped the bundle on to the table in
front of her.

'Please open it,' he said.

'But Johann, I couldn't! It's quite wonderful of you, but I couldn't take your money!'

'Please open it, Mrs Edward!'

In the face of his insistence she carefully untied the knot and spread out the kerchief, revealing a heap of money, mostly silver and copper coins plus a few ten-shilling notes.

'There is forty-two pounds seven shillings and fourpence,' Johann said. 'It would please me if you would take it.'

Tears, which she could not prevent, filled Cara's eyes.

'Johann,' she said. 'This is the nicest thing that's happened to me in many a long day. I shall never forget it. But I can't take your money. This is your life savings!'

'Please!'

Cara hesitated. There was a dignity about this man which she couldn't ignore, or dismiss lightly.

'We'll strike a bargain,' she said. 'I won't take it now, you must have it back, but I promise faithfully that if I find myself in need of it, I will ask for it.'

'You will promise that?' he insisted.

'I promise!'

She drew the corners of the kerchief together and tied the knots, then handed it back to him.

'Thank you a thousand times, Johann.'

'I will keep it safe until you need it,' he said. 'It will always be there.'

She told no-one of Johann's offer. He had chosen to make it when she was alone and she sensed that he wanted it kept secret.

'It's coming up to sales time,' she said to Mrs Hendry later that week. 'I must decide what to do.'

It couldn't be the same as in other years, when Edward, to increase the flock, had kept back the pick of the ewes for breeding, and had usually bought a ram or two.

'I can't possibly afford to increase the flock,' she said. 'And in any case we don't have the labour to look after what we already have. Anyway, I shall need every penny I can get from the sales to feed the rest of the animals through the winter.'

'Aye well, that costs a pretty penny,' Mrs Hendry agreed.

'As far as I can tell I'll have to sell all this year's lambs, and more older ewes besides,' Cara said. 'More than I want to.'

What she didn't quite trust herself to do, though she had learnt a lot about sheep in the last two years, was to sort out which lambs to keep and which to sell. Johann was willing to advise all he could but his knowledge was only fractionally better than hers.

'What shall I do?' she asked Grant Fawcett when he called to see them.

'I could take a look,' he said, 'but your best bet is to ask my Uncle Joseph. What he doesn't know about sheep isn't worth knowing. According to him, only Tom Hendry knew more.'

'Do you think he'd spare me the time?' Cara asked.

'I'm sure he would. I'll ask him, shall I?'

Joseph Fawcett came the next day.

'Now let's see what's what,' he said. It had never occurred to him that he'd ever be able to give advice about sheep to anyone at Beckwith.

He spent a long time walking around, examining the sheep.

'You've got a grand flock here,' he said, presently. 'Old Tom would have been proud.'

'And Edward had the same flair,' Cara replied.

'Aye, I know. It's a pity to sell too many.'

'Oh I agree,' Cara said. 'But I don't have much choice. I've got to make economies both in labour and in money. In fact I'd like to make enough profit from the sales, after I've made sure of the winter feed, to let me set on an extra man for the tupping, and then again in the spring for the lambing. Johann's willing, but one man can only do so much. And of course I shall help all I can.'

'And I don't doubt you'll do it well, but by now I don't have to tell you it's not easy work,' Joseph warned. 'Sheep can be awkward buggers – begging your pardon! You could certainly do with another pair of hands for the tupping. Fawcett's can't be much help because we'll be busy at the same time. Anyway, let's make decisions about these sheep.'

In the end, with Joseph Fawcett's advice confirming her own opinion, Cara decided to keep as many ewes as possible from last year's crop.

'They'll be ready to put to the ram come this year's tupping,' Joseph said. 'At least that'll give you a crop of lambs next spring.'

'Then I'll have to sell most of this year's lambs,' Cara said. It would be more than a year before they were ready to be bred from, and she couldn't afford to wait.

'I hope I'll be able to sell them for breeding, get a better price,' she said.

'Aye well, they're good stock. In fact I'll take a few myself,' Joseph offered. 'I'll give you the right price, and it'll save sending as many to market.'

And also save my face a bit, Cara thought. She wasn't keen on everyone knowing how far she had to cut down.

'It's very good of you,' she said.

'Nay, they're good lambs. I can do wi' em.'

'I'll sell the lambs from the chasers as fat lambs, for the butcher.'

'That's right, love. You'll get the subsidy for the fat lambs.'

'I'm very grateful for your advice, Mr Fawcett,' Cara said as they walked back to the house. 'I don't like selling so many, and of course I'll lose out when it comes to breeding next year, but it can't be helped.'

'You have to cut your coat according to your cloth,' Joseph agreed. 'You're doing the right thing, lass. Happen things will be better for you in a year or two's time. I hope so, I'm sure.'

The Hendrys had had it rough over the last few years, the first wife being killed like that, then old Tom dying. And as for Edward – well, it wasn't the first accident of its kind in these parts, it took but a moment to lose your footing. Everyone knew the dangers of the potholes but it was tragic all the same. Superstitious folks – which he wasn't himself – might reckon there was a curse on the family.

He liked Cara Hendry. She had pluck, that one, and common sense; but she also had beauty and sparkle. Such qualities didn't always go together. He knew Grant was keen on her, but he reckoned she'd not take anyone on in a hurry. In any case, his nephew wasn't in a position for that sort of responsibility.

'I dare say things will buck up,' he said.

'Perhaps.'

She didn't look too much into the future. She had found that most days she could only get through by concentrating hard on the present, on the job in hand, and by tiring herself out so that at the end of the day she fell asleep from exhaustion. It was better if she left herself no time to think.

But to live entirely in the present was not a sensible way to farm. She knew that. To be a good farmer you needed always to have an eye on the coming seasons, to look well ahead. Land and animals produced in their own good time, kept to their own cycles. By good husbandry you could help things along, but there was nothing you could do to change nature. Nature had her own pattern and it was up to you to fit in with it.

'I'll be off then,' Joseph said when they reached the house. 'No, I'll not come in, but give my best to Edith. And think on, if there's owt at all I can do, any bit of advice, you have only to ask.'

'Thank you,' Cara said. 'I appreciate that.'

'So what about giving the sheep a bloom dip before they go to the sales?' Mrs Hendry suggested that evening.

'I don't think we can manage it,' Cara said. 'It would take too long for Johann and me to do it between us. No, they'll have to sell as they are. They mightn't look as pretty but I reckon people know they can rely on Beckwith stock.'

'That's true,' Mrs Hendry agreed. 'Any road, a lot of people don't bother with bloom dips nowadays, so you'll be in the fashion. And what will you do about overwintering the sheep? Edward used to arrange that at the sales.'

'I can do nothing whatsoever,' Cara said. 'I can't afford it. They'll all have to take their chance here.'

In the event, the sale went well. It was an exceptionally busy market, crowded with bleating lambs and baaing ewes, but the Beckwith sheep sold quickly, and at fair prices, though it was with a heavy heart that Cara saw some of them go. It was ridiculous the way one got attached to animals, even sheep. Would a real farmer allow that to happen?

What pleased Cara particularly was the civility with which the other farmers greeted her. As far as she could see, she was the only woman farmer present, and Yorkshire farmers were a pretty conservative lot, didn't like anything the least bit out of the ordinary. Yet they treated her with respect and, except for the odd one or two, didn't talk down to her. She thought it likely that the respect was due to Edward and the Hendry family, not to her personally, but that was all right. By this time next year, she thought, I'll have gained it for myself. I'll show them what I'm made of!

Walking around the market, once the sheep were sold, she came face to face with Ralph Benson, the farmer from Nidderdale who had taken the Beckwith sheep for overwintering in the last year or two. He stood in front of her, barring her way with his huge presence.

'I hoped I'd see you, Mrs Hendry,' he said jovially. 'Now how many ewes are you going to be sending me come December?'

'I'm afraid none at all, Mr Benson,' Cara said.

'None at all?' He sounded surprised. 'So what have I done wrong? Did I not look after them well?'

'You most certainly did,' Cara assured him. 'I'd be more than willing to send them again. They always come back from you in fine fettle.'

'Well then?'

'The plain truth is, I can't afford it. I'm having to cut down all round – for this year at least. I hope you understand.'

'Aye. I understand.'

It was always the same, he thought. Town folk reckoned farmers were rolling in money. What they didn't understand was that the money was in the land, or in the future. It was seldom cash in the bank, there to hand when it was wanted.

'Well, I'd do you a special price for this year,' he offered.

'It's kind of you,' Cara said. 'It's very kind. But I really don't think I can afford it. They'll have to take their chance in Arendale.'

'Now hold on a minute,' he said. 'You'll have to feed them at Beckwith. Right?'

'Right.'

'So what do you reckon if I offer to take them for the cost of their keep, nothing more? That might not be as much as in Arendale. They can feed longer out of doors in Nidderdale, and they do well on the heather.'

'I know they do,' Cara acknowledged. 'And it's very kind of you, though I don't know why you should.'

'Let's say it's an investment,' Ralph Benson said. 'If I take them this winter for the cost of their keep, happen you'll send them to me in future years when you can pay the full price.' In fact, and he knew it, he was doing it for the sake of her pretty face and for her pluck in taking on Beckwith on her own. He admired her, but she wasn't the woman to thank him for showing it.

'Are you sure?' Cara asked.

'Quite sure,' Ralph Benson said.

'Well then, I accept, and I'm very much obliged to you.'

'And now can I get you a drink to seal the bargain?' he said. 'I don't suppose a lady like you drinks beer, but we could get a cup of tea.'

'That would be lovely,' Cara agreed.

Walking through the crowds towards the café, Ralph Benson was pleasantly conscious of the smiles, nods, and occasional winks he received from friends and acquaintances at the sight of his companion. They're jealous, he thought. So they should be!

Cara thought about the first year of her marriage when she had come to the sales with Edward. Remembering it, Kit Marsden sprang to mind. That was the first time she had set eyes on him. She had half expected he might be around today, but there was no sign of him.

'Do you know Kit Marsden?' she asked Ralph Benson.

'Who doesn't?'

'I just wondered. Where is he nowadays?' It was an idle question, so she was surprised with what interest she awaited his reply.

'I've no idea. He hasn't been around for quite a while. Up to no good, I dare say, wherever he is!'

'You don't like him?'

'Me? I'm neither one way nor the other. He'd never get the better of me, but he's as slippery as an eel. He needs watching.'

'He helped us with the Washing,' Cara said. 'He was all right then.'

'Oh I'm not saying he doesn't do a good job of work, when he has a mind to,' Ralph Benson conceded. 'I just say he wants watching.'

'I must go,' Cara said when she had finished her tea. 'I have some shopping to do in the town. Thank you very much indeed for your offer – and for the tea. I'll be in touch with you about dates.'

'Do that,' he said. 'If we can light on a date when I'm coming in your direction I could save you a bit on transport.'

'So it all went quite well,' Cara told her mother-in-law an hour or two later. 'I'll have to reckon things up, but I might just have enough to hire a man to help with the tupping.'

All the same, she thought, as she walked up the fell in the early evening of the same day, the flock looked sadly depleted. Edward would have been horrified.

'I couldn't help it, Edward,' she said out loud. 'There was nothing else I could do!'

In the days which led up to tupping time, fixed as always for early November, Cara was reminded continually of Edward and of the times they had done this together. Whenever a difficulty arose she found herself wondering what he would have done, how he would have dealt with it. Yet this was not how she wanted it to be. Though she would never wish to shut him out, and couldn't, the time must surely come when she must stand or fall on her own, when her decisions must be made on her own judgements, not on the memory of someone else's. Much as she cherished these memories, she would only find the strength she needed by making her own life.

'We could start bringing the ewes down from the top tomorrow,' she said to Johann. 'I'll help, of course, though we both know that Ruby and Bess will do the bulk of the work!'

Johann appeared to have inherited Bess, while Ruby worked almost as well for Cara as she had for Edward.

'If you do not mind, Mrs Hendry,' Johann said, 'there are still some parts of the wall which I should repair before we start to move the sheep. They escape through the smallest space, and then it will be a waste of time to have brought them down.'

Cara bowed to his judgement.

'You're quite right, Johann. How long will you need?'

'Two more days should see me finished,' he said.

After that the tupping would start in earnest. It would have to. The ewes were coming into season and the rams, which had already been separated from the flock, were growing day by day more restless.

'And I still haven't found any more help,' Cara said to Johann. 'How shall we manage?'

He shrugged.

'The best we can, that is all.'

She had tried everywhere to hire help for the tupping. It was frustrating in the extreme that she had saved the money from the sales for this purpose, but there was no-one to employ.

'It's been the same since the prisoners went home,' Mrs Hendry said when Cara fumed and fretted about it. 'What little labour there is has all been spoken for months in advance.'

'But I couldn't do that,' Cara pointed out. 'I didn't know if I'd have the money.'

She had asked Joseph Fawcett if he knew of anyone; she had visited the market in Shepton and asked everyone she knew there. All were sympathetic; no-one could help.

'The men don't want casual work any longer,' Mrs Hendry said. 'They want full-time jobs.'

'And that I can't offer, much as I'd like to,' Cara said. 'I couldn't be paying wages from tupping time to lambing time, the quietest period of the year.'

'I know,' Mrs Hendry acknowledged. 'That's why farmers prefer to depend on their families.'

'Well, as Johann says, we shall just have to do the best we can,' Cara said.

It wasn't just the farm. Emily, at thirteen months old, had started walking and was into everything. When Cara was on the fells Mrs Hendry saw to the baby, but that wasn't what Cara wanted. Oh, her mother-in-law was more than competent, and she loved the child, but Cara longed to spend just a little more time with her daughter at this fascinating age, instead of arriving back at the house each day, bone tired, to find Emily bathed and in her nightdress, ready to be popped into bed. That was exactly what had happened today, by no means for the first time.

'She gets more like her daddy every day, bless her!' Mrs Hendry said. 'Those big grey eyes, that dark hair.'

It was true, Cara thought. Edward would never die while his little daughter lived. Neither Susan nor David favoured their father to the same extent.

On the Thursday before they were to start the tupping in real earnest, Cara went into Faverwell to buy some household supplies and, at the same time, collect David from school. She stood by the school gates, waiting for the stream of children who would, any minute now, pour out of the small schoolhouse. David was one of the last to appear. How he had grown over the summer, she thought, though he was still too thin, and all her efforts and those of his grandmother to put more flesh on his bones hadn't worked. Also, his look was too serious, too worried, for a child only recently gone nine years old.

'Miss Pratt wants to see you,' he announced.

'See me? Why?'

'I don't know. She said I wasn't to let you leave until she'd spoken to you.'

'I wonder why?' Cara said. She couldn't imagine David in any sort of trouble. He got on well at school. He was by no means academically brilliant but he did well enough, liked Miss Pratt, had many friends and, as far as she knew, no foes among the other children.

She followed him back into the school and waited to one side while Miss Pratt carefully handed to a small girl a cardboard box with holes punctured in the lid.

'Thank you very much for bringing Marmaduke to show us, Hetty,' Miss Pratt said. 'It was most interesting, but I think you'd best not bring him again. You see, he might escape and then you'd be very upset!'

'And so would I,' she said to Cara when the girl had walked away. 'A mouse! Countrywoman though I am, and I don't mind them in the fields, I can't do with mice. If it got loose in the classroom I know I'd jump on the nearest desk!'

'He could have nibbled his way through the box,' David said.

'That's exactly what worried me!' Miss Pratt shuddered at the thought.

'David said you wanted to see me,' Cara said.

'Yes. How are you getting on at Beckwith these days?'

'Oh, all right. Busy, of course.'

'Of course. Tupping time. David says you're shorthanded.'

'We certainly are,' Cara agreed. 'What did you want to see me about, Miss Pratt?' She was sure it wasn't to make polite conversation.

'It's David,' Miss Pratt said.

'David? What's wrong?'

'Nothing much. Nothing at all. I just thought he'd been looking a wee bit peaky this week. I thought a day or two in the open air might do him good, if you see what I mean? Say a long weekend, Friday to Monday, come back Tuesday.' Miss Pratt looked Cara straight in the face. 'What do you think?' she asked.

Cara gave Amy Pratt an equally steady look.

'Why, I think perhaps you're right. But what about his schoolwork?'

'Oh, I think what he'll learn up there on the fells might be more useful to him than two days in school,' Miss Pratt replied. 'Of course I wouldn't like His Majesty's Inspector to hear me say that.'

'Well he won't, will he? Thank you very much,' Cara said. 'I'll see he gets lots of fresh air.'

'Does that mean I'll be able to help with the tupping?' David asked as they got into the car.

'I think that's the general idea,' Cara said.

'Terrific!' he exclaimed. 'What can I do?'

195

'I'm not sure. We'll discuss it with Johann.'

Johann's suggestion, which delighted David, was that with the assistance of Ruby, and with the minimum of oversight from Cara and himself, David might help to separate the ewes as and when necessary and get them into the fold where they were wanted; and even that, when the rams had been marked, he might help to put them with their chosen ewes.

'We'll see how it goes,' Cara said.

It went well. On Friday morning, after an early breakfast, David was out in the fields with Cara and Johann. All day he worked, reluctant even to go back to the house for a quick midday meal. He felt like a real farmer. But at the end of the short November afternoon Cara was quick to see his fatigue.

'Away with you,' she said. 'You've done a splendid day's work; now go and get your tea and then have a warm bath.'

'I am a bit tired,' he confessed. 'Can I help tomorrow?'

'I don't think we could manage without you,' Cara told him.

When David had left she went and joined Johann.

'How do you think we're doing?'

'I do not see how we could work any faster,' he said. 'But we are less than halfway through, and the more we delay, the more difficult the rams are.'

The truth was, Cara recognized, that neither of them had the speed and dexterity Edward had had.

'I shall have to go back soon, either to do the milking or to look after Emily while Ma does it,' she said. 'We can't leave the baby. She's too lively these days.'

'In any case it is almost dark,' Johann said.

When Cara wakened on Saturday morning she was stiff in every muscle. It was an effort to drag herself out of bed and dress. Susan was home, but rather than help with the sheep she would help in the house, and with Emily. So we face another hard day, Cara thought as she left the house. It was scarcely daylight.

Halfway through the morning Susan brought them tea and sandwiches.

'I will carry on, Mrs Hendry, while you take a rest,' Johann said. He did not like to see a lady work so hard but there was no help for it.

'Just a short one, then,' Cara said. 'I'll be glad of it.'

She dropped on to the grass and lay flat out, stretching her limbs. David sat beside her while Susan poured the tea into mugs and handed it round.

'There's a van coming along the lane,' David said.

'Just as long as it's no-one for us!' Cara said.

'Well, it is,' David said, 'because he's stopping.'

Cara sat up. The last thing they needed was a visitor. She watched with the children while, in the distance, the driver got out, neatly vaulted the nearest gate and began to climb towards them.

'Why, it's Kit!' David cried. 'It's Kit Marsden!'

He put down his mug and set off at a run to greet the visitor.

Cara watched them as they drew near, or, rather, she watched Kit Marsden. He climbed quickly, covering the ground with his long strides. There was spring in his steps, indeed his whole body seemed alive with energy. When he stood in front of her, smiling down, she felt the strength of him coming out to meet her.

She began to rise to her feet and he put out a hand to help her. Vitality flowed from his fingertips, bringing a surge of life to her body such as she had thought she would never feel again.

'The rumour is that you could do with a bit of help,' Kit Marsden said.

FOURTEEN

He was thinner than Cara remembered him; lean, and harder-looking, and he seemed taller. Yet, though the time before Edward's death seemed another life, it was only a matter of months. Her memory must be at fault.

'I heard it in the Ewe last night,' he said. 'I was sorry to learn about your husband. He was a good man.'

'Yes.'

As always, she searched for the right words to acknowledge people's sympathy – and once again failed to find them.

'I thought you might have heard sooner,' she said. 'Have you been away?'

'Yes.'

'I asked around after you. No-one seemed to know where you were.'

He offered no explanation, merely raised his eyebrows.

'You asked after me?'

'I needed some hired help.'

She would certainly not let him think she had been interested in his whereabouts. Indeed, she had not.

'And no-one knew where I was,' Marsden said. 'Ah well, that's the gypsy in me! But here I am now, just when you want me!'

'How long are you here for?'

'Who knows?' he replied. 'Perhaps as long as you like. I don't have any plans. But you'll have to find me somewhere to sleep. No point in wasting time going into Shepton and back every day. In any case, I've given up my lodgings there.'

'I can employ you until the tupping's finished,' Cara said. 'After that I don't know. I'll pay you the usual rate for the job and you can have the room over the stable.'

She spoke tersely. No doubt in his eyes he was doing her a favour just by turning up, and to be honest, maybe he was but she had no intention of being beholden to him. Give Kit Marsden an inch and he'd take a mile. She'd realized that a long time ago.

'Done!' he said.

'When can you start?' Cara asked.

'Now. This minute.'

'You'll need to go into Shepton and collect your things.' She assumed he was staying at the Ewe.

'Nope! I've got everything with me. I travel light.'

I'll bet you do, Cara thought. She couldn't imagine Kit Marsden being bound by anything or anybody. He was a free spirit if ever she'd met one.

'Then in that case we'll go up to Johann and sort out the jobs.'

'Johann? I thought you were the boss,' Marsden said. 'That's what I heard in the town. "A lady farmer", they said.'

'Oh, I am. A lady farmer *and* the boss. But Johann is my right hand. I wouldn't dream of not consulting him. I couldn't have got through the last few months without Johann.'

'You underestimate yourself,' Marsden said. 'I'd back you to get through anything.'

Her strength attracted him, which was strange, and against his nature. He didn't like women in charge. Women were meant for other things. Not that she wouldn't be good at those, he surmised, but she wasn't going to wrap him around her little finger like she did the German. He was his own man, always would be. There was no question of him taking orders from a Kraut, either.

Cara turned to Susan.

'You'd better get back and let Grandma know there'll be one extra for dinner.'

Susan, with the prospect of whiling away a little time in fresh company, was reluctant to leave, but her stepmother was clearly all agog to get on with the boring work. But boring or not, if she'd thought for a minute that Kit Marsden would turn up she'd have chosen it before helping in the house and looking after Emily.

'And I'd better get back to Johann,' David said. 'I'm helping him.'

The three of them set off together while Susan returned to the house.

'Are you really a gypsy?' David asked Kit. 'I mean a *real* gypsy?'

'My mother was, so a bit of me is. Or was. They say once a gypsy, always a gypsy.'

'Do you have a caravan?' David wanted to know.

Kit Marsden smiled.

'No. Only that old banger you see down there. But my grandmother had one. I remember it well, though I was younger than you. It was very cosy, surprisingly smart inside. Lots of cushions. Fancy tablecloths with fringes. And ornaments – dozens of ornaments. Flowers, too. She always had flowers.'

'Did it have a chimney, with smoke coming out?'

'I suppose it must have had. There was a stove.'

'I'd quite like to live in a caravan,' David said. 'Only I'd rather live on a farm.'

'Then you're a lucky lad,' Kit told him. 'You've got what you want. There's not many can say that.'

Johann looked up from his task and saw them coming. As they drew near his face was like thunder.

'Morning!' Kit called out.

Johann gave a curt nod.

Oh dear, Cara thought. Trouble! Men could be so childish, and right now she'd like to knock their heads together. But they'd have to put up with each other, there was too much work to be done to spare time for tantrums. To be fair, she didn't think Kit Marsden was one for tantrums, nor was Johann. It was the wrong word. Kit would want his own way, and he'd take it. Johann would sulk, and the atmosphere when the two men were together would be as heavy as lead, as it had been at the Washing.

'Kit's here to help through the tupping,' she said to Johann. 'It will be good to have some help, won't it? How shall we arrange the work?'

Johann shrugged his shoulders, said nothing.

'Very well,' Cara said. 'Perhaps for a start I'll work with Kit and David can continue to work with you. We'll see how that goes, shall we?'

At least it would separate the two men, and also it made sense. They had started to mark the tups, then loose them with their chosen ewes. David was too small to handle them, but he could help in various other ways which Johann had already started to teach him. It was also a job she herself found difficult to do on her own. The tups were heavy and restless animals and she didn't yet have the strength or the knack of both holding them and marking them. Nevertheless, she reckoned she could do her full share if she worked with Kit Marsden.

Johann turned away without a word.

Yes, he thought, it would be good to have help. They needed it if they were to get through. But not Marsden. He was the last man in the world he'd have chosen. Admittedly, he was a good worker, but he was arrogant, sometimes rude. Most of all, he didn't trust the man.

It was no more than an instinct, but it was strong. He had thought that Mrs Edward – he would always think of her as Mrs Edward – didn't like Marsden either, but it seemed he was wrong. As for the children, when the man had worked here before they'd doted on him.

He called to David.

'We'd better make a start.'

At least he would show that, even with the help of only a small boy, he could compete with Marsden. Before the day was out he'd match him, and a bit more besides.

'You've got a smaller flock,' Kit Marsden said to Cara. They'd been working together for more than an hour, not speaking much but getting on with the job. Kit was quick and skilled and Cara found it difficult to keep up with him.

'I sold some. Most of this year's lambs and a few older ewes.'

'Why? I thought Beckwith was always building up its stock.'

'It used to, but not this year. For one thing, we don't have the labour to deal with as big a flock: for another, I needed the money.'

That surprised him. He'd never thought the Hendrys were short of a bob or two.

'There's the winter feeding for the stock – and I still have the biggest flock in Arendale. Then there's three children to bring up. Vets' bills . . .' She stopped herself. Why was she saying all this to Kit Marsden? It was nothing to do with him and the last thing she wanted was his pity.

'But I manage very well,' she concluded. 'You don't have to worry about your wages.'

He looked at her in astonishment, his dark eyes flashing with sudden anger.

'I wasn't,' he snapped. 'We made a deal. I took it for granted we'd both stick to it.'

'I'm sorry!' She couldn't think why she'd been so sharp with him – except that that was the way she tended to be these days. She knew she must take herself in hand.

She looked at her watch, straightened her back, pushed the hair out of her eyes. 'We'd better go in for dinner,' she said. 'Grandma will have it ready any minute now. I'll call the others.'

Mrs Hendry, her face flushed with the heat from the cooking, looked up from the stove as Kit Marsden followed Cara into the kitchen. She smiled pleasantly at him.

'Well, well!' she said. 'Look what the wind's blown in! This is a surprise and no mistake. Oh, don't get me wrong, we can do with some help.'

Cara was looking at Johann. She read his thoughts as easily as if he

201

had put them into words. But not *your* help, the expression on his face said.

'Actually, Grandma, I came for your cooking,' Kit said, grinning at Mrs Hendry. 'I couldn't stay away a day longer!'

'Oh, did you indeed?' Mrs Hendry retorted. 'Well, kind words butter no parsnips, and you can leave off calling me Grandma for a start! I'm not your grandma, thank goodness. I'm grandma to these three children here, and that's all!'

Her words were fierce but everyone, including Kit Marsden, knew she was teasing. He went down on one knee in front of her, took her hand and kissed it.

'Forgive me, Madam Hendry!' he begged. 'Please forgive me!'

'Get up, you silly ha'porth,' Mrs Hendry said amiably, snatching her hand away. 'Get sat at the table, out of my way, afore I spill this stew on you!'

He did as he was told, sitting between Susan and David and across the table from Cara and Johann.

'Where's the baby?' he asked, looking around.

'She's asleep in her cot,' Mrs Hendry said. 'She usually takes a nap at this time of day, which means at least we get our dinner in peace.'

'But not much else!' Susan put in. 'I can tell you, it's a rest cure when I go back to school on a Monday!'

She didn't really mean that. She loved Emily, and she still hated school, still longed for the day when she could leave, and take her first steps on to the stage. But that was a subject she couldn't get the others to discuss seriously. It was so unfair. Laura Dunning's parents were doing everything they could to help Laura towards being a concert pianist. She was taking her exams, having special lessons. *I* could go to drama school, Susan thought. If my father had lived . . . But in her heart she knew he'd have been more against it than anyone.

'When you go back to school it's a rest cure for all of us!' David said pertly.

'That's enough of that,' Mrs Hendry said. 'No more arguing. Let your meat stop your mouth!'

'Just allow me to tell you, Madam Hendry,' Kit said, 'that this stew is food for the gods!'

'I don't know so much about that,' she replied. 'But it's good for farm workers on a nasty November day.'

'It certainly is,' Kit agreed.

'So you're planning on staying until the tupping's finished?' Mrs Hendry asked.

'That's right!'

'Well then, I'd best get your room ready this afternoon. It's a bit chilly up there but I think we have a spare stove somewhere. Only

202

you'll have to be a bit careful. We don't want the place set on fire, do we?'

'I shan't need a stove, not this side of Christmas,' Kit said.

'And you'll be gone before then,' David said.

'I'm warm-blooded,' Kit added.

Hot-blooded, I shouldn't wonder, Mrs Hendry thought. He was too attractive by half, though she couldn't help but like him. He had taking ways. She wondered how a chap who looked like Kit Marsden had escaped marriage – if he had, which she didn't know. She'd never heard him mention a wife.

'You're not married then?' she said.

If you wanted to know, she reckoned the best way was to ask.

'Plenty of time for that!' Kit said affably.

They ate in silence for a while, devoting themselves to the food.

'That sounds like Emily stirring,' Cara said eventually. 'I'll go to her. I'll follow the rest of you up just a bit later.'

'They're not going until they've had their pudding,' Mrs Hendry objected. 'Nor are you. You need a good lining to your stomach in this weather. Ginger sponge and custard should do that.'

The afternoon went quickly. At this time of the year the days were already short, and now, even before nightfall, the mist came down; a mist so thick that it shrouded not only the fell tops and the valley, but the sheepfolds in which they were working, so that they couldn't see even as far as the limestone walls which surrounded them.

'Mist is the very devil,' Cara said.

They could, and did, work through most weathers, but mist and fog put a stop to it.

'At least it's clean stuff here,' Kit said. 'Even as close as Shepton it's chock-full of black smuts, blown from the mills to the west. However, I think we'll have to call it a day.'

Johann was reluctant to leave. He wanted to satisfy himself that he could do as much as, and more than, Kit Marsden, though no-one but himself was making comparisons.

'I will work a little longer,' he said.

'As you wish,' Cara replied. 'But I think I'll take David home now. He looks tired.'

In fact he looked all in, and felt it, though he would never have admitted it.

'I'm quite tired myself,' Kit confided to David. 'I reckon we've done a good day's work!'

David sighed with relief. If Kit could admit to being tired, then so could he.

'Can you manage without me?' he asked Johann.

'Not quite as well as with your help,' Johann said kindly. 'But I shall manage for a little while longer, thank you.'

'I'll go and have a wash, and tidy up a bit before I present myself for supper,' Kit said as they walked back.

'Very well.'

Cara longed to get into a hot bath, to wash away the day's stiffness.

'Is the water hot?' she asked Mrs Hendry as she went in. 'I'm going to have a good soak. I'll see to Emily when I've cleaned myself up. Has she been good?'

'Good as gold,' Mrs Hendry said. 'And Susan has cycled into Faverwell to see a friend. She'll be back before supper.'

Minutes later, Cara lay in the deep old-fashioned bath, filled almost to the brim with steaming water. How she had hated those war years when everyone was put on their honour not to bathe in more than five inches of water! Her father, in his patriotic fervour, had painted a line precisely five inches up the inside of the bath, and Tom Hendry had done the same at Beckwith. Tom's line was still there, reproaching her as she luxuriated in this greater depth, lathering herself with the rose-scented soap, now in the shops again after so many years.

She wondered what Kit Marsden had done in the war. He never spoke of it. For that matter she wondered what he did in the peace, apart from odd jobs for needy farmers like herself, and shady dealings on the black market. Edward had described him as a horse-dealer, and a good one at that, but Kit himself never mentioned it.

Reluctantly – for she would have liked to have soaked for another twenty minutes, reading a book – she stepped out of the bath and began to dry herself. That done, she wrapped herself in a towel and went into the bedroom to dress.

Her room gave on to the yard at the back of the farmhouse. She went to the window, meaning to draw the curtains before she lit the lamp. It wasn't necessary in the country, but it was a town habit which stayed with her. She glanced out idly, not expecting to see anything. David would already have shut up the hens, and all that illuminated the fading day was a lantern, hanging from the barn door. In fact the mist had cleared, magically, as it sometimes did.

What she saw was Kit Marsden, stripped of all except his underpants, sluicing himself under the pump.

Almost against her will, yet compelled to do so, she stood and watched him. As in a painting from an Old Master, Dutch perhaps, or Italian, he was illuminated in a pool of light, shining out from the surrounding darkness.

Over the whole of his body, his arms and his legs, his skin was golden brown, and enhanced further by the soft light from the lantern. He looked as though he had spent long days in the sun.

Or, more likely, perhaps his colouring was an inheritance from his gypsy forebears?

His thick black hair was plastered to his head. Drops of water sparkled like crystals on his shoulders, and on the mat of dark hair which covered his chest and back. His thighs were long and muscular. The thought came to her that they would be hard, yet smooth, to the touch. He was not thin, but there was not an ounce of superfluous flesh anywhere on his body.

All this she observed in the space of a minute, and in the next minute she saw Susan ride into the yard and almost fall off her bicycle as she caught Kit in the added light from her cycle lamp.

At the sudden illumination, Kit looked up as quickly as a surprised animal, then, seeing Susan, waved a hand and went on with his ablutions.

'Like me to scrub your back?' Susan called.

Cara heard her quite clearly.

'Thanks! Another time,' Kit said, grinning. 'I'm about through.'

He straightened up and faced Susan. She stood there leaning on her bicycle, frankly appraising him.

As I have done, Cara thought. Exactly as I have done. She moved to draw the bedroom curtains together, and at the same moment he looked up and saw her. She stepped back quickly. Does he know how long I've been standing here? she wondered. But she'd not had the light on, so how could he? She was quite sure that Susan hadn't seen her, for she'd looked no further than Kit. Cara drew the curtains close and went to get dressed.

A little later, bathing Emily before the kitchen fire, she said, casually, to Mrs Hendry: 'Should we offer Kit Marsden the use of the bathroom? He doesn't really have a proper place to wash.'

'We could do,' Mrs Hendry replied.

'It just occurred to me,' Cara said lightly. 'While I was bathing Emily.'

A little later, Kit came in for supper. Perhaps he *had* seen her watching him as he washed. Not that he would care, she thought, not even if he was stark naked. He was bold enough not to mind *who* watched him – indeed she suspected that he might even enjoy showing off his physique, especially to the female sex. He had been quite unperturbed by Susan's frank look. As for Susan, her attitude had been almost brazen. For her own protection, Cara reckoned, Susan would have to be watched. She was not entirely sure that she could trust Kit Marsden not to take advantage of Susan's immaturity.

All this Cara felt as Kit, smiling pleasantly, gently teasing Mrs Hendry, took his place at the table. His hair was still damp, and

205

beginning to curl as it dried. He glowed with health and vitality. And with self-satisfaction, Cara thought.

'Have I missed Emily again?' he asked.

'I've just put her down,' Cara said.

Indeed, through the open door they could hear Emily crowing and crooning, making all the noises which were her preliminaries to falling asleep.

'She'll be talking afore long,' Mrs Hendry predicted. 'She says "Mama" and "Ganna" already.'

She used to say 'Daddy', Mrs Hendry thought with sudden bleakness. It was the first word she ever uttered. But not now, not any longer.

The moment the meal was over, Johann rose and excused himself.

'I will leave you in peace,' he said.

He would go, as always, to his own room, play his music, perhaps read a little German poetry or do some carving, before going early to bed. He thought, with some contempt, that Marsden would not have the manners to do likewise. He would stay on, whether invited or not. He did not know his place.

He was right. Kit Marsden stayed on for another hour, though it couldn't be said he had outstayed his welcome. Everyone seemed pleased enough to have him there and the talk flowed – except from Cara, who was for the most part silent. She almost resented him being there. She thought, like Johann, that he should go, and leave the family to themselves – yet at the end of an hour when he stood up and said, 'Well, I must be off!' she was disappointed. She couldn't understand herself.

'It's time you two were in bed,' she told Susan and David the moment Kit was out of the house.

'It's not really late,' Susan protested.

On most evenings spent at home she was glad enough to escape to bed. Everything was so dull. But this had been different.

'Kit is fun!' she said. 'He livens things up.'

'Yes, he does,' Mrs Hendry acknowledged. 'It must be a bit quiet for you children as a rule.'

'It's deadly!' Susan said.

'Well, you're nothing if not frank,' her grandmother said. 'And I can't complain because I dare say you get it from me!'

Every evening after that, while the tupping was in progress, the same pattern was repeated. Johann took himself off early; Kit stayed on, each night a little longer. Once, Cara invited Johann to stay but he pointedly, though politely, refused.

'I don't like it,' Cara said to her mother-in-law when Kit had at last gone to his room over the stables. 'I'm sure Johann feels pushed out. Kit has his bath here, then his supper, then stays almost until bedtime.'

'He knows we enjoy his company,' Mrs Hendry said. 'And he enjoys ours. Anyway, it'll not be for long. Tupping's nearly over. And Johann would be just as welcome, but it's not in his nature to join in. You can't change people's nature, love.'

Nevertheless, the next evening, twenty minutes or so after Johann had left them, Cara excused herself.

'Where are you going, love?' Mrs Hendry enquired.

'For a breath of fresh air,' Cara said.

'Then wrap up. It's the middle of November. The air's a bit too fresh if you ask me.'

Cara was conscious that Kit watched her as she put on her coat, and she had the feeling that he was on the point of suggesting he should accompany her. She didn't want that. She was going to see Johann.

She knocked tentatively on the door of Johann's lean-to, and when she observed the surprise on his face as he saw her standing there she thought she had done the wrong thing.

'May I come in?' she asked.

'Of course, Mrs Edward. Please do! Is anything wrong?'

'Nothing at all, Johann.'

It was sad that because she was paying him a visit he must conclude that something had gone wrong. It was perhaps natural, though. She and Edward had made a point of respecting Johann's privacy, as he had always done theirs.

'Nothing is wrong,' she repeated. 'I just thought . . .'

She hesitated. Now that she was here she didn't know what to say.

'I had the idea that I would like to listen to some music,' she said. 'I wondered if you might be playing your records.'

His face lit up in a smile. He didn't smile often and now, as he did so, she thought how much younger he looked. As a matter of fact, she realized, he was probably not yet thirty. It was his serious manner which made him seem older.

'Please come in,' he said. 'I play one or two of my records every evening. You are most welcome. What would you like to hear?'

'I'm not sure,' she said. 'Why don't you choose?'

'Then I will choose some Mozart,' Johann said. 'Perhaps a string quartet. Such music is perfect for a summer's evening, as the light is beginning to fade – though this is not a summer's evening. Nevertheless, the music is beautiful beyond compare and perhaps we will recapture the summer. Who knows?'

He showed her to the only armchair, which he had obviously just vacated, for it was still warm from his body. Then he wound up his gramophone, fitted a new needle, and put on a record. All his movements were careful and deliberate, as if he venerated the materials from which the music would come.

Listening, Cara's awkwardness left her. There was no need to think of anything to say. The music took over, the sweetness of the violins soaring, it seemed, to infinity, the rich sound of the cello following behind, the bass deep and resonant. The notes were now plaintive, now contemplative, now dancing. The shabby, cramped little room with its cheap furniture faded as she listened. She was transported, yet at the same time soothed, as she had not been for a long time.

When it was over they sat silently for a minute, then she dragged herself back to reality.

'Thank you very much, Johann,' she said. 'It was lovely. I'm not sure that I've ever sat still and listened to such music before.'

'You honour me by coming,' Johann replied. 'I would like to have offered you a glass of wine, but . . .'

'The music has much the same effect,' Cara said, smiling at him. 'Stimulating and soothing, both at the same time. But I must go now. Sometimes Emily wakens.'

At the door she turned back.

'Johann, I want you to know how much I appreciate all you do for me and my family. I wouldn't want you to think . . .' She broke off.

'The pleasure is mine,' Johann said. 'Good night. Mrs Edward.'

'Good night, Johann.'

It was raining as she left. Crossing the farmyard she came face to face with Kit Marsden. He stood in front of her, barring her way.

'Just turning in,' he said. 'Did you enjoy your walk?'

'Very much.'

'You seem to have avoided the rain,' he remarked. 'You must have walked between the drops!'

'I did,' Cara said lightly. 'But if I stand here we'll both get wet. Good night then!'

From her bedroom window, without lighting the lamp, she looked out across the farmyard. There was a square of light from Johann's quarters, but it was at Kit Marsden's window, not curtained, so that she could see him moving about, that she gazed longest.

She noted also, from the glow thrown down into the yard, that Susan's lamp was lit and her curtains not drawn. And then Kit came and stood by his window, clearly visible, smoking a cigarette.

What was happening? Probably nothing, she told herself – but she was uneasy. Susan was too familiar by far with Kit Marsden, and with his laughing and teasing, his sometimes flowery compliments, he encouraged her. There was no doubt that the child was attractive. Indeed, her thick mane of corn-coloured hair, the regularity of her features, and the curves of her slender, ripening body, added up to real beauty. And increasingly it was not the beauty of a child; already she could look a woman. She was a replica of her mother in the photograph she still displayed in her bedroom.

Cara's instinct now was to go to Susan's room on some pretext or other. But what pretext? It was not something she was in the habit of doing and she could think of no excuse. Nevertheless, she put on her dressing gown and went.

She knocked on Susan's door, then, hardly waiting for a reply, entered. Susan, looking absurdly childish in her striped pyjamas, was standing by the dressing table. She swung around, her eyes widening in surprise as she saw Cara.

'What in the world . . .?'

'I saw your lamp,' Cara said hesitantly. 'I wondered if you were all right?'

'I'm perfectly all right,' Susan said. 'I don't put out my lamp before I'm ready for bed!'

'You haven't drawn your curtains,' Cara said. 'You'll be cold.'

She crossed to the window and began to pull the curtains together. As she did so, she saw Kit Marsden back away and the next second his room was in darkness.

'If you don't mind, I don't like my curtains drawn,' Susan said angrily. 'If it's all the same to you!' She jerked back the curtains as she spoke.

'I'm sorry,' Cara said. 'Well, if you're sure you're all right . . .'

'Never better!'

'Go to sleep soon,' Cara said. 'School in the morning!' At least Susan would be out of the house for five days.

'You don't need to remind me,' Susan said crossly. 'And please don't interfere in my affairs!'

Lying awake in the darkness, Cara thought, I shall be glad when Kit Marsden leaves. He is a disruptive influence. Nothing at Beckwith has been quite the same since he turned up out of the blue.

Next morning Kit said to Cara:

'If you like, I'll give Susan a lift to school.'

'Thank you,' Cara said quickly. 'I plan to take her myself.'

'Since I have a bit of urgent business in Shepton, I thought I might as well save you the trouble,' Kit said smoothly. 'Oh, don't worry, I'll make up the lost time! We're nearly through anyway. Only the last of the ewes to see to.'

Susan looked smugly cheerful at the proposal, quite unlike her usual Monday morning self.

Cara had no answer. She owed him the time anyway. More than once he had worked well over the limit.

'In that case . . .' she began.

'I'll be back in a couple of hours,' Kit said,

Cara wondered what his business in Shepton could be, or if, as she suspected, he actually had any.

A little later she watched them drive away and then, on an impulse, she turned to her mother-in-law.

'Mother Hendry,' she said, 'do you worry about Susan?'

'I've worried about Susan practically since she was born!' Mrs Hendry said. 'What do you mean?'

'I'm not sure,' Cara hedged. 'I do wonder, though, if she's getting too familiar with Kit Marsden?'

'Oh *that*!' Mrs Hendry said comfortably. 'That's nothing but a bit of fun.'

'She's too provocative,' Cara said. 'And he encourages her. Look at the way he insisted on taking her into Shepton this morning!'

Mrs Hendry gave Cara a puzzled look. What was it all about?

'He was going into Shepton,' she pointed out. 'Where was the sense in both of you going? I think you've got things a bit out of perspective, love. As I said, it's a bit of fun.'

'Well, it doesn't seem funny to me!' Cara replied shortly.

'Cara, love,' Mrs Hendry said quietly, 'I think perhaps you're losing your sense of humour. I've noticed it once or twice lately, and it's not like you. Oh, I don't wonder at it! You've had a bad time. It's no joke, losing your man, and you so young. I know very well what it feels like. But things *will* change, they *will* get better.'

Cara left the house and went to join Johann. For the rest of the morning they worked together in companionable silence. As Cara worked she considered her mother-in-law's words. Perhaps Mother Hendry was right, after all. Perhaps she *was* losing her sense of humour. It was a depressing thought and she pushed it away.

It was satisfying to see the ewes now, almost all of them marked on the hindquarters by their tup. Only a few remained untouched, and these she and Johann were sorting out to put in a field with the chaser tups. They might well get through the job before Kit returned; and in that case, she decided, she would pay him off.

She was entitled to do so: she had only engaged him for the tupping.

She was truly worried about Susan, still more so when she thought about the child's mother. I *have* to be responsible, she thought. I *am* responsible.

It was mid-afternoon when Kit showed up, striding straight from his van to the field where she and Johann were.

'Sorry I'm late,' he said.

'No matter,' Cara replied brusquely. 'As a matter of fact, we're almost through. We'll finish this afternoon.'

The remaining sheep were soon dealt with, all except three which, finding a bit of newly-broken wall, had made the most of it and disappeared somewhere up the fell.

'I'll take Ruby and go after them,' Cara said.

'And I will mend the wall at once so that no more escape,' Johann said.

'Don't go too far,' Kit warned Cara. 'It'll be dark soon and there's a mist coming. In fact, since Johann will work better without me, I'll come with you.'

'There isn't the slightest need,' Cara said. 'I can look after myself.'

He took no notice, and when she began to climb, the dog running ahead, he followed behind. She climbed quickly, so that by the time she reached the top she was breathless. Ruby had found the sheep and was rounding them up. Kit had been right about the weather. The sun had gone down prematurely, and with the dusk the mist was closing in.

A minute later, as she leaned against a boulder to get her breath back, Kit caught up with her.

'You came up that fellside like a steam engine!' he complained. 'I could almost think you were trying to get away from me!'

'Why should I do that?' Cara asked. 'But speaking of getting away, since the tupping's now over I'm sure that's what you'll want to be doing.'

'Oh. I don't know . . .' Kit began.

'I only engaged you for the tupping. I can't afford to keep you on.'

He stood in front of her, putting out an arm on each side of her body, imprisoning her against the boulder. She tried at once to escape from him but he pushed her gently back again.

'Look at me,' he commanded. 'Look me straight in the face. It's got nothing to do with money. You want me to go, don't you?'

'Yes, I do!'

211

'Why? What have I done wrong?'

'I didn't say you'd done anything wrong. Let's not discuss it. I engaged you for the tupping, and it's virtually over. Now will you please stop fooling and let me go.'

'Not yet,' Kit said. 'I *want* to discuss it. Why can't you tell me? You owe me that much.'

'I don't owe you anything,' Cara said. 'But if you must know, I don't think you're good for Susan. She's only fourteen. She's impressionable. And she's not nearly as mature as she looks.'

'Is that it? Is that the reason?'

'It's enough,' Cara said.

'Then I can put your mind at rest,' Kit said. 'She's a nice enough kid, and she's fun. There's not too much fun around Beckwith at the moment, and I understand why, but she needs fun. But I'd not do her the slightest harm. To tell you the truth, I'm not interested in Susan.'

'Then why not leave her alone? Why were you showing yourself in front of her bedroom window last night?' Cara asked sharply. 'Why did you insist on taking her into Shepton this morning?'

'I took her into Shepton for the reason I gave you,' he said. 'I was going in anyway. As for the window bit – yes, I did see her. I knew she was watching me. But it was you I wanted. Don't you know that? Are you blind?'

'Stop it! You're talking nonsense!'

'No I'm not. And I won't stop until you've heard me out. I can't get you out of my mind. Why do you think I came back to Beckwith? And I believe you want me just as much!'

'How dare you!' She was furious.

'Oh, I dare all right. I saw you watching me at the pump that first night. And I've seen you watching me since – in and out of the house.'

'Me watch you!' Cara cried. 'You must be crazy!'

'Oh no! You want me and I want you. We're well matched, you and me. We want each other, Cara Hendry. We always have.'

He took hold of her shoulders in an iron grip and roughly pulled her close. Then he encircled her in his arms and opened her lips with a kiss which took the breath from her body and left her weak and spinning.

'*Now* tell me you don't want me!' he said at last. 'Say it if you dare – but don't expect me to believe you because I know what your body's telling me!'

She hardly heard his words. She was conscious only of his body and of her body, and of the deep longing of her body to drown in his.

She ran her hands in the thickness of his hair, pulled his head down to hers, and stopped his words with a kiss, a fierce, passionate, bruising kiss, of a kind she had never given, or experienced, before.

Oh yes, she wanted him. She wanted him more than she had ever wanted anything in her life!

FIFTEEN

It had been a call from Johann, a long-drawn-out 'Cooee' such as he might have used in the mountains of his native Austria, which had pierced the mist on the fell top, and the consciousness of Cara and Kit Marsden. Cara had had no idea of how long they'd been there. Time had lost its meaning. She'd become aware, then, that the mist had thickened until it shrouded the whole dale. There was a film of damp on her jacket and her hair hung in wet streaks around her face.

'We must go or Johann will come to look for us,' she said quickly. 'He knows the danger of the fell tops in the mist.'

She'd held on to Kit's hand as they picked their way down the hill – not because she needed his support but because she couldn't bear to let him go. Life and passion flowed from his fingertips into hers, setting her whole body alight. But when they'd seen Johann climbing towards them, she'd immediately distanced herself from Kit.

Johann, though as polite as ever, was white-faced and clearly angry.

'I was worried,' he said shortly. 'Ruby came back with the ewes several minutes ago.'

'I'm sorry, Johann!' Cara said.

She could think of no excuse to give him. Worse still, she feared that what had happened on the fell top must show in her face. She was another person, a changed person, from the woman who had walked up the hill earlier. How could it not be visible? How could the whole world not see the difference in her?

Kit had said nothing. The three of them had walked back in silence, but from the moment they had entered the house Kit had been his usual self again, laughing and joking with Mrs Hendry as if nothing at all had happened. As though, Cara thought, the whole world had not turned upside down.

214

'I'll see to Emily before I do anything else,' Cara said. She was surprised at the steadiness of her voice.

Picking up the child, clutching her almost desperately to her body, she carried her upstairs to the bathroom. Emily was old enough to go in the big bath now. It was good to be with her baby, Cara thought as she soaped the plump little body, made waves and splashes in the water, listened to the screams of delight from her daughter. It was cleansing and wholesome. To spend time with her baby might help her back to sanity, for surely what had so recently happened was insane?

She had calmed down a little, was ready to lift Emily out, when Kit came into the bathroom. Standing behind her as she leaned over the bath to steady Emily, he put his hands on her shoulders, then drew them down the length of her spine. As if at the touch of a switch, feeling flowed through her like a strong electric current. She held on hard to Emily, afraid that she might let her go.

'As I told your mother-in-law just now,' Kit said, 'I've never seen Emily in the bath.'

'Is that why you came?' Cara asked unsteadily.

'What do you think? Cara, I've got to see you, and not when you're juggling with a slippery baby. I've got to see you on your own.' His voice was urgent.

'It's not possible,' Cara said. 'You know it's not. How and when could I see you? There's no privacy here.'

'Tell me you don't want to be alone with me! Go on, say it!' he challenged her.

'How can I?' she whispered.

She longed for it. She longed for there to be no-one else in the world but the two of them – yet at the same time she was afraid, afraid to enter into something over which she might lose control.

'Tonight,' he said. 'After everyone's gone to bed. Leave the door unlocked.'

'No,' she protested. 'I couldn't do that! You mustn't come into the house. Supposing Grandma heard you?'

'She wouldn't,' he said. 'I know how to move quietly. That's in my blood.'

'It's impossible,' she said.

'Then you must come to me,' he ordered. 'You must do that. If you don't, I shall come here.'

He was still stroking her back. She felt weak with longing. Emily, annoyed because the splashing and the wavemaking had stopped, began to whimper.

'Please go,' Cara begged. 'I must see to Emily. If I leave her in the water much longer she'll catch cold.'

'Very well,' Kit said. 'But don't forget what I said. I meant it.'

She heard him run lightly down the stairs, heard him speak in pleasant tones to her mother-in-law in the kitchen. How could he sound so normal? What should she do? She felt desperate, torn apart, though there was no question of what she wanted to do. She wanted to go to him, to stay with him.

That night she lay awake, staring into the darkness. It was only a little after midnight, but as far as she could tell everyone in the house was asleep. Early to bed and early to rise was the rule at Beckwith. A few minutes ago she had crept along to David's room and found him fast asleep, the bedcovers close around his neck. Emily, who had been promoted to her own small room, had been asleep for hours, and in the normal course of events was unlikely to waken until morning. When Cara had passed Mrs Hendry's room she had heard gentle snores coming from behind the closed door.

Nevertheless, she thought, she could not allow Kit to come into the house. Though her body jangled with longing for his body, she could not countenance him in the bed she had shared, until only a few months ago, with Edward.

She got out of bed and looked out of the window. There was a square of light from Kit's room, where he lay waiting for her. Beyond that, Johann's quarters were in total darkness.

She would go to Kit, she had no alternative, but it would be for the first and last time. She would go to him and make it plain that the whole thing was impossible.

She put on her dressing gown and crept down the stairs, praying that Emily would not waken. The dogs heard her but, being used to her, made no sound. When she climbed the rickety old steps to Kit's room his door was open, he was waiting. Without a word he took her in his arms and pulled her down on to the bed, but she pushed him away.

'No!' she said. 'No!'

'Don't be silly,' he said gently. 'I don't believe you can be afraid!' He was unfastening the buttons on her dressing gown.

'I'm not being silly, and I'm not afraid. I just can't go through with it, Kit, that's all.'

He tried to smother her words with his kiss, but she pulled away. 'No, Kit! I mean it!'

'Stop playing games,' he said. 'You know what you want. We both know why you're here!'

'I know why I'm here,' Cara said. 'I'm here because I couldn't allow you to come to the house. And I came to tell you . . .' She hesitated. 'I came to tell you that this has got to end before it goes any further. I can't do it!'

'End? Don't be silly, sweetheart! We've hardly begun.'

216

'I know,' Cara said. 'But I can't have an affair with you. How could I live in Arendale, how could I be with my family – my children, my mother-in-law – and at the same time be having an affair with you? This isn't London or Paris. This is the dales. Marriage is what happens in Arendale.'

He drew back from her, sat upright.

'Who said anything about marrying?'

'I only meant . . .'

'I'm not the marrying kind,' Kit said. 'It's not in me to be tied down.'

'And it's not in me to have a clandestine affair.'

'This has the flavour of blackmail to me,' Kit said tersely.

'How can you say that?' Cara demanded. 'It's nothing of the kind. I'm not blackmailing you into anything. Even if you wanted to, even if you asked me, I couldn't marry you. Not yet. It's only a matter of months since Edward died. It would cause a scandal.'

'So you don't want marriage because it's too soon, but you're too prudish to have anything short of marriage!' He pushed her away, sprang to his feet and began pacing the floor, up and down in the small room.

Then he stopped, and stood in front of her, his face suffused with anger.

'Do you know what you are? You're a tease – and I don't mean that as a compliment. Are you so stupid that you don't know how much I want you?'

'Of course I know,' Cara retorted. 'I'm flesh and blood like you. Do you think I don't want you, that I don't ache for you, right now, this very minute? Do you think I don't feel anything?'

'I thought you did,' he said bitterly. 'I thought I knew that much. I didn't know you could turn it on and off like a tap.'

'I can't!' she shouted. 'I can't!'

'Have you thought,' he said, 'that I could just take you, here and now? Do you realize that?'

For a moment, which to Cara felt like an hour, they stared at each other. She was suddenly afraid.

'Yes, I realize that,' she said, breaking the silence. 'You have the strength. But you won't, will you? You wouldn't do that?'

He continued to stare at her. She was cold with fear. Then he turned away and went and sat on the bed, burying his head in his hands.

'Get out!' he said. 'Get out!'

The fear went.

'Not like this, Kit!' she pleaded. 'Oh Kit, why don't you love me enough to wait – just for a little while? We could be so happy together, I know we could!'

217

She realized as she spoke that he had not mentioned love. She had assumed it because she knew for certain that she loved him. Body and soul she loved him, as it seemed to her she had never loved anyone before.

'I'm not a patient man,' he said. 'I don't care to wait for what I want. Now go!'

'Very well, I will,' Cara said. 'And you had better leave Beckwith.' She felt drained of strength, turned to stone.

She was at the door when he came after her and took her in his arms again.

'Cara, *please*! This is mad!'

In his arms she thought, what a fool I am! Why can't I just take what he wants to give? Why can't I take it this once, here and now?

It was no good. She twisted out of his embrace.

'I must go,' she said dully. 'Emily might waken.'

Her eyes were blinded by tears as she went back to the house and crept stealthily up the stairs to her room. There was not the slightest stir from anyone. How can they sleep so soundly, she asked herself, while my life is being torn apart?

In the morning, by the time she came down to breakfast, Kit was gone.

'He didn't even stop for a bite to eat!' Mrs Hendry said, mystified. 'Said he had urgent business to see to. What's so urgent that a man goes without his breakfast? Anyway, he's left you a note.'

Cara's hands trembled as she unfolded the piece of paper. She was aware that Johann's eyes, as well as her mother-in-law's, were on her. She read the note and then dropped it on the table. There was nothing in it the whole world couldn't see. Not a word.

'It's a bill for what I owe him,' she said. 'He asks me to send the money to the Ewe and Lamb.'

Johann, though he said nothing, and immediately ceased to look at Cara, concentrating instead on the substantial breakfast Mrs Hendry had placed before him, was not deceived.

He had observed Cara's face when she came down from the fell top with Marsden yesterday, and again in the evening as they'd sat at supper. It had all been there in her look. And this morning it was in her voice; her words and her tone just too casual to fool him.

She didn't know, nor would she ever, that to him she was an open book. They all were, this family who had given him a home.

Because he was quiet, stayed in the background and said little, they didn't realize how much he saw. It wasn't that he wished to pry; rather that he watched over them, would, if he could, have guarded them from all harm.

Possibly they thought his English was still not good enough to understand everything, but they were wrong. Although he wasn't as fluent in speech as he would have liked, he understood almost every word, even the strange Yorkshire phrases they used, which in the beginning had caused him so much confusion.

But this time no subtle understanding had been necessary. Last night, from his room, he had heard their voices, Cara's and Marsden's, raised in anger. He had not heard the words, he hadn't wanted to, but he had heard Cara's distress and had wanted to break in on them and beat Marsden to a pulp. He had kept on the alert until, with great relief, he had heard Cara leave.

This morning he had been in the kitchen when Marsden, with the pleasantest of farewells to Mrs Hendry and a curt nod to himself, had left. He was glad to see the back of him. Marsden spelt trouble and unhappiness.

'Fancy not waiting for his money!' Mrs Hendry said. 'I wouldn't have thought that was like him. Any road, I shall miss him. He was lively around the place.'

'We only engaged him for the tupping,' Cara said.

Back in her room, she had not slept again, and this morning she was utterly weary.

'You sound tired, love,' her mother-in-law said. 'Did you not sleep well?'

'Not very well,' Cara admitted.

'Was Emily troublesome?' Mrs Hendry asked.

'No. She slept through. I looked in on her a minute ago. She's still asleep, and so is David, though I'll have to waken him or he'll be late for school.'

There had been moments, during the night, when she had thought that she could easily run away from Beckwith, live in one room, anywhere, with Kit. But almost immediately the claims of Beckwith – the farm, the animals, children, her baby – had asserted themselves. She was tied by silken cords to Beckwith. And aside from that, she reminded herself grimly, Kit had not asked her to leave!

'I shall not need help this morning, Mrs Edward,' Johann said. 'There is not a great deal to do and I can manage it.'

'Well in that case,' Cara said, 'when I've taken David to school perhaps I'll go into Shepton. There's some shopping I'd like to do.'

'And you could drop in Kit's wages at the Ewe at the same time,' Mrs Hendry suggested.

Donnerwetter! Johann cursed silently. I have spoken too soon! I should have said I needed help.

'I suppose I could,' Cara said. She had already thought of it.

When Cara reached the Ewe it was not yet opening time. She wandered, once again, around the market stalls, willing the time to pass more quickly. When the town hall struck the hour she set off down the High Street, then halted. She must give him time to get there. She couldn't sit in the bar, a woman on her own, waiting for him, though she was sure he would come.

She dallied, looking into shop windows and seeing nothing, for another fifteen minutes, then made for the Ewe.

'Why, Mrs Hendry! Good morning!' the landlord greeted her. 'It's a long time since I saw you in here! How are you?'

'I'm very well thank you, Mr Thwaite.'

'Can I get you a drink, then?'

'No thank you. I thought I might see Kit Marsden here. He's been working up at Beckwith and he left something behind.'

'Nay, I'm sorry love, you've missed him!' Thwaite said. 'He's been and gone.'

'Been and gone? I thought you'd only just opened?'

She felt as though she'd been hit in the face. On the drive in from Arendale she'd persuaded herself, until she was quite certain of it, that Kit's note was an invitation to meet him in the Ewe. She knew she shouldn't, that it would get her nowhere, but she would allow herself one more time. At the very least they could part on better terms.

'We have,' Thwaite said. 'He came quite early, picked up a few things he'd left here while he was working in Arendale, and went.'

'Will he be in again?' She tried hard not to show her bitter disappointment, not to appear anxious.

'Who knows?' he said, laughing. 'Nobody ever knows when they'll see Kit Marsden again.'

'I see. Then when he does come in, will you give him this envelope?'

He was clearly curious about the contents as she handed the envelope over to him.

'It's his wages,' she explained. 'He left without them.'

'Left without his wages!' Thwaite exclaimed. 'I reckon that's not like him!'

Except he usually leaves in a hurry, he thought, and more than once with an irate husband after him. But Mrs Hendry wasn't in that class. Even Marsden couldn't be lucky enough for that. She was a cut above it.

'Well, I'd be grateful if you'd hang on to it and give it to him when you do see him,' Cara said.

She went home at once. There was nothing to stay in Shepton for now. She felt she never wanted to see it again. After dinner, since Johann repeated that he had no need of her, she decided she would take Emily out in the pram, walk along the lane.

'You do that,' Mrs Hendry said. 'It'll be a nice change for

both of you. The little love doesn't often get to go out with her mother.'

'I know – and I feel guilty,' Cara said.

'No need for that,' Mrs Hendry assured her. 'No-one could do more than you do. You're holding this place together!'

'But not on my own,' Cara said.

What would you think if you could see into my heart, she wondered. Oh, Mother Hendry, what would you think of me? Then on an impulse she put an arm around her mother-in-law and kissd her on the cheek.

'Now what's that about?' Mrs Hendry said, flushing with pleasure. They didn't often show their feelings in this part of the world, not unless it was to children.

'Would you like to come with us?' Cara asked.

'I think I won't, love. I think I'll have a few minutes with my feet up, if it's all the same to you.'

'Of course,' Cara agreed. 'You haven't often had the chance lately. I'll not be long, and I'll do the milking today. In fact, now that the tupping's over I'll have time to do it every day. Give you a break.'

She was glad, pushing the pram along the lane, that her mother-in-law had decided not to come. She had a terrible need to be alone, a need not easy to satisfy at Beckwith. She would be pleased, too, to take over the milking again for the next few months. It was a task, performed in solitude, she enjoyed.

Wheeling the pram along the lane Cara observed, though it was still November, signs of the coming winter, which always arrived early in Arendale. The trees which lined the river bank were almost bare. What few withered leaves still remained would be stripped by the next autumn gale. Though the new grass was through on the river meadows, it had none of the life and brilliance it would show in the spring, and every slight hollow in the land was filled with floodwater which had remained after the heavy rains of October.

It was the least beautiful time of the year in Arendale, though nothing could diminish the grand contours of the landscape, the rocky outcrops, the walls. They were proof against all seasons. They didn't need colour.

'Not much longer now and it won't be fit to bring you out,' Cara said to Emily.

Emily smiled happily; said 'Ganna', 'Mama', and a few more words from her repertoire. It was her way of carrying on a conversation.

'The snow will come,' Cara informed her. 'Any day now it will cover the fell tops, and later on the whole dale.'

Usually, she didn't mind the winter. There was less to do on the

221

farm, more time for reading and other pursuits. Last winter she had taken up tapestry. And if they were snowed up, as at some stage they usually were, well, the house was warm and weather proof. As for the dale itself, it was never more magnificent than under a blanket of snow. Also, with less work on the farms, winter was the season for social gatherings: dances, parties, concerts. Dalesfolk knew how to enjoy themselves.

'But what will *I* do?' Cara said out loud. 'What will *I* do, little Emily?'

Last winter Edward had been alive. Last winter everything had been different.

'Why did you leave me?' she cried out. 'Why did your daddy leave us?' she demanded of Emily. A startled blackbird, perched on the wall, took flight at the sound of her voice.

Yet what troubled her this November afternoon as she pushed her daughter's pram over the uneven ground, was that it was Kit Marsden, not Edward, she was missing so desperately. She felt swamped by guilt and desolation. How could she, so soon after Edward, have even looked at Kit?

She knew the answer to that. She had known it for several days now. The truth was that even while Edward was alive, even while they were happy together, Kit Marsden had insinuated himself into her thoughts, pricked at her feelings.

There had been the Washing, when they had danced together. There had been the days when the snow of that never-to-be-forgotten winter had marooned them in Shepton. But even before that there had been the very first meeting in Shepton, after the sales, when he'd caught up with her outside the cinema. She had felt his attraction even then, and there had been no moment of meeting with him since of which she didn't recall every detail.

Was she never to be free of him? But did she want to be? Yet could she bear this raw, wounded state she was in now? How could she carry on?

She knew the answer to that last question. She would carry on because she had to. There was no way out of it. Whether she should, or could, tear Kit Marsden out of her heart, or whether she should keep the hope alive that one day he would come back to her, and all would be well, were the questions she couldn't answer.

'It's blowing colder,' she said to Emily. 'We'll go home.'

When they reached home Mrs Hendry said: 'Grant Fawcett phoned while you were out. He's in Faverwell, so he'll give David a lift home from school.'

'Good! Then I needn't turn out,' Cara said.

The two of them arrived ten minutes later.

222

'It's a while since we've seen you, Grant,' Mrs Hendry said. 'The kettle's coming up to the boil. You'll stay for a cup of tea, I hope?'

'Thank you,' Grant said. 'Yes, it has been a while. We've been busy with the tupping. Who hasn't?'

He turned to Cara.

'Did it go well?'

'Quite well,' she replied. 'Not many left for the chasers. We should have a good crop of lambs next spring.'

'I hear you had Marsden to help,' Grant said. 'Did that work out all right?'

'Yes. He's left now.'

'Uncle Joseph wasn't too happy when he heard Marsden was up here at Beckwith,' Grant told her. 'He thought he might try to hang on through the winter.'

'Well, tell him not to worry,' Cara said steadily. 'He left the minute the tupping was over.'

She poured a cup of tea and handed it to Grant.

'We might never see him again,' she said, torturing herself with the words.

'Oh I doubt that,' Mrs Hendry said comfortably. 'He'll turn up one day!'

'Apart from giving David a lift,' Grant said to Cara, 'I came with a purpose. I came to ask you if you'd go with me to the Farmers' Ball in Shepton.'

'The Farmers' Ball? Oh, I don't think . . .' she began.

The ball, which had ceased during the war years, had been started up again last winter. It was the biggest social occasion of the year. She and Edward would have attended last winter but for the fact that she'd been nursing Emily.

'Why not?' Grant asked.

'It's . . . well, it's too soon. By rights I'm still in mourning.'

'I don't think anyone else is going to worry about that,' Grant said. 'Anyway, there'd be a party of us. Aunt and Uncle are going, and some friends of theirs from Faverwell.'

'I think you should go, love,' Mrs Hendry put in. 'It would do you good. You need to get out a bit.'

'And *you* wouldn't think it was disrespectful?' Cara asked her. 'You especially?'

'Not if you were going with a party.'

'Well,' Cara said hesitantly. 'I'll think about it. Thank you for asking me, Grant. When do you need to know?'

'As soon as possible,' he said. 'It's on the third of December and the tickets are limited.'

223

She didn't want to go. She didn't really want to go anywhere. However, she would keep her word, she'd think about it.

'I'll let you know in a day or two,' she promised. 'Will you excuse me now? It's milking time and I don't need to tell you cows seem to have clocks built into them!'

Grant watched her anxiously as she left the house.

'She doesn't look too well,' he said to Mrs Hendry. 'Is she all right?'

'I think so,' Mrs Hendry said. 'It's not an easy life, what she's taken on – added to which she has her sorrows to bear. And there's none of us can do that for her. We each have to come to terms with our own life.'

I would bear Cara's sorrow for her if I could, Grant thought. I would do anything for her. But that wasn't something he could say to Mrs Hendry, or to Cara. Not yet. Not yet to either of them.

'Try to persuade her to go to the ball,' he urged,

'Oh, I will,' Mrs Hendry assured him.

She brought up the subject again that evening, after supper.

'Why not go, love?' she said. 'It always used to be a lovely affair. Me and Tom went regular when we were younger. We danced every dance!' Her voice softened with pleasure at the memory.

'That's the point,' Cara said. 'You went with Tom.'

'And do you think I don't wish you were going with Edward?' Mrs Hendry said. 'I know you'll miss him, and it won't be the same. But you'll be in a party. You'll not be lonely. And you'll not lack partners, I'll be bound. I think you should make the effort.'

Shall I ever not feel lonely? Cara asked herself. Out loud she said: 'What would I wear? It's a very dressy do, isn't it?'

'I expect so,' Mrs Hendry admitted. 'It always used to be.'

'Well I've neither money nor coupons for a ball dress,' Cara said. 'So there we are!'

'Then why don't you wear your wedding dress?' Mrs Hendry suggested. 'Oh, I don't mean as it is,' she said, seeing Cara's look of astonishment. 'I mean have it altered and have it dyed.'

'I'm not sure that I could do that,' Cara said doubtfully.

Before going to bed that night, she took her wedding dress from the wardrobe, removed the clean white sheet in which it was draped, and hung it from the picture rail. Then she stood in front of it, looking at it. It smelled sweetly of the lavender sachets fastened to the coathanger, and it was the scent, as much as the sight of it, which brought back the rush of memories of that August wedding day. The best years of her life had stretched before her then, seemingly endless, all waiting to be lived with Edward by her side.

She flung her arms around the dress and buried her face in the soft white satin. Oh Edward, she thought desperately, I did love you so much, and I *do* love you. I would have been faithful to you for ever. Please forgive me now, Edward!

Suddenly, without warning the tears were flowing as they had not done since Edward's death. She flung herself down on the bed and gave herself up to her grief; indulged in it, welcomed its manifestation. She was tired of being strong, of being so strong for everyone. You've been so brave, they all said – but inside she wasn't. She was weak and afraid. She wanted someone to recognize her weakness, and no-one did.

She lay on the bed for a long time, too weary to undress and get into bed. Her pillow was wet with the tears she had shed. And then, strangely, slowly, she felt better – as if with the tears she'd shed some of the poison of the last few months. She rose to her feet and began to undress.

She had loved Edward, *did* love him, and had lost him. She loved Kit Marsden and she had lost him too. But she knew, in this moment, that she wouldn't be defeated. She would win. It was like the moment when she'd resolved to keep the farm. No-one and nothing, nothing that fate had to throw at her, would defeat her from now on. She was stepping back into life.

And the first thing I shall do, she decided, is go to that ball! She would prove to herself – other people didn't come into it – what she was made of. From now on she would *live* her life, not drag herself wearily through it.

Edward would approve, she thought. I know he would, my dear Edward. As for Kit Marsden, he could go to hell!

She finished undressing, got into bed, turned over her pillow to the dry side (as if she was turning her life, she thought). The last thing she saw before falling into the best sleep she had known for months was her wedding dress hanging on the wall, its shining whiteness caught in the shaft of moonlight which streamed in through the window where she had forgotten to draw the curtains.

'Why don't you get your ma to give you a hand with the dress?' Mrs Hendry suggested next morning when she heard Cara's decision about the ball. 'She's a dab hand with a needle, which heaven knows I'm not!'

'Perhaps I'll do that,' Cara said. 'It needs to be taken in, and the train will have to come off and the skirt be shortened a bit.'

When she'd wakened this morning all her doubts and fears of the previous day had rushed back again. Her grief for Edward and her longing for Kit Marsden had been as strong as ever. She'd wanted to close her eyes and sink into oblivion again. But then she'd looked at the dress, hanging on the wall, and her resolve had returned with a rush of strength. The dress, she thought, had become a symbol.

'You'll have to get on with it. There's not much time since you'll want to have it dyed,' Mrs Hendry said. 'Why don't you go into Akersfield after breakfast? We're not busy, you could even stay the night.'

'I'll not stay over,' Cara said. 'But I'll give Ma a ring, and if she can do with me I'll get the train this morning. Are you sure you can manage?'

'Of course I am,' Mrs Hendry said.

'I'll be glad to do it,' Beth Dunning said on the phone. 'Get here as soon as you can.'

The rush over the next hour suited Cara. She wanted no spare time in which to think, in which to change her mind. She packed the dress, telephoned Grant Fawcett to tell him the news, and set off for Akersfield.

'You're too thin, love,' Beth Dunning said critically, pinning the dress on Cara. 'You must have lost a lot of weight. I'm having to take these seams in more than two inches. Have you not been eating properly?'

'Oh, I think I have,' Cara said. 'It's been a busy time on the farm.'

But there was more to it than that, Beth thought. Aside from the fact that she had lost weight, and with it the bonny roundness of her face and figure, her daughter looked pale and drawn. Perhaps the struggle was too much? Perhaps Arnold had been right, and she should have got out of the farm, into something easier.

'You must look after yourself,' she cautioned. 'At any rate, I'm glad you're going to have a bit of fun, go to the farmers' do. I've always fancied going to a function like that.'

'Would you like to come?' Cara said quickly. 'You and Dad, if I could get tickets?'

For a brief moment Beth's dreams took off and rose sky-high. I'd have to have a new dress, she thought. And new shoes. Blue would suit me! Then her dreams floated gently down again and settled on the ground.

'I don't think so, love,' she said. 'It's a nice idea, but in any case I don't think your dad would agree. And it's a long way to go for an evening.'

'Lots of people will be coming just as far,' Cara told her. 'They come from all over the dales to the Shepton Farmers' Ball. Why don't we ask Dad when he comes home for dinner?'

'We'll see,' Beth said. 'What colour had you thought of having your dress dyed?'

'I'm not sure,' Cara said.

To have her wedding dress altered and dyed, to plan to wear it in

226

public, had been more an act of defiance, the cocking of a snook at life, than anything else. She hadn't thought of the details.

'Perhaps a deep green. A very deep emerald, or a sea green. I dare say I ought to choose black, but I'm not going to.'

Beth nodded approval.

'Quite right! A rich, dark green would suit you. And I reckon this material will take the dye well. I'll finish the sewing tomorrow, then I'll post it to you and you can take it into Shepton to get it dyed. Now step out carefully. It's full of pins.'

Cara took a last look at herself, in the long mirror, in her shining white wedding dress. As she stepped out of it she felt as if she was saying goodbye to a precious part of her life.

'I can guess what you're thinking,' her mother said. 'Try to tell yourself that with your beautiful green dress you'll be stepping into a new bit of life. Life goes on. Trite, but true.'

When Arnold Dunning came home at dinnertime Cara asked him about the ball.

'Why not?' he said after the briefest pause. 'Why not? It would do us good!'

Beth gasped in astonishment.

'I'd have to have a new dress,' she ventured. 'And shoes!'

'So what?' Arnold said. 'You can have my coupons!'

SIXTEEN

On Friday, Susan came home from school. Cara met her at the station, then returned by way of Faverwell to collect David.

'Kit said he'd come to meet me,' Susan said. 'I enjoyed it when he took me to school. He drives very fast!'

'Well, this time he's driven fast away!' Cara said. She tried to keep her tone light. Susan was going to miss him.

Susan turned on her with a not-unexpected vehemence.

'What do you mean?'

'He's left,' David said.

'Left?' Susan cried. 'I don't believe it! Why would he do that?'

'He left because we finished tupping,' Cara said, keeping her voice calm. 'He was only engaged for the tupping.'

'You sacked him!' Susan accused her. 'How could you? You knew he didn't have another job!'

'I did *not* sack him,' Cara said.

'You must have,' Susan contradicted. 'When he took me to school on Monday he said "See you Friday". He didn't plan to leave!'

If that had been his plan, if he'd even thought of such a thing, he would have told her; she knew he would.

'I don't know anything about that,' Cara said. 'Perhaps he didn't think we'd finish tupping so soon.'

'You could have kept him on. You're always saying there's too much work to do. Why didn't you keep him?'

'Susan,' Cara said firmly, 'I engaged Kit to help with the tupping. I simply can't afford to employ him for anything else. You know that.'

Please stop, she wanted to shout! Why must Susan go on and on? She wished only to forget Kit Marsden, she was trying her hardest to do so, and as quickly as possible.

228

'Everything's much more fun when Kit's here,' Susan said.

What she couldn't stand the thought of, though she'd not let Cara know, was that he hadn't said goodbye to her. He'd gone without a word. If he had *had* to leave at a moment's notice, then he could have sent her a note to school. Or . . . Suddenly, she thought of it. He *would* have left her a note! How silly she was. He'd have left it in her room. She would find it as soon as they got back to the house.

'Oh well!' she said, in a voice which closed the subject.

'So what sort of a week have you had?' Cara enquired.

'Not as bad as usual,' Susan admitted. 'We've been rehearsing every day for the end-of-term play.'

They were doing *The Merchant of Venice* and there was to be a performance for families and friends two weeks from tonight.

'Is it going well?' Cara asked.

'Oh yes. Of course, mine's a very big part,' Susan said loftily. She was playing Portia. 'I shan't be able to help much this weekend because I'll have to swot at my lines! Will you hear them?'

'Of course,' Cara agreed. She'd hear them fifty times over if it would take the child's mind off Kit Marsden.

When they reached Beckwith, Susan was first out of the car. She hurried into the house and, passing through the kitchen like a whirlwind, made for her room.

'There she was – gone!' her grandmother said in astonishment as the others came in.

'I rather think she's going to pitch straight into *The Merchant of Venice*,' Cara said.

'Without a bite to eat? That's not like Susan!'

'Can I have something to eat?' David asked.

There was no note on the dressing table. Perhaps, Susan thought, he had hidden it from prying eyes, slipped it into a drawer? She opened the top drawer, but even among the conglomeration of combs and brushes, cream and powder, beads and brooches, it was clear there was no note. Nor was there one in any of the other drawers, nor on any shelf or surface. Nothing.

She flung herself face down on the bed, deflated and unbelieving. How could this be? She knew, she just *knew* that he was – well – very fond of her, almost in love with her, she reckoned. As for her, she doted on him. She had told some of her friends at school all about him and they were wildly jealous. What was she to think now? Why had he done this?

Had Cara suspected? Had she given him a lecture about her stepdaughter being too young, only a schoolgirl and all that rubbish – then sent him packing? If she has, Susan vowed, I will get it out of her. I will find out.

Or could Cara have been into her room, seen the note (which she was more and more certain he must have left) and confiscated it?

She jumped up from the bed, took off her coat and dropped it on a chair. She dropped her satchel on the floor and her hated school hat on top of the debris which piled another chair, and went into the kitchen.

'Has anyone been tidying my room?' she asked.

'I picked up some dirty underwear from the floor and put it in the wash,' Mrs Hendry said. 'Otherwise you'd have had no clean knickers! But as for tidying your room, I wouldn't know where to begin. It's like a rubbish tip! I don't know how you find your bed at night!'

Susan looked enquiringly at Cara.

'I haven't been near your room,' Cara said. 'Why do you ask?'

'It's nothing,' Susan replied evasively. 'I thought I left a library book on the dressing table. I must have left it at school.'

'Sit down and get your tea,' Mrs Hendry said.

Susan doubted she'd be able to eat a thing. Her appetite was quite gone, but at the sight of the spread on the table she persuaded herself to change her mind. It was a great strain playing Portia. She had to keep up her strength.

'We're all coming to see you in the play,' David said. 'Even Grandma's coming!'

'I wouldn't miss it for all the tea in China,' Mrs Hendry said.

'It's a pity Johann can't go,' David said.

'It is,' Cara agreed. 'But someone has to look after the animals.'

'I know,' David said. 'If Kit had still been here, he'd have gone to the play. I'm sure he would.'

Cara wanted to scream. Why must every conversation with the children include Kit Marsden?

But David's remark lit a new lamp of hope for Susan. Kit knew about the play. She'd told him about it when she'd been picked for the part. It was almost certain, therefore, that he'd come!

'And Mam is going to the Farmers' Ball,' David announced.

With a piece of gingerbread halfway to her mouth, Susan stopped and stared.

'The Farmers' Ball?'

It was the dream of her life – well, next to playing Portia on the West End stage – to go to the Farmers' Ball.

'Yes,' Cara said. 'I'm going with the Fawcetts – and Grandma and Grandpa Dunning are joining us.'

'Oh, can I go?' Susan begged. 'Oh, Cara, please, *please*!'

'I'm sorry, love. You're too young,' Cara said sympathetically. 'When you're sixteen you can go.'

'But I *look* sixteen,' Susan said. 'Everyone says I do!'

Yes you do, Cara thought. Every day of sixteen, if not more. And so pretty. In a year or two her stepdaughter would be the belle of the ball.

'Not this year, love. I'm really sorry. Now if you've finished your tea would you like me to hear your lines? We can do it in the parlour. I lit a fire earlier on.'

'Oh, all right,' Susan conceded. 'But I do think it's quite stupid that I can't go.'

When they were settled in the parlour, Susan said:

'We'll do the bit where Bassanio chooses the casket. I keep getting it wrong. Here it is.' She pointed out the page. 'Give me the cue.'

'Right! "But let me to my fortune and the caskets,"' Cara read.

'"Away then, I am locked in one of them,"' Susan began – then hesitated.

'"If you do love me you will find me out,"' Cara prompted.

'Oh yes! "If you do love me you will find me out,"' Susan proclaimed.

The words hit her with a sudden force. Wasn't it a message straight from the gods? Of course! It was exactly what he *would* do. Kit would be at the play, she was certain of it. And not only did she want to see him, she wanted him to see *her*, up there on the stage. When he saw her as Portia he wouldn't think she was too young, even if he did now.

'As well we're not busy on the farm,' Cara said to her mother-in-law when the weekend was over. 'I've spent most of the last two days listening to Susan's lines. And it'll be the same next weekend. But she really is good, you know!'

The performance, two weeks later, was quite splendid. As the final curtain descended, the applause rang around the packed school hall.

'I thought Susan was the best of all,' David said loyally, clapping until his hands were red.

From what could be heard on all sides that seemed to be the general opinion, and when the cast took the curtain call there were cries of 'Portia! Portia!' from the audience. After a moment or two Miss Ellwood, the headmistress, who had also produced the play, gave Susan a gentle push forward to take the call on her own. As she stepped to the front the applause swelled.

'She was very good,' Mrs Hendry said with satisfaction. 'I can't say I understood every word, but our Susan was very good!'

When the final curtain fell a flushed Susan rushed backstage. There were to be light refreshments in the dining room for all who wanted them. If Kit had attended the play, he'd have stayed to see her. She hadn't seen him, but then while the play was on she hadn't thought of him. She'd been Portia, not Susan Hendry. It was better than being Susan Hendry.

231

'Remember,' Miss Ellwood called out, 'no girl is to leave this room with her make-up on. It is *most* unprofessional to appear in public wearing stage make-up!'

There were moans and groans from the cast. They longed to be seen in the full glory of their make-up. Susan looked at herself in a corner of the crowded mirror and sighed at the thought that Kit couldn't see her like this. On the other hand, if it was unprofessional, then for the sake of her career she wouldn't do it.

She creamed and wiped her face as quickly as possible, and went out to join her audience.

There was no sign of Kit in the crowded room, though she could see her family in the far corner. She crossed towards them, looking all the time for Kit.

'It was wonderful!' Cara said enthusiastically. 'You did *so* well. And you didn't forget a single word. I told you you wouldn't!'

'I was quite proud of you,' Mrs Hendry said.

'Thank you. Thank you very much,' Susan said. She was touched and pleased by her family's appreciation. All the same, she wanted to find Kit.

'Have you seen Kit?' she asked David, trying not to sound too eager.

'No. Is he here?'

'I thought he might be,' she said. 'Have *you* seen him?' she asked Cara.

'No. I don't think he's here.'

I would have known if he was here, she thought. I wouldn't have needed to see him. I would just have known.

Susan was about to break away – to go in search of him, Cara guessed – when Miss Ellwood joined them. She put an arm around Susan's shoulders, thus rooting her firmly to the spot.

'So what do you think of our Portia?' she asked.

'We thought she did very well,' Cara said. 'We're proud of her.'

'So you should be,' Miss Ellwood said. 'She was magnificent! She's very young to play such a part – indeed it isn't a play I'd choose for schoolgirls, but everyone else wanted it. However, she handled it with a fair degree of maturity, wouldn't you say?'

'I certainly would,' Cara agreed.

'Well, Mrs Hendry, I hope you're not going to allow this talent to go to waste,' Miss Ellwood said briskly. 'It should be nurtured and trained.'

It was such a pity about the girl's father, she thought. The step-mother looked far too young to deal with a girl as high-spirited as Susan. But she'd been determined to talk to Mrs Hendry who, she suspected, didn't recognize the kind of talent she was dealing with.

232

'I want to do the best I can for Susan,' Cara said quietly. 'As I do for all the children.'

'Of course! But with respect, Mrs Hendry, it's Susan who has the need right now. Your other children, I'm sure, will get their turn.'

Cara turned to her stepdaughter.

'Susan, love, I think you and David should take Grandma and find her a cup of tea and a sandwich, while I talk to Miss Ellwood.'

'But Cara . . .' Susan protested.

Miss Ellwood's words were music to her ears. She wanted to go on listening.

'I think that would be a good idea,' Miss Ellwood said firmly. 'Mrs Hendry, perhaps you and I would find my office a better place for this conversation. There's too much going on here.'

'I'm going to be quite direct,' Miss Ellwood said five minutes later in her robust voice. 'I hope you won't mind.'

She was a tall, broad-shouldered woman, with her greying hair scraped back from her face in an old-fashioned bun. Seated behind her large desk, with Cara placed in front of it, she seemed more imposing than ever. Except that I've been offered a chair, Cara thought, I feel like a delinquent schoolgirl hauled up for a wigging from the Head.

'Not at all,' Cara said. 'Naturally, I want to do the very best I can for Susan. But she's not . . .'

'She's not an easy child,' Miss Ellwood said. 'Yes, I know.'

'She's not had an easy life,' Cara said. 'To lose both one's parents in tragic accidents is dreadful. And a stepmother can never be the same.'

'I dare say not. But I'm pleased to see you have some understanding,' Miss Ellwood said, softening a little.

'I try,' Cara said. 'I don't always succeed.'

Miss Ellwood leaned forward and gazed intently at Cara.

'Mrs Hendry, let's get down to brass tacks, shall we? I have to tell you frankly that Susan is wasting her time here. She is frittering away an important part of her life which will never come again. She doesn't work unless she really wants to, which isn't often. She's insubordinate – oh, never with me of course! Some of the staff find her extremely difficult and she does *not* have a good influence on her classmates. She is not only wasting her own time, she is wasting everyone else's.'

'I'm terribly sorry to hear that,' Cara said.

'But not entirely surprised, I dare say. In fact I've been on the point, more than once, of asking you to remove her from my school. That's not a thing I do lightly, but I have to think of others, teachers and pupils, and Susan is disruptive.'

'Oh please, Miss Ellwood!'

A huge wave of helplessness swept over Cara. She felt drowned in it. I've failed, she thought. I've tried so hard, I've even learned to love Susan, but I've failed her. Oh Edward, I'm sorry!

Miss Ellwood held up her hand.

'Don't worry, Mrs Hendry. I'm not going to do that, not yet anyway. I see Susan as needing support, and unless things get too difficult I promise you I won't withdraw mine. Susan is a clever child. Sometimes she can be a surprisingly nice child. Perhaps child is the wrong word. In some ways she's mature. For instance . . .' Miss Ellwood hesitated, her cheeks reddened. 'I have reason to believe, from what she is reported as saying to the other girls, that she is sexually mature beyond her years. But that isn't what I want to talk about.'

'She's romantic,' Cara said. 'I think that's all.'

Miss Ellwood dismissed the subject with a nod.

'The thing is, Mrs Hendry, that Susan has needs which this school cannot supply. Only you can help her fulfil them.'

'What does she need?' Cara asked.

'She needs a purpose – and she doesn't see it here. She needs to use her very real talent so that it absorbs all her energies, and in that she's frustrated. In short, Mrs Hendry, send her to stage school! Let her try out her talent!'

'Stage school?'

'There's a very good one in Manchester. The Magda Dale School. A percentage of the pupils are boarders, but that would be all right with Susan, she's a boarder here. Or if you happen to have friends in Manchester she could live out, in approved lodgings.'

'I'm not sure . . .'

It wasn't the first time stage school had been mentioned. Susan had been on about it for some time. And I dismissed it as a childish fancy, Cara chided herself. But now, with Miss Ellwood spelling it out, it took on a new significance.

'Would it be expensive?' she asked. 'I have limited means.'

Miss Ellwood shrugged.

'It depends what price you put on a child's future. No money is better spent than on education and training.'

'I agree,' Cara said. 'If you happen to have the money in the first place.'

'There are a few scholarships each year,' Miss Ellwood added. 'Susan might well win one, if not in the first year then in the second or third.'

'But I couldn't rely on that,' Cara said.

'I'll give you the address of the Magda Dale and you can send for a prospectus,' Miss Ellwood said. 'References will be required if you make an application, and I shall be pleased to supply one.'

'Thank you. I'll send for details,' Cara said. She felt as though she had been swept along by a rushing tide.

Miss Ellwood rose to her feet. Clearly, the interview was over.

'Good!' she said. 'And I do urge you, for Susan's sake, to give this matter serious thought.'

'Oh I will,' Cara promised. 'I will!'

When she rejoined her family the dining hall was almost empty. Mrs Hendry, Susan and David sat at a small table, awaiting her.

'We didn't find Kit,' David said at once.

'Kit? Did you expect to?'

'Susan did,' he replied. 'We looked everywhere but we didn't find him.'

'Shut up, will you!' Susan said fiercely.

I understand how she feels, Cara thought. Poor Susan! But she'll grow up, she'll meet someone else. She'll forget she ever knew Kit Marsden. Could that be said of me?

'I'll be glad to be off, Cara love,' Mrs Hendry said. 'It's been a lovely evening and a rare treat, but I'm a bit tired now.'

'I'm sorry, Grandma,' Cara said. 'I'll bring the car around to the front door. I'll be there in ten minutes and we'll be home in less than an hour.'

'So what did Miss Ellwood want?' Susan asked as Cara drove back to Arendale.

'She suggested that perhaps you should go to stage school,' Cara told her.

The yell of surprise from Susan almost caused Cara to swerve into the hedge.

'She also said that you didn't work hard, you were insubordinate and – what was the word? – disruptive!'

'Oh Cara, I wouldn't be any of those things if I went to stage school!' Susan cried. 'I'd work like a demon, honest I would! Please Cara, *please*!'

'It would also cost money,' Cara said. 'As yet I don't know how much. A scholarship would make all the difference.'

'Indeed yes,' Mrs Hendry agreed. 'But you've got to tell her whether or not she can apply.'

'I said I'd send for the prospectus. The Magda Dale School in Manchester. We can't decide anything until we have that.'

'Will you write tonight?' Susan begged.

'No, but I'll write tomorrow.'

'Cara, you're an angel! When do you think we'll get a reply?'

'Not for several days, I imagine. You'll have to possess your soul in patience.'

If Susan went to stage school, Cara wondered, would it help to take her mind off Kit Marsden? Not that that was a good enough reason for sending her. There had to be more to it than that.

The following day she wrote the letter and Susan, not content to wait for the postman to call at Beckwith, cycled into Faverwell to take it to the post office. The prospectus arrived by return of post. Reading it through, Cara was impressed by the curriculum it offered, but dismayed by the fees.

'Take a look,' she said, handing the brochure to Mrs Hendry. 'It sounds very good, very comprehensive, but I just don't think we can manage the fees.'

When she had studied it Mrs Hendry said: 'Well somehow, love, we've got to! This is just the thing for Susan. Stage management, lighting, costume, speech, acting, auditions, radio . . . Good gracious! I never knew there was so much to it! Once she sees this it'll break her heart if you refuse. We could scrimp and save, cut down.'

'How?' Cara demanded. 'The main thing we spend money on is the animals. We can't cut down on them. And you know I've planned to buy a tractor. I don't want to use my tractor money. We need it badly, to save labour.'

'I know,' Mrs Hendry said. 'Well, I've got fifty pounds. You can have that and welcome. I reckon it would be money well spent.'

'Oh, Mother Hendry, how could I take it?' Cara said gently.

'It's not for you,' Mrs Hendry pointed out. 'It's for my granddaughter. If I want to spend what I have on my granddaughter, who's to say I shouldn't? It won't go far, but it'll help. Of course I'd have nothing left for David.'

'David will have the farm,' Cara said. 'Eventually, that is. But as Miss Ellwood said, Susan's need is now. Anyway, I'll think it over between now and Friday. I think I'll have to tell Susan then, one way or another.'

The following day's post brought her dress from Akersfield. It had been skilfully and carefully altered, the sleeves taken out and the neck lowered, and seemed quite perfect.

'I'd best take it to the dyer's right away,' Cara said. 'The ball is on Friday week.'

'Aren't you going to try it on first?' Mrs Hendry asked.

'No. I'm sure it'll be all right.'

The truth was, she couldn't bear to put it on yet again, she didn't want to see herself in it. The sight of it, in its pristine whiteness, both saddened and reproached her. She fervently hoped that by the time it was dyed it would be so changed as to hold no reminders of its original purpose, though she supposed that was too much to hope for. Not for the first time, she wondered whether she had been right in agreeing to go to the ball.

'Come to Shepton with me,' she said to Mrs Hendry. 'The change will do you good. And you can help me choose the colour for my dress.'

'What about Emily?'

'We'll take her with us. We'll put her pushchair in the car. She's never been to Shepton.'

'Right then, I will,' Mrs Hendry said. 'I wouldn't mind seeing the shops.'

'Can you be ready in half an hour?' Cara asked.

'Five minutes, love! Just watch me!'

In Shepton the two of them looked through the swatch of materials in the dyer's shop.

'I can't decide between the midnight blue and the green,' Cara said. 'What do you think?'

'Most definitely the green,' Mrs Hendry said. 'You'll look a treat in that.'

'Let's go for a coffee,' Cara suggested when they left the dyer's. 'If we can find a place we can take the pushchair in.'

The thought of how to scrape together enough money to send Susan to stage school was never far from Cara's mind these days. As they sat in one of Shepton's many cafés, she returned to the subject.

'All I can think of so far,' she said, 'is to sell a couple of cows.'

'I'm not so sure about that,' Mrs Hendry said dubiously. 'Tom never liked selling stock, and we don't have much of a herd as it is.'

'I know,' Cara agreed. 'I just don't know what else to do.'

'Which would you part with?' Mrs Hendry asked, unwrapping the two small sugar lumps which had arrived with the coffee. She looked at them with disgust before dropping them into her cup.

'Here, you can have my sugar,' Cara offered. 'I can take it or leave it in coffee.'

Mrs Hendry sighed.

'I wish I could. Sugar's about the only rationing that worries me. I wish I hadn't such a sweet tooth. Which cow would you part with?' she repeated.

'I don't know,' Cara admitted. 'Not Marigold or Daisy, that's for sure.' She would hate to see any of them go, but those two were special.

'There'll be something to come from next summer's shearing,' she went on. 'But I can't be sure how much I'll be able to spare. Of course, we shan't need the money until the end of the summer, when the first term's fees have to be paid, but I reckon Susan should have her answer this weekend.'

'Oh yes,' Mrs Hendry agreed. 'You've got to tell her whether or not she can apply.'

'What I don't want to do,' Cara said, 'is break into my tractor money.

I'm saving hard for that and I want to order it before too long. If you want a new one you have to go on a waiting list.'

They left the café and walked around the market, Cara manoeuvring the pushchair over the cobbles. She found herself wondering all the time whether Kit Marsden was in the town, whether at any moment he might materialize in front of them.

As they passed the Ewe, at the bottom end of the market, she watched the entrance, hoping he might walk in or out. She longed to go in and enquire about him, but with what excuse? Oh, God, why can't I just forget him? she asked herself angrily.

'I said, is there anything else we need?'

Cara knew by her mother-in-law's voice that it wasn't the first time she'd asked the question.

'I'm sorry! No, I don't think so. Shall we go back to the car?'

'Well all right, but if we see a queue on the way, we'll join it,' Mrs Hendry said. 'You never know what you'll get!'

To Mrs Hendry's disappointment they didn't meet with one. Queueing, which to most women was a daily drudgery, was to her an exciting novelty. Living at Beckwith, she seldom went shopping.

Driving back, Cara deliberately pushed Kit Marsden out of her mind and concentrated on the problem of Susan. Money, or rather the lack of it, was a pest. She would like just to get on with the farming, not to spend her time worrying about profit and loss.

On Friday morning Grant Fawcett telephoned.

'I have to go to Faverwell again this afternoon,' he said. 'Would you like me to pick up Susan and David?'

'This is getting to be as regular as a taxi service,' Cara said. 'But yes, I'd be grateful. I have a load of paperwork I'd like to get to.'

It was a chilly November day, with a drizzly mist, not quite rain, not quite fog, which blacked out the hills and drained whatever colour there was from the landscape, leaving it a dull grey. It wasn't a day for working out of doors. Johann, taking advantage of the poor weather, had embarked straight after breakfast on his programme of whitewashing the insides of the farm buildings.

'That young man's being very obliging these days,' Mrs Hendry remarked as Cara put down the receiver.

'He's a good neighbour,' Cara said. 'He has been ever since he came to Fawcett's.'

'Yes, well, folks can do with good neighbours when they live in a place like Arendale,' Mrs Hendry said. 'You never know when you'll need 'em.'

At teatime Susan burst into the house like a tornado.

'Has it come?' she cried. 'Where is it? Let me look!'

238

'Yes, it came. Don't you want your tea first? You have all weekend to look at it,' Cara teased.

'Oh Cara, don't keep me in suspense! Where is it?'

'On the sideboard.'

'What's all the excitement about?' Grant enquired.

'I sent for a prospectus for the Magda Dale Stage School,' Cara explained. 'Susan might, just *might*, go there. Nothing's decided but that's what all this is about.'

Susan, still wearing her hat and coat, was absorbed in the brochure. Gasps of delight came from her as she turned the pages.

'Oh, but this is wonderful!' she exclaimed eagerly.

'Look at the last page where it mentions the fees,' Cara said drily. 'That's not quite so wonderful.'

She turned to Grant.

'You don't suppose your uncle would like to buy a couple of cows from me, do you? They're good milkers.'

'It's like that, is it?' Grant asked.

'It's like that.'

'I'll sound him out, let you know.'

'If he happens to want them it would save me taking them to market. I don't like people seeing me selling off stock,' Cara said.

'I'll let you know. In the meantime, roll on next Friday. Are you all ready for the ball?'

'Not yet, but I will be,' Cara promised.

When Grant had left she turned to Susan.

'Well, young lady?'

Susan bounded across the kitchen and flung her arms around her stepmother.

'Oh Cara! Cara, please say I can go! *Please!*'

Cara looked at Susan's eager face, her bright, shining eyes. How terrible, she thought, that I have the power to wipe that happiness from her face! How terrible the power one person can have over another. But it wasn't a power she was going to use; quite the contrary. She had decided days ago, perhaps from the moment she had walked out of Miss Ellwood's study, that Susan should have her chance. If in the end it meant that she must use the tractor money, then so be it. Susan was more important.

'Yes love, you can go! If they'll have you, of course! We'll have to send off the application form and see what happens.'

To everyone's astonishment, Susan burst into noisy tears. It was a rare sight.

'Oh Cara, it's wonderful!' she sobbed. 'How can I thank you!' Every harsh thought she had ever entertained about her stepmother vanished into thin air in the joy of this moment.

'I can tell you that,' Cara said. 'You can thank me – *and* your grandma – because she's had a part in this – by working really hard for the rest of the time you're at school here. It's important. I know Miss Ellwood will *want* to give you a good reference, but you'll have to earn it. It's not enough to do well in the end-of-term play. You must really settle down at school for the next two terms.'

'Oh I will, I will,' Susan promised. 'I'll work every hour God sends!'

'Don't be too rash,' Cara said, smiling at Susan. She handed her a handkerchief. 'Here, dry your eyes and blow your nose!'

'I'm so happy!' Susan said.

'I don't know why you're crying if you're happy,' David said.

'She's crying *because* she's happy,' Mrs Hendry told him wiping a tear from her own eye with the corner of her apron. 'It's what women do.'

'Well, it's daft!' David said.

'So we'll fill in the form this weekend,' Cara said to Susan. 'Then you can take it to Miss Ellwood on Monday morning, with a letter from me. There's a place she has to sign before it's posted. I know she'll be pleased, but don't be surprised if she gives you a good talking-to.'

'I shan't mind in the least,' Susan said. 'I shan't mind *anything* now.'

For the day of the ball Cara had booked an appointment with Miss Eva Pinckney who, in the front room of her Faverwell cottage, permed and snipped and waved those ladies of the district who, while still wishing to look good, had neither the time nor the inclination to go to Shepton.

'She's not exactly Paris or London, or even Leeds,' Cara said to her mother-in-law as she was about to set off. 'But she's not bad. And I can't remember when I last went to the hairdresser, so it'll be a treat anyway.'

'I expect you're going to the Farmers' Ball. All my ladies today are going to the ball,' Miss Pinckney said. 'Do you want a bit off the length?'

'Yes I am. And no, I'll keep the length. I thought I'd have it put up at the back if you can manage it.'

'Lovely,' Miss Pinckney said. 'What colour is your dress?'

'Emerald green. A rather dark emerald.'

'Oh my! Emerald green and red hair. How striking!'

'I wonder if it isn't a bit obvious,' Cara confessed. 'But it's too late now.'

'There!' Miss Pinckney said an hour later. Her eyes, meeting Cara's in the mirror, were filled with admiration. 'I reckon that's lovely, though I say it as shouldn't. You'll be the belle of the ball, Mrs Hendry.'

It was obvious from the look he gave her when he called for her, and saw her standing there in the dress, that Grant was equally admiring.

'You look . . . breathtaking!' he said.

'She's come up a treat,' Mrs Hendry declared.

'Oh, Mother Hendry, you make me sound like a sponge cake,' Cara said, laughing.

'You would look very good on the stage,' Susan said. It was the highest praise she could offer. She still wished she was going to the ball, but for the past week the thought of the stage school had sustained her through all other disappointments, even the inexplicable silence of Kit Marsden.

The ball was being held at the Golden Pheasant, Shepton's largest hotel. Its pride was its real ballroom, with a high moulded ceiling picked out in gold, and a sprung maple floor, claimed to be the best in the North of England. Regular patrons swore that as the evening went on and the dancing became more vigorous you could feel the floor move beneath your feet like a trampoline.

On the large stage a five-piece band, banked by a lavish display of chrysanthemums and assorted greenery, played all the latest hits for dancing.

'This is very posh!' Cara said as she foxtrotted with Grant. 'I was too young to go to anything like this before the war, and this is my first time since.'

She looked around with appreciation. The women's dresses, most of them now full-skirted, and cut low, were incredibly smart, as though clothing coupons and shortages didn't exist, and never had. The men were, if anything, more miraculous in that most of them were in tails or dinner jackets, dug out of pre-war wardrobes, newly bought, or even hired. Except for the healthy outdoor colour of their skins, which couldn't be disguised, they didn't look the least bit like a crowd of farmers.

'You dance very well,' she said to Grant. She hadn't expected it. 'Do you like dancing?'

'Love it,' he said. 'I could dance all night.'

'So could I.'

'Then I hope you'll dance with me most of the night.'

'We'll have to see. I don't want to monopolize you.' She didn't expect many invitations to dance. She hardly knew anyone here, except that she recognized some of the men from having seen them at the market.

'I'd be more than happy to monopolize you,' Grant said.

A little later she waltzed with her father, who looked splendid, while Grant took her mother around the floor. The older Fawcetts had elected not to dance, but to sit and watch.

'Except for the last waltz,' Mrs Fawcett insisted. 'I must have the last waltz with Joseph.'

The supper refreshments, like the clothes, gave the lie to rations. They were lavish. No-one asked how or why.

They were still at the supper table, Cara talking to her mother, when a man's voice said 'Good evening, Mrs Hendry!' Cara looked up and saw Ralph Benson.

'May I have the pleasure?' he requested.

'And may I tell you,' he said, the minute they started to dance, 'that you look ravishing?'

'Thank you,' Cara said. 'I was surprised to see you. I didn't think of anyone coming from Nidderdale.'

'Oh, there's quite a party of us,' he said.

'Is your wife here?'

'I'm not married. Or not any longer. My wife died two years ago.'

'I'm sorry.'

'So you see, I know what it's like. But I'm glad to see you looking better than when I saw you last, at the market. Which brings me to the question, when am I going to get your ewes for overwintering? It's about time.'

'I know,' Cara said. 'But if you are to have them I'll have to take you up on your offer of a low price. It's just been decided that my stepdaughter's to go to stage school and I shall have to find the money for that.'

'As I told you, you can just pay me the cost of their keep,' Ralph Benson said. 'I don't go back on my word. I'll tell you what, I'll come over to Beckwith one day next week – say Wednesday – and we'll sort it out. Then I'll send one of my men to bring them over. How will that do?'

'Splendid,' Cara agreed. 'I'm most grateful.'

'And since we've spent most of this dance talking shop, which wasn't at all what I had in mind,' he said, 'I'll expect you to give me at least one more dance later on.'

She danced the next few dances with Grant. He could do anything, any step, and with no more than the lightest touch he could indicate where she should follow. They didn't talk. He held her close and they moved as if the two of them were one. She gave herself up to the music and the rhythm, feeling as if she was floating in time and space, happier than she had been for a long time.

'That was wonderful,' she said when the music stopped.

'For me too,' Grant said. 'And I don't just mean the dancing, Cara.'

242

She wished he hadn't said that. She had known, before Edward had died, that Grant was too fond of her. Since then she had seen his feelings grow. Everything would be so easy, she thought, if she could fall in love with Grant; so convenient, so *right*. But she couldn't. He was a dear friend and that was all. She didn't want to lead him into thinking anything else.

'Oh dear, a Paul Jones,' she said as the band struck up again. 'I hate the Paul Jones.'

'Then let's sit it out,' Grant suggested. 'Let's find a quiet corner.'

'Oh no!' Cara said quickly. 'We mustn't be anti-social! Think of all those ladies out there, dying to dance with you!'

Reluctantly, they joined the two circles.

But when the music changes, she thought, I shall sneak away to the cloakroom. Anything to miss the Paul Jones. In the confusion of matching up partners a few minutes later, she slipped away from the ballroom. I've left some poor man without a partner, she thought remorsefully.

To reach the cloakroom she had to cross the hotel's large entrance hall, towards the rear. It was there that she came face to face with Kit Marsden.

She froze to the ground. So did he, except that he swayed a little on his feet. He had obviously come from one of the hotel's bars. The fumes of beer and whisky hung around him like a cloud.

He stared her in the face for a second, his eyes meeting hers, then his gaze swept her from head to foot, lingering deliberately on the low-cut neck of her gown which revealed the curve of her breasts. He lifted his eyes to her face again.

'Very nice!' he said. 'Very nice indeed!'

His voice was full of the mocking tone she knew so well. She felt weak and trembling at the sight of him, and at the same time furiously angry at the way he was looking at her.

'Good evening, Kit,' she said. She marvelled at the steadiness of her tone, when her mind and body were in turmoil.

'Good evening, Cara!' he replied formally. 'May I have the pleasure of this dance?'

Before the words were out of his mouth he had stepped forward and taken her in his arms, and to the strains of the music which could be heard from the ballroom, he whirled her down the long hall. She had no choice but to go with him. The half-dozen people in the hall stepped aside, laughing, as the couple moved swiftly forward.

'Stop it!' Cara said furiously. 'Let me go at once!'

'Oh no!' Kit said. 'The band's still playing and I'm enjoying this. Tell me, do you come here often?'

'I wouldn't have come near if I'd known I'd meet you! Now stop fooling and let me go! Everyone's looking at us.'

'And if I may say so, you're well worth looking at, my love,' he said. He held her tighter now, so that however she struggled, she couldn't get away. With clenched fists she began to pummel him on the chest.

'Let me go!' she cried. 'Let me go!'

It was then that one of the onlookers came to her aid, a tall, heavy-set man, who stood in their way.

'Is this man annoying you, madam?' he asked.

'Go away! Go and mind your own business!' Kit said thickly.

'Not unless the lady tells me to,' the man said.

'Let me go,' Cara pleaded quietly with Kit. 'We don't want a scene.'

His answer was to hold her closer than ever, so that her body was crushed against his. The man seized Kit by the shoulders and jerked him away. Kit swerved around, swiped at the man with a clenched fist, and missed, staggering into the wall.

Cara escaped, and ran to the cloakroom. Trembling from head to foot, she sat down in front of the mirror. A woman standing near looked at her with concern.

'Are you all right, love?'

'Yes thank you. I felt a bit faint. It's hot in the ballroom.' She felt sick.

Yet also, to her disgust, she knew that she had enjoyed being held in Kit Marsden's arms, that the feel of his body against hers had been exciting. Even while she'd struggled for freedom she'd known that with part of her she never wanted to be free.

SEVENTEEN

The telephone rang.

'Don't answer it!' Susan begged. 'Let Grandma! If we don't set off we'll miss the train!'

Cara had already picked up the receiver.

'Of course we won't,' she said. 'Arendale two seven two. Oh, hello Ralph!'

'It's Mr Benson,' she told Susan. 'I won't be long.'

Susan gave a groan of despair.

Cara listened, then said, 'Well as a matter of fact, it's not convenient. I'm just setting off for Manchester, with Susan. She's got an interview at the Magda Dale. Yes, she's very excited. I think she'll probably explode. But if you happen to be this way next week . . .? Wednesday, then. Must go now!'

'He wanted to meet me for lunch tomorrow, in Shepton,' she said, replacing the receiver. 'He wants to discuss about the ewes coming back to Beckwith.'

'And of course he couldn't do that on the phone, could he?' Mrs Hendry said gravely.

Cara gave her a quick look.

'It's all right,' Mrs Hendry said. 'I was only teasing. He's a nice man, Ralph Benson.'

'I'm only having lunch with him, to talk business,' Cara protested.

'Oh aye, I know,' Mrs Hendry said.

Susan broke in impatiently.

'Cara, if we don't go now I just *know* we'll miss the train. Johann's been waiting in the car for the last ten minutes.'

'I suppose, in the circumstances, it's too much to ask you not to fuss?' Cara said. 'Anyway, I'm ready.'

Susan had been fussing ever since the letter had arrived, fixing the interview and an audition. She had posted her application in December, bitten her nails through Christmas and the New Year, until she'd heard that she'd be sent for in March, when the interviews were to take place for admission in the following September. As far as Susan was concerned, time had stood still for the last two months or more.

'We're off then, Grandma. We'll be back tomorrow afternoon.'

Mrs Hendry, unusually for her, took Susan in her arms and gave her a hug and a kiss.

'I wish you luck, love. Don't be nervous. Just do your best and I'm sure you'll be all right.'

'Thanks, Grandma,' Susan said. She was nervous already. By the time of the interview she knew she'd be a quivering jelly.

Johann drove them to the station in late March sunshine which lit up the pearl-grey walls and intensified the green of the spring grass, the brilliance of its colour derived from the limestone landscape. February's profusion of aconites and snowdrops had given way now to early primroses, themselves heralds of the myriad wild flowers which would follow them. Fleecy clouds, chased by the wind, scudded across the sky, casting fast-moving shadows on the hillside. Those sheep which had not been sent to overwinter in Nidderdale stood out white against the lower slopes of the fells, and in the river meadow the cattle grazed on the new grass. They were two fewer now, since Joseph Fawcett had kindly bought Primrose and, at his insistence and despite Cara's reluctance, Marigold. It was not a day to be leaving the dale for the smoke and grime of Manchester, Cara thought.

Susan thought otherwise. Though she had never been to Manchester, it represented Nirvana, El Dorado, the Heavenly City. The interview was due to start at eleven o'clock and would last until teatime. When Cara had delivered Susan to the school she would go off to meet her mother – now presumably on her way from Akersfield. At teatime they would all, including Laura Dunning, meet up. The four of them were to spend the night at Laura's lodgings, which Cara was interested in seeing. There was no real need for them to stay the night, it wasn't a long journey on the train, but it was to be a treat.

'We might decide that it'd be better for you to share rooms with Laura rather than stay at the Magda Dale hostel,' Cara said as the train sped towards Manchester.

The landscape had changed soon after they'd left Shepton. Sometimes it was flatter, but always with hills in the distance; at other times the railway ran in deep cuttings between the hills. The stone of the walls and the buildings, the rocky outcrops, were no longer pale and shining. The dark millstone grit of the area was further overlaid with a black coating, carried by the west wind from the mill towns of Lancashire.

'Please don't talk as though it's a foregone conclusion that I'll even get in!' Susan said anxiously. 'I'm sure that's unlucky. It's tempting providence!' She felt in her pocket for the lucky pebble she had fished out of the river at Beckwith, taking comfort from its smooth solidity.

What would she be given for an audition, she wondered for the hundredth time? There was no question of choice; she would have to take whatever they threw at her, some of it undoubtedly with other would-be pupils. For the poem of her own choosing she had decided on a Shakespeare sonnet, just to be on the safe side. She leaned back in her seat and said the first few lines out loud.

'"How like a winter hath mine absence been
From thee! . . .
What freezings have I felt, what dark days seen . . ."'

Then she lapsed into silence, continuing the rest in her head, against the rhythm of the wheels and the noise of the steam.

And I have not seen Kit Marsden since the night of the ball, Cara thought bleakly. Neither sight nor sound, though she had been to Shepton several times. Once she had called in at the Ewe, ostensibly to ask if he had ever collected the envelope she'd left. He had, quite some time ago, the landlord said. More than once she had attended the market, mixed with the other farmers, but there had been no sign of him.

Why do I want to see him, anyway? she asked herself yet again. He is nothing but trouble, best avoided.

She had told no-one of the episode in the Golden Pheasant. When she'd returned to the ballroom the first person she'd met had been Ralph Benson, who had immediately claimed her for a dance. If he'd noticed she wasn't herself he had tactfully said nothing, and by the time she danced with Grant Fawcett again she was, to all appearances, back to normal.

She had seen Ralph Benson a few times since then. True to his promise, he had visited Beckwith in the week following the ball, and made smooth arrangements to move the ewes to Nidderdale. He had stayed to dinner, remaining long enough to make a good impression on Mrs Hendry.

'He's what I call a real man,' she'd commented after he'd gone. 'A man's man.'

'A woman's man also, I reckon,' Cara said. 'I imagine he misses his wife very much.'

No sooner had the ewes been safely transferred than a bad spell of weather set in: freezing fog and icebound roads which dislocated

247

traffic all over the region. And then in mid-December the weather changed again: the fog cleared, the ice melted, the temperature soared into the high fifties.

'Why don't you take advantage while the weather holds and drive yourself over to see my place?' Ralph Benson suggested on the telephone. 'You can take a look at your sheep, see I'm treating them right!'

Surprised at herself, she had done so. He farmed on a south-facing slope between Pateley Bridge and Harrogate. Although it wasn't a great distance from Arendale, the countryside was different: the hills high, but gentler; the valley wider. That December had been unbelievably mild, almost like late spring. She had enjoyed her solitary drive along the traffic-free roads, her tour of his farm, which was as large as Beckwith, and the substantial meal which his housekeeper had cooked for them. She'd been sorry when, in mid-afternoon, he'd said: 'I don't like to say it, but I think you'd best be going. I wouldn't want you to drive all the way in the dark.'

'I know my car is old, but it does have lights,' she said. 'But you're quite right. I should go. Thank you very much for a lovely day.'

'Promise you'll come again,' he said.

She had made the promise, but so far she hadn't kept it, though she had seen him at the market more than once.

Yes, she thought now, he was a nice man. She looked forward to seeing him next Wednesday.

Grant Fawcett had been assiduous in his attentions, telephoning or calling at Beckwith almost every day. At Christmas he had given her a beautiful brooch, an amethyst set in silver, which had belonged to his mother. Though he never put them into words, he made no secret of his feelings for her. They were obvious in all his actions. She hoped he would not put them into words. She was not ready.

The view from the train was now entirely of buildings: factories, the backs of houses, smoking chimneys, scarcely a glimpse of sky.

'We must be almost there,' Susan said.

'A couple of minutes at the most, I think.'

The principal of the Magda Dale School, Madame Simonetta, greeted Cara pleasantly, then dismissed her, together with several other parents, in a matter of minutes.

'There is no need for you to stay,' she announced. 'Your children will be better without you, and we shall look after zem well. You may collect zem at four o'clock. Please be punctual.'

She was a tall, generously proportioned woman, with hair blacker than nature had designed, parted in the centre and heavily fringed. Indeed, she was fringed all over: the hem and sleeves of her jumper, two vividly coloured scarves, and the decoration on her handbag and shoes. She spoke with a strange accent which could have come from anywhere in Europe, but included distinct sounds of Liverpool.

'Funny old bird,' a parent said to Cara as they were leaving. 'Of course, no more Madame Simonetta than you or me, dear. She's Mrs Alfred Simons, widow of the Great Alfredo, conjuror. But she's a fine teacher and she runs a good school.'

It was not far from Magda Dale to the station. Cara was there in time to meet her mother from her train.

'So what would you like to do, Ma?' she asked. 'We've got until four o'clock.'

'Oh, as it's Manchester we must look at the shops!' Mrs Dunning said without hesitation. 'Lewis's, Kendal Milne's – there's nothing like them in Akersfield!'

'Did you manage to get the theatre tickets?'

'I did. I telephoned, so we have to pick them up. Seats in the Dress Circle for *A Midsummer Night's Dream*. I hope they'll be pleased.'

It was to be a surprise. Neither of the girls had an inkling.

'Was Susan nervous?' Mrs Dunning enquired.

'As a cat,' Cara said. 'But I suppose that's no bad thing. They say anyone who's any good at acting is nervous.'

The time flew by in an orgy of pseudo-shopping, punctuated only by a Welsh rarebit in a coffee house. They viewed, priced, discussed, were dazzled by, tried on – while spending next to nothing – until it was time to collect first Laura, then Susan. Back at the Magda Dale, Cara was shown into Madame Simonetta's room, where Susan awaited her.

'She 'as done very well!' Madame Simonetta announced. 'I will allow 'er a place in my school. By the time I 'ave finished with 'er she might be an actress – but only if she works very 'ard indeed! No slacking!'

She turned to Susan.

'You promise you will work 'ard?'

'Oh yes, Madame Simonetta,' Susan said fervently.

'You 'ave all ze details,' Madame told Cara. 'Ze fees must be paid one month in advance. Lunches are extra. Will Susan be staying in ze 'ostel?'

'I'm not sure,' Cara said. 'My younger sister is studying music in Manchester and she lives in very good approved lodgings. She's well looked after. I thought Susan might join her there. I'll let you know quite soon.'

'Please do,' Madame Simonetta said. 'And we shall see Susan in September.'

'*N'est-ce pas, ma petite?*' she added, in Scouse-accented French.

Cara's impression of Laura's lodgings was a good one. She liked Mrs Hargreaves, the motherly landlady, and certainly Laura's own appearance was a tribute to her care. She looked healthier and happier than Cara had seen her for a long time. She had even put on a little weight.

'No need to tell you I'd look after Susan as if she was my own,' Mrs Hargreaves said. 'And she'd be company for Laura. They'd be company for each other.'

'May I think it over, and I'll let you know in a day or two?' Cara asked.

'Of course, love. You must do whatever's best for Susan,' Mrs Hargreaves said.

Cara and Susan discussed that, and every other facet of the previous day, on the train going home next morning.

'There's a lot to do at Magda Dale,' Susan said. 'After the first year I'll have to choose whether I want to go in for more drama, or more dancing. And what kind of dancing: tap, ballet, whatever. Oh joy!'

'It all sounds exciting,' Cara said. 'I'm so pleased for you.'

'And I'm very grateful to you,' Susan replied, serious for a moment.

'So what do you think about lodging with Laura, at Mrs Hargreaves?'

'I'd like it. I think I'd prefer it to the hostel.'

'Then we'll not choose ze 'ostel,' Cara decided. 'I expect Madame Simonetta will have to give her approval, but I see no difficulty about that.'

On the following Saturday a letter came, addressed to Susan and bearing a Manchester postmark. She took it from the postman and held it by the tips of her fingers, as if it might burn her.

'Oh Cara, what can it be?' she cried. 'I daren't open it! I just daren't!'

'Then you'll never know, will you?' Cara said. 'I expect it's just to confirm what was said the other day.'

Gingerly, as if something might jump out and bite her, Susan opened the envelope and extracted a letter. It was, as Cara had forecast, a confirmation of what Madame Simonetta had told them – until she reached the last paragraph. When she read that, Susan leapt into the air with a blood-curdling yell.

'I've done it!' she screamed. 'I've done it!'

'*What* have you done? For heaven's sake tell us!' Cara begged.

'I've won a bursary! Here, read it!'

Cara took the letter.

'The tuition fees for the first year! But that's wonderful, Susan! That's really wonderful!' She passed the letter to Mrs Hendry.

'It's a result of the audition,' Susan said. 'I was so nervous, I didn't know how I'd done. Oh, what a fantastic surprise!'

'It doesn't surprise me in the least,' Mrs Hendry declared with satisfaction. 'Not in the least! Well done, love!'

'It will make such a difference,' Cara said.

The following Wednesday Cara went into Shepton to meet Ralph Benson for lunch. She was half afraid that he might take her to the Golden Pheasant and was relieved when he said, 'I've booked a table at the Hare and Hounds. It's a bit quieter.'

'I'm going to enjoy this. It's got to be one of my last jaunts for a long time to come,' Cara said when they were seated. 'I'm going to be much too busy, and I still only have Johann. Not that he isn't worth any two other men.'

'Why didn't you hire an extra hand?' Ralph asked.

'To tell you the truth, I didn't see how I could pay for it, because of saving for Susan,' Cara admitted. 'Now that she's won the bursary, things will be easier financially. But I'll still be up to my eyes in work.'

'Come to that, so will I,' Ralph Benson said. 'Now which day shall I send the ewes over? We've already left it a bit late. Would next Monday suit?'

'Fine!' Cara said.

They lingered over the meal until they were the last people left in the dining room, and the waitress, who had already presented the bill, was hovering.

'I must get back,' Cara said.

As Ralph helped her on with her coat his hands rested for a moment on her shoulders. With her back to him, she stood perfectly still, fighting the temptation to turn around and face him. His hands slid from her shoulders, down her arms. He drew her imperceptibly closer, and she allowed it.

'When *shall* I see you again?' he asked quietly.

'I don't know.'

Gently, almost reluctantly, she eased herself out of his grasp.

'I won't let you go that easily,' he said.

She made no reply. They left the hotel and he walked back with her to where her car was parked.

'Take care of yourself,' he said.

'You too!'

'I'll be in touch,' he promised.

I'm glad I'm going to be busy, she thought as she drove home. She had had too much time to spare since the turn of the year, too much time to think and feel. She knew, from previous experience, that from now on there would be so much to do that every minute would be filled. Before long she would be grateful to crawl into bed, at whatever time the exigencies of lambing allowed, and sleep; devoid of sensation and too tired to dream.

When she walked into the kitchen at Beckwith, had she not been suddenly deprived of the power of movement, she would have turned and run out again.

Sitting on a chair drawn up to the fire, a mug of tea in his hand, was Kit Marsden. She went hot, and then cold, at the sight of him, then cursed herself and him for the power he had to make her feel like this. He put down his tea, but continued to sit there. There was no sign of Mrs Hendry and Emily.

'Please don't bother to get up,' Cara said. 'Unless you're getting up to leave.'

'I wasn't planning that,' he said amiably. 'Your ma-in-law kindly gave me a cup of nice strong tea and a curd tart. She's taken Emily to the bathroom.'

'You have an infinite capacity for turning up out of the blue,' Cara said. 'Not to mention disappearing in a similar fashion. Can I be the only one who finds it irritating?'

'The thing is,' Kit said, 'I tend to turn up when I'm needed. It's a gift the gypsies have.'

'Well, I don't need you and I don't want you,' Cara said harshly. 'I suggest you go. I'll make your farewells to my mother-in-law.'

'Oh, I couldn't leave without a word to her,' Kit said. 'Mrs Hendry has always treated me well. Anyway, I don't believe you.'

He got up, slowly, and came and stood close in front of her, his eyes searching hers. She was angry with herself that she had no power to turn away from him. If he so much as touched her, she would crumple.

'I reckon you both need me *and* want me,' he said.

'You're a poor judge of character,' Cara said. 'As I once was, but not any longer!'

'Anyway,' he said, 'your ma-in-law says you're going to be desperate for help on the farm. So I'm your man!'

'You are *not* my man!' Cara retorted. 'I'm not that desperate!'

'Oh, come on, Cara,' he said with a change of tone. 'You know what lambing time's like. How can you and the Kraut manage that lot between you?'

'I'll thank you not to refer to Johann in that manner!' Everything he said rubbed her up the wrong way, yet, even while telling him to leave, she had this insane desire to keep him talking, not to let him go.

'I beg your pardon! Herr Johann Eisl!' Kit said with mock solemnity. 'And how is the Kraut?'

'Still worth ten of you!' she snapped.

He shrugged.

'Possibly. But not when it comes to work. You know as well as I do that you'll not find a harder worker than me. You'd be daft not to

252

employ me. Besides, I'm neat and clean in my habits, and if it suits you I'll speak only when I'm spoken to!'

'Why can't you be serious?' Cara demanded.

He looked at her for a moment without speaking, then said:

'All right. I'll be serious, if that's what you want. I came because I *had* to see you. I couldn't keep away any longer. Perhaps you don't need me, perhaps you don't want me, Cara Hendry – but I need you, and I want you. Is that serious enough for you?'

Mrs Hendry walked into the room, holding Emily by the hand.

'I didn't hear you come in, love,' she said to Cara. 'Have you been here long?'

'Only a minute or two,' Cara said. It seemed like hours.

'And what about this one?' Mrs Hendry went on, indicating Kit. 'I told him, he turns up like a bad penny!'

'I couldn't have put it better,' Cara said.

'But he seems to know just when to turn up,' Mrs Hendry said. 'I reckon he has second sight.'

'You know I have,' Kit said. 'So what about it? Do I stay or don't I?'

'Don't be daft! Of course you do!' Mrs Hendry said before Cara could speak.

He turned to Cara, a smile of satisfaction on his face.

'So?'

'Until the end of the lambing only.'

Her mother-in-law had no business to make the decision, and it was unlike her to do so. But to Mrs Hendry it would be common sense. She knew how much he was needed on the farm. As for me, Cara thought, where would I find the strength to send him away?

'It's nice to be welcome,' Kit said. 'Same arrangements as before?'

'I'll look to your room,' Mrs Hendry said. 'I'll need to air the bed. It hasn't been slept in since last tupping.'

'I'm going to see Johann. Please give me a few minutes.' Cara stalked out of the house.

Johann wouldn't welcome the news, she was well aware of that, but they *did* need help. However willing Johann was, there were limits for both herself and him, to time and strength.

'I know how you feel about Kit Marsden,' she said when she had located Johann. 'I don't blame you. But please try.' She didn't need to add 'for my sake'. He would do it for that reason only.

'I think I'll start him on the walling,' she said. 'There's still quite a bit of work to be done before we can be sure of keeping the sheep just where we want them.'

The dry-stone walls were a constant source of work and worry, not least because there was such a length of them. They climbed and crisscrossed and divided every acre of the land. Since they had been there for hundreds of years, with not an ounce of mortar in them, it was hardly surprising that there was always some part of them needing repair. The fierce weather also did its part, as did the animals themselves. They would widen the narrowest gap in no time at all.

'Before the war,' Cara told Johann, 'my father-in-law would have called in the Waller to do it. Now it's next door to impossible to find a Waller. They're a dying breed. But I suppose if we could, we'd not be able to afford him.'

She went back to the house and told Kit what she had decided.

'The in-lamb ewes will be back from Nidderdale next week,' she said. 'I'd like us to get through as much as possible before then.'

'Show me the way!' Kit said.

They walked, side by side, to the particular stretch of wall Cara thought most urgently in need of repair. Neither of them spoke, though to Cara the air between them was charged with feeling. She knew, in the marrow of her bones, that it was the same for him. Hadn't he said he needed her, wanted her?

He surveyed the broken wall and shook his head.

'It shouldn't have been allowed to get into this state.'

'Do you think I don't know?' Cara snapped. 'Johann works like a slave, but even he can't do everything. And so far I've never done walling, though I can quite see I might have to.'

'It's not woman's work,' Kit said. 'It needs brute strength as well as skill. Some of those stones weigh a ton!'

He strode around, kicking a bit of wall here and there, picking up stones and examining them.

'I reckon the foundations weren't put in properly,' he said. 'I'm going to start from the beginning, clear out this lot, give myself a space to work in. Then I shall dig out the bottoms before I lay the foundations.'

'Can you do that?' Cara asked doubtfully.

'Of course I can!'

'It's going to take a long time.'

'Do you want a good job doing, or don't you?' Kit demanded.

'I suppose I do,' Cara acknowledged. 'Shall I ask Johann to give you a hand?'

'I reckon not,' Kit said, grinning. 'We don't want to start another war, do we? But if you'd like to work with me, I'll not refuse. You could be helpful.'

She wanted to leave him, to be as remote from him as possible over the next few weeks. But stronger than that was the desire to be with him every minute. He had a power over her she could neither explain nor deny.

'What can I do?' she asked.

'You can help to sort the stones. We'll move the ones that have fallen, and take the rest down to the bottom. I'll show you the different sizes and shapes – they all have their functions – and you can put them in their categories. Don't try to move the big ones. Leave that to me.'

He picked up a stone from the heap on the ground.

'See this, for instance? This is a topping stone. You can see it's green along one surface, where the air's got at it. Topping stones aren't easy to find if we should happen to need new ones, so sort them out carefully.'

While Cara sorted and lifted, and laid the stones out on the grass, Kit began to build the wall. He was quick and deft, picking up the largest boulders as though they were no weightier than marbles and, with a sure touch, putting the stones into place in the wall. As far as it was possible, he locked them together like pieces in a jigsaw puzzle, angling them slightly upwards so that they were less likely to sink, and the 'fillings' – the small stones which he would tip down the centre of the wall after both sides had been built – would stay in place.

'Arendale stones are stinkers,' he said. 'They're about the worst you could have for building walls. So many of them are rounded boulders. Flat stones are best.'

'There are a few very big flat ones,' Cara said.

'Those are the "through" stones,' Kit explained. 'Every so often we put a stone through the whole depth of the wall, to keep it together. When you reckon that this wall is four feet through at the bottom and over two feet at the top, you can see why we need great big through stones. I hope they're all here. They're difficult to come by.'

'How do you know all this?' Cara asked. 'Where did you learn it?'

'I don't rightly know,' he admitted. 'I suppose I picked it up, here and there, as I went along.'

They worked, from then on, in near-silence, but it was a companionable silence, such as Cara had never known before with Kit Marsden. It seemed to her that every encounter to date had been antagonistic, or charged with the excitement of sexual attraction, or indeed, both. It was too much to hope that the present state would last, but for this brief period her antagonism had melted away. She felt in harmony with him; with the place, with the work they were sharing, with the whole of nature.

The sexual attraction was still there, still strong. Whenever she handed him a piece of stone, and their fingers briefly touched, a thrill ran through the whole of her body. She accepted the situation. She neither sought it, nor pushed it away. All she knew was that she wanted the afternoon to go on forever.

255

'It'll soon be dusk,' Kit said. They were the first words he had spoken for a long time.

And this will be over, Cara thought. Oh, not the wall – there were still some hours of work on that – but the perfection of the afternoon. If she helped him on the wall tomorrow, would they recapture it?

She stood upright, stretching the muscles of her back, and saw Johann, a couple of field-lengths away, making his way back to the house. Kit followed the direction of her gaze and also saw him.

'We should happen call it a day,' he suggested.

'It's not quite too dark to see. We could work a bit longer,' Cara said.

'Very well.'

They worked for a few minutes more then, as if driven by the same thought, they stood and faced each other. Neither of them spoke. There was nothing to be said. She was locked in his gaze, assaulted by the hunger in his eyes, while knowing that he must read the same message in hers.

He held out his arms and she stepped forward and went into them. He lifted her up and carried her across the stone-strewn ground to a clear place, where he laid her on the grass. She had no more resistance in her than a piece of stone he might have picked up to build the wall.

He came down on top of her, and his hands were everywhere; exploring, exciting. His kisses were fierce and demanding, and hers no less so. She felt as if she was drowning, and she had no desire to be saved, only to drift away on this tide of ecstasy.

Even so, it was she who came back to the present first. She sat up quickly, fastening the buttons of her blouse.

'We must go at once!' she said. 'It's almost dark.'

'Please, Cara! Not now!' Kit begged.

She jumped to her feet, felt the dampness from the moist ground on the back of her clothing, wondered if it was visible.

'We have to go,' she said. 'They'll wonder what's happened to us. Johann will be out with the dogs, looking for us.'

'Ah, Johann!' Kit said, recovering himself. 'Well, it would never do for Johann to see what we were up to, would it? He'd likely tan the hide off me – or try to!'

She had already set off at a run, but he caught up with her.

'Cara, listen to me,' he pleaded. 'It can't stop at this. You know that as well as I do.'

'It's got to,' Cara said in a flat voice. 'Things can't go any further. We've gone into all that before, and nothing's changed.'

'Yes it has,' he said urgently. 'I love you, damn it!'

'Oh Kit! And I love you!'

'Then how can you say nothing's changed?'

'I loved you before, though I wouldn't admit it, even to myself. But nothing else has changed. The circumstances are the same.'

They were almost back at the house.

'I've got to be alone with you,' Kit said. 'When can I see you alone, for heaven's sake?'

'I'll work on the wall with you tomorrow. I can't say any more than that just now.'

'Open to the whole of Arendale! Do you call that being alone?'

There was nothing more to be said. They were entering the house.

'We were wondering what had happened to you,' Mrs Hendry said.

'Nothing,' Cara replied, trying to sound surprised. 'We were just so busy, we didn't notice it was getting dark.'

How can I say that nothing happened, she thought, when Kit told me he loved me? She wanted to shout it out to the whole world.

Next morning they had been working together on the wall no more than a few minutes before Kit brought up the subject again.

'So I suppose, like all women, you've got terms and conditions? All right then, let's hear them!'

'I don't want to have terms and conditions,' Cara said. 'You make it sound horrible. I want to be free to do exactly what I want, but life isn't like that. At least, mine isn't. You have no ties, you're answerable to no-one. You come and go without having to give a thought to anyone else.'

'I don't believe in answering to anyone,' he said.

He picked up a large stone, examined it, and fitted it into place.

'You're conventional,' he accused her.

'I know I am. My life's a bit like that wall. It has to have a solid foundation, and all the pieces have to fit.'

'Dear God!' he exclaimed. 'Why did I have to fall in love with you?'

Or I with you, Cara thought. Grant Fawcett would have been much more suitable. But by the side of Kit Marsden, all other men paled. They were bickering, almost quarrelling, yet she felt she had never loved him more.

'Well, since we have,' Kit said, 'come on. I know what I want of you. What do you want of me?'

'Not an affair,' Cara said. 'Not here at Beckwith, not with my family around me. Not in Arendale, where everyone knows what everyone else is doing. It's not in me. Oh Kit, I love you so much, but that's impossible!'

'You mean you want marriage? That out-of-date, man-made state? Or woman-made,' he added. 'No man in his right mind wants marriage.'

'That's what I want,' Cara said. 'But not just for me. It has to be that for the sake of my family.'

Angrily, Kit threw down the stone he was holding, then turned and grasped Cara by the shoulders, his fingers digging into her flesh until she wanted to cry out.

'Then damn you, woman! I'll marry you!' he shouted.

He released her, and she stood still, staring at him.

'Do you mean that? Really mean it?'

'Damn and blast it, of course I do!'

'It's a very strange proposal,' Cara said, her voice trembling. 'But I accept it. Oh, Kit, I can't believe it!'

'All right,' he said. 'So when? It's got to be soon. I'll not wait!'

'Just a little while longer, my love. Only a little while. In a few months from now Edward will have been dead a year. Then I'll marry you, and be the proudest woman in the world to do so!'

'A few months? How can I wait a few months? Do you know what you're asking? Do you know what it's like, working here alongside you?'

'I do,' Cara said. 'Indeed I do! But you can leave when the lambing's over, and return in September. During that time I'll break the news to my family. It won't be easy for Mrs Hendry.'

'You've got it all cut and dried,' he said.

'When you come back in September we'll be married. It will be for the rest of our lives, my darling. We can surely wait a little while for that?'

EIGHTEEN

Kit Marsden and Cara Hendry were married on the third of September. It was a quiet wedding which took place, at the earliest possible time of day, in Shepton Registry Office.

'We don't want any fuss,' Kit had said.

Cara was happy to agree. There was rejoicing in her own heart, and that sufficed.

Two days earlier she had taken an incredibly excited Susan to Manchester, for the start of her first year at the Magda Dale. Cara had worried about how her stepdaughter would react to the news of her impending marriage to Kit Marsden. She had been careful not to make the announcement until a short time beforehand, reckoning that the less time she allowed for repercussions, the better.

'*You*, marry *Kit*!' Susan said. 'I don't believe it!'

'It's true,' Cara said. 'Why can't you believe it?'

'Well, because . . .' Susan floundered, searching for words. Why would he choose Cara? She'd already been married; she had a child; she was a farmer. She wasn't all *that* young. It wasn't the least bit romantic.

Cara could read Susan's thoughts. In some ways she was a transparent child.

'I'm still only twenty-three,' she said with amusement. 'A year or two younger than Kit, actually. Life isn't over for me yet, you know!'

'So what will happen here at Beckwith?' Susan wanted to know. Not that it would make much difference to her. She would be living in Manchester most of the time over the next three years. After that, who knew? She could be anywhere: on tour, playing in the West End, even abroad! There was no end to the exciting possibilities. In fact, she might never *really* live at Beckwith again, not really *live* there – though of course she would visit when her engagements allowed it.

'Kit will live here,' Cara said. 'I have no intention of leaving Beckwith, and he's happy to be here.'

'I suppose he would be,' Susan agreed. In her mind she had already relinquished Kit. She couldn't afford to be tied down.

'And you're not upset at not being here for the wedding?' Cara asked. 'It isn't easy to arrange things when we're busy on the farm.' The truth was that Kit hadn't wanted anyone at the wedding. The registrar could supply witnesses, he'd said. No-one else was necessary.

'Not a bit,' Susan said truthfully.

Then for a moment her thoughts turned away from herself.

'Cara,' she began hesitantly.

'Yes?'

'Cara, you won't forget Daddy, will you? You won't ever forget him?'

Cara took Susan's hands in her own.

'Of course I won't! I could never forget him! I loved your father very much.'

'That's all right then!'

So Susan, who Cara had thought might be the most difficult person to deal with, had proved the opposite.

Mrs Hendry had been another matter. Cara had thought it right to break the news to her early. She was the one person who shouldn't be kept in the dark, nor could Cara live in the same house with her while keeping such a secret.

'Tell her right away, while I'm here,' Kit suggested.

'No! That won't do. There are things to be said between us, things to do with Edward. It will be easier for her if you're not there.'

'Have it your own way,' Kit said. 'Mind you, you're having too much of your own way at the moment. It's got to stop when we're married!' His manner was joking, but Cara didn't miss the glint in his eye.

'Don't expect me to be a doormat,' she said, equally lightly. 'I never will be!'

The lambing had gone well. There were several pairs of twin lambs and very few mishaps. She, Kit and Johann had worked night and day. Sometimes she had wondered whether it was worth undressing for bed at all, so little time did she have for sleep, but at the end of it the sight and sound of the fields full of ewes and their lambs was a more than adequate reward.

When it was over, Kit left. The day after he'd gone, Cara broke her news to Mrs Hendry. She waited until the children were in bed and she and her mother-in-law were sitting in the kitchen, she doing the books, Mrs Hendry knitting.

Cara laid down her pen.

'Mother Hendry,' she said, 'I have something to tell you.'

'Oh yes, love?' Mrs Hendry rocked gently in her chair and continued to knit.

'Please stop knitting!' Cara said. 'This isn't easy.'

Mrs Hendry looked up swiftly, and at the sight of Cara's face she put down her work.

'What is it, love?'

As Cara told her, she watched the colour drain from the older woman's face, saw her hands gripping the wooden arms of the chair until her knuckles were white. There was a silence, then the words poured out with a passion Cara had not suspected in her mother-in-law.

'Oh no, Cara! No! Not yet! Not so soon! Oh, I know you won't want to stay single forever, I'd not expect it. And I've seen the way Grant looks at you, I've seen what's in his mind. But Edward's not been gone a year. Surely Grant will wait?'

'Mother Hendry,' Cara said gently. 'It's not Grant. Much as I like him, I don't want to marry Grant Fawcett.'

'Not Grant? Then who? Not . . .' She was about to say Ralph Benson when Cara broke in.

'Kit. Kit Marsden.'

Mrs Hendry stared at her.

'It can't be true! I don't believe it! That's a thousand times worse!'

'I thought you liked Kit,' Cara said.

'Of course I like him. But not as a husband for you. He's not right. And not as a man who'll take the place of my son!'

'He won't,' Cara said. 'Edward had a very special place in my life. No-one will ever take it, I promise you.'

'And what about the farm? What about the children?' Mrs Hendry cried. What about me? she wanted to say. What's to happen to me?

'Everything will go on just the same,' Cara assured her. 'Kit will live here. He'll help with everything on the farm, and you know what a difference that will make.'

'You don't have to marry the man just to get help on the farm!'

'I'm not doing so. I love him, Mother Hendry. Please try to understand. I love him. As for the children, they already get on well with Kit.'

'And there'll be other children,' Mrs Hendry said sharply. 'That's nature.'

In an instant, all expression left Cara's face.

'No,' she said. 'There won't be other children. Kit doesn't want children.'

It was stronger than that. When Cara had brought up the subject

261

he had adamantly refused to have children. She'd been, and inside herself still was, deeply saddened by this. She wanted his child. She told herself he would change his mind, but in her heart she knew he wouldn't.

'Things will go on just as they are,' she repeated. 'Except that Kit will live here.'

And sleep in my son's bed, with my son's wife, Mrs Hendry thought. She didn't know if she could bear it.

'Kit won't want me here,' she said.

'Oh, Mother Hendry, of course he will! I *know* he will!'

'I expect you've discussed that too,' Mrs Hendry said. 'I expect you've had a talk about what you'll do with me!'

'You're wrong, we haven't. We've taken it for granted that you'd be here, as always. Please let's not quarrel, Mother Hendry!'

'We're not quarrelling,' Mrs Hendry said. 'But nor can you take me for granted. I have to give this some thought. It's been too sudden. I had no idea this was going on, and right under my nose. I must be a blind old woman!'

Little more was said that day. The atmosphere in the house was heavy, with the two of them polite to each other, but hardly speaking. Mrs Hendry embarked on a bout of fierce cleaning of rooms which had no need of it: Cara went out on the fells, taking Emily with her.

The next morning when Cara came down Mrs Hendry was waiting for her.

'I've been thinking about all this, Cara. In fact I've thought about nothing else. I've hardly slept.'

That, Cara thought, was evident in her mother-in-law's white face; in the droop of her body, usually so straight and upright; in the lassitude of her movements. Now she *did* look an old lady.

'I shall go and stay with my cousin Bertha in Wensleydale,' Mrs Hendry announced. 'Oh, I don't plan to go for good!' she said, answering Cara's gasp of dismay. 'I'll go for a few weeks, see how it works out. I'll not desert you through the summer, I know just how much there is to do and I'll be here to help. But if you're getting married in September, I shall go at the end of August. You'll not expect me to attend the wedding. You can't expect that!'

'I understand,' Cara said. 'Oh, Mother Hendry, I shall miss you! Please don't stay away too long!'

'We shall have to see, shan't we,' Mrs Hendry said.

She could not endure the thought of being there when Kit Marsden brought his bride home. She couldn't be in the house with the newly-weds, with the man who, however much she liked him, was going to usurp her son. She was not so old that she'd forgotten what the early days of marriage were like. Tom had been an ardent lover.

262

She couldn't be in the house, in the next room, when it was happening. It was more than flesh and blood could stand.

'And there's another thing,' she continued. 'You've got to tell Grant Fawcett what you've just told me. It's only right. You know perfectly well what he thinks of you.'

'Of course I'll tell him,' Cara said. 'But not just yet. It can wait awhile.'

'No it can't!' Mrs Hendry contradicted. 'People close to you have a right to know. There's Johann also. He's worked his fingers to the bone for this family. Is he to be kept in the dark until the last minute?'

'Of course not,' Cara said. 'You're quite right. I'll tell them both – but I must find the right moment.'

'That won't be difficult,' Mrs Hendry said. 'Now that lambing's over, Grant will be here oft enough. As for Johann, you see him several times every day. There's no excuse there.'

As it happened, Grant called at Beckwith the same afternoon.

'I thought I'd come and take a look at your new lambs,' he said. 'Are you pleased with how it all went, then?'

'Very pleased,' Cara said.

They left the house and walked together to the lower fields where the ewes and lambs were folded, and where they would remain until the lambs were older. This way, both ewes and lambs could more easily be inspected every day.

'They look pretty good to me,' Grant said. 'More twins than I'd have thought.'

'Yes, we've done well this year. But Beckwith always did have its fair share of twins.'

'Any troubles?'

'Not really. We've still got one sickly lamb we're looking after in the house, but she's on the mend.'

'Well, it's good to get the lambing over,' Grant said. 'Though I don't know why I say that, because it's my favourite time of the year – on the farm, I mean. It makes everything else worthwhile. Did Marsden do a good job?'

'Very good.'

'I'm glad he's gone. He's not a man to have hanging around.' He spoke casually. Cara stood still and faced him.

'I'm sorry you feel like that, Grant,' she said quietly. 'I'm going to marry him.'

She knew her words wouldn't please him, but she was taken aback by the violence of his reaction.

'Marry Marsden! You can't! Are you out of your mind?'

This normally quiet-voiced, gentle man was red-faced and shouting. He grabbed her by the arms and thrust his face close to hers.

263

'It's not true! Tell me it's not true!'

'It *is* true,' Cara said. 'I'm going to marry Kit Marsden. Grant, I know how you feel . . .'

'You do *not* know how I feel,' he contradicted. 'You think I'm jealous, don't you? Well maybe I am, but what I feel right now has nothing to do with jealousy. It goes far beyond that. I wouldn't be exactly delighted at the thought of you marrying anyone but me – I expect you know that – but I'm appalled that it should be Kit Marsden. He's no good!'

'That's not true!' Cara said hotly. 'How can you say that? You don't know him!'

'I know enough. Ask anyone you like, you'll get the same opinion.'

'You mean the same prejudice!'

'It isn't prejudice.'

'I think it is. You're all the same here. You don't like anyone who doesn't conform. You want everyone to be the same. Well, one of the things I like about Kit is that he *doesn't* conform. He's his own man.'

'Oh, he's that all right,' Grant said bitterly. 'But he's not the man for you.'

'I think you must allow me to be the best judge of that,' Cara said.

'That's just it! You're not showing any judgement at all!'

He turned away from her, paced angrily across the field like a lion in a cage, then turned around and paced back, to face her again. Cara had never realized that there was so much anger in him; and now, seeing it released, though she wasn't pleased to be at the receiving end of it, made him suddenly more attractive, more real.

'Cara, think again,' he pleaded. 'Wait a little! You've been widowed less than a year; it's too soon to make such a decision.'

'I mean no disrespect to Edward.'

'I'm not talking about disrespect to Edward. I'm talking about *you*. You've got to give yourself time. Why do you think I've not told you I love you?'

'Please, Grant!'

'I won't be silenced, Cara. Not now! I've kept silent to give you time, so as not to take advantage. You know I love you, you know I want to marry you – but when you're ready.'

'But Grant,' Cara said gently, 'I can't marry you. I'm honoured that you should ask me, and I have the greatest regard for you, but I love Kit Marsden and I mean to marry him. Believe me, I know what I'm doing!'

'I believe you *think* you do,' Grant said. 'I'm equally sure that you're wrong. I warn you, Cara, that from now until the day you actually marry Kit Marsden – and I hope that day never dawns – I shall do everything in my power to prevent you!'

'You won't prevent me, Grant. It's a waste of your time trying,' Cara said. 'I am going to marry Kit Marsden.'

Grant turned abruptly, and walked away down the hill in the direction of Fawcett's farm. Cara watched him until he was out of sight, then she flung herself down on the ground and buried her face in the cool dampness of the grass. She felt shattered by Grant's attitude, by the strength of his objections.

Why was everyone so against the marriage? Why did they dislike Kit so much? She could find no answer to either question and she tried to console herself with the thought that Grant Fawcett and her mother-in-law didn't, after all, add up to 'everyone'. But there was still Johann to tackle, and she had little hope of support in that direction.

There was also Ralph Benson. It would be less than polite not to tell him beforehand, but perhaps she would telephone, or write a letter. Then there was the question of her parents. It would be best, she thought, for Kit to go with her to Akersfield and meet them there. She would be thankful when all these preliminaries were over, and she and Kit could get on with their new lives.

I'll tell Johann now, she thought. Nothing could make this day worse than it had been so far. She picked herself up and began to climb the slope to where Johann was working.

Johann's reception of her news was quite different from Grant's. He was a man who knew how to keep his feelings under control, and he would not forget his place. When Cara made her announcement he showed no outward sign of the turmoil which raged suddenly inside him – except that in his cheek a muscle twitched uncontrollably, and beneath his eye a tic appeared. Both of these signs Cara observed.

'Will you wish me to leave?' he asked her.

If the worst came to the worst – and what could be worse than Mrs Edward marrying that man? – he would go back to Austria. What he would do there he had no idea, but he would find something.

'Leave?' Cara was astonished. 'Why should you leave? I'd be devastated if you did such a thing. How would I manage without you?'

'May I ask who would be employing me?' Johann queried.

'Why, I would be, of course!'

'And I would take my orders from you?'

'Oh yes! That is . . . there might be the odd occasion . . .' She stopped in mid-sentence.

'I will think about it, Mrs Edward,' he said, with his usual dignity.

All that day and all night, Johann thought about what he would do. In the end it was loyalty to Cara, and to the Hendry family – Tom Hendry, who, though Johann was an enemy alien, had freely taught him all he now knew about farming; Edward Hendry, who had been a fair and considerate employer; Mrs Hendry, who had treated him like a son – which made him decide to stay: that, and the thought that one day Cara might have need of him. But he dreaded that Kit Marsden might soon become the boss, that he would be obliged to take orders from this man whom he – on little more than instinct – despised.

'I'm grateful,' Cara said when he told her. 'Beckwith wouldn't be the same without you.'

Mrs Hendry wrote to her cousin and made arrangements for a long visit.

'She says she'd be delighted to have me,' she told Cara when the reply came. 'She says she gets bored on her own.'

'Well, it'll be a change and a rest for you, I don't doubt. And you deserve it,' Cara said. 'But don't let her keep you too long!'

I'm not going for a change and a rest, Edith Hendry thought. I'm going because I can't bear to stay. There's no place for me at Beckwith any longer. Would there ever be again?

Two days after Cara had seen Grant, Joseph Fawcett paid a surprise visit to Beckwith. Mrs Hendry, through the window, saw him walking towards the house and guessed what his errand might be. Cara had already told her that she had spoken with Grant.

'He wasn't pleased,' was all her daughter-in-law would say, when discreetly questioned.

'I'm going to take Emily to help me feed the hens,' Edith said now. 'She enjoys that.'

She didn't want to be present when Joseph came in. He was a good man, but you couldn't call him tactful. Many were the arguments he'd had with her Tom. Anyway, it was clear that nothing was likely to move Cara.

'Now then, what's this I hear?' Joseph Fawcett demanded of Cara, the moment he marched into the house.

'What *do* you hear?' Cara asked – not that she didn't know. 'Will you have a cup of tea?'

'No I won't. No tea. Just a bit of straight talking between you and me, lass. Grant tells me you're set on marrying that good-for-nothing Marsden.'

'That's true – except that he's not a good-for-nothing,' Cara replied. She would try to keep her temper. Joseph Fawcett was an old man; she respected him and he'd been kind to her.

'Well, he's not good for you, and that's for sure!' Joseph said. 'Nay, love, what's gotten into you?'

266

'I'm sure Grant's told you that I'm in love with Kit Marsden and that's why I intend to marry him. What have you all got against him?'

'He's light-minded. He's a fly-by-night, like his mother before him.'

'So you know him, do you?'

'I knew his folks,' Joseph said obstinately. 'His father was a decent enough man until he met this gypsy woman at Shepton Fair. He was potty on her, but she left him after a year or two, went back to her own lot, said she couldn't stand living in a house.'

'And she left Kit behind?'

'Oh no!' Joseph said. 'She took him with her, travelling around. No life for a child. He didn't come back to these parts until she died, by which time his father was dead.'

'Well this is very interesting, but what's the point?' Cara asked. 'Nothing you've said tells against Kit.'

'The point is, he's never settled down. There's bad blood there. What's bred in the bone will always come out in the flesh. I haven't spent all my life breeding sheep and cattle without knowing that much. He'll not stand by you.'

'I think you're wrong. You can't possibly know that. Anyway, the risk – if there is a risk – is mine, Mr Fawcett. It's one I'm more than willing to take.'

Joseph Fawcett sighed, a deep sigh.

'Aye, well, I can see our Grant was right. He didn't want me to come here, told me I'd be wasting my time. You know, Cara love, we thought you and Grant would make a go of it in the fullness of time. There's everything in its favour. Two farms, marching side by side. And Grant's a good lad. He'd make any woman the very best of husbands.'

'I know that,' Cara said. 'I like Grant, and I admire him. I count him one of my best friends. The difference is, I'm in love with Kit!'

'Being in love has a lot to answer for,' Joseph said. 'I can only hope that it'll work out for you.'

'It will,' Cara assured him.

It would have a better chance, she thought when he'd gone, if they were all more accepting of Kit. But probably if he knew, he wouldn't care two hoots. He'd laugh that slow laugh of his. And I won't care either, she determined.

But David, when the news was broken to him, made up for everything.

'I like Kit,' he said. 'It will be nice to have him living here. He won't be my dad, of course. More like an uncle or a friend.'

Cara hugged him close.

267

'You are a joy, David Hendry!' she told him.

'You'll be Mrs Marsden, won't you?' he said. 'You won't be Mrs Hendry any more.'

'But there'll still be Hendrys at Beckwith,' Cara said. 'When you're grown-up, the farm will be yours. Then you'll marry and have children and it will still belong to Hendrys.'

In the event, she met Ralph Benson, unexpectedly, in Shepton. Earlier in the morning, Kit had telephoned.

'I've got to see you,' he'd said. 'I'm coming up to Beckwith.'

'Please don't!' Cara begged. 'Things aren't easy here. It's better if you don't come just now.'

'But I want to see you!' he insisted.

'Then I'll come into Shepton. Where shall I meet you?'

'All right then. In the Ewe, at noon.'

'Please be there,' Cara said. 'I can't sit in a public house on my own.'

Mrs Hendry was agreeable to being left with Emily at a moment's notice, but she had her suspicions as to why Cara was suddenly dashing off to Shepton. The plea of essential shopping didn't wash with her. However, she thought, there's nothing more I can say.

Cara had parked her car and was walking into Shepton High Street when she ran, almost full tilt, into Ralph Benson.

'I thought you couldn't find the time to come into Shepton these days?' he accused her. 'I thought you were too busy.'

'It's a very quick visit,' Cara said. 'There was something I needed. Anyway, I'm glad to see you; I was going to write to you.'

'Write to me? Whatever for?'

She informed him as casually as possible, just the bare facts. They were, after all, she tried to tell herself, not old friends, not that close. She was sick of making the announcement and being met with opposition. If Ralph Benson protested, she would be tempted to tell him to mind his own business.

To her surprise, somewhat to her chagrin, he showed no emotion whatsoever. Watching him, she saw nothing more than an upward tilt of his chin.

'I see,' he said steadily. 'A bit sudden, but if that's what you want . . .'

'It is.'

'Since you're in a hurry, I'll not keep you,' he said.

'Oh! All right! Goodbye then.'

He turned, and was gone, while she stood there, looking after him.

When he got to his car, to the astonishment of two women standing nearby, he gave it a deliberate and vigorous kick. Then he got in, slammed the door with a force which nearly sent it off its hinges, and drove off. The two women jumped out of his way.

'You're late,' Kit said when she walked into the Ewe.

'Not more than a minute or two. Oh, love, it's so good to see you!' She wanted him to take her in his arms and hold her close, but there was nowhere in the whole of Shepton they could be alone together. 'Why did you want to see me?' she asked.

'Do I have to have a reason? I just want to see you, that's all. Make sure you haven't changed.'

'I'll never change,' Cara said. 'Where you're concerned, I'll never change – not even if I live to be an old, old lady.'

'You'll be a beautiful old lady,' he said. 'You've got the bones for it. But there's a lot of living to do between now and then. I'm sick of waiting.'

'So am I. But it won't be long now, my love. Two more weeks. Anyway, you've got to meet my parents. They'd not want me to marry a man they'd never met.'

'Do I have to?' Kit protested. 'Can't I do all that later? It's you I'm marrying, not your family and friends!'

'Well, in this case I'm afraid we've no choice,' Cara insisted. 'Why don't we go early next week, get it over?'

Cara telephoned her mother, and made plans. Beth Dunning was shocked, and not a little upset at the news. 'It's so sudden, love!' she protested. 'Of course we want your happiness, but this is something we didn't expect, not yet, anyway. I don't know what your dad's going to say.'

'Ask him to reserve his judgement until he's met Kit, and please do the same, Ma! None of this is easy, but I'm sure you'll both like him.'

As it happened, they did. Kit was easy and pleasant with them, and they took to him exactly as Mrs Hendry and the children had done on *their* first meeting. But before she and Kit left at the end of the afternoon, her father took Cara into the dining room, on her own.

'He seems very nice, Cara love. I reckon he'll look after you, and it'll make life a bit easier for you on the farm. But are you sure it's what you want? You've got to be sure.'

'Absolutely sure, Dad! I was never more sure of anything!'

'Well then, you have my blessing, and your mother's,' Arnold said. 'She's a bit disappointed at not coming to the wedding, but I dare say you're right, in the circumstances.'

And now she was Mrs Kit Marsden, and had been for one month and six days. They had been deeply happy days and even more blissful nights. Kit was a wonderful lover: ardent, passionate, tender, and sometimes, it seemed, insatiable. Every night they made love, often more than once. Cara was sometimes thankful, when she came down in the morning, that Mrs Hendry was not there to witness what lovemaking, and lack of sleep, had done to her.

Mrs Hendry had been away six weeks now, and her letters gave no hint of when she might return.

'I miss Grandma,' David said. 'I wish she'd come home!'

'I miss her too,' Cara confessed. 'But I think she's still enjoying her holiday.'

Her mother-in-law's absence had made a tremendous difference in the house. From the moment she had left for Wensleydale, all the work of the house and all the care of Emily had fallen to Cara. There were not enough hours in the day to get through it all, as well as to spend time on the outside work she so much preferred. In the end, because Kit no longer had to be paid a wage, they scraped enough money together to employ a woman to come and help.

Mrs Violet Eliot cycled in from Faverwell every weekday morning and cycled back again after tea. She was honest and reliable and she adored Emily, who returned the compliment. She skimmed lightly through the housework, on the principle that tidiness was all, pushing everything into drawers and cupboards. In no time at all, when left to herself at weekends, Cara could find practically nothing she sought.

Mrs Eliot also made meals, but on a limited menu, so that the same dish came round too often.

'I could forgive her all that,' Kit said, 'if she didn't make lumpy custard! When I think about Mother Hendry's custard, smooth as satin, I could go right over to Wensleydale and drag her back by the hair!'

'I'll make us all a nice meal at the weekend,' Cara promised.

'I'm sorry, love,' Kit said. 'I know you're willing, and God knows you're a cut above Mrs Eliot, but you'll never have Mother Hendry's touch.'

'Well, I miss more than her cooking,' Cara said. 'I miss *her*. I miss her down-to-earth nature and her pawky sense of humour. She just *belongs* here!'

'Do you think she'll come back for my birthday?' David asked. 'Shall I write and ask her?' He would be nine years old in ten days' time. 'I wish Cousin Bertha was on the telephone, then I could talk to Grandma.'

'Yes, do write,' Cara said, though she had a feeling that her mother-in-law wouldn't come. 'Tell her if she can't come, you and I and Emily will go over to Wensleydale one day next week. Kit and Johann will have to manage without us, for once.'

David wrote the same day, and had a reply two days later.

Mrs Hendry said she'd like it very much if they'd come over to Cousin Bertha's.

They went on Saturday morning.

'Can we go over Fleet Moss?' David asked. He loved the feeling of the little car climbing and climbing, sometimes sounding as though it would never make it up the next steep slope of the narrow, twisting road as they went higher and still higher. At the summit, Cara stopped the car while they looked at the scene, at the high hills and deep valleys spread out before them, everything sparkling in the October sunshine.

'Is this the top of the world?' David asked.

'Not quite,' Cara said. 'But it's the top of your world and mine.'

Cousin Bertha lived in a small cottage on the edge of Hawes, from the window of which Mrs Hendry had been watching the road since shortly after breakfast. When she saw the car approaching down the lane, she rushed out to meet it. Not since the day Edward had come home from the war had she so looked forward to seeing anyone. She didn't know whom to embrace first.

Cousin Bertha waited in the doorway to greet them. She was a tall, stiff woman, with no apparent curves in the whole of her body. Her iron-grey hair was drawn back tidily from her face and her brown dress was covered by a spotless white apron. Everything about her was as neat and shining as a new pin; and, Cara noted the moment she stepped into it, so was everything in her house. Plumped-up cushions were symmetrically set on the three-piece suite, clearly not to be leaned against. Every chair had its hand-crocheted antimacassar. Ornaments in pairs balanced each other on the mantel piece and on the well-polished sideboard, and the small fire in the grate burned neatly, its flames even, scattering no ash.

'If you'll excuse me,' Cousin Bertha said pleasantly, 'I have things to do in the kitchen. The dinner won't cook itself, as we all know. Why not take the children into the garden to play?'

'We'd better,' Mrs Hendry said when Cousin Bertha had left the room. 'She's likely to have a fit if they leave so much as a fingermark in here.'

The garden was also as neat and tidy as its owner. Flowers and vegetables grew in regimented rows, and no weed dared raise its head. As a concession to the weakness of others there was a bench at the bottom of the garden, and there Mrs Hendry and Cara sat while David played with Emily on the square of manicured lawn.

'So how are you?' Cara asked. To her eyes, her mother-in-law didn't look well. It was not so much that she looked unhealthy as that she had a dispirited air, with none of her usual liveliness.

'I'm all right,' Mrs Hendry said. 'The trouble is, there isn't enough for me to do. Bertha does it all – cooking, cleaning, washing, shopping. She won't let me help, says I'm here for a rest. The fact is, she doesn't trust me to do anything to her standard. She's a born martyr, that woman. She enjoys working her fingers to the bone while I sit and do nothing. Or knit!'

She was sick to death of knitting. Sometimes she felt like stabbing one of those perfect cushions with the point of her long steel knitting needle.

'I wish you'd come back to Beckwith, Mother Hendry. Oh, not just to work!' Cara assured her. 'You could sit and do nothing there if you wanted to. We just want you back – Kit, as well as me and the children.'

For a brief moment Mrs Hendry's face lit up – then darkened again.

'I don't know, Cara love. I'm not sure I'd fit in any more.'

'Of course you would!' Cara said. 'Beckwith is where you belong. I'd like to take you with me this very day!'

'I couldn't do that,' Mrs Hendry said. 'I'd have to think about it. Strangely enough, Bertha does like having me here. And she's not all bad, you know. She means well.'

'I suppose so. But please remember that we want you back. You've only got to say the word and I'll come right over and fetch you.'

After dinner Cara said:

'We'd better leave soon. I want to be back before dark.'

'You're not going over Fleet Moss, I hope?' Mrs Hendry asked.

'No. It might come in misty. I'll stick to the low road.'

The sadness in Mrs Hendry's face was there for all to see when they took their leave. She couldn't hide it. She found it difficult to let the children go, especially as David was in tears.

'Just remember what I said,' Cara called as she drove off.

272

NINETEEN

Cara had decided, and Kit approved wholeheartedly, that for his ninth birthday David should have his own pony. She had been saving for it, a little at a time, and only hoped that she would have enough money.

'Don't worry about that,' Kit said. 'When it comes to a pony, if anyone knows where to get a bargain, I do!'

'I want him to have a good one,' she emphasized.

'Of course! And he shall have.'

Most dales children had their own pony long before they were nine years old, but what with one thing and another, David had missed out.

'I know it's not the best time of year to be buying a pony,' Cara said. 'It's only October, but before we know where we are the winter'll be on us. It won't get enough feed out of doors.' It would need its share of the stored winter food.

Part of the idea of David having his own pony was that he would, like many dales children, be able to ride it to school, leave it in the school field to graze while he was at his lessons. But there would be many days when the roads were too icy, or the snow too deep, for him to do this.

'There's not much you can do about that,' Kit said reasonably. 'The lad's birthday is in October. Mind you, it might knock the price down!'

'It seems Susan never wanted a pony. She's not one for the country life,' Cara said.

'In that case it's as well she hasn't got one,' Kit said. 'She'd not look after it.'

'I'd like it to be a surprise for David,' Cara said.

'Then I'll go into Shepton when he's at school,' Kit said. 'We can have it delivered on his birthday.'

'I'd like to go with you to choose it,' Cara said.

'There's no need, love. I can judge a pony!'

'I know. But I'd like to go.'

'If you must,' Kit said. Cara thought he sounded reluctant. 'We'll do it tomorrow, market day.'

The main ewe sales were over in Shepton, but the market was still busy. Cara had done well in the sales though, mercifully, she'd not been forced this year into selling far more stock than she wanted to. The shearing had brought her in more cash than she'd hoped for, and there'd been a good hay harvest. They wouldn't have to spend as much on winter food as in some years.

'We should look for a Dales pony, or maybe a Fell pony,' Kit said. 'I reckon a Fell pony might be best. It's a bit lighter, a bit smaller, but not so small it won't last him for many a long year. A man or a child can ride a Fell pony.'

'You think it's preferable to a Dales?' Cara asked.

Kit shrugged.

'There's not a lot to choose. My opinion is it's better for riding, and the Dales pony is better for pulling, or carrying weights. The Dales ponies were used in the lead mines hereabouts.'

'Prince is a Dales,' Cara said. 'But of course you know that.'

Prince was the last remaining horse on the farm. He was old now, and when she bought her tractor he would be put out to grass.

They went to Shepton the next day, leaving Emily to Mrs Eliot, knowing that she would spend her time with the child and do the minimum of housework. Cara wondered if she might see Ralph Benson at the market. She hadn't set eyes on him since before her marriage and she was unhappy about the way they'd parted then. She didn't want to be at cross purposes with Ralph; she regarded him too highly.

'We'd best go up to the horse field first,' Kit said.

They walked to the top of the High Street, then turned right past the church to Top Field. This was where the men selling domestic livestock – puppies, white mice, rabbits and the like – congregated. Kit led her to the far end of the field where Jack Butterfield, the horse-dealer he was looking for, traded.

Butterfield watched them approach. He'd known the Hendry family, at a distance, most of his life, and he'd seen this lady at Kilnsey Show and Askrigg Show, but he'd never spoken to her. She was a bit out of his class. But she was a corker! What a figure! Ripe. What a face! A cross between Merle Oberon and Margaret Lockwood, with a bit of Vivien Leigh thrown in, and red hair to boot. And now that lucky bugger Kit Marsden had landed her! Trust him to fall on his feet!

'We're looking for a good pony,' Kit said. 'A Fell, or happen a

Dales – and no fancy prices, think on! He's no worse for watching, Jack Butterfield isn't! Slippery as an eel!' he told Cara.

All the same, Kit reckoned, the smile Cara gave Butterfield was worth at least a fiver off the price.

'So have you got one?' Kit asked.

'It's your lucky day,' Butterfield said. 'I've just what you're looking for. About three years old, thirteen hands, give or take.'

'I can't afford to pay a lot,' Cara put in.

'Well, you tell me what you can afford and I'm sure we can come to some arrangement,' Jack Butterfield said. He was amazed to hear himself uttering the words, and with sincerity. His usual arrangements were strictly for the benefit of Jack Butterfield. But there was something about her that sent him right off his course.

'Let's be seeing him, then,' Kit said.

'Her. Her name's Bella. She's tethered up at the top. There's a bit more room there and the ground's not so muddy.' He turned to Cara. 'Do you know owt about horses?'

'She doesn't, but I do, and don't you forget it!' Kit said.

'Oh aye, we all know that!'

They walked to the top of the field and Jack Butterfield pointed out the pony.

'There she is then. There's Bella.'

They stood in front of the pony, surveying her. Cara raised her hand and gently scratched the animal's shoulder and neck, and it rubbed against her in appreciation.

'You know more than you let on, missus,' Butterfield said. 'Most folks would have patted her, but they like to be scratched.'

'Are all Fell ponies black?' Cara asked. This one was jet black, except for a white star on her forehead.

'The majority are,' Kit said. 'Some say the blacks are best. You find them mostly in the Lake District; they're the same colour as the rocks.'

'She's got everything you'll be looking for,' Butterfield said. 'Eyes wide-set, nice soft mouth, well laid back shoulders, and a deep chest with plenty of room for heart and lungs. You need that in a pony for hilly ground. And a short, broad back and strong, straight legs.' It was to Cara he reeled off all Bella's points, well aware that Kit would miss none of them.

'She looks very sturdy,' Cara agreed.

'Yes, well, that all sounds very fine, but let's see how she moves,' Kit said.

He began to walk her around. She walked with an easy, swinging gait, her long thick tail set high. After a while Kit began to run, and man and beast matched each other, both with co-ordinated ease, no strain. Then, hardly slowing the pony down, Kit leapt on to its bare back and began to ride it. At the far side of the field he allowed it to break from a trot into a canter. In spite of the fact that the pony was new to him, he showed total skill and confidence. He was, Cara thought, a pleasure to watch.

Presently pony and rider came back and Kit dismounted.

'Well, what do you think?' he asked Cara.

'I'm impressed.'

'You'll not find her wanting,' Butterfield said. 'She's as hard as iron and as gentle as a dove. It'll break my heart to part with her!'

Kit gave him a withering look.

'Will you be wanting tackle?' Butterfield asked.

'Yes. Good second-hand, and a fair price,' Kit replied.

'You know me,' Butterfield said in an injured tone. 'My prices are allus fair. Sometimes I think I'm a fool to meself.'

'Would you be able to deliver Bella on my stepson's birthday – Saturday?' Cara asked. 'We want ɔ surprise him.'

'Certainly,' Butterfield said.

'Beckwith Farm, Arendale.'

'I know the place. I'll be there early.'

Kit and Cara went back to the market, moving around together, looking at livestock, meeting people. There was, Cara felt, something different about the atmosphere; there was little of the warmth and friendliness she was used to. No-one was rude, but she sensed a distance, an air of coolness, verging on hostility. She was sure some people had avoided speaking to her.

'Is it my imagination,' she asked Kit, 'or am I right in thinking we're not too popular?'

'It's not your imagination,' Kit said. 'But does it matter? I've never been all that popular, but I don't let it affect me. They can all go to hell!'

'Not for me, they can't!' She was troubled. 'I thought a lot of these people were my friends. It upsets me to think they're not.'

'Well, that's what comes of marrying me!'

Kit put his arms around her shoulders and gave her a squeeze, at the very same moment as Ralph Benson emerged from the crowd in front of them.

'Oh Ralph, I'm so pleased to see you!' Cara cried. 'I hoped we might. Do you know Kit?'

Ralph Benson gave a curt nod in Kit's direction, after which Cara and Ralph carried on a desultory conversation for a minute or two, Kit saying nothing, clearly impatient to be off.

'Would you have my ewes again for overwintering?' Cara asked Ralph.

Before he could reply, Kit broke in.

'I don't think so, Cara. I thought I'd send our ewes down Kildwick way next time.' There was a faint, but unmistakable, emphasis on '*our* ewes', not lost on either Cara or Ralph.

'It'd cost less,' Kit added. 'We can't afford fancy prices!'

Cara flushed with embarrassment.

'But last winter . . .' she began.

She would have said that last winter Ralph Benson did the job for next to nothing, but he interrupted her.

'Well, if a cheap job is what you want, you're right to go elsewhere. I don't do cheap jobs on animals. Anyway, I doubt if I could have taken them. I'm very busy. Good day to you both.'

He walked away and was swallowed up in the crowd.

Cara rounded on Kit.

'How *could* you? How could you be so rude? You know perfectly well how kind Ralph Benson was to me. He took my sheep for practically nothing.'

'Yes, well, we don't want to be beholden to his sort, do we?' Kit said.

'What do you mean, his sort?'

Cara was suddenly aware that she had raised her voice and that people standing nearby had broken off their own conversations to listen, but she was too annoyed to care.

'Ralph Benson is my good friend,' she said. 'I value my friends, and I'll thank you to be polite to them!'

'You don't need men friends any longer,' Kit said in a hard voice. 'You've got me.'

'And right at this moment, I don't want you!' Cara snapped. 'I'm off! I'll see you at the car in one hour from now. If you're later than that I shall leave you!'

'Suit yourself!' he said.

She left him standing, and rushed out of the market, seeing no-one through the angry tears which blurred her eyes; not seeing Ralph Benson, who made as if to stop her, then changed his mind and drew back.

Outside the market area she went into a small café. She would have a cup of tea and pull herself together. Was this their first married quarrel? Was it really a quarrel? But she'd take back nothing. She was still furious with him.

The café was crowded – clearly she would have to share a table. She chose the darkest, farthest corner of the room, and said, 'Excuse me, may I join you?' to a woman already sitting there. Not until the woman replied did Cara realize that she knew her, though not well. She was the wife of a farmer in Faverwell, and she had children at school there.

'Oh, Mrs Chalmers, I hadn't seen it was you!' Cara said. 'It's a dark corner.'

Nor, if she had seen the woman in advance, would she have chosen to join her: not that she had anything against Mrs Chalmers, but she was sure that her own upset feelings showed in her face, and she didn't want to parade them.

'A busy market today,' Mrs Chalmers said.

'Yes. We've been buying a pony for David's birthday.'

'Well, if I may say so, Mrs . . .' Freda Chalmers floundered over Cara's new name, couldn't bring herself to utter it. '. . . you don't look all that pleased. Did you not get what you wanted?'

'Oh yes, we got a very good pony. It was just . . .'

Cara hesitated. She had no intention of mentioning her argument with Kit, but there was something else she'd like to get to the bottom of while she was in the mood. Should she or shouldn't she?

'Yes?'

'To tell you the truth, I *am* a bit upset, Mrs Chalmers. I found the atmosphere at the market a little . . . cool. Towards me, I mean. I don't think it was my imagination. I wondered . . .?'

'Well, Cara . . . May I call you Cara?' Mrs Chalmers said. She wasn't going to call her Mrs Marsden. 'You must know why. You'd be very naïve not to.'

'Is it because of Kit?'

'Marsden? To be frank, yes. You see, we were all very fond of Edward, we respected him and all his family. We took to you, not only for yourself – which we did – but because Edward Hendry married you.'

'And was I expected never to marry again?' Cara asked quietly.

'It wasn't that, love, though a big part was that it was so soon.' He's not cold in his grave, was what people had said, but she'd not repeat that. 'You see, dalesfolk are very loyal to their own, and very conventional. Old-fashioned maybe. It was partly that you married . . .' She stopped before mentioning Kit's name.

'There's always been Hendrys at Beckwith,' she went on. 'We've always looked up to them and I suppose we don't find it easy to think of anyone else taking over. Now even Edith Hendry has left. That's upset people, also.'

'I live in hopes she'll return,' Cara said. 'But don't forget my stepson. David is a Hendry through and through, and one day the farm will be his. All I'm doing on the farm – all my husband will be doing – is in the end for David. The minute he's old enough there'll be a Hendry in charge again.'

'Well, I hope you don't mind me speaking out,' Mrs Chalmers said. 'But you did bring it up. No offence meant!'

'And none taken,' Cara said.

I have behaved badly, she thought. Selfishly and without thought. It came to her suddenly, with remorse, and it had taken a comparative stranger to make her aware. She hadn't considered what harm she might be doing to Mother Hendry, to the children, even, it seemed, to the dalesfolk. All she had thought of was what she had wanted so desperately – Kit Marsden. Nothing else had mattered. It was all too soon after Edward's death, and Emily's birth. She should have recognized that she was still in shock, not seeing straight. She should have waited.

'I must go,' she said.

'But you haven't finished your tea!' Mrs Chalmers protested as Cara rose.

'I know. I've remembered something I must do.'

It was not true. All she wanted was to get away. She went immediately to the car. It was fully twenty minutes short of the hour but perhaps Kit would already be there, waiting for her.

There was no sign of him. She got into the driver's seat and prepared to wait. She was upset and saddened by what Mrs Chalmers had said, but the woman was right, it would be naïve of her to be surprised. She had lived in this place long enough to know how people reacted. If she had thought about it, she would have realized the effect her marriage to Kit would have, but she wouldn't have acted any differently. She loved Kit, she wouldn't have been prepared to lose him by waiting. And if she had to choose, she'd do the same thing all over again.

When the hour was up there was no sign of Kit, and then ten minutes passed, and then twenty. By the time he was half an hour late she was torn between annoyance and anxiety. He was doing this on purpose to punish her. She was sure of it. On the other hand, something *could* have gone wrong. An accident? But that was silly, they would have found her.

When the twenty minutes had extended to an hour, she was frantic, but she daren't leave the spot in case something awful had happened and they came to look for her. Five minutes later she saw, with great relief, a friend of Kit's walking in her direction. She jumped out of the car at once, and was amazed when he simply nodded a greeting and walked on.

'Norman!' she called after him. 'Norman, do you happen to have seen Kit? I think we must have missed each other.'

'Yes, I *have* seen him,' he said hesitantly.

'Where? Do you know where he is now?'

'I just left him in the Ewe. I expect he'll be on his way any minute now.' He didn't believe what he was saying. Marsden had looked well dug in, and he'd had a fair drop to drink.

'Thank you,' Cara said.

She got back into the car. There were two things she could do – three, actually. She could go on waiting here, which she wasn't prepared to do; she could go to the Ewe and drag him out, and she wasn't going to lower herself to do that; thirdly, she could go home and leave him to his own devices, leave him to find his own way when the spirit moved him. It took her no more than two seconds, during which time her anxiety and annoyance turned to blazing anger, to decide on the third.

She slammed the car door and drove out of the town far too fast.

She was back at Beckwith in record time. The fast drive had not cooled her rage in the slightest. She didn't care if he had to walk every foot of the way back, and if it came on to rain and he got soaked to the skin she'd be doubly pleased. But knowing him, she thought bitterly, the sun would continue to shine and he'd be fairly certain to get a lift.

She got out of the car, slammed the door again, and marched into the house. Mrs Eliot looked up from where she was playing with Emily on the rug. Johann was in the kitchen, finishing his tea.

'Mr Marsden not with you?' Mrs Eliot asked.

'He was detained on business,' Cara said shortly. 'Can you stay on until I've done the milking?'

'Of course,' Mrs Eliot said agreeably.

'I could do the milking,' Johann offered. He had noticed Cara's manner, but there was nothing to be said.

'No, I'll do it,' Cara said.

It was the one task which could soothe her, and to a certain extent it did that now. She was still filled with a mixture of anger and anxiety, and not a little fear as to Kit's reaction when he found himself abandoned. But he had asked for it. She had told him what she'd do and he'd deliberately put her to the test. She'd also told him she'd never be a doormat and now he'd know she meant it.

Then gradually, as she milked, other thoughts came into her mind. In any case, it didn't do to milk the cows in an angry mood. They felt it, and it upset them. She thought about her resolve to buy, as soon as she could, another cow, in calf. She would dearly like to buy back Marigold from Joseph Fawcett. Would he agree? Beckwith no longer kept a bull, but she could have her inseminated by what the dalesfolk, not yet used to the idea, called 'The Artificial Man'. Marigold's calf would be a honey.

Her anger cooled a little. She would have a calm, rational talk with Kit about the matters which had led to their quarrel. He had to learn that the farm was not his, that she didn't even think of it as hers. It was for David. Though she hoped they would eventually change, she would put up with what the local people thought of her, because she loved Kit, but she was *not* prepared to lose her few friends, and she would *not* tolerate Kit's rudeness to them. These things Kit would have to understand, and she was sure he would. She longed, now, for him to come home soon, so that they could make up. He would put his arms around her, and kiss her, and everything would be back to normal, only better.

When she went back into the house David had arrived home from school, and shortly after that Mrs Eliot left.

'Where's Kit?' David asked.

'He had something to attend to in Shepton. I had to get home for the milking,' Cara said.

'How will he get back?'

'He thought he might get a lift,' Cara extemporized. 'There's sure to be someone who would give him a lift to Dale End, and he'd walk from there.'

'That's what I did,' David said.

Should I telephone the Ewe, Cara wondered. She would do it quite tactfully, say she had to come back into Shepton and would pick him up. She could leave Emily with David, and Johann would keep an eye open for them. But she would have to go through the local exchange and they'd know exactly where she was phoning. It couldn't be helped. Anyway, it was no-one else's business.

She asked for the Shepton number, and recognized Billy Thwaite's voice as he answered.

'Nay, we're closed, Mrs Marsden,' he said. 'It's after hours. Kit left a while back.'

'Of course! How stupid of me!' Cara said. 'I'd forgotten about closing time.'

'Well, we do keep open longer on market days, but we've been closed a while now.'

'I dare say he'll be home any minute, then,' Cara said. 'Thank you very much.'

She'll not thank me when she sees him, Billy Thwaite thought. The man had gone home with a skinful!

So what shall I do? Cara asked herself. She could set off in the car and go to meet him, but if he'd hitched a lift then she might miss him. She wanted to be here when he arrived. Cold common sense told her that he'd have drunk a bit too much.

It was more than an hour later, Emily had been put to bed and was already asleep and David had gone to join Johann on the fell, when she saw Grant Fawcett's car along the lane. It turned into the farmyard, and stopped.

Cara watched as Grant got out of the car and then opened the passenger door for Kit, offering a hand to assist him. With an angry gesture, Kit pushed past Grant and began to weave his uncertain way over the short distance to the house. Grant came close behind and followed him into the kitchen. He looked at Cara, and she at him, neither of them speaking.

Kit lurched towards Cara, thrusting his face against hers. The smell of drink almost choked her.

'Where were you, you bitch?' he said thickly. 'By God, you'll pay for this!'

He grabbed her roughly by the arm, and Grant stepped in and pulled him away.

'Come on, old chap,' he said. 'Bed's the best place for you! I'll give you a hand.'

Kit shook him off as if he were a troublesome fly. It was surprising, Grant thought, that drunk as he was, Kit was still as strong as an ox.

'I don't need you to put me to bed,' Kit said. 'If anybody puts me to bed, it'll be a woman! It'll be my wife!' He leered at Cara.

'I'll make some strong coffee,' Grant offered. He crossed to the sink and picked up the kettle.

'You'll do no such thing!' Kit said. 'This is *my* house. An Englishman's home is his castle! You will kindly leave at once. Take your hook!'

At that moment David burst into the kitchen, closely followed by Johann.

'Ah!' Kit said fondly. 'The crown prince! The little crown prince. But I'm the king, of course. I'm the king of the castle! Don't you ever forget that, little prince. I'm the king!'

David looked at Cara in bewilderment.

'Kit isn't too well,' she said. 'He's just about to lie down for a while.' She turned to Johann. 'Didn't you tell me you wanted to show David some of your woodcarvings?' she asked.

'I did certainly,' Johann replied promptly. 'I'll do so now. Come, David!'

They left at once. Grant looked at Cara, a question in his eyes.

'I think you should go,' Cara said steadily. 'I'll be fine. Thank you very much for giving Kit a lift.'

'If you're sure,' Grant said. He was reluctant to leave her.

'Quite sure!'

'Then I'll call in and see you in the morning.'

'Don't trouble,' Kit said. 'Not needed!'

'Now Kit,' Cara said when Grant had left, 'I think you ought to go to bed. You look quite tired.'

She took his arm and led him upstairs to the bedroom. He went as meekly as a lamb, but in the bedroom, where she helped him on to the bed and began to take off his tie and unfasten his collar, his mood suddenly changed. As she leaned over him he seized her by the shoulders and pulled her down. Then he rolled her over so that she was underneath him, all his weight on top of her, and his hands began snatching at her blouse. When his fingers proved too clumsy to undo the buttons, he tore savagely at the fine cotton and ripped it to the waist. While with one hand he dug clumsily and painfully at her breasts, with the other he unfastened his trousers and lifted her skirt.

She had never experienced such force in him. She was powerless beneath him, unable to escape his grasp. Then at the very moment he would have entered her, revulsion gave her a rush of strength. With all her might she twisted violently away from him, and was free.

She moved quickly, but not quickly enough. He came after her and, in a frenzy of frustration, he lashed out. His fist caught the side of her face and sent her spinning. She crashed into the wall, and a searing pain shot through her right arm. When she sank to the ground she lay there, unable to move. She knew that blood was trickling from her face; she could taste it on her lips, but there was nothing she could do about it. She lay on the floor, waiting in terror for the next blow, which didn't come.

There was total silence for a minute, and then the sound of Kit's sobs. Cara raised herself cautiously. Her right arm was a mass of pain, and when she raised her left hand to her face it came away wet with blood.

She had no idea what to do. Why had she sent Grant away? Should she try to get to the telephone and call him? But her lips, she realized, were so swollen, and her face so painful that she wasn't sure she could even talk. Nor did she want Grant, or anyone else, to see her like this.

Slowly, painfully, she got to her feet. Kit was lying face down on the bed, still sobbing.

'I'm sorry! I'm sorry!' he mumbled. 'I didn't mean it! It was your fault! You left me!'

She stood by the bed, watching him. There was no need to be afraid any longer, he had no fight left in him. Strangely, in spite of what he had done to her, she could still feel pity. While she watched him, he fell asleep.

It was then that she remembered David. Any minute now Johann would bring him back. Neither of them must see her in this state.

She crossed to the washbasin in the corner of the room and looked at herself in the mirror over it. Her lips were very swollen, and bleeding where the lower one was split. The side of her face was bruised, showing the marks where Kit's knuckles had caught her.

With her left hand – her right one was no good – she turned on the tap and began to bathe her face, wincing as the water stung her. That done, with great difficulty she took off her torn blouse and soiled skirt. She wanted to tear off every shred of clothing, and burn them: she wanted to immerse herself in hot water, wash away the pain and the shame, but it was physically impossible for her to do so.

She dressed as well as she could, and tidied her hair, then powdered her face in a hopeless attempt to hide the bruising. Kit lay on his back, snoring loudly. The room stank of drink. Her arm was more painful than ever and she knew she must have it attended to. At the moment when she had gathered enough strength to go downstairs she heard Johann and David come into the house.

'I'll not be a minute!' she called. 'I'm just coming!'

Johann stared at her in horror as she came into the kitchen, and David ran across the room and flung himself at her.

'Cara! Cara, what happened?'

She tried to smile, which caused her lip to bleed again.

'I was so stupid!' she said. 'I tripped over the bedroom rug and fell against the wall! It's nothing. Just a bruise. And I've hurt my arm a bit.'

Johann's eyes met hers in total disbelief.

'I shall telephone for Dr Speight,' he said.

'Oh, I don't think we should trouble him,' Cara protested. 'I'm sure it will be better by morning!'

But he was already on the phone and she didn't have the strength to stop him; nor, to be truthful, the inclination. Her arm was so painful.

'Where's Kit?' David asked.

'Kit? Oh, he's all right. He's sleeping like a baby,' Cara said brightly.

Dr Speight was there within the hour.

'How in the world . . .?'

'As I've already explained to David and Johann, I tripped over the bedroom rug and fell against the wall.'

'I see.' For the moment he would pretend to believe her. 'Well, I'd better take a look at you.'

'It's just my arm.'

When he had examined her he said: 'It's not broken, but it's a nasty sprain – often more painful. And you seem shocked. I'll give you some tablets. You won't be able to use your arm for a day or two. And if I were you, Cara love, I'd get rid of that bedroom rug!'

The next morning Kit awoke with no more than a slight headache and a dry mouth. Cara had had very little sleep, kept awake not only by his drunken snores but, even more, by the pain in her body and the tumult in her mind. How could this have happened? The day had started out so well.

She had fallen asleep towards morning, and wakened to see Kit, propped on one elbow, staring down at her.

'How in the name of . . .!'

'I'm not a pretty sight, am I?' Cara said.

'How did you . . .?'

'I didn't,' Cara said tersely. 'You did.'

'No!' he was vehement. 'No, I couldn't have!'

'You did. You were drunk.'

'But I only had a few pints, a drop of whisky!'

'Whatever you did or didn't have, you were very drunk. If you hadn't been, I couldn't face what you did to me.'

He put out a hand to touch her shoulder and she winced.

'Don't touch me! My arm is painful.'

'Oh Cara love, I'm sorry! What can I say? I'm sorry! Please forgive me!'

'I forgive you because you were drunk,' Cara said. 'If you'd done it in cold blood, I couldn't have. I told the doctor I'd tripped over the bedroom rug and crashed into the wall.'

'The doctor?'

'Johann sent for him. I was in a lot of pain.'

'What about Johann?'

'Whether he believed the story or not, Johann won't say anything. You know Johann. Nor will Dr Speight or Grant Fawcett.'

'Grant Fawcett? What has he to do with it?'

'He brought you home. I don't suppose you remember that either? He's sure to be around this morning. David, bless his heart, *does* believe I tripped over the rug!'

Kit buried his head in his hands and groaned at the thought of David.

'Oh Cara! What can I say? What can I do?'

'I've thought a lot during the night,' Cara said. 'You did it because you were drunk, and I dare say you got drunk because we quarrelled. So it's what we quarrelled about that's important now. What you can do is listen to me while I lay down a few ground rules.'

'Rules? What do you and me want with rules?'

'In the first place,' Cara said, 'Beckwith Farm doesn't belong to you and never will. It *does* happen to belong to me, but I keep it in trust for David. That's what Edward would have wanted. I love you, and I want you here. I'll listen to what you have to say about the running of the farm, but you're not going to take over. Do you understand that?'

He said nothing.

'And the second thing is that you will be polite to my friends. I'm not asking you to like them – though I don't see why you can't – but you'll treat them decently.'

'And?' he queried.

'Nothing else. And now, for everybody's sake, we'll pretend I really did trip over that rug. We'll be as we were before. It's David's birthday the day after tomorrow. Nobody's going to spoil that.'

'And no hard feelings?'

'You're asking a lot, Kit Marsden. But very well, no hard feelings. It's behind us.'

David's delight at the gift of the new pony was endless.

'Her name is Bella but you can change it if you want to,' Cara told him.

'It's a perfect name! *She's* perfect!' David cried. 'When can I ride her?'

'I'll give you your first lesson, and you can ride her this very day,' Kit said. He was entirely back to his normal self, as if nothing untoward had happened.

'She's gentle,' Jack Butterfield said. 'You treat her well and she'll do the same by you.'

'Oh I will, I will!' David promised.

Jack Butterfield stole another glance at Cara. With her right arm in a sling and the bruises on her face she looked as if she'd been in the wars, and no mistake. If it had been some couples he knew he'd have taken her tale of falling over a rug with a pinch of salt, but there seemed nothing wrong with these two. Quite lovey-dovey they were, in fact; standing hand in hand, she gazing up at him as if she could eat him. I wish someone would look at me like that, he thought.

'Well, I'll take my leave,' he said. 'I've done as promised. I hope all goes well.'

'Thank you very much, Mr Butterfield,' Cara said. 'You can see David's delighted – indeed, we all are.'

They were still in the bottom field, which had been chosen as the best place for David to learn to ride his pony, when Cara saw Grant's car coming up the lane. She waved to him to slow him down; he would no doubt be bringing David a birthday present.

What he was bringing was Mrs Hendry.

'Mother Hendry! I don't believe it!' Cara cried. 'How did you get here?'

'Grant brought me,' Mrs Hendry said. 'He telephoned me yesterday and came to fetch me this morning.'

'Why doesn't he mind his own bloody business?' Kit said, but in a low voice, for Cara's ears only.

Cara gave him a fierce, warning look.

'He said you'd had a bit of an accident,' Mrs Hendry said. She said nothing of the fact that it was his very real anxiety which had persuaded her to come. He'd told some flimsy story about Cara falling, which his manner said he didn't believe. Looking at Cara's face, she wasn't so sure herself. Spraining her arm was one thing, that face was another.

'Anyway, I wanted to come for David's birthday!' she said brightly. 'So how is my birthday boy, then?'

'Can you stay for a day or two?' Cara asked presently. They were back in the house now, Kit remaining with David to give him his first lesson.

'You look as though you can do with me,' Mrs Hendry said. She looked with critical eyes around the kitchen. 'So does this place. I'll stay for a little while, as long as I can be useful, love.'

TWENTY

It was to be a full house at Beckwith this weekend. Susan was coming home from Magda Dale for a visit, and in the two years and more she'd been there her visits to Beckwith had become fewer and fewer. It was not that the school didn't allow it, but Susan chose to remain in Manchester, where there was more going on. She spent a lot of time with Laura, now her closest friend. Sometimes she went with her to spend the weekend in Akersfield.

'My ma sees a lot more of Susan than we do,' Cara remarked to Mrs Hendry. 'And she always did get on with Dad, right from the start.'

'Well, she'll come to no harm in Akersfield,' Mrs Hendry said. She felt less sure about Manchester. She'd never been there. 'All the same, it'll be nice to have her home for once. The house seems quiet these days, with David away most of the week.'

David was now a boarder at school in Shepton and, in common with several of the dales' children of his own age, came home only at weekends.

'Nothing's quiet with Emily around,' Cara said. 'She's the liveliest four-year-old in existence!'

'Another year and *she'll* be off to school!' Mrs Hendry said ruefully. 'It's awful, the way they fly the nest.'

'Oh, Mother Hendry!' Cara said laughing. 'How can you talk about flying the nest? It'll be years and years for Emily, and not at all for David.'

'You're right, love,' Mrs Hendry conceded. 'It's just that time goes so fast. Anyway, David's settled well at his new school.'

'He would,' Cara said. 'He's got a friendly nature, and he's good at his lessons. All the same, he can't get home fast enough at weekends, though I suspect it's Bella he's keenest to see, not us! Buying Bella was one of the best things ever.'

However, she didn't like to think of the day she and Kit had done that. She had, as she'd promised, tried to put the memory of Kit's violence behind her, but the small blue mark, just below her right cheekbone, was a reminder every time she saw her face in the mirror. There seemed no reason why it shouldn't have faded; it wasn't disfiguring, no more than a beauty spot, but she wished it would go away.

Kit had not been physically violent since that day, or at least not to any extent. Sometimes he would grasp her arm in too rough a fashion, or push her out of his way, but at least he hadn't thrown her against the wall again. She had learnt by now to cope with the sudden flaring of his temper, not least because at other times he could be so charming, and because she loved him passionately.

She tried to avoid quarrels, not only because of a lingering fear of what they might lead to, but because of her mother-in-law. Mrs Hendry had lived with them again since she'd come back from Wensleydale on David's birthday, two years ago. She was glad to be there and they were pleased to have her, but it was not easy for Cara to quarrel within earshot of a third person. Kit had no such qualms. Either he was oblivious of, or didn't care about, the effect of his temper on anyone else.

'It doesn't bother me,' Mrs Hendry said once, when Cara apologized for him. 'I can stand up to Kit any day of the week. But I worry for David. It upsets him. I'm glad he's away at school.'

She had seen the way the wind blew on that birthday weekend. Grant Fawcett hadn't been wrong in his suspicions, which he'd hinted at but not voiced. Cara's face couldn't have been bruised like that from falling against the wall. Not possibly. She had also read the truth in Johann's eyes; still did. Johann went through his days trying never to look at Kit Marsden, but when he had to, there was no disguising the contempt and hatred he felt for him.

Even if she hadn't been made as welcome as she had, Edith Hendry thought – and to be fair to him, by Kit as well as by Cara – even if she hadn't had the excuse of Cara's injured arm, she'd have found some good reason for staying. She'd reckoned she was needed in this home, and that feeling had never left her.

'They shouldn't be long, now,' Cara said.

Kit was collecting David and two Faverwell children from school, and after that, meeting the Manchester train. He had left Beckwith before lunch, saying he had a bit of business in Shepton.

What his bits of business were, Cara never now enquired. She had done so once, and he'd flared up, snapped at her roughly, 'Ask no

289

questions and you'll get no lies!' She was fairly certain they were black-market deals. There was still plenty of scope for them; six years after the war had ended, rationing was as severe as ever. He made no attempt to bring home any of the gains, and since there was no way she could put a stop to the business, it was safer to remain in ignorance. He was never short of money.

'Don't spend too long in the Ewe,' she'd said as he left home. 'Remember you have to drive the children home.'

'Don't talk to me as though I'm an idiot!' he retorted.

Perhaps she shouldn't have said it, she thought as she watched him drive away. He wouldn't be careless about the children. The trouble was, he was no judge of his own competence when it came to drinking. He would claim, and often did, that he drove better with a pint or two inside him.

'I'll be glad to see them home,' she said to her mother-in-law. 'In the meantime I'll get on with the milking. Johann's brought them in.' It wouldn't be many weeks now, especially if the winter came early, before the cows would have to be kept in.

To her surprise and pleasure – and to Kit's annoyance, for he wanted nothing to do with the family – Joseph Fawcett had allowed her to buy back Marigold. The artificial insemination man had called in July, and Marigold would have her calf next March.

'I could have got you something much cheaper,' Kit grumbled. 'Old Fawcett's charged you top price.'

'I didn't want any cheap old cow,' Cara said. 'I wanted Marigold.' To her, being able to buy back Marigold was a sign that things were going well at Beckwith, better than she had ever expected in those bleak months after Edward's death. 'Anyway,' she added, 'Joseph asked a fair price and I was willing to pay it. He had to be compensated for all the months he'd fed her and looked after her – which he did well.'

'You shouldn't be buying shorthorns,' Kit argued. 'Friesians are the beasts to go for now. People who know are changing over. They're better milkers.'

'Well here's one who isn't changing,' Cara said. 'I still reckon dairy shorthorns are best for this dale. As for milking, I've no complaints.'

In the Shippon, as she moved around, she talked to the cows, especially to Marigold.

'I expect you'll have a beautiful baby,' she said. 'You're lucky! I wish I was having a baby.'

Kit was totally adamant that they should not have children. There was no moving him. They made love often, with passion and pleasure – these were the best times in life – but he would never allow her to be the one to take precautions against her becoming pregnant. 'I

don't trust you,' he said. 'You're capable of cheating. All women are.'
Perhaps he was right, she conceded; about her, at any rate.

The three of them arrived as she was crossing the yard from the
Shippon. David jumped out of the car and rushed past her like an
arrow in flight, making straight for the stables and Bella.

'I've got time for a ride!' he shouted.

'What about your tea?' Cara called after him.

'It can wait. But save me plenty. I'm hungry!'

Cara followed Susan into the house. Mrs Hendry embraced Susan,
then held her at arm's length.

'Now let's have a look at you, young lady. Let's see if you're up to
the mark!' The warmth of her voice took away any idea of criticism.

Susan stood still while her grandmother eyed her.

'Well, Grandma, will I do?'

'You will that,' Mrs Hendry said. 'You're a sight for sore eyes and
it's a treat to see you. Mind you,' she added, 'you're too thin!'

'Oh Grandma, I'm not!' Susan protested. 'You need to be thin to
be on the stage.'

'Are you eating enough, I want to know?'

'Of course I am! Masses! You always said I ate like a horse, and I
still do.'

'We'll see,' Mrs Hendry said. 'Tea will be on the table in two
minutes.'

'Can you make that one minute, Ma Hendry?' Kit said. 'I'm
starving!' He picked up Emily and swung her high above his head.

'Shall I hang you on the hook?' he threatened. 'Shall I then?'

She screamed with delight.

Why doesn't he want children, when he's so good with them? Cara
asked herself.

'Emily had a ride on Bella this afternoon,' she said. 'She enjoyed
it.'

She had promised David that while he was at school she would look
after Bella and give her some exercise. Some days she rode the pony
herself, other days she walked her on a leading rein around the bottom
field, with Emily mounted. Sometimes Bella would take them both on
her back, so accommodating was she.

'I saw Jim Armitage today,' Kit said. 'I arranged he'd take the ewes
for overwintering.'

'Oh! I don't remember discussing it,' Cara said.

Jim Armitage was the farmer who had taken the ewes for the last
two winters. Kit had had his way in this matter, and now he assumed
he always would. Armitage farmed between Brogden and Shepton, in
Airedale. There was no disputing that the weather was milder there
than in the more northerly Arendale, but Cara had the feeling that

the sheep overwintered better in Nidderdale. There was nothing she could put her finger on, and she was willing to believe that she might have a certain amount of prejudice because Kit had managed – she was not sure how – to take the decision on himself.

Also, she admitted to herself, she was still upset that she seemed to have severed her friendship with Ralph Benson. In the last two years she had seen him no more than three or four times at the market, and only on one occasion had he been within speaking distance. Kit had been with her, and Ralph had raised his hat, bidden her a polite good day (without looking at Kit), and passed by.

'There's nothing to discuss,' Kit said shortly.

He turned away, avoiding the sharp look Cara gave him. All right, I won't make an issue of it now, she thought, not with everyone here for the weekend.

After supper, when all the animals had been settled, everything closed up for the night, and Johann had gone to his own quarters, they went into the parlour. It was already dark; the nights were closing in, getting chilly. It was good to see the logs blazing in the wide fireplace.

'Now,' Mrs Hendry said, settling in her favourite chair, 'tell us what you've been doing, Susan love. It's been a while since we saw you.'

'Oh, this and that!' Susan said. 'It's not as exciting as it was, we seem to be doing a lot of the same things over again. In fact . . .' She paused, and looked around the room. One thing she had learned at Magda Dale was that a pause in the right place was a sure-fire way of getting everyone's attention. Well, it had certainly worked this time. They were all waiting expectantly for her next words.

'In fact,' she announced, 'I want to leave!'

Cara was the first to voice her astonishment.

'*Leave*? Whatever do you mean?'

'Leave Magda Dale. Not continue. What else could leave mean?'

'Don't you want to go on the stage, then?' David asked.

'Of *course* I do, silly! I never said that. I want to leave Magda Dale *because* I want to go on the stage. I want to do it now, not wait.'

'But surely there's more to learn?' Cara objected. 'What's the point in not finishing the course, especially as you've started your last year?'

'That's just it,' Susan said eagerly. 'I don't think there's a lot more I *can* learn there. I'd learn a lot more in a proper job. Anyway, you'd save money. You'd save two terms' fees, not to mention expenses.'

'Saving money isn't the most important thing at this stage,' Cara said. 'I'm not happy at the thought of you giving it up. I don't think your father would have liked it.'

'I'm sure he wouldn't,' Mrs Hendry put in.

292

Susan looked defiantly from one to the other of them. 'How can either of you be so sure?' she demanded. 'Daddy might have understood perfectly. We don't know.'

'Just when do you want to leave?' Kit asked mildly.

'Now!' Susan said. 'This coming week. That's why I came home. I wanted to tell you.'

'And there we thought you wanted to see us for our pretty faces!' Mrs Hendry said.

'So what would you propose to do next?' Cara asked, trying to keep her voice level. It was another of Susan's wild ideas, but to oppose it too strongly at the beginning would only strengthen the girl's resolve.

'If I move quickly, I'm sure I can get a job in pantomime,' Susan said. 'But it really would have to be quickly. They'll be starting rehearsals any day now. I can't afford to wait. And there are lots of places I could try. Bradford, Liverpool, Newcastle, Bristol . . .'

'*Bristol!* Why, that's hundreds of miles away!' Mrs Hendry was horrified. 'You're too young to go to Bristol. You're only seventeen!'

'Oh Grandma, it doesn't have to be Bristol,' Susan said impatiently. 'There are lots of places.' And I'll not be daft enough to tell anyone I'm only seventeen, she thought. She knew she could easily pass for nineteen or twenty. Nor would she tell them, not at this stage, that she'd already written to Bristol and Leeds in search of a job. She favoured Bristol. It was further away from interference.

'I don't expect to get much of a part,' she admitted. 'I'll do whatever's offered. I'll sweep the stage and make the tea if there's nothing better.'

'Well, I reckon two years' training should just about qualify you for sweeping up and making tea!' Kit said, grinning.

Susan glared at him.

'I thought you at least would have been on my side,' she accused him.

'Oh, I dare say I would be, if I were to take sides,' he said.

'Please, Kit, do be serious,' Cara begged.

'I don't regard it as all that serious,' he said equably. 'I reckon two years' training is enough. I believe in learning on the job.'

'That's what I mean,' Susan said eagerly. 'I'd learn far more by doing it.'

'You mean you'd learn more about making tea and sweeping up?' Mrs Hendry said. 'Well, happen that would be something. You've not shown much aptitude for such tasks here.'

'Oh Grandma, you know very well that isn't what I mean. You're being stupid!'

'I'll thank you not to speak to your grandmother in that fashion!' Cara said sharply.

'But why can't she understand?' Susan persisted. 'Why can't *you* understand?'

'You have rather sprung it on us, haven't you?' Cara said. 'Perhaps I'll understand better when I've had time to think about it.'

'But I can't afford to wait,' Susan said desperately. 'I've explained that.'

'All right. But I'm not going to be rushed into a decision this minute. I'll give you a firm yes or no before you go back to Manchester on Sunday.'

'I don't see what there is to think about,' Susan protested. 'It's my life.'

'I want to do what's best for your life,' Cara said. 'For the future, not just for the present. So we won't talk any more about it this evening, but we will tomorrow.'

When she and Kit were getting ready for bed later that evening, Kit said: 'Let the lass go. Why do you want to tie her down?'

'I don't. Not in the least,' Cara replied. 'I want what's best for her. She's always been a child who's wanted her own way, but she's had to be guided. I'm trying to think what Edward would have wanted.'

'Oh, Edward, is it?' Kit said dismissively. 'Well, get into bed and think about what *I* want!'

'Don't I always?' Cara asked.

But when they were in bed, and he made love to her, nothing else mattered and everything was perfect. Why can't things always be like this, Cara asked herself as she drifted happily into sleep.

'What shall I do about Susan?' Cara said to Mrs Hendry next morning. It was ten-thirty. Susan, seizing the chance of a lie-in, was still in bed. David had long been out with Bella.

'What do you think Edward would have wanted?' she asked.

'Oh, I don't doubt what he'd have wanted,' Mrs Hendry said. 'He'd have wanted her to finish the course. Whether he'd have been able to make her do so is another matter. He could be as soft as putty where Susan was concerned. I don't have to tell you that.'

'But you think he'd have wanted her to carry on?'

'I'm quite sure of it.'

'Then that's what I must try for,' Cara said. 'I don't enjoy the prospect of telling her.'

'No,' Mrs Hendry agreed. 'And I don't envy you.'

Susan appeared half an hour later, yawning and rubbing her eyes.

'Well,' she began, the moment she set eyes on Cara. 'Have you made up your mind to let me leave?'

'No,' Cara said. 'I'm sorry, Susan, but I've decided you must stay on and finish. I think it's important, and I think it's what your father would have wanted.'

'I don't believe it!' Susan cried. 'How can you be so mean?'

'It's only a few months,' Cara said. 'It will soon pass.'

'It will *not* soon pass. It'll be an eternity!' Tears of frustration filled Susan's eyes.

'Grandma, can't you make her see sense? Can't you persuade her?' she begged.

'I don't know whether I could or not,' Mrs Hendry admitted. 'I just happen to agree with Cara. You should finish what you've started.'

'Why?' Susan demanded. 'What's the point if it's doing no good? I've learnt all I can at Magda Dale. Anyway, I'm telling you both, here and now, if you make me stay on, I'll not work. You'll be wasting your money.'

It was money which, in the end, stood between her and her ambition to get a job. If she had it she wouldn't wait for permission. As it was, she would need the fare to Bristol – or wherever – and she would need some money to live on until the first payday. She would probably have to pay for her lodgings in advance. Also, she could do with a new coat and hat to make herself presentable. She couldn't manage on less than fifty pounds, which, if Cara had agreed to her plan, she was sure she'd have advanced her. Now, she had next to nothing. Two pounds ten shillings, to be exact.

She stood face to face with Cara. At that moment she hated her.

'I think you're rotten!' she said. 'You only care about what *you* want. You don't care two hoots about me!'

'That's untrue and unfair,' Cara protested. She was shocked by the intense dislike she saw in Susan's face. She'd thought that that had died a long time ago. 'You may remember that it was I who agreed to you going to Magda Dale when you were so keen on the idea. It wasn't easy. All I want now is for you to finish what you were so desperate to start.'

'But can't you see, there's no point in finishing?'

'I'm sorry, Susan,' Cara said. 'I'm not going to argue any further. You must go back to Magda Dale, make the most of what's left of your time, and when you *do* leave I'll give you all the help possible. Willingly. I *want* you to succeed.'

'Well, you have a funny way of showing it!' Susan said furiously.

She jumped up from the table and ran out of the house. Cara turned to her mother-in-law.

'Oh dear! I didn't manage that very well, did I?'

'You couldn't have,' Mrs Hendry said. 'No-one could. But you did the right thing. She's got to learn that she just can't pick up things and then throw them away, and she can't always have her own way.'

'Well I must say, doing the right thing doesn't make me feel good. Should I go after her?'

'Certainly not!' Mrs Hendry said firmly. 'Anyway, she'll not stay out long. She dashed out without a coat and there's a sharp nip in the air. There was a frost this morning.'

Susan, marching along the lane in a fury, was feeling the chill. She hugged her arms around her and walked quickly, trying to keep warm. She didn't know where she was walking to, she just knew she wanted to get away. She wished she had wings and could fly. She wanted to be rid of Beckwith and everyone in it. She wanted to get away from Arendale, whose high fells and limestone crags hemmed her in. It was too narrow, like the people who lived in it. They hadn't the slightest idea what went on in the real world.

Looking up the hillside, she spotted Kit, and immediately she saw him the idea came to her, as if straight from heaven.

Kit was not like the rest of them. He wasn't stuffy, or narrow-minded. She'd always got on well with Kit and he'd never made any secret of his liking for her. I expect that's at the bottom of it, she thought. I expect Cara is jealous, so she's taking it out on me.

She climbed the slope towards Kit, and as she neared him she began to cry. It wasn't difficult. They'd had more than one lesson at Magda Dale on how to show your emotions. She didn't need to think, now, of all the sad things in the world, she needed only to think about how miserable *she* was, to start the tears flowing.

'Good heavens, what's all this about?' Kit said. 'Why the water-works?'

'Oh Kit, I'm so unhappy!' She was, too. She wasn't acting that.

'Whatever in the world . . .?'

'I can't make Cara understand! She doesn't seem to realize how miserable I am at Magda Dale!'

'I didn't know you were unhappy there. I thought you just wanted to get into a job,' Kit said.

'Oh I do, I do! But I hate it there. I try to hide it. I've tried not to complain. Oh, if only I had someone to help me!'

'Dear me! So what do you mean by help?'

'If only I had some money of my own!' She saw the flicker of interest in Kit's eyes. 'If only I had fifty pounds!' she said, judging it best to name the sum.

'So you reckon all that stands between you and happiness is fifty pounds?' There was a definite twinkle in Kit's eyes now.

'That's all,' Susan said mournfully. 'But who do I know who would lend me fifty pounds? Cara could, but she won't. And I do mean lend. I'd definitely pay it back.'

'And how would you use this passport to happiness?' Kit enquired. Then he held up his hand and stopped her as she was about to reply. 'No! Don't tell me. Best not to know.'

'*You* don't know where I could borrow it?' she asked hopefully.

'As a matter of fact,' he said, 'I could let you have the money – but on one condition . . .'

'Anything! Oh, I'll do anything you like!'

'Will you now?' he said grinning. 'Well, perhaps better not! The condition is that you don't mention a word of it before you go back to Manchester, and even then you don't let on it was me.'

'I won't! I won't!' Susan promised. 'Oh, Kit, you are so good!'

'I can guess what you have in mind,' he said. 'And it's a risk. But you're a clever girl and I dare say you'll pull it off.'

Too clever by half, he thought, and too attractive for comfort, especially when she looked at him as she was doing now. But he didn't want to soil his own doorstep.

'Be careful,' he added. 'It's a wicked world out there.'

'Oh, I will,' Susan assured him. 'When . . .?'

'I'll drive you back to the station tomorrow. You can have it then. In the meantime, behave yourself, don't cause any more trouble. Best not to say you've seen me.'

When Susan got back to the house, frozen to the marrow, she made no mention of what had earlier driven her out, nor was it mentioned during the rest of her short stay. She was subdued, as befitted one who had reluctantly accepted her disappointment, but nothing more. In the afternoon she got out her bike and cycled into Faverwell, where she recounted the glories of Magda Dale – which, to be honest, she had quite enjoyed – to her envious friends. She would have liked to have boasted of her wonderful plans for the future, but she decided on discretion. Once she was on the stage, everyone in Faverwell, and far, far beyond, would hear of her.

Cara made no objection, in fact she was rather relieved, when Kit, on Sunday afternoon, offered to drive Susan to the station. There seemed to be a strange, unexpected truce between herself and Susan and she would just as soon not risk breaking it.

'Mind you're not so long before your next visit,' Mrs Hendry said as Susan was leaving. 'This is your home, you know!'

'Oh I won't be, Grandma,' Susan promised. Little did they know!

Sitting in the car beside Kit, being driven out of the dale, leaving it all behind her, Susan's spirits lifted to the sky. She was as happy as a lark.

'I didn't think you'd set your sights on pantomime,' Kit said. 'That surprised me.'

'Oh I haven't,' Susan said. 'Not in the end. It's a stepping-stone, and something I thought I could get into quickly.'

'I hope you're right,' he said.

'But I do like pantomime. I think it must be fun.' She would never forget the pantomime in Helsdon, in the winter of the great snow. Cara, if only she knew it, had actually been the means of getting her stage-struck.

'You'll let us know how you get on?' Kit said.

'Of course!'

When Kit returned, Cara said, 'Let's take a walk around.'

It was something she had loved to do with Edward. They would visit every part of the farm, every field, almost every animal; see how things were going, discuss problems, talk about what they would like to do or, more to the point, what they could afford to do. And it was not only the practical matters which claimed their attention: they discovered the first primrose, caught the swift, iridescent blue flash of the kingfisher down by the river or, because sometimes it was evening before they could spare the time to walk, they watched the first stars appear. Edward's love of the land had made every small thing important, and Cara had caught this and learned it from him.

This was not in Kit's nature. Once started on a job he worked every bit as hard as Edward would have done, he was skilled, but when the task was over that was it. He didn't want to go any further.

'Must we?' he said now.

'Not if you don't want to,' Cara replied. 'It's a nice evening. I thought it would be pleasant.'

The truth was that having so recently pressed fifty one-pound used notes into Susan's eager hand, to be spent in a way which he knew would upset Cara considerably, he judged it best to keep a safe distance. It seemed highly likely that on such a walk the conversation would turn to Susan, and that he wished to avoid.

He didn't regret what he'd done. He reckoned it was high time the girl left that fancy school. She was too mature, too much of a woman, to be there. It was time she spread her wings. His only real regret was that she wouldn't be flying in his direction. He'd have liked to have shown her what a certain bit of life was like.

'I thought of going down to the Dragon,' he said.

The Green Dragon was the more popular of Faverwell's two pubs. He didn't like it as well as the pubs in Shepton – he knew he wasn't as acceptable in Faverwell as in the town – but it was better than spending a Sunday evening at home.

'As you wish,' Cara said. 'You won't mind if I take a stroll on my own?' She was disappointed, though not surprised, by his decision. She sensed Kit's boredom with Beckwith. Sometimes she wondered if that boredom extended to herself, but then when he made love to her she was convinced it did not.

When Kit reached the Dragon it had only just opened for the

298

TWENTY-ONE

Kit came in at the door with all the noise and bluster of a storm wind, then immediately tripped over the sill and fell flat on his face, momentarily deflated.

Cara looked silently down at him. Blazing anger outdid the relief she felt at the sight of him, but she hid her emotions behind a stony expression.

'Well, come on, you bloody silly cow!' he said when he'd regained his breath. 'Help me up, can't you? Do you want me to lie here all night?'

'As far as I'm concerned that's just what you *can* do,' Cara said tightly. 'You're disgusting!'

With difficulty he scrambled to his feet, then stood there swaying, looking as though he might topple over again any second. Cara refrained from putting out a hand to help him. She didn't want to touch him.

'I won't ask where you've been, because it's obvious,' she said. 'And Billy Thwaite is in for trouble, allowing drinking after hours.'

'Not Billy Thwaite! Not the Ewe. And not the bloody snooty Dragon neither. Found a new water . . . watering hole!' He stumbled over the words.

'Didn't it occur to you I'd be worried sick? How was I to know you hadn't met with an accident?' Cara demanded. 'And how could you drive in that condition? You could have killed yourself – or worse still, someone else.'

'Well I didn't, did I?' He was ponderously cheerful now. 'And don't you critic . . . critic . . . say anything bad about my driving!' He lurched towards her. 'Best driver in Yorkshire, bar none! Ask anybody!'

He took an uncertain step forward and grabbed her by the shoulders, pushing his face against hers.

'How about a nice welcome home? How about a kiss?'

'Don't touch me!' Cara snapped. 'You're revolting!' She pushed him away, and as he staggered backwards, so his mood changed. He swayed towards her again.

'Revolting, am I? Untouchable? Well I've known times when I wasn't, and so have you! You, my lady, can be like a bitch on heat! That's it, a bitch on heat!'

'Keep your voice down. You'll waken everyone in the house.'

'And why not?' he blustered. 'Why not waken the lot of them? I live here don't I? A man has a right to raise his voice in his own home, even when everything belongs to his bloody wife!'

'That's beside the point. Now will you . . .?'

'Oh no, it's not beside the point!' he interrupted. He was shouting now. 'I know what they all say. I know what those bloody bastards in the Dragon say. There's a man who's kept by his bloody woman. That's what they say!'

'Will you please shut up and go to bed before everyone wakes up?' Cara said wearily.

She was too late. The door to the stairs opened and Mrs Hendry stood there in her nightdress. A second later, before anyone had time to speak, a startled, white-faced David appeared behind her. He rushed across the kitchen to Cara and she took him in her arms, holding him close and stroking his hair.

'It's all right, love,' she said. 'There's nothing to worry about. I'm sorry we woke you.'

'Will I make a cup of tea?' Mrs Hendry asked calmly.

'Bloody cup of tea!' Kit bellowed. 'Is that all you ever think of? Bloody cups of tea! Where's the whisky? Don't tell me you haven't any.'

'I'd say you'd had enough whisky for one night,' Mrs Hendry observed dispassionately.

'And who the hell are *you* to say? You're like me, you're here on sufferance. We're here to serve madam – only we serve her in different ways. She likes *me* best in bed!' He leered at Cara, and made a grab for her, missing her and falling against David, who cried out in fear.

'Wash your mouth out, Kit Marsden,' Mrs Hendry said fiercely. 'There's a child present!'

'Oh yes! The little lord and master. Who could forget the little lord and master, heir to the kingdom?'

'What does he mean, Cara?' David whispered. 'Why is he so cross? Is he drunk?'

302

'I'm afraid he is,' Cara said. 'And I reckon we should all go to bed, leave him to cool off.'

'Cool off, is it?' Kit said angrily. 'I'll show you best how to cool off!'

He moved rapidly, considering his state, towards the door, and took his shotgun from the rack, holding it at shoulder height, waving it about from one to the other of them.

'Get out, the three of you!' he ordered. 'Out of the door. Chop chop! You'll cool off out there all right. Get out!'

He poked his gun menacingly in their direction. Cara, her arms around David – she could feel his body trembling – made for the door, and Mrs Hendry followed. As they stepped outside, Mrs Hendry and David in their night-clothes, Cara without coat, the freezing cold of the night assaulted them like daggers.

'Emily?' Cara cried. 'What about Emily? I can't leave her!'

'She was sound asleep,' Mrs Hendry said. 'In any case, he'd not harm Emily. Also,' she added quietly, 'I doubt he could get up the stairs in his present state.'

'I don't like leaving her,' Cara said anxiously.

Behind them they heard the clatter of the gun as, inexplicably, Kit threw it out, and then the banging of the door as he closed it on them.

'Quick! Into the shippon,' Cara ordered. 'It's warm in there. We'll be all right, David love.'

Before they reached the shippon Johann came running across the farmyard. He wasted no time in asking questions.

'Into my room,' he said.

It was not easy for Mrs Hendry to climb the rickety ladder which led to his quarters, but desperation gave her strength. Once there, Johann wrapped her, and David, in the blankets from his bed.

'I don't have a third blanket,' he apologized to Cara. 'You must wear my coat.' It was his old army greatcoat which he had somehow managed to keep. He held it while Cara slipped her arms into it, grateful for the warmth. She was shivering from top to toe, her teeth chattering.

'What can I say, Johann?'

'There is no need to say anything. I heard him arrive. I was not asleep.'

'He threw his gun out. It's lying there on the ground.'

'Then I will get it,' Johann said.

'Please be careful!' Cara begged.

He was back in minutes.

'In fact,' he said, 'the gun is not loaded, though perhaps he did not realize that. It is my opinion that I should drive into Faverwell and

303

bring Constable Potter. It is not fitting that you should be banished from your home in the middle of the night, welcome though you are in my room.'

'Oh I don't think so,' Cara said quickly. 'I don't want to involve the police.'

'I think Constable Potter will be discreet.'

'And I think my husband will fall asleep quite soon,' Cara said. 'Then we can go back. In any case, I must soon. I'm anxious about Emily.'

'If you were to go back on your own I would worry for you,' Johann said. 'Let me go with you.'

'I really don't think you need, Johann. I suspect the worst is over.'

Cara was not sure that she believed what she was saying. She said the words partly to comfort David, who still looked sick with fear.

'I'd like to stay here,' David said.

'Then we will for a little while,' Cara promised. 'But then we must all go back to bed and get some sleep. Don't forget you have to go back to school in the morning.'

'Shall I put on some music?' Johann suggested.

This time he chose not Mozart, but Brahms; gentle, soothing melodies. David relaxed against Cara's shoulder and almost fell asleep.

When the music finished they sat in silence for a while. There was no sound from anywhere. All seemed quiet at the house.

'I think he must be asleep,' Cara said. 'In which case he won't waken until morning. I *must* go back.' She looked at her watch and saw that it was ten past two. 'You should also get some sleep, Johann,' she added.

'Please let me come with you,' he asked again.

Cara shook her head.

'Better not.'

The three of them crossed the farmyard in silence. Cara, in front, opened the kitchen door carefully and looked in. Kit was fast asleep in the armchair, snoring loudly. She turned around and beckoned Mrs Hendry and David to follow her, and they passed swiftly through the kitchen and went upstairs. Cara went at once into Emily's room. The little girl lay in a tranquil sleep, oblivious to anything that was happening. Cara felt dizzy with relief at the sight of her.

'Now I shall make you both a drink of hot milk,' she said to the others. 'It will help you to sleep.'

'You're not going down there again!' Mrs Hendry objected.

'He won't hear me. He's well away.'

'Can I sleep with you, Grandma?' David asked.

'Of course you can, love,' Mrs Hendry said. 'In fact I was just going to suggest it. We'll keep each other warm.'

Cara, moving quietly, heated the milk and took it upstairs with some biscuits, then came down again, having forgotten to check that the fire was all right. It was as she walked into the kitchen that Kit stirred – and woke.

'Where the hell have you been?' he asked.

She stared at him. His handsome face was red and bloated. He was not a pretty sight.

'Where do you think we've been? You turned us out, remember? At gunpoint. Johann took us in, thank goodness.' She spoke quietly. The last thing she wanted was to disturb the others again. 'We were quite comfortable – no thanks to you.'

'I forbid you to go near that Kraut,' Kit ordered. 'He has his eye on you.'

'Don't talk rubbish! Anyway, I'm going to bed, and I advise you to do the same. I shall sleep in Susan's room.'

That roused him thoroughly. He stood up, waving his fist at her.

'Oh no you won't! Your place is in my bed, and don't you forget it! You've been glad of it up to now.'

'Not tonight,' Cara said. 'You're not fit to sleep with.' The way she felt at this moment, she never wanted to sleep with him again. She wished he would just go away and leave them all in peace.

Instead he seized her wrist in a grip from which, though she tried, she couldn't escape. She was surprised at his drunken strength.

'Let go!' she protested. 'Don't be so stupid! Let me go!'

'I'll soon show you who's stupid!' he retorted.

Pulling her by the wrist, he forced her out of the kitchen and then up the stairs. She wanted to cry out, but far more than that, she wished not to disturb Mrs Hendry and David again. They had had enough for one night, for which she felt the guilt.

In the bedroom he closed the door, then threw her roughly on to the bed and was on top of her, his mouth fastened on hers, his hands tearing in a frenzy at her clothes. And now he was hurting, hurting, hurting; and when she could no longer contain her moans of pain, he snatched a pillow and held it across her mouth to silence her.

'Twitch as much as a muscle,' he threatened, 'and it goes across your face! I'll show you who's boss in this house!'

She recognized with a cold certainty that it was no idle threat, that he had it in him, at this moment, to smother her. He was in thrall to a savagery which was beyond her knowledge and beyond her comprehension. He was no longer himself, and for the first time in her life she was truly terrified. She knew that if she struggled any further, she was lost. For her own safety, she must allow him to abuse her as he wished.

She lay as limply as a rag doll, but she was afraid to close her eyes.

She wanted to; she wanted to shut out the sight of the sickening lust on his face, she wanted to lose herself in unconsciousness so that she could no longer feel the pain, but fear compelled her to keep a watch on him.

His assault on her, though it seemed to Cara to go on forever, was mercifully short. He was in no state to sustain it. When it was over he collapsed on top of her, his face in her neck. A wave of nausea swept over her. She wanted to throw up at the drunken stink of him, and then the knowledge that she could no longer keep it down gave her the strength to push his inert body away, and to dash for the washbasin.

Next, she dragged herself to the bathroom. She had no strength to take a bath, but she bathed herself as well as she could. She was bleeding. When she had staunched the blood, she took a long drink of ice-cold water, then went to Susan's room, where she lay under the eiderdown, shivering, not sleeping, until morning.

When she heard her mother-in-law go downstairs, heard the sounds of her raking the fire into life, she wrapped herself in the eiderdown and followed her. She was desperately in need of two things: human comfort and hot tea.

Mrs Hendry gasped at the sight of her.

'What in the world . . .'

'Oh, Mother Hendry! Oh, Mother Hendry!' Cara sobbed.

At once, Mrs Hendry's arms were around her and she was leading her to the armchair.

'Oh love!' she said. 'Oh, love! What did he do to you?'

She had no need to ask and she didn't know why she'd done so. She knew very well what he'd done. I should never have left her, she accused herself. I should never have gone to bed and left her. She had seen it in his eyes.

Cara was weeping, rocking herself to and fro, to and fro, in the chair.

'I'm sorry!' she said. 'I'm sorry!'

'You've no need to be sorry,' Mrs Hendry said. 'And you cry, love. Let it come out. A good cry never did anybody any harm!'

She was conscious, as she said them, of the triteness of her words, but what *could* she say? She wasn't clever with words, but even if she had been, how could words heal this poor lamb right now?

'The kettle's on,' she said. 'I'll have you some hot tea in a minute. And a drop of whisky in it.'

'Not whisky!' Cara said, shuddering. She wanted never to smell whisky again as long as she lived.

They sat together and drank the tea, not saying much. In the end, Cara said, 'I must go and get dressed. There's the milking.'

No matter if it was the end of the world, the cows had to be milked.

'I'll ask Johann to do the milking,' Mrs Hendry said. 'He'll not mind.'

'No,' Cara said quickly. 'I want to do it. It will help.'

'I know what you mean,' Mrs Hendry acknowledged. 'I always reckoned tending the animals was the most healing thing I knew. But are you sure, love?'

'Quite sure.'

The hot drink and, even more, her mother-in-law's understanding presence, had calmed her. 'In any case,' she said, 'I must get dressed. I don't want David to see me upset, and he'll have to be up before long.'

Mercifully, she thought, this time there were no outward bruises to be seen. Both the physical pain, which still tore at her but would heal, and the mental pain, which was infinitely worse, were invisible.

Only the first streaks of gold and orange daylight banded the sky as Cara crossed the yard to the shippon. Dawn came later every day now. It was going to be a beautiful day, and she didn't know whether that would help her, or mock at her feelings.

A light showed in Johann's room. She wondered if he had slept after they'd left. Dear, good Johann! What would they ever do without him?

She was not to know, he would never tell her, that he had kept vigil most of the night. Nor would she know that, to spare her feelings and calm her fears, he had lied when he'd said that Marsden's gun wasn't loaded. But it wasn't now. He had emptied it.

His own gun, though, *was* loaded, and he knew that, if necessary, he would use it. In the war he had shot men against whom he knew nothing. He was sorry for it and always would be, but that was war. If it became necessary – and he had not defined in his mind what he meant by necessary – he would shoot Marsden with no more compunction than he would pot a rabbit on the fellside. There always had been, and always would be, shooting accidents where there were guns.

While Cara was milking, Johann left Beckwith and walked along the lane to where the field path led to Fawcett's farm. In the night he had decided, rightly or wrongly, that he must tell Grant Fawcett what was happening at Beckwith. Someone who could talk to Mrs Edward – as he still thought of her – must be made aware. However much he worried – and he did worry, for this was not the first time – he himself was not in that position. He could not presume either to comfort or advise her.

He would not tell Mrs Edward that he had been to Fawcett's and he hoped to be back at Beckwith before she had finished milking. He hoped by going so early that Grant Fawcett might be the first person he would meet there, and in that he was lucky. Grant was actually in the farmyard.

'Good heavens!' he exclaimed. 'Johann! Is something wrong at Beckwith?'

'No. That is to say . . . May I speak with you in private, Mr Grant? I won't come into the house, and I have to get back quickly before I'm missed.'

'Then I'd best walk part of the way back with you while you tell me whatever it is,' Grant said.

He listened with growing anger as Johann told him of the previous night's events.

'I have his gun, and it is no longer loaded,' Johann concluded. 'But he will get it back, and eventually he will reload it. There is nothing either you or I can do to prevent that.'

'Well, we must think of something,' Grant said. 'Though I can't see what. Oh God, why did she have to . . .' He broke off.

Johann knew well enough what he would have said. 'Why did she have to marry him?' Anybody with eyes in their head could see that Grant Fawcett wanted her, and always had, Johann thought, even when Mr Edward was alive.

'It is inexplicable,' was all Grant said.

When Cara came in from the milking, David was already up and having his breakfast. Aside from his pallor, and the smudgy dark shadows under his eyes, he gave no outward sign of being any the worse for his disturbed night. He looked up from his food, which he was eating with seeming appetite, and smiled at Cara as she sat down at the table.

'You're up in good time,' Cara said lightly. It was important, she thought, to restore everything to normality as quickly as poss-ible.

'I wanted to help with the milking, but I wasn't soon enough for that.'

'Never mind, you can help me both days next weekend. I'll be glad of it. We'll be all hands aloft with the sheep.'

'Where's Kit?' David asked hesitantly.

When he'd wakened this morning and, to his surprise, found himself in his grandmother's bed, and her not there, the memory of last night had come rushing back. Hurrying downstairs to check that everything was all right, he'd been reassured by finding that his grandmother looked and sounded exactly the same as always, and that Cara was busy with her usual milking. When she'd come in from the shippon a minute ago she'd seemed all right. Perhaps last night had not been as bad as he'd remembered?

All the same, he'd been really frightened, terrified of Kit. He remembered that well enough. Only when Johann had taken them in had he felt safe again. Now he didn't want to see Kit; he'd asked where he was simply so that he could keep out of his way. From last night, Kit had changed. David wondered if he might always be a bit afraid of him from now on.

'He's fast asleep in bed,' Cara said. 'And I reckon when he wakens he'll have quite a headache!' She tried desperately to make it sound a bit of a joke, but David couldn't accept that.

'I thought he was going to shoot us,' he said.

'Oh no, love! He'd not do that. The gun wasn't loaded, you know. He'd just had a drop too much to drink. I expect he met a lot of friends in Shepton and they all bought him drinks. You mustn't worry – everything's going to be all right.'

She hoped she sounded more convincing than she felt. How could everything ever be all right again? And how could David not be affected by what they'd gone through?

'Who's taking me to school?' David asked. He hoped it wouldn't be Kit.

'I am, of course.'

Well before it was time to leave, Grant Fawcett arrived at Beckwith. He looked at Cara keenly, observed her ashen face and the dullness of her red-rimmed eyes, but there was little he could say in front of the child. Mrs Hendry, also, gave not the slightest sign that anything was amiss.

'Are you all right?' he asked Cara.

'All right? Yes, of course.' He couldn't know anything and she had no intention of telling him. Thank heaven Kit was still sleeping it off.

'Where's Kit?' Grant enquired.

'He's not too well. He's having an extra hour in bed. Did you want him? Did you come for anything special?'

'Not really, except that I'm going into Shepton and I thought I'd offer David a lift to school.'

'That's kind of you, but I have to go in anyway,' Cara said.

She wanted to take David herself. She hoped to use the journey time to give him some of the reassurance she was sure he needed. Also, she thought she might tell David's teacher, in private, that there had been an upset over the weekend, and ask if David might be allowed to telephone home if he seemed not quite himself in the week.

Why had Grant enquired about Kit, she wondered. There was no love lost between them. Though they didn't quarrel openly, they avoided each other like the plague.

'Fine!' Grant said. 'Then as we're both going to be in Shepton, I'll treat you to a cup of coffee. Poppy's Pantry at ten o'clock.'

'Oh, I'm not sure . . .' Cara began.

'A good idea!' Mrs Hendry interrupted. 'Do you good.'

'All right,' Cara said.

It suddenly seemed to her that the one thing that might do her some good would be spending a little time with someone as nice and kind as Grant Fawcett. Also, any time today away from Kit would be a godsend. She had, as yet, no idea how they would face each other when he finally appeared. She knew she didn't want to see him – and she knew she would have to.

When Cara walked into the café, Grant was already there, seated at a table in the corner. So far, they were the only customers. She sat down and he ordered.

'A lovely day,' Grant said.

'Perfect for the time of the year,' Cara agreed. 'Have you finished potato picking?'

He nodded. 'Last week. A good crop. They'll see us through.'

There was an awkward silence. I shouldn't have come, Cara thought. She was in no mood for polite chat.

The silence was broken by the waitress with the coffee, but when she had left it fell again. Cara watched Grant unwrap his two small cubes of sugar, drop them into his cup, and begin to stir as intently as if his life depended on it. She pushed her own ration across the table.

'You can have mine. I don't take sugar.'

'Thanks.'

'I don't think . . .'

'Look here! . . .'

They spoke simultaneously, then Grant continued.

'Look, Cara, I didn't ask you here to talk about the weather, or potato crops.'

She could tell by the tone of his voice, by the anxious look on his face, that he knew something. But how?

'What can I do?' he asked.

'About what?'

'Cara, you know what! About Kit.'

'How do you know?' she asked. 'Who told you?'

'Does it matter?'

'It could only have been Johann,' she said. 'He shouldn't have.'

'Yes he should,' Grant contradicted. 'He'd have been wrong not to. He was deeply worried – *is* worried. And so am I. We can't stand aside and do nothing.'

'There's nothing you *can* do. It won't happen again, I'm sure.'
Thank God he had no idea what *had* happened. No-one would ever
know that, though her mother-in-law had guessed. 'He'd had too much
to drink, that was all,' she added.

'All? And what if he has too much to drink again? How can you
stop him? Last night wasn't the first time, was it?'

'What do you mean?' Cara said. 'What are you talking about?'

'David's birthday weekend. You didn't really think anyone believed
you'd fallen against the wall, did you? Oh Cara, *why* did you marry
him?'

'Because I loved him,' she said in a dull voice. 'I still do.'

'You can't!' Grant protested. 'How can you possibly love a man
like that?'

'I don't know, but I do. We don't choose who we'll love.'

She drained her coffee and put down her cup.

'I must go, Grant. There's nothing more to be said. Believe me,
I'm grateful to you, but there's nothing *you* can do.'

'I could give him a bloody good hiding, knock some sense into him!'
Grant said angrily. 'I think I'd enjoy that.'

'That wouldn't be any use to me,' Cara said. 'It would simply make
things worse. He doesn't like you, I'm sorry to say.'

'Oh, I'm aware of that!' Grant said. 'That's why I don't often come
to Beckwith. But let me tell you, from now on I'm going to be a
frequent visitor. I shall be keeping an eye on things.'

'You know I always like to see you, Grant, but it won't do any good,'
Cara said.

'We'll see! Cara, why don't you send him packing? He's not safe.
A man who threatens with a gun . . .'

'It wasn't loaded,' Cara said. 'He must have known that. He was
just frightening us.'

'Oh yes it was loaded! Johann didn't want to upset you any further
last night, but it was loaded all right. Cara, I'm not convinced that
you're taking this seriously. . .'

Not taking it seriously, she thought. My God, if I were to tell him
what happened afterwards!

'Just think what might have happened to you – to any one of you,
all three of you!'

How could she tell him what had happened to her in the
bedroom? The savage brutality which she still felt in her bruised
body had almost driven out the thought of what had happened
earlier. But Grant was right, the situation between herself and
Kit had put the others in danger. Facing that now, she froze with
horror.

'I'll not be happy until you see the last of him,' Grant said. 'But please promise you'll take care. And please promise you'll tell me if there's the least way I can help. You know there's nothing in the world I wouldn't do for you? You know my feelings. They don't change.'

'I know,' Cara said. 'I promise I'll come to you if I need to. I *am* truly grateful, Grant!'

'Gratitude doesn't come into it,' he said roughly.

She picked up her gloves and her handbag, and rose.

'I must go.'

'I'll go back with you.'

'Oh no!'

Whatever was to be faced, it would be best to face it alone.

Kit was sitting at the kitchen table, propping his head in his hands. Mrs Hendry was not in sight. She was probably in the dairy, Cara thought, keeping out of the way. He raised his head as he heard her, and peered at her through half-open eyes, as if he couldn't bear the light of day.

He looked horrible. What Cara could see of his eyes were bloodshot and bleary. His face, which last night had been mottled red, was now the colour of lard, with blue shadows where he needed a shave. Around him, so strong that it was almost tangible, the stink of stale whisky polluted the air.

'Pour me a drink, Cara love!' His voice was subdued, as if he couldn't bear the sound of it in his head.

'I'll do no such thing!' Cara said, taking off her coat and hanging it behind the door.

'Just a small whisky,' he pleaded. 'Hair of the dog!'

'If I thought there was so much as a teaspoonful of whisky in this house, I'd pour it down the sink!' Cara said fiercely.

She walked past him, towards the sink, and as she did so he caught her by the hand and held her in his strong grasp. At his touch, a shiver of revulsion ran through her. Yet hadn't she just told Grant Fawcett that she loved this man? 'How could you?' he'd said. And now she asked herself the same question.

'Let me go,' she said. 'At once!'

She hated him. Yet how could that be? This time yesterday she had loved him. How could she change so quickly? *He* had changed, but in the last twelve hours she had recognized that the changes in him had been taking place over many months, ever since she had married him, in fact.

It was something she had been unwilling to recognize: his drinking, his streak of cruelty, his antagonism to most people; his ruthless determination to have his own way in everything, to rule and run the farm, to make everything his.

312

But because she loved him, because he could charm her, because at first the changes in him were gradual, and most of all because the magic that was between them in their bed transcended all the problems of the day, she had closed her eyes to what was happening. It would all come right, she had told herself.

He let go of her wrist.

'Don't be like that, Cara,' he said.

'Don't be like that!' she shouted. 'Do you know what you've done? Do you know what you did to me?'

'I'm sorry if I was a bit rough.'

'Rough? Is that what you call it? A bit rough? You were an animal, a wild beast. What you did to me was rape!'

'Oh, come on,' he said. 'You're my wife. All I wanted was a bit of love!'

'Love? You don't know the first thing about love. All you know is power and greed and force and lust. Rape isn't love.'

'You're talking rubbish now,' he said. 'A man can't rape his own wife.'

'You did just that,' Cara said. 'And never mind me, what about the rest? What about turning us out of the house? What about threatening us with a loaded gun? An old woman and a child! What about scaring David half out of his wits?'

He looked confused, as if he didn't know what she was talking about, but she sensed he was putting on an act.

'Don't pretend you can't remember,' she said. 'I can see through that.'

'I wouldn't have fired,' he said. 'You know that.'

'I don't know that,' she contradicted. 'I no longer know what you'll do when you're in drink. I reckon you're capable of anything, and I can't take the risk. I have to think of the others. I had to leave Emily in the house with you. How do you think I felt about that?'

'Oh, come on Cara,' he said in a wheedling voice. 'You know I wouldn't harm a hair of little Emily's head.'

'I don't know that either. I can't trust you any longer. The fact is . . .' She hesitated. How could she bring herself to say it?

'But you do love me, Cara?'

'Damn you, yes I do! I wish I didn't, but I do!'

'Then that's all that matters. We can sort out everything else. I'll turn over a new leaf. I'll never get drunk again. I promise, hand on heart!'

'How can I believe you?' Cara said. 'No, Kit, it's best if you go.'

313

'Go?' He was astounded. 'Go where?'

'I don't know. Just leave Beckwith. Leave us in peace.'

The pain in her heart as she forced out the words was worse than any bodily pain. She felt as if she was tearing herself to pieces, giving her life away. Yet, underneath the agony, instinct told her that it was what she had to do. There was no doubt of it.

Kit stared at her in disbelief, which quickly gave way to anger.

'Oh no, madam! You can't do that! You can't turn me out just because you've got tired of me.'

'I haven't tired of you,' Cara said. She felt numb. She didn't want to argue, all she wanted now was for him to go. 'And I'm not turning you out. I'm asking you to go, of your own free will.'

'You're mad!' he said. 'Just because I take a drink once in a while . . .'

'Take a drink? You get roaring drunk, you threaten our lives, you rape me – yes, I said *rape* – and you call it taking a drink! And it's not the first time, is it? Look at this mark on my face. Remember how I got it? There'll be a third time, and a fourth and a fifth. What's going to happen to us?'

'I thought you loved me,' he said. 'I suppose you've got some other man lined up the minute you get rid of me.'

'How dare you?' Cara flared. 'You know I've never looked at another man!'

'Well, you're not getting rid of me that easily.'

Then his mood changed and he began to plead.

'Please, Cara. I don't want to go. I'll stop drinking. I'll turn over a new leaf. Give me another chance!'

This was not the Kit Marsden she knew. That one would beg for nothing, he was too proud. He would take what he wanted as his right.

'I can change,' he said eagerly. 'Let me show you, Cara!'

She hesitated. He saw her hesitation and pressed his advantage.

'I'm your husband, Cara. You're my wife. At least let's give it another try!'

She sat down, buried her head in her hands. How could she know what to do? A minute ago she had been certain, and now she no longer was. She couldn't kill her love for this man, not in an instant.

'Give me another chance,' he begged. He was standing at the side of her, not touching her. After a while she looked up.

'Very well,' she said. 'A fresh start for both of us.' She felt no joy in the decision. 'There's just one thing . . .'

'Anything!' he promised.
'I can't sleep with you. Not yet.'
'But Cara . . .!'
'Not yet, Kit,' she said.

TWENTY-TWO

On the following Friday morning the telephone rang.

'It's for you,' Mrs Hendry said, handing the receiver to Cara.

It was Madame Simonetta, almost incoherent with emotion, so that Cara found it difficult to understand her.

'In fifteen years it 'as never 'appened to me before!' Madame Simonetta cried. 'I am desolated! It is the honour of my school!'

'*Please* Madame Simonetta, please tell me what *has* happened,' Cara said anxiously. 'Is Susan ill? Has she had an accident?'

'Not ill, but out of 'er mind, I reckon! To do such a thing she must be. Your stepdaughter 'as run away!'

'Run away! Where? How? Do you mean she's on her way home?'

'She 'as gone to Bristol, to join a pantomime!' Madame Simonetta said in tones of deep disgust. 'A *pantomime*! Oh, when I think of the plans I 'ave for 'er – Shakespeare, Shaw, even Ibsen – and she chooses pantomime. *Red Riding 'Ood!* Not even *Cinderella*!'

'I still don't understand,' Cara said. 'When did you learn about this? Has she actually got a job?'

'I learned of it when she did not turn up for 'er class this morning. And then, be'old, in the post is this letter. She 'as not got a job, she 'as got an interview only, but she seems sure she will be taken on and I daresay she is right. I believe we 'ave seen the last of 'er at Magda Dale, Madame 'Endry. Do you know nothing of this?'

'Nothing. Except . . . that is . . .' Cara broke off. There was nothing to be gained by mentioning Susan's attitude last weekend. 'I've not heard from Susan,' she said truthfully. 'But I shall get in touch with my sister Laura. She and Susan share lodgings, as you are aware. If anyone knows about this it will be Laura. I will telephone you the minute I hear anything.'

'Per'aps you will come to Manchester,' Madame Simonetta said firmly. 'There are other matters to be settled.'

'I'll do whatever seems best,' Cara promised.

'It 'as never 'appened to me before, such a thing!' Madame Simonetta repeated. 'Never! You cannot imagine what . . .'

'I'm so sorry,' Cara interrupted. 'I'll be in touch.'

Mrs Hendry had listened to the one-sided conversation with anxious interest.

'For goodness sake, what's it all about?' she asked.

'Susan's run off from Magda Dale, or, presumably, from her lodgings. She's gone after a job in Bristol.'

'Bristol!' As far as Mrs Hendry was concerned it was the far side of the moon. 'But that's past London!'

'Considerably,' Cara agreed. 'I must telephone Ma at once, see if she's heard anything from Laura; though surely Laura would have phoned me?'

'It's news to me,' Mrs Dunning said a few minutes later. 'Actually, Laura's been home for a couple of days with a cold. She only went back this morning. I'm sure she knew nothing. In fact, she told me she'd invited Susan for this coming weekend, but Susan refused, said she had other plans.'

'She most certainly had,' Cara said grimly. 'Well, Ma, I shall go to Manchester and see what I can sort out. I can't just do nothing. Madame Simonetta is hopeless on the telephone. Also, Mrs Hargreaves might know something, and she's not on the telephone.'

'I'll go with you,' Mrs Dunning offered.

'Thanks. I'll pick you up,' Cara said.

Mrs Hendry was totally in agreement with Cara's decision to go to Manchester, but Kit was not.

'What can you do?' he said. 'You can't do anything. You can't fetch her back.'

'I can and I will if I think that's best,' Cara said decisively.

He shook his head.

'Wrong! You can't *make* her come back. She's old enough to leave home legally, even if she's given her real age, which I doubt. You'd best leave her be.'

'Leave her be? Take no notice? Are you mad?'

'She'll get in touch with you,' he prophesied. 'As soon as she has something to tell you, you'll hear from her.'

'I can't take it quite so calmly,' Cara said. 'But then, I have the responsibility and you don't. And another thing – where did she get the money to go to Bristol? She was complaining at the weekend that she was stony broke.'

Kit shrugged his shoulders, and went off to work.

Cara and her mother arrived in Manchester early in the afternoon and went straight to Laura's lodgings. Mrs Hargreaves was out, but as luck would have it, Laura was there.

'I don't have to go in this afternoon,' she explained. 'I have an evening session. But honestly, Cara, this is the first I've heard of it, except Susan's kept on about wanting a job. And I've not seen Mrs Hargreaves today.'

'Perhaps Mrs Hargreaves doesn't know,' Beth Dunning said. 'If she saw her leave, she'd think she was just going off to Magda Dale.'

'Could we look in Susan's room?' Cara asked.

Susan's room was the same untidy kind of heap as her bedroom at Beckwith. She had certainly not packed up her entire belongings and taken them with her. What they did see, however, propped up conspicuously against the dressing-table mirror, was a note addressed to Laura. She tore it open and read it.

Cara held out her hand.

'Do you think I might see it?'

'I suppose you'd better,' Laura said reluctantly. Cara read it out loud.

'I'm going to Bristol after a job, and I just *know* I'll get it. Have written to Old Mother Simonetta but not yet to Cara. Will do so when I know more. Don't want her chasing after me. Be a chum and stall her. I'd do the same for you.

    Yours till hell freezes,
Susan.

(Henceforth Suzanne Delamere. Do you like it?)

PS If I get the job, which I will, will you be an angel and pack my stuff and send it on?'

'Well! The little minx!' Mrs Dunning said.

Cara sat down on the bed.

'What do I do next? It looks as if Kit was right; there isn't much I can do until we hear from her.'

'She says she'll write,' Laura pointed out.

'I still can't work out where she got the money. It's not just the fare; she'll have had to stay overnight.'

'Don't look at me!' Laura said. 'She didn't get it from me because I don't have much. And I know she was short; she said so.'

'I suppose I'd better go and see Madame Simonetta,' Cara said. 'Sort things out there.'

An awful idea was beginning to form in her mind. Though Madame Simonetta had said nothing directly about money on the telephone, she had said, 'There are other matters to settle.' What exactly did she mean? But I've never known Susan be dishonest, Cara thought.

Madame Simonetta, when Cara was shown into her room, was still deeply offended that a pupil of her school had chosen to leave, and to go into *pantomime*.

'It is an insult!' she said dramatically, her small black eyes flashing with indignation.

She was also sharply aware that there were two terms' fees in the balance. About what might happen to Susan she seemed less perturbed.

'I shall be obliged to charge you to the end of the school year, Madame 'Endry,' she said firmly. 'There is no way I can fill Susan's place in the middle of it.' (But perhaps I can, she thought. We'll have to see. But first make sure of the money.)

'I understand that,' Cara said. 'I'll let you have a cheque the minute it's due. Of course I'm hoping that Susan will return, and that when she does you'll have her back.'

'We shall 'ave to see,' Madame Simonetta said. 'I can make no promises. Oh, 'ow *could* she?'

'That's what I ask myself, but for a different reason,' Cara said. 'I don't understand how my stepdaughter raised the money to go to Bristol.'

'Well certainly not 'ere!' Madame Simonetta snapped. 'I would 'ave known of it! I know all that goes on at Magda Dale.'

Quite obviously you don't, Cara thought – but let it pass.

'Well the minute I hear anything, I'll let you know,' she promised.

In the entrance hall she collected her mother and Laura, and returned the latter to her lodgings before starting back for Akersfield. There she stayed only long enough to greet her father. He looked at her with concern.

'You don't look quite the thing,' he said. 'Are you all right, love?'

'Quite all right,' Cara assured him. 'Just a bit tired, that's all. And worried.'

'Dashing off to Manchester after that little monkey won't do you a lot of good,' he grumbled.

'I expect you'll hear something soon,' Mrs Dunning said. 'Let us know when you do.'

'I will,' Cara promised. 'Anyway, I must be off now.'

'Always rushing away,' Arnold Dunning complained.

'Well there you are, that's farming for you,' Cara said.

Arnold Dunning had thought from the very first that farming was no life for his daughter, let alone taking on two stepchildren. As for her second husband, he couldn't do with him at all. He didn't trust him as far as he could throw him, but it was no use saying so to Cara. Love was certainly blind there.

Cara drove west, towards a sun sinking over the horizon like a ball of red fire. When the last curve of it had gone, she turned north for Arendale. It was not of Susan she thought as she drove, but of Kit. There was no more she could do about Susan until they heard from her, though if that didn't happen soon, nothing would prevent her taking off for Bristol. She had to know that the child – and in some ways she *was* quite childish – was all right. But for the time being, and quite deliberately, she pushed Susan from her mind, and thought of Kit.

In the last five days there had been no more scenes, no quarrels, no recriminations – and very few words of any kind between them: but she couldn't bear him near her, she couldn't stand it if he so much as touched her in passing. When would it end? Would it ever? She had seen the anger in his eyes when she flinched from his proximity, yet she couldn't help herself. How long would he stand it? Patience was not one of his virtues.

When she arrived at the house, supper was over, but there was a place laid for her at the table. Only Mrs Hendry was in the kitchen.

'Where is everyone?' Cara asked.

'I've just put Emily to bed,' Mrs Hendry said. 'She's had a fractious afternoon; I think she's starting a nasty cold. I gave her half a Fennings powder. As for the others, Johann has gone to his quarters and Kit . . .' She hesitated.

'Where is Kit?' Cara asked quickly.

'Kit's gone into Faverwell. As soon as he'd finished his supper. He didn't say what for, but he did say he wouldn't be late.'

'He didn't say why?'

'No love, he didn't.'

But they both knew that there was nothing to do in Faverwell with a dark evening except spend it in the Dragon.

'He *did* say he'd not be late back,' Mrs Hendry repeated. 'I'm sure he meant it.'

'I expect he did,' Cara said. 'Well, we'll see.'

'So what happened in Manchester?' Mrs Hendry enquired.

Cara gave her all the details.

'So I didn't get much further, except that I saw the note to Laura. Susan must have had it all worked out beforehand. She must have known when she was here last weekend.'

'What are we going to do?' Mrs Hendry said, clearly troubled.

'We'll give her time to write, but if we don't hear from her in a day or two I shall certainly go to Bristol. It shouldn't be difficult to find her. Even if there's more than one theatre, someone is bound to know which one is putting on *Red Riding Hood* at Christmas.'

'Bristol seems such a long way off,' Mrs Hendry said.

'It is. And it'll be highly inconvenient for me to leave Beckwith, with tupping so near. But of course I shall go.'

'Well, let's hope we hear from her soon,' Mrs Hendry said. 'And now I'm going to pour you a nice glass of sherry while your supper's heating up. You look all in.'

'I *am* tired,' Cara admitted. 'I'd like an early night.'

Nevertheless, she thought, she wouldn't dare to go to bed before Kit returned.

For the rest of the evening she watched the clock anxiously – and was aware that Mrs Hendry was doing the same. To her intense relief, Kit came in shortly after ten o'clock. He had had a few drinks, she could smell it on his breath, but he was a long way from being drunk.

Mrs Hendry rolled up her knitting and said, 'Well, I'll be off then. It's seemed a long day.'

'I agree,' Cara said. 'I shan't be long after you. I'm tired.'

'So you're tired!' Kit said when Mrs Hendry had left the room. 'Well, we know what that means, don't we?'

'It means exactly what I say,' Cara said. 'I *am* tired. It's been a trying day. In fact, if you'll excuse me, I'll be off to bed.' She could see his mood. He was truculent. Any minute an argument would start, and she couldn't do with it.

'I hope that means you're going to your own bed – *our* bed,' Kit said gruffly.

Cara hesitated. She wanted to do as he asked; she wanted to bridge this awful gulf between them, or life would be intolerable. But it was too soon; she couldn't do it; it was too much to ask.

'I'm sorry, Kit, I can't. Perhaps in a little while – but not yet. It's too soon.'

She was no longer using Susan's room. It had occurred to her that Susan wouldn't like it, she would see it as an intrusion. She had, therefore, fixed up a single bed in Emily's room.

'Too soon, is it?' Kit said nastily. 'And when does madam think she might return to being a proper wife?'

'When sir seems more likely to be a decent husband,' Cara retorted. 'Who drove me from my own bed? And you're not the least bit sorry about anything. All you do is *demand!*'

Oh dear, she thought. Why did I say it? We're quarrelling, and I can't bear it!

'And all you do is refuse,' Kit said.

'I'm going to bed,' she told him firmly.

'Go to bed then,' Kit said. 'Go to hell!'

Emily was sleeping, though there were round red patches on her cheeks, hot to the touch. Cara pulled the covers over her daughter, then climbed into her own bed, into the warm comfort of the flannelette sheets Mrs Hendry insisted on from October to the following May. In spite of her troubled mind, she fell quickly into a deep sleep.

She had no idea how long she had been asleep when she awoke – and saw Kit. He was standing in his pyjamas by the side of the bed, looking down at her. She was not sure, either then or later, whether he had wanted her to wake, or had hoped that she would remain asleep while he did whatever he had come for.

'What is it?' she asked sleepily.

'I want you! Cara, I want you! Don't turn me away!'

She sat up, fully awake now, and with consciousness came fear. He loomed over her, his eyes hard with passion.

'Go back to bed,' she said.

'No,' his voice was urgent. 'No, I'll not! I want to come into your bed!'

Then he looked suddenly pathetic, his mouth trembling, like a child seeking comfort. To her surprise and dismay, pity for him swept over her. But it was nothing more than pity. She didn't want him near her and his sudden weakness repelled her more than ever.

'Please, Cara! Please!'

She was immeasurably distressed to hear this once so-strong man pleading with her, grovelling.

'Please!' he begged. 'I just want to lie beside you. I won't force you. I'm lonely, Cara!'

'Please go back to bed, Kit. You'll waken Emily.' She tried to keep her voice steady, calm.

'Don't send me away! For pity's sake don't send me away!'

It was for pity's sake only that she overcame a reluctance which almost amounted to revulsion, and turned back the bedclothes to let him come in. She lay on her back, as rigid as iron, while he took his place beside her. He smelled strongly of drink; now he *did* seem drunk.

'Oh Cara,' he said, 'you don't know what it's been like!'

'Yes I do,' she said. 'Please go to sleep.'

'Let me hold you,' he said. 'You've got to let me hold you!'

When he put his arms around her already stiff body she clenched her fists and bit her lips to stop herself crying out, but when he began to caress her, stroking her neck and her breasts, she could bear it no longer. In one swift move she flung the bedclothes away and jumped out of bed, stood there shivering in her nightdress.

'No!' she cried. 'I can't, I can't! It's no good! Go back to your own bed. Leave me alone!'

He was no longer suppliant. 'I'll show you!' he shouted, his voice loud with anger, his face contorted with it. He leapt out of bed and grabbed hold of her.

'Please don't!' she begged. 'Oh Kit, please leave me alone!'

'Why should I?' he shouted. 'Why should I leave you alone? You're my wife. I've got my rights. The law says I've got my rights – and you've got your duty.'

She escaped from his grasp and ran swiftly out of the bedroom and down the stairs. In the kitchen she picked up the heavy iron poker and stood there, holding it aloft in front of her, waiting for him. Even when he didn't come she continued to grip it firmly, holding it high.

It was thus that Mrs Hendry, wakened by the quarrel, and by the sound of Cara running downstairs, found her. When she took the poker from her, Cara fell in a dead faint at her feet.

When Cara opened her eyes it was to see Edith Hendry bending anxiously over her, chafing her hands to bring warmth into them.

'There you are, doy,' Mrs Hendry said. 'Now I'm going to sit you in the armchair and fetch a blanket, then you're going to have a sup of brandy.'

She asked no questions. Now wasn't the time.

In moments, she had Cara wrapped in a blanket and had rekindled the fire. Then she took down a glass from the shelf and went to the sideboard cupboard for the brandy.

'That's funny!' she said. 'It's not here. I must have put it back in the wrong place, though I don't remember when we used it last.'

Yet why would I have put it back in the wrong place? she asked herself. The brandy had been kept in the same spot on the same shelf, ready for emergencies and seldom touched otherwise, since she had come to Beckwith as a bride. It came as no surprise to her that it wasn't in the second cupboard. Why should it be?

'It's gone!' she said. 'The brandy's gone.'

She and Cara looked at each other.

'Well,' Cara said steadily, 'I'd as soon not have brandy anyway. I'd rather have a hot drink.'

There was no need for either of them to discuss the whereabouts of the brandy bottle. It was quite obvious.

'You should get back to bed, love,' Mrs Hendry said presently.

'I couldn't sleep,' Cara protested. Yet she was so tired, so unbelievably tired. 'Oh, Mother Hendry, what am I going to do?' she cried.

'I don't know, and that's a fact,' Mrs Hendry said. 'I just know something's got to be done. Do you mind if I ask you a straight question, Cara?'

'Ask anything.'

'Do you love him? I mean really love him?'

'I no longer know,' Cara admitted. 'I *did* love him, I think I was besotted by him, but now I don't know. I wish I did!'

'I think besotted is right,' Mrs Hendry said. 'Oh, I'm not blaming you, it's not something we ask for, is it? But it's not the same as love.'

'Yet while it lasts . . .'

'Oh yes, while it lasts . . . but how long is that? I don't know, I'm sure.'

'I think *you* should go to bed, Mother Hendry,' Cara said gently. 'It's selfish of me to keep you up like this.' At this hour of the day her mother-in-law looked old. And she is old, Cara thought. She shouldn't be troubled by my worries.

They went upstairs together. Passing Kit's bedroom they could hear him snoring. Whether I love him or not, Cara told herself, he cares nothing for me.

Next morning Kit, surprisingly, was down to breakfast at his usual time. He was pasty-faced and silent, but he showed none of the fatigue which sat on Cara like a ton of lead. It was an unusually silent meal. Johann, of course, never had much to say. He spoke when he was spoken to, as if, even after all these years of taking his meals with the family, he was still far apart from them. But usually the others talked, mostly about the work of the day ahead.

This morning there was none of that. Cara could think of nothing to say – how could she indulge in small talk? Kit glowered at his plate, and ate steadily. Mrs Hendry seemed far away and even Emily was quiet, though in her case happily so, enjoying her scrambled eggs and toast fingers.

It was a relief when Rob Sellars, the postman, delivered the mail.

'A letter from Bristol!' he said chattily. If it had been a postcard he would have told them the news before they read it. Postcards were public.

'I'll take that,' Cara said.

Usually, she would open her letters while he drank the tea which Mrs Hendry always offered him. This morning there was none forthcoming.

'I'd best get on,' he said – and left.

The moment he was out of the door Cara tore open the envelope and read the letter. Mrs Hendry's face was one large question mark; Kit did not even raise his head.

'She got the job,' Cara said. 'Assistant to the stage manager – so I suppose she *will* sweep the stage and make the tea!'

She read the remainder of the letter out loud.

'I am going to be very happy here. I've got some good digs, cheap, and with a nice landlady who reminds me of Grandma. Love to everyone, not forgetting Kit.'

The truth hit Cara the moment the words left her mouth.

'*You* gave her the money!' she accused Kit.

'So what?' he said laconically.

'So what!' Cara cried. 'You had no business to do that! You know perfectly well that we didn't want her to leave Magda Dale. We discussed the whole thing.'

'*You* didn't want her to leave,' he contradicted. 'It's always what you want, isn't it?'

'Of course not,' she protested. 'But I *am* responsible. You went behind my back, you undermined what I was trying to do. You'd no business to give her the money!'

Kit brought his fist down hard on the table, so that the crockery rattled. Emily, startled, began to cry.

'What I do with my money *is* my business!' he shouted. 'It's one of the few rights I have left in this bloody place!' He glared across the table – and met Johann's steady gaze.

'And you can get out, Kraut!' he said furiously. 'This is a family affair. You're the hired help. You're not wanted. Leave the sodding house and get to work!'

Johann turned to Cara.

'Mrs Edward, do you wish me to leave?' His voice was controlled but his eyes were like steel.

Kit jumped to his feet.

'What do you mean, Mrs Edward? She's Mrs Marsden, Mrs Marsden, Mrs Marsden! Don't anybody forget it – including *you*!' he said to Cara.

Cara thought Johann might just have used the wrong name intentionally. If so, it was no help to her.

'If you've finished your breakfast, Johann,' she said pleasantly, 'then you might prefer to leave. Who could blame you? But only when you're ready.'

'Thank you,' Johann said. 'I will go.'

'So you think it's clever to show me up in front of that Kraut bugger!' Kit thundered, when Johann had left. 'Well if I had my way he'd be out of here, lock, stock and barrel!'

'You showed yourself up,' Cara said. 'You don't need any help from me in that direction. You never do. Why don't *you* just go, lock, stock and barrel? I've had all I can take.'

'Oh no, madam! You don't get rid of me that easy! I'm here to stay. Don't you kid yourself otherwise.'

Emily was crying noisily, her face crumpled, the tears racing down her cheeks. Cara held her close.

'It's all right, pet! No-one's going to hurt you.' She stroked the child's head, trying to soothe her.

'For your information,' Kit said, 'I'm going out now. Never mind where, and I'll be back when it suits me and not before.'

'Drunk, I suppose!' Cara said bitterly.

'Wait and see!'

'Well, let me remind you that it's Friday,' Cara said. 'David is due home this afternoon and I don't want him frightened out of his wits again. What sort of a man would frighten children?'

He pulled his chair away from the table with a force which sent it flying backwards. Emily screamed with new fright. Then he strode out of the kitchen, and a minute later they heard his van start up, and be driven away.

Cara held Emily tightly, laid her cheek against the child's silky hair. Tears rolled down her cheeks and mingled with the child's.

Mrs Hendry touched her briefly on the shoulder.

'I'll make a fresh pot of tea,' she said helplessly.

It was thus that Grant Fawcett found them a minute or two later.

'What's with Kit?' he asked. 'He all but ran me down in the lane. If I hadn't jumped smartly, he would have.'

'The mood he's in, he'd run down his own mother!' Mrs Hendry said.

'We had an argument,' Cara said.

Emily was quiet now. Exhausted by her crying, she had fallen asleep against her mother's shoulder. Cara laid her gently on the sofa and covered her with a shawl.

'I'm sorry,' Grant said.

He couldn't bear to see Cara like this, defeated and miserable. It was so totally unlike her. He had called at Beckwith every day since the episode with the gun, trying to find excuses, always fearful of what he might walk in on. He tried to time his calls so that Kit would be out of the house, but he wasn't always successful. Kit Marsden hated him. He was like a red rag to a bull, and that was no help to Cara. But he had to know, though Johann had promised to telephone him at once, day or night, if things got out of hand.

'Susan has run away from Magda Dale and taken a job in Bristol, in pantomime.' Cara showed him Susan's letter. 'I discovered that Kit had lent her the money to do this. I was angry.'

But she knew, and she wondered if Grant Fawcett knew, that this was not really what it was about. It went much deeper. At times it seemed to her that all this was happening so suddenly, like a ball set in motion down a steep hill. At other times she felt it had been going on forever, so that it was difficult to remember the good times. But over every other emotion was the feeling of helplessness, of being trapped in something from which there was no escape. She had no realistic hope that Kit would change his ways.

'Cara, I have to say it . . .'

She cut him short. 'There's nothing to be said, Grant.'

'Yes there is. You must get rid of him. You must send him packing. For the children's sake, not just yours.'

'I know,' Cara said. 'I've tried. He refuses to go.'

He would, Grant thought bitterly. He was on to a good thing at Beckwith. He had always seen Marsden's advent in that light.

'Where has he gone now?' he asked.

'I don't know. Nor do I know when he'll be back. Ironically, we need him here. We start tupping next week, and I don't have to tell you there's a lot to do beforehand.'

'I'll see if I can spare Len for an hour or two,' Grant promised. 'But we're rather in the same boat. Shall I ask around in Faverwell, see if there's anyone available for casual work?'

Cara shook her head.

'It wouldn't do. Not with Kit here. It would be asking for more trouble. Thank you all the same, Grant. I do appreciate everything.'

'If you want to send David over to Fawcett's any time this weekend, we'd be pleased to have him,' Grant offered.

'Thank you,' Cara said. 'I might just do that, though I know he's looking forward to helping Johann.'

After Grant had left, she worked all day on the fells. There was healing in seeing to the sheep; everything seemed less complicated with animals. When it was time to collect David from school, Kit had not returned.

David was excited by the thought of Susan being in pantomime.

'Just imagine,' he said proudly, 'my sister on the stage! Shall we be able to go and see her?'

'I doubt it,' Cara replied. 'Bristol's a long way, and we're very busy.'

'We won't be busy when the tupping's over,' David said. 'I think she'd like us to go. After all, it's the first time ever!'

'I'll think about it,' Cara promised.

All evening, attending to the children, doing her chores, she had her mind on Kit, and an ear cocked for the sound of his van along the lane. He didn't come.

At midnight she said to Mrs Hendry: 'I think we should turn in.'

She was afraid to go to bed, though her body craved rest and sleep – and there would be a long, hard day on the farm tomorrow.

While still listening – the country night was full of sounds – she fell asleep quickly. It was dark when she awoke, but when she looked at the clock on her bedside table, she was amazed to see that it was six o'clock. She had slept through the night; she had not heard him come in.

She pulled on her slacks, and a heavy sweater, and hurried to the shippon for the milking.

TWENTY-THREE

An hour later Johann, crossing the yard, seeing the light in the shippon, stopped to look in.

'Do you want any help?' he asked.

'No thank you, Johann. I'm almost through,' Cara said. 'I just have to tidy things up.'

When she went back to the house it was still not quite daylight, but in the east the sky was lightening. Mrs Hendry and Johann were at the breakfast table, but there was no sign of Kit. She wasn't surprised. Over the last few weeks he had come down later and later, and no doubt this morning he was sleeping off last night's excesses. It suited her. She would be glad to be out of the house before he appeared.

The moment he had finished eating, Johann pushed his chair back, said thank you, as always, to Mrs Hendry, put on his jacket, and left – Bess at his heels.

'I'll be up very soon!' Cara called after him as he went out of the door.

'I'll let the children lie as long as they will,' Mrs Hendry said. 'The rest will do David good. I thought he looked a mite peaked when he came home yesterday.'

She poured herself another cup of tea, strong and milky, the way she liked it, and sat down again at the table. She enjoyed these snatched moments of leisure before the real work of the day began. When she'd seen to the children there'd be the work in the dairy, all the pans and churns to be cleaned and scalded, and a dozen other jobs. The dairy was still her responsibility, and after that there was plenty to do in the house.

'So what time did his lordship come in last night?' she asked Cara. 'I must have fallen asleep the minute my head touched the pillow.'

'I don't know,' Cara admitted. 'I wasn't long myself. I was dead tired. Anyway, thank goodness he came in quietly for once. I suppose he's sleeping it off.'

'Well, I'm not going to waken him,' Mrs Hendry said. 'If he sails down when breakfast's cleared he'll have to fend for himself.'

'Quite right!' Cara agreed. 'And I must go. There's a lot on today. Tell David he can come up and give us a hand as soon as he's ready.'

When she left the house and walked towards the lane she was conscious that something was not as it should be. She stopped, and looked around, not certain of herself. Then she realized what was wrong. There was no sign of Kit's van. He always parked it in the same spot, and it wasn't there. Nor was it anywhere else in the yard, nor by the gate.

Could it be further down the lane? Could he have run out of petrol and had to walk the last bit? But from the gate she could see a long stretch of the lane in the Faverwell direction. There was no sign of any vehicle.

She turned around and walked back into the house.

'Kit's van isn't there,' she told Mrs Hendry.

'Not there? Are you sure, love?'

'Quite sure. There's no sign of it.'

Mrs Hendry smiled, a broad smile which puffed out her cheeks and crinkled her eyes.

'Don't tell me he had to walk home! No wonder he's sleeping it off!'

'I don't think . . .'

'Or perhaps he got a lift?' Mrs Hendry suggested.

But somehow, Cara knew that that wasn't the answer. She crossed the kitchen and went upstairs to the bedroom. The bed was empty, the bedclothes totally undisturbed.

She ran down again.

'He's not there! His bed hasn't been slept in!'

Mrs Hendry looked at her in disbelief.

'Are you *sure*?'

'Of course I'm sure!' Cara said.

'Yes, it was a stupid question. Could he . . .' Mrs Hendry hesitated, searching for a logical reason. 'Could he have gone out very early this morning?' She knew as she said it that it was highly unlikely.

'Even if you can see Kit getting up and going out in the dark,' Cara said, 'can you envisage him making his bed before he left?'

'Of course not!' Mrs Hendry agreed.

Cara sat down suddenly on the nearest chair.

'So he didn't come home! What's happened to him? What shall I do?'

Is he being perverse? she asked herself. Or had he decided, after all, to leave – and chosen this way to do it? But when he'd gone from the house yesterday he'd taken none of his belongings with him.

'What shall I do?' she repeated.

Perhaps he was lying somewhere, injured . . . even . . . She pushed the thought away from her. Someone would have found him, wouldn't they? But perhaps not. It was only just daylight, even now.

'Shall I telephone Grant?' she asked.

'I'm not so sure about that,' Mrs Hendry said doubtfully. 'There might be a simple explanation, and if Kit turns up and finds Grant on the trail there'll be trouble.'

'You're right,' Cara agreed. 'As you say, there might be a simple explanation. Perhaps his van broke down in Shepton. Perhaps . . .' But no explanation she could think of need have prevented him telephoning, letting her know.

'I'll be off to work,' she said. 'I'll give him time. But if he doesn't turn up before dinnertime then I shall call the police. I shall just have to!' She wondered if it wasn't leaving things too long, to wait even until dinnertime.

'You could phone the pubs,' Mrs Hendry suggested.

'Yes, I could. Well, I'll give it two or three hours and then maybe I'll do that before I ring the police. If anyone telephones about him while I'm on the fell, you'll let me know, won't you?'

'Straight away,' Mrs Hendry promised.

'I shall be working in Scarbottom,' Cara said, naming the field. 'So if he comes along the lane I'll see him for myself.'

She left the house aware that her anxiety was more evident than she would have liked and walked, deep in thought, to join Johann where he was inspecting the ewes on the lower slopes. Most of them had now been brought down from the higher pastures, and by tomorrow they would all be down.

'Kit didn't come home!' she said.

Johann, on his knees examining a ewe, looked up startled, then rose to his feet. His face showed concern. But for me, Cara thought, not for Kit.

'Do you wish me to do anything, enquire anywhere?' he asked.

'Not just yet. I'm not quite sure what we *should* do. We'll give it an hour or two, then I'll go back to the house and telephone.'

For the next couple of hours they worked side by side, neither of them saying much. That was not unusual. Johann never had much to say, but this morning the silence between them was uncomfortable, on Cara's part filled with an anxiety she couldn't quell. She felt relieved when Johann, moving higher up the fell to bring down more ewes, left her on her own.

She straightened up and looked around. It was a beautiful morning, crisp and clear, with the sun touching the white walls with gold, and turning the few remaining leaves which clung tenaciously to the trees by the river to even deeper shades of bronze and purple. She loved this time of the year in the dale, though one had to savour each day's good weather to the full, knowing that winter was near. Then, as she stood there, she saw Kit's van approaching down the lane.

Relief surged through her that, after the horrors she had envisaged, the pictures her imagination had conjured up since she'd discovered his absence, he was safe and sound. Her relief, however, was swiftly followed by a fierce anger that he had subjected her to this anxiety. How could he do this? But of course he could; Kit Marsden was a law unto himself, no-one else counted. She realized now that no-one else ever had.

She watched while he parked the van in the lane and began, with long athletic strides, to climb the hill towards her. At this distance he was still the strong, attractive man she had first met. It was only as he drew near, when she looked at his face, that she saw the difference between her one-time illusion and the present reality. What she had seen as the strength of his expression, she now saw as obstinate and cruel; and as well as sensuality in the curves of his mouth, she now recognized weakness. His eyes, always attractively mocking, were sharp and hard.

He came quite close, and took hold of her. She pushed him away, but not before she had smelled the cheap scent which clung to his clothes and his person.

'Where have you been?' she demanded. 'No, on second thoughts, don't bother to tell me where you've been – I can smell that a mile off. Just explain why you couldn't let me know!'

'Let you know?' There was mock surprise in his voice. 'I didn't think it was something you'd want to hear, but of course if you do, I can tell you!'

'I don't!'

For a brief moment, the smell on him, the knowledge that he'd been with a woman, had filled her with jealousy; but it had not lasted for more than a moment. Almost immediately she'd known she didn't care.

'I don't want to know about your whore,' she said. 'She has atrocious taste in scent, though that, and she, are beside the point. But you could have telephoned me.'

'Don't tell me you were anxious, my love!' Kit retorted.

332

'I am not your love, and I'd be anxious about a dog if it disappeared for twenty-four hours.'

'You'd be more anxious about a dog,' Kit said bitterly. 'As for my whore – and I admit she was, Shepton isn't without its amenities – at least she didn't cheat me, at least she gave value for money, which is more than can be said for the likes of you! God preserve me from virtuous women!'

'God preserve *them*!' Cara said. 'Did you pay her with a black eye?'

'You know I never meant that,' Kit said savagely. 'I was drunk! But I'm stone-cold sober now, so let me tell you that as you refuse to be a wife to me, I shall go where and when I like.'

'Kit, why don't you go away and stay away?' Cara implored. 'You're not happy here. I'm not happy.'

'I'll go when, if ever, it suits me,' Kit said. 'I shall come and go as I please, and there's not a damned thing you can do about it! Now if you've finished I suggest we get to work.'

'Very well,' Cara said quietly.

He was right. There was nothing she could do. The sensible thing, for the sake of everyone in the house, was for her, as far as she could, simply to keep the peace.

'Very well,' she repeated. 'Though I'd appreciate it if you'd let me know when you're not coming home. *I* don't care, you understand, but at least I could then have some reasonable explanations for David and Mother Hendry. And by the way, I think you should let her know you're back. No!' she corrected herself. 'On second thoughts you'd better not. David will be up, and you smell like a brothel. I'll go down myself.'

David was not in the house when she got back.

'He went out on Bella and took Emily with him,' Mrs Hendry said. 'I'm surprised you didn't meet them.'

'They must have gone up dale,' Cara said. 'Does he know Kit wasn't home?'

'No. He'd assume he was on the fell.'

'Which is where he is now,' Cara said. 'So no need for David to know any different.'

'Where's he been?' Mrs Hendry asked.

Cara hesitated. She had intended to make up a story about the van breaking down, telephones being out of order – anything other than the truth – but suddenly it was all too much for her. Engulfed in loneliness and misery, drowning in it, she buried her face in her hands and wept bitterly; and as she wept, so it all came out.

'The skunk!' Mrs Hendry said furiously.

She thought, as she stroked her daughter-in-law's hair – for she

333

still regarded her as her daughter-in-law and, indeed, almost as her daughter – of how it should have been: her son and Cara, so good together, so well-suited, he had thought the world of her. There would have been more children growing up at Beckwith, keeping the place happy and alive. That a sudden, swift accident should so change Cara's life (and rob me of my only son, she thought) was cruel beyond belief. Where was God's justice and mercy in that?

'Skunk is a good description,' Cara said, 'considering how he smelled!'

'I could flay him!' Mrs Hendry declared. 'If I had him here . . .'

She felt that if he stood before her right now she would assault him physically. Her anger sent strength flowing through her veins; nothing would have been beyond her.

'Just let him wait until I see him!' she threatened.

'I know how you feel,' Cara said. 'I understand only too well!' The thought of smallish, elderly, rounded Mother Hendry setting about Kit, probably with a rolling pin, like someone in a pantomime, almost brought a smile to her lips and a lift to her heart.

'All the same, it's not the way we must go about things,' she said. 'If life's going to be anything other than impossible, all you and I can do is try to keep the peace. I can't shield you, much as I'd like to because you shouldn't have to put up with this, but I do want to shield David. I don't want either of the children to be any part of it.'

'You're right, love,' Mrs Hendry conceded. 'It's as well David is only home at weekends, and since that's the case we should manage. I'm glad Susan's where she is. You'd not keep anything from her.'

They had had another letter from Susan. She was settling in, making a friend or two, and enjoying rehearsals. It all seemed a world away from Beckwith.

'I don't know what to say to Johann,' Cara confessed.

'Leave him to me,' Mrs Hendry offered. 'No need for you to say anything.'

Cara dried her eyes, then went to the sink and splashed her face with cold water. She wouldn't give Kit the satisfaction of knowing he'd made her cry.

'I'd best get back to work,' she said.

'Must you? Dinner will be ready in a half-hour. Give yourself a break until then.'

'Oh, very well,' Cara agreed.

Johann came into the house before Kit. Cara left her mother alone with him, to say what she had to. It was clear, when she returned, that he knew. He said nothing; his look was so kind, so compassionate, that she wanted to break into fresh tears. But tears would get her nowhere, and in any case David and Emily arrived at that moment, closely followed by Kit. He breezed in as if he'd been away from the house no more than ten minutes.

'Now then, Ma!' he said. 'I hope it's something good? I'm famished!'

Without speaking, Mrs Hendry took the large pot from the oven and deposited it with unnecessary violence on the table. Cara sent her a warning look.

'It's Irish stew,' she announced.

'Irish?' Kit queried. 'Now would that be foreign or wouldn't it? Why not good honest Yorkshire stew? We don't want foreign stuff at Beckwith, do we?' He stared pointedly at Johann who stared back at him impassively.

'Call it anything you like,' Mrs Hendry said. 'Do you want some or don't you?'

'Oh dear! Who got out of bed the wrong side this morning?' Kit said.

'At least . . .' Mrs Hendry bit back the words. At least I got out of my own bed, she wanted to say.

'You smell all scenty, Kit,' David said. 'Like pink soap!'

Kit scowled at him.

'Get on with your dinner and mind your manners,' he said sharply.

'I wasn't being rude,' David protested. 'I *like* pink soap.'

'Let your meat stop your mouth!' Kit thundered. 'You have too much lip!'

'I wasn't . . .' David began.

Cara touched him gently on the arm.

'Not now, love. Get on with your dinner; don't let it get cold.'

Two minutes later the accident happened, though it was only a small accident.

Emily now sat to the table to meals, with two cushions on her chair to bring her to the right height. The top cushion shifted, causing her to slide, and her arm caught her full mug of milk and sent it flying. Kit, sitting next to her, received the full contents in his lap. Emily herself slid to the floor.

Kit sprang to his feet.

'You brat! You little fool! You're not fit to sit at the table, not fit to eat with decent people!' he shouted.

As he spoke he picked her up from the floor and began to shake her, so that she screamed.

Johann, Cara and David jumped up at once, but it was David who got to Kit first, striking at him with clenched fists.

'Stop it! Stop it!' he yelled.

'Give her to me,' Cara said to Kit. 'At once!'

'Gladly! She's all yours! They both are, thank God!'

'I echo that,' Cara said quietly, taking Emily into her arms. 'David, get back to your seat and eat your dinner, love. It was all a silly accident, nothing for anyone to make a fuss about.'

'Your ma's right,' Mrs Hendry said as she mopped up the spilt milk from the floor. 'Now who's going to have some pudding?'

'He shouldn't call Emily a brat,' David persisted. 'She's not a brat, and *I'm* not a brat.'

'Neither of you are.'

Cara spoke with a calm she was far from feeling. It *was* no more than a silly accident, but there had been a moment when it might have turned ugly. When she'd seen the temper on Kit's face as he'd shaken Emily, she had gone cold with fear. She knew, without a doubt, that they must tread very, very carefully.

In the middle of the afternoon, Grant Fawcett called. Aside from Emily, Mrs Hendry was alone in the house.

'They're working in Scarbottom,' she said to Grant. 'At least, Cara is. I don't know about the others. David will likely be with Johann and Kit will be wherever the mood takes him.'

'I'll take a walk up there,' Grant said. There was something in the tone of Mrs Hendry's voice he wasn't used to hearing.

'I wouldn't if I were you,' Mrs Hendry said. 'You'd not improve matters.'

He gave her a searching look.

'Is there something you should tell me?'

She sighed.

'I don't know. I'm moithered to death, and that's a fact. I don't really know what I should do any longer.'

'Then tell me,' Grant said. 'Trust me!'

There was a pause while she looked at him, trying to make up her mind. How much of it was her business? What would Cara want? In the end it was the scene over the spilt milk which decided her. She'd been more frightened than she'd cared to show about that – not about what Kit had actually done, but the rage and hate he'd shown.

'Very well,' she said, 'I'll tell you.'

She watched the anger rise in him as she gave him the facts. So much anger everywhere, it was frightening!

'I no longer feel we're safe,' she admitted. 'I've never been really frightened before, but now I am.'

'I would like to strangle him!' Grant said.

She was startled at the venom in his voice. He was the most good-tempered of men. She watched his hands – strong, capable-looking hands – jerk and clench and grasp at the air, as if he held Kit Marsden's throat between them. I believe he really means it, she thought – and was not comforted. The air of her usually calm kitchen seemed, these days, to be contaminated with violence.

'Anyway, I've told you,' she said. 'Though whether I've done right I don't know.'

'Of course you've done right,' Grant assured her. 'And I want you to promise me one thing. If *ever* you're afraid, or even apprehensive, you'll let me know at once. Just telephone. Promise!'

'I promise,' Mrs Hendry said. 'And I really think you'd best not go up there. You know you'll only provoke him.'

'Very well,' Grant agreed. 'Please tell Cara I was here. She knows I'll come whenever she wants me.'

Then he looked at her and smiled.

'Cheer up, love!' he said. 'I dare say it'll turn out all right.' He didn't believe a word he was saying, but he couldn't bear to see this old lady so troubled.

On the fellside the afternoon's work went well. There was a great deal to do and by the time the day began to draw in and they returned to the house, everyone was tired. Cara still had to milk, and on this occasion she accepted Johann's offer of help.

'Two of us will do it in half the time,' he pointed out.

They worked in near silence, except that at one point, without raising his head from his task, Johann said:

'If there is ever anything I can do for you, Mrs Edward, you know I will do it. No matter what it is.'

'I know you will,' Cara replied. 'Thank you, Johann.'

'Marigold seems to be doing well,' he said, changing the subject. 'She should have a fine calf.'

'I look forward to it,' Cara admitted.

Surprisingly, and mercifully, supper passed in peace. Kit was taciturn, his shoulders hunched, his head lowered over his food; Johann was silent, but Cara and Mrs Hendry kept up a flow of inconsequential chatter in an effort to lighten the atmosphere. The only note of dissension came when Mrs Hendry said: 'Oh, I almost forgot! Grant called in to say that if David wants to ride over to Fawcett's this weekend, they'd be pleased to see him.'

'I'd like that,' David said. 'Bella would like it too – if I can be spared.'

'You're not to go,' Kit growled, immediately looking up.

David looked from Kit to Cara, questioning them both.

'You may go tomorrow,' Cara said firmly. 'But you must be back before dark.'

'I've said he shouldn't . . .'

'As you reminded me this morning,' Cara interrupted Kit, 'the children are my responsibility.' There was a finality in her voice with which Kit, for once, didn't argue.

The minute supper was over he elected to go out.

'Will you be late back?' Cara asked, trying to keep the anxiety out of her voice.

'No,' he said. 'I'm going to Faverwell. There's nothing to keep anybody late in Faverwell.'

Cara bathed Emily and put her to bed, then played rummy with David until it was his bedtime.

'I shall have an early night too,' she said. 'I'm quite tired.' The last thing she wanted was to be up when Kit returned.

In her bed in the spare room, which she had now made her own, she lay awake, thinking. She thought of the earliest days of her marriage to Kit, of the happy nights they had spent in each other's arms. Body and soul, she longed for it to be as it had been then. She had been so much in love with him. Was he ever as much in love with me? she asked herself.

But in her heart she knew she couldn't blame Kit for everything. He hadn't wanted to marry her, she had bullied him into it. She had wanted her own way, and had taken it, with scant thought for anyone else. Perhaps Kit had always been as he was now, but she had been too besotted to see him clearly. Why didn't I realize he never really loved me, she wondered. In the quietness of the night she faced the fact that she had made a serious mistake, for which she must now pay. And she alone must pay; not her family, not even Kit. The fault was hers. It was up to her to protect her family, and she would.

She was still awake when she heard him return. Except that he never bothered to climb the stairs quietly, he made little noise. When she heard him go into the bedroom and bang the door shut, she sighed with relief, and allowed herself to drift into sleep.

On Sunday afternoon David rode Bella over to Fawcett's. She was glad to see him go. There was an uncomfortable atmosphere between himself and Kit. In the evening, after a busy day on the fells, Cara sneaked time to go to evensong. It was not yet dark as she walked through the churchyard where Tom and Edward, and generations of Hendrys before them were buried. She could tell by the diminishing sound of the five-minute bell that any second now George Dacre would stop ringing, but nonetheless she paused for a second in front of the headstone which bore Edward's name. Years of fierce dales weather had all but obliterated so many names, but his was still clear.

I haven't been the best Hendry in the entire family, she thought: but perhaps David will be, and I'll be forgiven. She hurried into the ancient building when the last stroke of the bell had died away, and the choir, five boys and four rather elderly men, were already in procession down the aisle.

By the time she was home again Kit had gone out, but as on the previous night, he returned before she fell asleep. A day without incident! How strange, and how awful, she thought, that a day should be seen as something special merely because it had been without incident! It wasn't exactly living life to the full – and she was young, and strong and – yes – passionate. But at least it was a level with which she could cope, and she thanked God for it.

'I thought I'd take David all the way to school today,' Cara said to Johann as he sat at breakfast next morning. 'There's some shopping I need to do in Shepton, and I'd like to change the library books. I'm sure you can manage without me for a couple of hours.'

'Certainly,' he said.

When she left with David, though Johann was already at work, Kit had not put in an appearance. At least she knew where he was, she had heard him come in. She had ceased to complain about his late start to every day, he did as he liked. And actually, once he made a start, he worked hard. The hours he spent with the sheep, or driving the new tractor, or indeed doing anything on the farm, were the one part of his life which had not changed.

In Shepton, having delivered David, she did her shopping and then wandered around the market while waiting for the library to open. There was a stall which, among other bric-à-brac, sold a few secondhand gramophone records. She searched through them, and found some clarinet quintets which she thought were sure to please Johann. It was while she was paying that out of the corner of her eye she saw, further down the High Street, Ralph Benson. He was almost out of sight, but there was no mistaking his tall, broad figure, even from behind. She almost snatched the record from the stall-holder, and set off in pursuit.

She was too late. It was as if he'd vanished from the face of the earth. There were several narrow turnings and alleyways leading off the High Street and he could have taken any one of them. She was disappointed. She would very much have liked to have seen him again, to have had a conversation. Also, she had half a mind to overrule Kit and send the ewes to Nidderdale this coming winter, if Ralph would have them after Kit's rudeness to him. She wouldn't expect him to take them on the cheap, she would pay the going rate.

Oh well, she thought, I can telephone him if that's what I decide. But it would have been nicer to have seen him face to face.

It was in the library that she met up with Grant Fawcett.

'Everybody seems to be in Shepton this morning!' she said.

'Who's everybody?'

'Not really everybody. I saw Ralph Benson, or at least I thought I did.' Now she felt less sure it had been he. 'I'm surprised to find either of us in the library at such a busy part of the year. When do we find time to read?'

'Speaking of time,' Grant said, 'will you come and have a cup of coffee with me?'

'I can't, much as I'd like to,' Cara said. 'I really must get back.'

'Then I'll walk with you to your car,' Grant persisted. 'There's something I have to say to you, unless you want me to say it here?'

'We'll get thrown out if we don't stop talking,' Cara told him. 'But *must* you say it?'

'Yes,' he said, 'I must.'

He waited until they were clear of the building, but only just.

'Cara, I know exactly what the situation is. Never mind how I know – but I do. Cara, love, you can't go on like this. You've got to send him packing, you've got to get rid of him, divorce him.'

'I sometimes wonder how I'll go on,' Cara admitted, 'but divorce is a big word in the dales. A disgrace. It's quite different from the towns.'

'But you're not the guilty party!' Grant protested. 'Nobody's going to blame you!'

'Oh yes they would, Grant. And you know it. There's never been a divorce in the Hendry family in more than two hundred years. I'd be the first to bring that disgrace. As for sending him packing – I've tried, and he won't go. So I shall just have to do what I'm already doing, take life a day at a time.'

'That's no way to live,' Grant said roughly. 'Divorce him, blow the disgrace – if that's what you call it – and marry me. People forget. It will all blow over!'

'I'm sorry, Grant. I can't think that way just now,' Cara said. 'Don't press me!'

'Very well,' he agreed reluctantly, 'though I don't promise never to mention it again. And you must promise me one thing. If you need me, promise you'll call on me, at once, whenever and wherever.'

'I promise,' she said.

For the next fortnight at Beckwith, since tupping time was on them, there was scarcely time to eat or sleep, and the hard work was intensified by the fact that Kit did not take his full share. Most days, as soon as darkness fell, he went off to Faverwell or Shepton to drink, driving dangerously home after the public houses closed, waking late next morning, long after both Cara and Johann were on the fells.

He showed no further physical violence, except that once – and in the presence of the children – he had taken her by the shoulders and shaken her roughly. Apart from that occasion, his weapon now was words. He shouted abuse, hurled insults, and the loudness of his voice constantly frightened Emily.

Three times in that fortnight he failed to come home until the next day, and though she knew he had been with a woman – he made no attempt to conceal it – Cara almost preferred such occasions. The day was less frightening than the night.

On the last day of tupping – they had put the remaining ewes in with the chasers – Kit left before nightfall. As she watched his van disappear down the lane, Cara turned to Mrs Hendry.

'I wish he would never come back!' she said. 'However wicked that is, I wish he would never come back!'

TWENTY-FOUR

'It's nearly eleven,' Cara said. 'I think we should go to bed. I don't know about you, but I'm dead tired.'

'Same here,' Mrs Hendry agreed. 'Would you like a cup of cocoa before you go up?'

'No thank you. Nothing. Oh, Mother Hendry, I'm glad the tupping is over. Usually I enjoy it, but this year it's seemed a hard slog. I think . . .'

Her words were interrupted by a loud shriek. Cara sprang to her feet.

'Emily! Another nightmare!'

She hurried out of the room and ran up the stairs to her daughter.

'Poor lamb!' Mrs Hendry said. The child had had far too many disturbed nights of late and the cause wasn't far to seek. Until Kit had started his tantrums and his shouting she'd been the most placid of little girls – but not any longer.

He wasn't back. Would he be back? There was no telling. At least if he didn't appear there'd be peace, but it was only postponing the evil hour. She agreed whole-heartedly with Cara, it would be better if he just never returned.

Emily was still crying noisily – some nights, and this was clearly one of them, it took an age to settle her again – when the telephone rang. Mrs Hendry snatched it up quickly. In her opinion no news which came after ten o'clock at night could be anything other than bad.

'Hello!'

After that she did no more than listen. The message was short, sharp, and to the point.

'Thank you,' she said. 'Thank you for ringing. I'll let her know.'

As she put down the receiver she glanced towards the stairs door.

Emily was still crying, though less noisily now, but Cara was certain to stay with her until she fell asleep again. With any luck she would have time to do what she had immediately decided she *must* do, and be back before anything was discovered.

Swiftly, she left the house, crossed the yard, and knocked on Johann's door. He came quickly, and as he opened his door she could hear the soft music from his gramophone. Signalling him not to speak, she stepped inside.

'The landlord of the Ewe just telephoned,' she said urgently. 'Kit is on his way, and he's fighting drunk. Very nasty, the man said. What shall we do?'

'The landlord should not have let him get so,' Johann said. 'He has a duty . . .'

'He didn't. He was very quick to say that. It seems Kit arrived at the Ewe already in a state and the landlord refused to serve him more. He was very worried about him driving his van home. What are we going to do?' she repeated. 'Cara doesn't know. She's upstairs with Emily.'

'Then there is no need to tell her,' Johann said. 'I will see to everything.'

'I promised I'd let Grant Fawcett know if anything like this happened,' Mrs Hendry said. 'I can't telephone him for fear Cara hears me.'

'Leave it to me,' Johann said firmly. 'I will do what has to be done.'

'Not without telling Grant,' Mrs Hendry insisted.

'I will do that,' Johann promised. 'And you must go back at once. Say nothing. Both of you go to bed. We will see to everything. He will have a lesson he will not easily forget.'

'Very well, then. But be careful. Don't let anything get out of hand.'

She was deeply troubled. She'd long been aware of Johann's hatred for Kit Marsden, and Grant's was scarcely less. But something had to be done.

As she went back into the house Cara was coming into the kitchen. She looked startled at the sight of Mrs Hendry entering from the yard.

'What is it? Where've you been?'

'Nowhere,' Mrs Hendry said. 'I thought I heard the henhouse door banging. I didn't want them getting out.' Her voice was flat calm. She gave no sign that her heart was beating fifty to the dozen.

'Was it open?' Cara asked. 'I could have sworn I closed it properly.'

'False alarm!' Mrs Hendry said dismissively. 'It's a bit rattly though.

343

I reckon Johann should look at it when he has a minute. I can't stand a rattling door. Is Emily all right?'

'She is now. She's gone off to sleep again.'

'Then we'd best get to bed while the going's good,' Mrs Hendry said. 'In case she wakens later.'

Cara agreed. 'I reckon *he's* not coming,' she said.

'I reckon so too,' Mrs Hendry nodded.

Moving quickly, she made the fire safe and started to turn out the lights.

'Come on, love,' she urged Cara. 'Let's be having you. You look all in.'

They parted at the top of the stairs.

'Sleep well, Mother Hendry,' Cara whispered.

'And you, love!'

I'll not sleep a wink, Mrs Hendry thought, closing her bedroom door behind her. In fact, she wouldn't even undress. Who knew what was to happen or when she might be needed? She had a terrible foreboding on her.

From the top drawer of the chest she took out a candle and a box of matches which had lain there, ready for any emergency Hitler might have liked to inflict on them, right through the war. When she had lit the candle and set it on the table by her bed she switched out the light, then she wrapped herself in a blanket and sat down in the armchair to wait. She was uncertain what she was waiting for, and the uncertainty made her even more afraid.

Johann hurriedly put on his jacket, picked up his torch and, as he left his quarters, wound a scarf around his neck. It was a cold night, but dry, no sign of rain. The sky was velvet-dark, and high, thick with bright stars. By the time Cara looked out of her window, as she did every night before getting into bed, Johann's room was in darkness. He had left the farm and was already running as fast as his legs would carry him towards Fawcett's. There was no moon and he cursed as, twice, he stumbled as he ran.

He would have liked to have carried out this mission on his own, without involving Grant. For a long time now, spurred on by a hatred which daily grew deeper, he had longed for the opportunity. Now that it had arrived he was reluctant to share it. He was fit and strong, undoubtedly fitter than Marsden, though not quite as young. In normal circumstances he was sure he could have done all that was needed, but perhaps the man would be stronger in drink. There was also the question of stopping the van. Everything had to be done properly, so for Mrs Edward's sake he would stifle his desires and be prudent, seek other help.

Grant Fawcett came to the door on Johann's first, sharp rap, almost as if he had been waiting, though that was impossible, Johann thought. Quietly, urgently, he gave him Mrs Hendry's message.

'Then we must hurry,' Grant said. 'If he's driving like a maniac it won't take him long from Shepton.'

As he spoke he took down his jacket and scarf from the hook, put his heavy torch in his pocket, and was already on his way out. At the barn he stopped long enough to collect a small coil of rope, then they left the farm and began to run down the lane, to meet the road along which Kit must travel to reach Beckwith.

They wasted no words, saving their breath for running. In any case there was no need for talk. They both knew what they had to do. It had been planned between them some time ago, and since then they had impatiently waited for the opportunity, which sometimes it seemed would never come. But now it had.

'God bless the landlord of the Ewe!' Grant said fervently.

They ran until both Fawcett's and Beckwith were left well behind, to where the road curved close to the river and was out of sight or hearing of any dwelling.

'This is the place,' Grant said.

For quite some time Mrs Hendry had succeeded in keeping awake, though it was difficult. She bemoaned the fact that she had left her knitting downstairs; it would have helped. She read her nightly verses from the bible, then she picked up her prayer book.

'Lighten our darkness we beseech Thee, O Lord,' she read. 'And by Thy great mercy defend us from all perils and dangers of this night.'

But whom would the Lord defend? Would He defend Cara, or would He defend Kit Marsden?

She was overcome by weariness, and couldn't sort out the answer. Against her will, her eyes closed. She was asleep.

Grant vaulted the gate into the river meadow, Johann following suit. Grant shone his torch to reveal, behind the wall close to the gate, a heap of boulders, large pieces of limestone. This was on the edge of Fawcett land. No-one was to know, except the two men now examining them, that none of the stones had been here a very few weeks ago. They had been gradually and painstakingly deposited, one or two at a time, by Grant Fawcett and Johann, until the heap was now large enough for its purpose.

'Away we go then!' Grant said. 'Don't forget, the really big ones we handle between us.'

He opened the gate, then quietly they set to work, the only sounds being the grunts of the two men as they picked up the heavy stones and moved them into the road. They moved quickly, conscious of working against time, all the while watching the road down the dale along which Kit Marsden must soon appear.

It would have been quicker, they knew, to have taken the wooden gate off its hinges and used it as a barrier across the road, but a drunken Marsden might be reckless enough to drive into and through the gate, or even around it. There was no possibility that he could dodge the barrier of boulders which they had now built across the road. Breathless, they stepped back and surveyed their work.

'He is trapped, like the rat he is!' Johann declared.

'We both know the drill,' Grant said. 'It won't help if he recognizes us, so wrap your scarf around your face and no speaking. We don't need words. The moment he stops, we shine the torches in his face and blind him. After that . . .'

He stopped in mid-sentence as, in the distance, they saw the headlights of the van coming towards them, waving erratically from one side of the road to the other.

'Quick!' Grant ordered. 'Behind the wall! You that side, me this. As soon as the van stops, we move!'

Each on his own side of the road, hidden by the wall, they watched while the van drew nearer. It was not being driven fast, which suited the two watchers. It was no part of their plan to have Kit Marsden injured in an accident.

The van's headlamps were efficient and Marsden, even in his drunken state, must have retained something of his driving skill. He pulled up, with a squeal of brakes and a string of curses, within a yard of the barrier. Still swearing, he fumbled with the van door then started to get out. It was then that Grant and Johann moved, swiftly as tigers, silent as cats.

Kit held up his hands to shield his eyes from the blinding light of the torches, and as he did so he was set upon by the two men. It was a moot point how many of the hard blows to the different parts of his body he felt before he slumped, unconscious, to the ground. Until that moment, though his arms had flailed out wildly, he had made almost no contact with his assailants.

Johann, standing over his body, observing the blood from his nose dripping on to the stones, thought, I could have dealt with him by myself.

'The rope,' Grant said. 'Quickly! He might come to.'

'Oh no, I think not,' Johann said with satisfaction. 'I think it will be some time before he comes to. And when he does he will be very, very sore.'

'You think we don't need the rope?' Grant queried. 'You think we can carry him as he is?'

The rope had been brought to tie him up should he attempt to struggle. There was clearly no struggle in him.

'No need at all,' Johann said. 'I'll take his head and you take his feet. It will be easy.'

They picked up the unconscious man and carried him through the gateway and across the meadow to the edge of the river. At a point where a small current left the main stream and lapped into a bay, they laid him on his back in the shallows. A trickle of blood ran down his face and stained the water.

'I would prefer to put him face down in the river!' Johann said savagely. 'He is a blight on the world!'

'I agree with the feeling,' Grant said grimly. 'But that's not on! The most we can do is give him a sharp lesson. And if he doesn't learn from it, it can be repeated.'

Johann nodded.

'You are right. Now we must remove the stones!' Yet before they turned away he gave Marsden a short, sharp kick. 'There's one from the Kraut,' he said. Kit didn't stir.

As quickly as they had assembled the barrier, they pulled it down again and moved the stones away, no longer heaping them behind the wall, but dispersing them as widely and naturally as possible. When they had finished the road was completely clear, except for the van, which was undamaged.

'I doubt if he'll ever remember why he left the van,' Grant said. 'But if he does, there's no sign of anything. He'll think he dreamt it. And he certainly won't know how he came to be in the river!'

They began the walk back. As they parted company Grant said: 'I'll be over at Beckwith mid-morning.'

Mrs Hendry wakened with a start. She was cold, shivering almost. She thought it was that which had wakened her. For a moment she didn't know what she was doing here, sitting in a chair, fully dressed, in the middle of the night, with the light out and a half-burned candle on the bedside table.

Then she remembered, and shivered, but this time not with cold. She picked up her prayer book from where it had fallen to the floor, and went to the window.

There was a light in Johann's room, but as she stood there watching, it went out. So he was home again! But where was Kit? Was he with Johann? Had Grant taken him? Surely he couldn't be in the house or she would have heard. She didn't intend to find out about that.

The house was quiet. As far as she knew, Cara was asleep, and best left so.

And there's nothing more I can do, she thought. Unutterably weary, she undressed and climbed into bed. When the new day came she would face things, but not yet.

Next morning she was down at her usual time, and Cara not long afterwards.

'A quiet night after all,' Cara observed. 'He didn't come home. I looked in his bedroom on my way down. Did you sleep well?'

'Like a top!' Mrs Hendry lied.

Johann came in to breakfast. Mrs Hendry gave him an enquiring look and he replied with an almost imperceptible nod. So it's been dealt with, she thought. How, she daren't ask.

The three of them ate breakfast in near silence. Emily was still asleep. When Johann was about to leave, Cara said: 'I'll be out shortly. As for Kit, I can't say. He didn't come home.'

She had given up all pretence with Johann that things were normal. He wasn't stupid, he could see how the land lay, and it would be an insult to him, she thought, to pretend otherwise.

'There is less to do today,' he said. 'I can manage.'

He hoped she would not come out too soon. He badly wanted to go down to the river to see what, if anything, had happened.

He was too late.

As he opened the door, Kit Marsden was coming up the path. Johann stopped, and stared at him, and for a moment had the feeling that he was staring at a ghost. With half his mind he had wondered if Marsden would survive the night. They had left him on his back, in very shallow water, but who knew, Joann had asked himself many times since then, whether a very drunken man, when he began to stir, would not turn over, face downwards in the water.

But if he does, he had reasoned with himself, it will be nothing to do with me, it will not be my fault; it will be his own action and no-one can say otherwise. Moreover, he had concluded, he did not care. In the war he had perforce killed men whose bootlaces Kit Marsden was not fit to tie.

But now, stumbling up the path, was the evidence that Marsden had not turned over in the water and drowned himself. He was alive all right. Though a sorrier sight I have never seen, Johann thought with satisfaction.

Kit was soaking wet from head to foot, the water still dripping from his clothes and leaving a damp trail on the flagstones where he walked. His right eye was so swollen and bruised as to have almost disappeared beneath the purple flesh. His nose was also swollen, and encrusted around his nostrils, with dried blood, as was his upper lip. There was a cut on his lip, still bleeding. Indeed, there was hardly an inch of his face which was not bruised and contused, and his left arm hung limply from the shoulder, clearly painful.

There was, however, nothing wrong with the volume of his voice, and it was his bellows of pain and rage which brought Cara and Mrs Hendry running to the door.

'What in heaven's name . . .?' Cara began as she rushed to meet him.

'Get out of the way!' he roared.

His words were slurred, as if even his sojourn in the cold waters of the Aren had not fully sobered him.

'What happened?' Cara cried. 'Whatever happened? Where have you been?'

'I've been in the bloody river, stupid!' he shouted. 'Where do you think I've been? And some bugger's set about me!'

'But who? When?' Mrs Hendry asked in trepidation, dreading the answer.

'How the hell do I know?'

That was the trouble. He could remember practically nothing between leaving the Ewe and waking up this morning, lying on the edge of the river, soaking wet and a mass of pain.

'But I'll find out!' he added. 'Don't think I won't find out! And when I do the bugger'll get what's coming to him. *He'll* not wake up this side of Christmas!'

'Never mind that now,' Cara said. 'Come in at once and get out of those wet clothes. You'll catch pneumonia!'

'Can I help?' Johann asked Cara. He hated the thought of her having to deal with this lout.

'Get out!' Kit thundered. 'Get out and stay out!'

'Thank you, Johann. I can manage,' Cara said. 'I'll see you later.'

Kit walked stiffly into the house. His head was thick and buzzing with pain. If only his head would clear he would be able to remember everything, he knew he would. As it was, he didn't even know where his van was – yet he knew he had left Shepton in it. There was something at the back of his mind to do with lights, and stones – but right now he could not make the effort to think about it. It would all come back to him later.

'You should go straight upstairs and change,' Cara said. 'Preferably have a hot bath, before you get into some dry clothes. Then I'll see to your face. I don't understand this at all. How did you come to fall in the river? What were you *doing* by the river?'

'For God's sake, woman, stop asking questions,' Kit complained. 'I've already told you, I don't know. I don't believe I fell in the river. It's my belief some bugger put me there.'

'For heaven's sake,' Cara said, 'who would do that?'

She had hardly said the words when something struck her as not being quite right, something which had happened – or not happened – in the last ten minutes. But what is it? she thought. What's wrong? What's niggling at me? Then suddenly she knew!

Johann had been there when Kit had first appeared, soaking wet, bruised and battered. He had shown not the slightest surprise. She and Mother Hendry had been shocked and astonished, firing questions. Johann had said nothing. He had remained totally impassive. As soon as the idea came to her she knew she must ask no more questions, though they were hurtling around in her mind.

Kit dragged himself upstairs, leaving a trail of river water, for he refused to take off his boots in the kitchen. Cara followed close behind and started to run the bath for him. He really did look terrible.

'You'll have to help me,' he said. 'It's my arm. I can't get my clothes off.'

She helped him with his jacket, shirt and vest – all soaked through and through – until he was stripped to the waist. She was leaving the bathroom when he put out his right, uninjured, arm and stopped her, pulling her close.

'How about a kiss and a cuddle?' he said thickly. 'You can't refuse me now! I'm an injured man!'

'I can and I do!' Cara snapped. 'Don't you touch me!'

She ran out of the bathroom and he picked up his wet clothes and flung them after her.

'You're a hard-hearted bitch!' he yelled as she ran downstairs. 'That's what you are, a hard-hearted bitch!'

'When he's had his bath he should go to bed,' Cara said to Mrs Hendry. 'I don't think his face needs anything other than bathing, which he can do for himself. Oh, Mother Hendry, *am* I so hard-hearted?'

'Of course not, love,' Mrs Hendry assured her. 'And if you were, you'd have good reason. Don't worry, I'll see to him when he's out of the bath.'

'What do you suppose *really* happened?' Cara asked. 'What's *your* idea?'

'My idea? Oh, I don't know, love. I suppose he left his van for a call of nature, wandered down to the river, fell in and cut his face on the rocks. He was blind drunk, after all.'

'He's got a lot of cuts and bruises just from falling,' Cara said thoughtfully.

The telephone rang. Cara answered it.

'It's the landlord from the Ewe,' she whispered to Mrs Hendry.

Mrs Hendry flushed scarlet and busied herself with something at the sink.

'Yes, he's home,' Cara was saying. 'He's in the bath at present. But thank you for asking about him.'

When she had put down the receiver she turned to Mrs Hendry.

'Mr Thwaite wanted to know if everything was all right. He said Kit left Shepton at closing time last night, drunk as an owl. He was worried because of him driving the van.'

She said nothing of the fact that Thwaite had mentioned last night's call, and that Mrs Hendry had answered it. Though her mother-in-law's guilt was visible in her face, now was not the time to ask questions.

'That was very civil of him,' Mrs Hendry said steadily.

'Wasn't it?' Cara said. 'The thing is, where is the van now? When and where did Kit leave it?'

As soon as his breakfast was over, Grant left Fawcett's farm, making his excuses to his uncle.

'I'm going to check the wall in Riverside,' he said. 'When I drove past yesterday it didn't look quite right to me. We don't want the ewes getting out – it's too close to the road.'

He had spent a restless night, and wakened this morning with a worried mind. He was not convinced that they should have dumped Marsden in the river; it was part of the plan he had never been sure about. He had no regrets, none at all, about beating up Marsden, though he had not known that such violence was part of his nature. With each blow he had landed he had felt he was avenging Marsden's blows to Cara, as she was unable to strike back herself. That was reason and incentive enough to him. If it came to it, he would do it again. There was nothing he would not do for Cara: she was the sun and the moon to him.

But the river was another matter. He was aware that if while Marsden was unconscious, or if he half came to and was fuddled, he might all too easily turn over in the shallows. It would not take long, lying face downwards in the water, for a semi-conscious man to drown.

He thought it unlikely that he or Johann could be implicated – though Marsden's bruises would have to be accounted for – but he would know himself, and even if she never found out, it would be a barrier between himself and Cara which he could never break down.

Besides, and all that apart, and even though he hated Marsden's guts, he drew the line at what would be precious near to murder.

It was therefore with the utmost relief that, when he reached the river, there was no sign of Marsden. The river was too shallow here, and the current not strong enough, for him to have drifted downstream. No, Grant concluded, he must have left under his own steam.

Marsden had not, however, taken the van. It was still there, slewed across the road and partly blocking it. It would be wise to move it before anyone came along and asked questions.

He climbed into the driver's seat. It started on the third attempt. He drove it to Beckwith, parked it by the side of the road, and walked up to the house.

He went straight into the kitchen – neighbours in Arendale did not knock on doors – and was surprised not to see Marsden. Surprised, but not displeased. He would certainly not have been welcome, and he still had some doubts about what Kit might or might not remember; or whether, even without remembering, he might put two and two together. The last thing Grant wanted was for Cara to have any knowledge of last night's events. The less she knew, the safer she would be.

'I came across Kit's van down the lane,' he said. 'I drove it back. It's parked outside.'

'Thank you,' Cara said. 'I was wondering about it. Kit's in bed.'

'In bed?'

'He arrived home in a terrible state; soaked to the skin and badly bruised and battered. He'd been in the river, he said. He seems quite sure someone put him there.'

She watched Grant's face closely as she spoke, but his expression gave nothing away.

'How do you think it could have happened?' she asked. 'His face is awful.'

'I should think the explanation is fairly simple,' Grant said. 'I suppose he was drunk. He got out of the van, wandered down to the river – it runs quite close to the road just there . . .'

'Just where?' Cara asked quickly.

'Close to where I found the van, of course. He fell in, cut his face on the stones, got a soaking.'

'That's exactly what Mother Hendry says,' Cara told him.

'And I'm sure I'm right,' Mrs Hendry broke in.

'It's not at all what Kit thinks.' Cara looked Grant straight in the eye and he met her look with a steady gaze.

'Actually, Cara, from what you say, he doesn't sound in any state to think. Does he actually *remember* anything?'

'Not at the moment,' Cara acknowledged. 'But he will. Later on he will.'

Until she'd learned that the landlord of the Ewe had spoken to Mrs Hendry, it had not occurred to her to suspect Grant of any part in what had happened. He despised and disliked Kit, that she knew, but he had never experienced the daily jibes and insults which Johann had had to bear. He wouldn't have stood for them. He was in a position to answer back, to get rid of his anger. In Johann it had been building up for a long time. Nevertheless she suspected Grant. His observations were altogether too smooth, too pat. She suspected all three of them, but they weren't giving anything away and, as yet, she wasn't going to ask outright.

'He's uttering fierce threats against whoever did it,' she warned. 'I'm sure he means it.'

'If anyone *did* it,' Grant said. 'Don't let it worry you.'

He accepted a cup of tea, stayed for a little while, then went home. He was not happy to leave. It was possible, just possible, that they had not so much taught Marsden a lesson as incited him to further violence. If that was so, then Cara would be the one to suffer.

'Don't worry,' he repeated. 'Phone me if you want me. Promise?'

'I promise,' Cara said.

It was an hour later. Kit was stirring and Mrs Hendry had taken him up a cup of tea. Cara looked out of the window and saw a woman walking along the lane towards the house. It was an unusual sight, unusual because Cara didn't know her, nor did she recognize the two small children she had with her, one on either hand. She thought she knew everyone in Arendale.

Nor was this on the way to anywhere. Above Beckwith the road petered out and the steep fells closed in the dale.

She must be lost, Cara thought.

She watched as the woman stopped, looked around her, then came on again. She halted briefly by the van, then began to walk up the path to the house. By the time she reached the door, Cara was there to meet her.

'What can I do for you?' Cara asked pleasantly. 'Have you lost your way?'

The woman was tall, full-bosomed, wide-hipped. Wisps of coal-black hair escaped from a brightly-coloured headscarf, and her eyes were as black as her hair. The children, a boy of about six and a girl a little younger, clung tightly to her hands.

'Oh no, we haven't lost our way,' the woman said confidently. She had an arrogant air about her. 'No, I reckon this is it. Beckwith Farm – am I right?'

'Quite right,' Cara replied. 'So what can I do for you?' She hadn't the slightest idea who the woman might be. Perhaps she was looking for work?

'You can fetch me my husband,' the woman said.

'Your husband? We don't have any men working here – except one who's been here for years, and he's not married.'

'Oh, he's here all right,' the woman said. 'Kit Marsden I'm talking about. He's my husband. These are his kids.'

TWENTY-FIVE

Cara stared at the woman on the doorstep in total amazement.

'*What* did you say?'

'You heard, love! I said I've come for my husband. You didn't really think he was your husband, did you?'

'He married me . . .' Cara began.

Her voice seemed not her own. She couldn't believe that this was happening.

'Well he married me first, lady. In Appleby in 1945. And he's still married to me. There's been no divorce, I don't hold with it. We've split up from time to time, but he comes back in the end.'

'I can't believe it!' Cara whispered. 'I don't believe this is happening!'

'I suppose it is a bit of a shock,' the woman conceded. 'But if you can't believe it, take a look at young Sidney here.' She thrust the little boy forward. 'Tell me if he isn't the spitting image of his dad!'

Cara looked at the child. What the woman said was true; his hair, his eyes, the shape of his face, even the sturdy lines of his body combined to make a small replica of Kit. And if that was not enough, there was the look in the child's dark eyes: bold, sparkling, yet wary. He looked at her now with exactly the same impudent gaze which had first attracted her to Kit. Oh yes, he was his father's son all right.

'He is like him,' she acknowledged.

'He's the living, breathing double,' the woman said proudly. 'Who could deny it?'

Was this a hoax, Cara wondered? Was it some plan to get money

355

out of her? The fact that the boy was Kit's was no proof that he was married to this woman.

'I know what you're thinking,' the woman said. 'You're thinking that I don't have to be Kit's wife just because I've got his son. Well, that's true enough – but you're wrong. Sidney is legitimate, not born the wrong side of the blanket. Kit and me was married. Just in time,' she added with good humour.

'You'd better come in,' Cara said. 'This isn't something we can discuss on the doorstep, Mrs . . .'

'Mrs Marsden,' the woman said. 'The *real* Mrs Marsden. Oh, I've got my marriage lines all right!'

So have I, Cara thought. And it seems they might be worthless. The thought that she was not married to Kit, and never had been, was difficult to take in. Yet somehow she believed this woman. She rang true.

'I'll be glad of a sit-down,' the woman said. 'We got a lift to Faverwell – I was told in Shepton where he'd be – but we've walked from there, me and the kids. It's a tidy step, and me six months gone.'

'You're . . . pregnant?' She hadn't noticed under the woman's loose coat, but now it was evident. 'Is it . . .?'

'Oh it's Kit's all right! They all are. I'm not a loose woman.'

She motioned to Emily who was playing at the table with her wooden farm animals.

'She's not a bit like Kit, is she?'

'She's not his,' Cara said. 'I was married before. Since you've come so far, would you like a cup of tea, and some milk for the children?' The woman, in spite of her confident air, looked tired.

It was now that Mrs Hendry came in from the dairy. She looked at the visitors in surprise. They must be lost, she surmised.

'Mother Hendry, this is Mrs Marsden,' Cara said.

'Mrs Marsden?' She thought for a second. 'Then you must be Kit's sister-in-law. We didn't know Kit had a brother, did we Cara?'

'He hasn't,' Cara said. 'Mrs Marsden says she is his wife, and these are his children.'

I do not believe this is happening, she thought, filling the kettle. This is some bizarre tea-party in a mixed-up, crazy dream, and any minute now I'll waken.

'I don't just *say* I'm his wife! I *am!*' the woman said sharply. 'So where is he? He'll soon tell you who I am.'

'He's in bed,' Cara said.

'In bed? At this time of the day?'

'He's had a bit of an accident.'

'An accident? Oh Lord!'

'Nothing serious,' Cara said. 'He came back from Shepton drunk. Somehow he wandered as far as the river, and fell in. He's bruised his face and hurt his arm.'

'That sounds like my Kit,' the woman said with a grin. 'He never could hold his liquor!'

Mrs Hendry seated the children and gave them mugs of milk and pieces of oatcake. 'That's the best milk you'll ever have tasted,' she said. 'Better than you get in the towns.'

It was something to say; otherwise she was at a loss for words. The little lad was exactly like Kit, and somehow she believed the woman.

'My husband's been away long enough,' the woman said. 'He's strayed once too oft and it's time he came back. We need him, me and the kids. I've got the chance of a nice little house in Appleby. He can shake the dust of Shepton off his feet. Anyway, he likes Appleby because of the horses. So I'd like to see him now, if you please.'

Cara turned to Mrs Hendry.

'Could you get Kit downstairs? Make some good excuse, but don't tell him why.'

'That's right!' the woman said. 'We'll give him the surprise of his life!'

While Mrs Hendry was upstairs the woman continued to chatter, but Cara scarcely heard her. I'm not married, she thought. I'm not married to him and I never have been. It all fell into place. He'd never wanted to marry her, she'd pushed him into it, and he'd never let her have a child. At least she could be thankful for that.

He was going out of her life. It was the end of a nightmare. It was also the end of a dream – which had turned into a nightmare.

She heard his heavy tread as he came down the stairs, cursing volubly at being disturbed. She jumped to her feet. Suddenly she wanted to run away, escape from it all.

He came into the room, then stopped short and stared at the woman, but it was a stare of recognition. Under the ugly red and purple bruises his face went the colour of uncooked pastry.

'What the bloody hell . . .!'

'My word, Kit, you do look a mess!' the woman exclaimed. 'Whatever have you been doing to yourself?'

'What the hell are you doing here?' he demanded. 'What in God's name . . .'

'I came to fetch you,' the woman said. 'You'd be surprised how many people were ready to tell me where you were. Anyway, we need you, me and the kids. You've had your fling – a pretty long one this time, I reckon – and now it's time you came back. I can't manage.'

Kit looked at Cara for the first time.

'It's all true, isn't it?' she challenged him. 'She *is* your wife. Your real wife. And I'm not, and never have been.'

'I can explain . . .' he began.

'Don't bother.'

'If I'd told you the truth you wouldn't have had me,' he said.

'I certainly wouldn't,' Cara agreed. 'Now please leave.'

'I want to stay with you. I don't want to leave you,' he pleaded. 'We were happy enough, you and me. I'll be different! I'll turn over a new leaf!'

'Where have I heard that before?' his wife said. 'No my lad, you're coming with me, and don't you think different.'

'If you think there's the slightest likelihood of staying here, you're mad,' Cara told him.

'I'll not go,' he blustered. 'There's neither of you can force me!'

'I can,' Cara said. 'This time I can!'

She had found a strength she hadn't known she possessed, yet underneath that strength, though she would not allow it to surface, she was bruised and crying inside.

'You know what you've done,' she said. 'You must know what you've done. You've committed bigamy. Bigamy is a serious crime. You could go to prison for quite a long time for bigamy. If I go to the police . . .'

'You wouldn't dare! You wouldn't show yourself up like that!' Kit said.

'Oh, I'd dare all right,' Cara assured him. 'Make no mistake about that. As for showing myself up, what *you* did is no disgrace to me. I might look a fool but I'll get over that.'

There was a moment's utter silence, as if everything in the world had stopped. It was broken by Cara.

'I'm going out. There's nothing more to say, except I'll be back in an hour, and if you're not gone by then, lock stock and barrel, I shall call the police. And if you leave anything behind I shall burn it.'

'He'll be gone,' his wife promised. 'I'll see to that, lady!'

'Oh yes, there is one thing more,' Cara said. 'If you so much as set foot on Beckwith land ever again, I shall have you charged with bigamy. So get out, and get out quick!'

She turned to the woman.

'I wish you joy of him!'

She walked to the door, took her coat from the peg, and left the house, walking quickly, putting the distance between herself and Kit Marsden. From the lane she went through the lower fields and on to the fell. She climbed and climbed, almost to the top. When there was no more strength left in her, she flung herself face down on the short-cropped grass and cried as though her heart would break.

Presently, it seemed a long time after, she sat up, dried her eyes and looked around. It was a clear day; she could see down the length of the dale. Far below in the valley the river ran, no longer hidden now that the trees along its bank had lost their leaves. Parallel to the river ran the narrow road, and along the road she saw Kit's van being driven out of the dale. She rose to her feet and watched until it was a speck in the distance, and finally out of sight.

So it was over? It was all over. But how could it ever be over for her? Three years of marriage, of tempestuous marriage, with its love, passion, hate, fear; wonderful times, terrible times. And in the end, not marriage at all. One great falsehood, a trick played on her. How could the fact that she had sent him away, watched him leave, ever wipe out the last three years? They were with her for always.

Fresh tears coursed down her cheeks as she began to descend the fell towards home.

Halfway down the fellside she saw Johann in an adjoining field. I'll tell him at once, she decided, while we're on our own. He would be the first of many people she would have to tell, but with Johann it would be less difficult. He had the gift of making everything easier than it might be.

She walked across to where he was examining a stretch of wall.

'I've something to tell you, Johann,' she said.

She has found out, he thought at once. She has found out what I did. He hadn't wanted her to know, not for his sake – he didn't care, he would do it again – but for hers. It would be easier for her to think that what had happened was an accident.

He straightened up, and looked at her. Before he could say a word she began to talk. He listened almost in disbelief.

'So he's gone,' Cara concluded. 'And this time he won't be coming back.'

'I'm sorry,' Johann said.

'Sorry? I thought you'd be pleased.'

'Not sorry that he has gone. About that I *am* pleased. Grieved only that you have been hurt.'

'Thank you,' Cara said.

She left him, and went down to the house.

'Oh, Mother Hendry,' she said, 'I'm sorry I left you to cope with the last of him. I just couldn't take any more.'

'Of course you couldn't, love,' Mrs Hendry replied. 'And let's hope it *is* the last of him.'

'I'm sure he won't come back,' Cara said. 'I meant what I said and he knows it.' But in her heart would she ever know the last of him?

'Well, my next job is to clean that bedroom and make sure he's taken all his stuff with him. *She* helped him to pack, went through everything like a dose of salts!'

I'm not sure I shall ever go back to that room, Cara thought. It held too many memories, good and bad.

'We can settle down to a bit of peace,' Mrs Hendry said. 'No more being afraid to go to bed. No more frightening the bairns.'

'A bit of peace is what we all need,' Cara agreed. 'But you know, Mother Hendry, he wasn't all bad.'

'Nobody is, love. But quite a lot of him was. Don't you kid yourself about that!'

'We had some good times,' Cara said. 'In the beginning.'

'I know that, Cara love. But it didn't last, did it? It was over well before his wife turned up. Be honest with yourself. And don't look back,' Mrs Hendry pleaded. 'Face the future now!'

'I'll try,' Cara promised. 'But how can I not look back? I can't pretend three years of my life never existed.'

'I know, love, I know.'

'I shall telephone Grant,' Cara said. 'He has a right to know. And what am I to say to David? I have to collect him this afternoon for the weekend.'

Mrs Hendry gave a deep sigh. There was so much to be gone through yet. Cara was right. It didn't end with Kit Marsden walking out of the house.

'I reckon it might be best to tell David the truth, as simply as you can. If you don't tell him, you can depend on it somebody else will. And at his age facts are perhaps something he can cope with, especially coming from you. He thinks the world of you, you know.'

'As I do of him,' Cara said. 'Most of the time I totally forget that he isn't my own son.'

'I'll get on with that bedroom,' Mrs Hendry said.

While Mrs Hendry was working upstairs, Cara telephoned Grant. She had given him no more than the barest details before he interrupted.

'I'm coming right over,' he said. 'At once!'

When he walked into the house he embraced her, and for a moment she laid her head on his shoulder and gave herself up to the secure feeling of his arms around her.

'Oh Cara, it's the best news ever!' he said.

She jerked herself out of his embrace.

'Oh no!' she contradicted him. 'It's not at all like that. To believe you were married, to go through three years of marriage with all its

360

ups and downs, and to find it was all a lie – that's not the best news ever. I dare say I should feel relieved, and in a way I do, but I also feel angry, sad, humiliated, cheated. There aren't enough words to say how I feel.'

'Oh, I'm sorry, love! I'm a fool! I was thinking no more harassment, no more fear. I've seen you afraid so often over the last few months.'

'I have been,' she acknowledged. 'And I'm glad that's gone, of course I am. But I can't feel jubilant.'

'You know I want to talk about the future,' Grant said. 'But I won't rush you.'

'Please don't,' Cara said. 'The future is something I can't contemplate, not yet. Please be patient, Grant. There's so much I have to think through – and in the meantime there's a farm to run.'

'You'll need extra help,' he said. 'Shall I look around for you?'

'I'll wait a bit. We're coming up to the quietest time of the year. Johann and I might manage between us.'

'All right.'

He left soon afterwards. Cara tried to turn her mind to the demands of the farm. It was a relief to do so. And I must do something about the overwintering of the ewes, she thought. I can't drive it much later. Could she pluck up courage and ask Ralph Benson? Why not? The worst he could do would be to refuse.

She picked up the telephone there and then and asked for his number. She was put through quickly and, as luck would have it, he himself answered.

'Benson!'

She was unaccountably taken aback by the sound of his voice, and for a moment couldn't find her own.

'Benson!' he repeated. 'Who is it?'

There was the same slight note of impatience that she remembered.

'It's me, Cara. I wondered . . . that is, would you take my ewes for overwintering?'

It was his turn to pause. Then he said: 'What about your husband? I seem to remember he wasn't too keen, to put it mildly.'

'He doesn't come into it.'

'Doesn't come into it?'

'Not any longer,' Cara said. 'But it's too complicated to go into on the telephone. Can we meet? I shall have to go into Shepton on Monday to take David back to school. Might you be there?'

'I can be,' he said.

When she put down the telephone she was shaking. She couldn't think why. Though he was never a man of many words, he had been pleasant enough when she'd announced herself. Indeed, he'd seemed pleased to hear from her.

In the afternoon, setting off for Shepton to collect David, she was still wondering how to put things to cause her stepson the least upset. Probably Mother Hendry was right; the plain facts would be best. He was waiting for her at the school gate and she was pleased to see that, for once, there was no other child with him to whom she must give a lift. She would have him to herself.

She negotiated the traffic – Shepton was always busy on a Friday – and drove out of the town. Not until they were on the open road, heading for the upper dales, did she attempt to say what occupied every corner of her mind.

'I've got something to tell you, David,' she began.

She hadn't meant to sound ominous, or too serious, she'd intended to keep her feelings firmly under control, but from David's instant and alarmed response she knew she'd failed in that. He clutched at her arm so fiercely that she almost swerved into the ditch.

'It's Bella! It's Bella, isn't it? Something's happened to Bella?'

She righted the car, then pulled into the side of the road, and stopped.

'She's had an accident? She's ill?' He was frantic.

'No! No, darling! Bella is absolutely fine! Honestly!'

'Then it's Grandma! She's poorly!'

'Grandma is fine, too. She was the picture of health when I left her an hour ago! So if you'll calm down I'll tell you.' She paused.

'Kit has left me,' she announced. 'No, wait, let me finish, then say anything you want to. He's left us for good, he won't be coming back to Beckwith. But that's not all, David. I found out this morning that I wasn't really married to him. He has a wife and two small children. They came to fetch him back.'

There was only the slightest hesitation before he answered, and his voice was totally matter-of-fact.

'Did he want to go?'

'Actually, he didn't. But they needed him.'

'We don't need him,' David said firmly. 'I'm quite glad he's gone.'

'Glad?' This was not what she had expected to hear.

'Yes. I used to like him, but not any more. He frightened me, *and* Emily. He frightened you sometimes, didn't he?'

'Sometimes,' Cara admitted.

'So you must be glad he's gone? I once heard you telling him to go, and he wouldn't.'

How much more had he heard, Cara wondered. He must have lain awake in bed, listening.

'It's not quite so simple,' she said. 'But yes, all right, I suppose I *am* glad in a way. Relieved, more like. But I'm pleased you're not too badly upset.'

'He's not my father,' David said. 'You're my mother but he's not my father.'

'I'm . . .'

She opened her mouth to say 'I'm not your mother', then stopped. She had told Mother Hendry this morning that she thought of David as her son, usually forgot that he wasn't, and now the same thing had happened to him, in reverse. He thought of her as his mother. It was a moment which made up for so many of the bad things. She started the car again and drove off.

'I'll be the man of the house,' David said. 'Or will Johann be the man of the house?'

'You will be, love!'

It seemed that he had nothing more to say or to ask on the subject until, later, as they were turning into Arendale, he enquired: 'Have you written to Susan?'

'Not yet,' she answered. 'It only happened this morning. Actually I thought I might not tell her while she's rehearsing for the pantomime. I don't want to upset her. She was fonder of Kit than the rest of us.'

'I *do* wish we could go to see the pantomime!' David said. 'Can't we possibly?'

'Oh David, what a question! All the way to Bristol? It's hundreds of miles.'

'I know,' he said. 'I checked it on the map. We'd have to stay overnight, of course. Or perhaps we could come back on a sleeper!' His eyes shone at the thought.

'You're really serious, aren't you?' Cara said. 'Do you really want to go so much?'

'You bet I do! Do you know, I've never been *anywhere*! Not anywhere that counts.'

'Well, I don't even know how I'd manage the money,' Cara said. 'But I'll promise to think about it.'

'You could tell Susan then,' David suggested as they approached the farmhouse. 'About Kit, I mean. You needn't write.'

As soon as the car stopped he was out with a bound, making for the stables to see Bella. 'I've got time for a short ride before it gets dark,' he called.

'So how did he take it?' Mrs Hendry asked Cara the minute she stepped into the house.

Cara said: 'I would say he took it in his stride! It was amazing. He was so sensible.'

'There you are, you see, you needn't have worried,' Mrs Hendry said.

'What's really buzzing around in his head is that he wants to go to Bristol!'

'To Bristol?'

'To see Susan in the pantomime. Of course I can't possibly afford it.'

'Of course not,' Mrs Hendry agreed.

'I wish I could, though. I'd like to give him a real treat. Do you know what he said? He said I was his mother!'

'And to all intents and purposes, so you are,' Mrs Hendry smiled.

'I must telephone Akersfield,' Cara said. 'Tell them what's happened.'

Mrs Hendry looked at Cara with deep concern. For someone who had had a crushing blow only a few hours ago she was being far too practical, much too brave. She was trying too hard; it would only tell on her later.

'Must you do it today, love?' she protested. 'Give yourself a rest. It will keep until tomorrow.'

Cara hesitated. She didn't want to do anything, or talk to anyone. She was desperately weary.

'No, I must get it over,' she said. 'I can't rest until it's done.'

Her mother answered the phone. When Cara had broken the news there was a long silence at the Akersfield end.

'Are you still there?' Cara said.

'Yes. I'm sorry, love. I just couldn't believe what I was hearing. Oh, Cara, my love! What a terrible thing to happen! Are you all right? Do you want me to come over? I will.'

'I'll be all right,' Cara said. 'Try not to worry about me, Ma.' Her parents knew nothing of Kit's drinking, or of his violence, and she thought it better not to tell them. Also, she didn't want to go into the details, to relive them.

'Your father's here,' Mrs Dunning said. 'He wants a word with you. I'll put him on.'

'Is this true?' Arnold Dunning demanded. 'Are you all right?'

'It's true,' Cara said. 'And I'm all right. Don't worry!'

'I never liked the fellow! It shows I was right. He wasn't your class! You'll go to the police, of course. I'll come with you.'

'No, Dad. I won't go to the police.'

'You mean you'll let him get away with it?'

'As long as he stays away, yes. It will do no good to prosecute.'

'He deserves a stiff sentence, and he'd get it!' her father said angrily.

'But I'd be worse off. Everything would be made public, even more public than it's bound to be. And his wife and children would suffer. It's best left.'

'I suppose that's one way of looking at it,' Arnold Dunning admitted grudgingly. 'But I don't like the idea of him getting off scot-free. He's a scoundrel!'

'It's the best way,' Cara said.

'You're a brave girl,' her father said. 'But then you always were.'

'Oh, Dad. I don't feel a bit brave!' Cara said. She didn't know what she felt: weary, confused, perilously near to tears again.

'Your ma wants another word,' Arnold said. 'Keep your pecker up, love. If there's anything at all I can do . . .'

'I know. Thank you, Dad. I'll be over to see you before too long.'

'Your dad's very upset,' Mrs Dunning said. 'How is David taking it, poor lamb?'

'Surprisingly well,' Cara replied.

'And Susan?'

'She doesn't know yet. I'm going to write. David is hankering to go to Bristol to the pantomime.'

'So is Laura,' Mrs Dunning said. 'It seems they promised to be at each other's performances whenever they could. But Bristol's a long way off.'

'I know,' Cara said. 'I can't possibly afford it.'

'Take care of yourself, love. I'll telephone you again tomorrow,' Mrs Dunning said.

She did so on Sunday afternoon.

'I've got something to cheer you up,' she said. 'Your dad says he'll pay for the three of you to go to Bristol: you, David and Laura. All expenses!'

'But that's marvellous!' Cara cried.

'He thinks it will do you good. It will have to be after Christmas because Laura has a concert in Manchester on Christmas Eve.'

'After Christmas is best all round,' Cara said. 'Oh, David will be so thrilled! Can I write and tell Susan? She'll need to find us somewhere to stay.'

'Oh yes, it's definite,' Mrs Dunning assured her.

On Monday morning Cara met Ralph Benson, as arranged, in Shepton. He seemed taller and broader than ever, and still attractive. She realized now how much she had missed him. She was astonished by how little surprise he showed when she gave him her news.

'It was a bolt from the blue,' she confessed. 'Totally unexpected. But if I may say so, Ralph, you don't seem the least bit taken aback.'

'I'm not,' he said.

'You don't mean . . . you didn't *know?*'

'Of course I didn't. Wouldn't I have told you if I'd known? It's just that I didn't trust Marsden. I didn't know him well, but his reputation wasn't good. Do you remember what I said to you three years ago?'

'I'm afraid I don't.'

'I said, "he's as slippery as an eel. He needs watching." As I remember it you weren't too pleased with me, and I doubt you took a blind bit of notice.'

'I didn't,' Cara agreed. She had never met anyone who'd had a good word to say for Kit. She hadn't cared a hoot – quite the contrary, it had made her rush to his defence.

'Well, I'm not here to say I told you so,' Ralph said. 'I'm just glad it's over. Let me know if you have any more trouble from that quarter. I'll deal with him.'

'So will you take my ewes?' she asked after a while.

'On one condition.'

'Which is . . .?'

'You'll come over to Nidderdale and have some lunch with me.'

'I'd like to,' Cara said.

'How soon?'

'I think fairly soon, before the weather gets bad.'

'Next week? Wednesday?'

'Why not?'

She would be glad to escape from Beckwith, if only for a few hours. In Nidderdale no-one knew her; no-one would look at her and think 'There goes Cara Marsden, only she wasn't, poor thing!' Anyway, she liked Ralph Benson. She had forgotten just how much she did like him. She would be glad to spend time with him, whatever the reason.

'A good idea,' Mrs Hendry said when Cara told her. 'Get you out of yourself.'

But was it a good idea? she wondered as the week went by. Ralph Benson was an attractive man, with a lot to offer a woman. It was her deep-down belief that sooner or later he would offer it to Cara. And who could blame her if she took it? She was a young woman, she couldn't be expected to live like a nun for the rest of her life.

She pushed the thought out of her mind. It was not one she could bring herself to contemplate. Time enough to face that if and when she had to. Also, she reminded herself, there was always Grant Fawcett. He wouldn't let Cara go without a fight.

TWENTY-SIX

It was a fine, clear day when Cara drove over to Nidderdale. By now all the trees had lost their leaves, so that their bare branches stood out against the landscape and the sky in intricate patterns of black lace. She had always preferred trees in winter to the lush, heavy green of summer.

As she parked her car in his drive, Ralph Benson came out of the house to greet her.

'Same car!' he observed.

'Oh yes,' Cara said, smiling. 'And likely to be for some time yet! But I did get my new tractor, some time ago now. That's more to me than a car.'

'And do you drive it – the tractor?'

'Of course I do! Johann and I practically fight over who's to have it!'

'He's a good man, Johann.'

'The best,' Cara agreed.

'Do you want to look around before lunch?' Ralph asked. 'Would you like to see your own sheep, check I'm treating them right?'

'I would rather,' Cara said.

He had a wonderful farm, she thought, following him around: clean, well-managed, productive. He was full of quiet enthusiasm for it, full of plans for the future, what he would do, where he would improve. But what delighted Cara was that when they came to where her sheep were grazing, she recognized them – not by their marks, but by their individual appearances.

'Tom and Edward used to know all their sheep just by looking at them,' she said. 'I *never* thought I'd reach that stage.'

'Well, now you have. You're a real shepherd. And now, if you're quite satisfied with the appearance of your flock, we'll go back into the house. We'll have time for a drink before lunch.'

They sat in deep leather armchairs, sipping fine sherry from delicate glasses. Tantalizing smells of cooking drifted in from the kitchen.

'This is a beautiful room,' Cara said. 'In fact, it's a beautiful house.'

'It needs a woman,' Ralph said. 'Oh, my housekeeper is very good, but that's not what I mean. Maybe it's beautiful, but it's not alive.'

'Do you miss your wife very much?' Cara asked gently.

'I do miss her. But it's five years now. You come to terms with it as time goes on. It's not that you forget, but you learn to live again.'

'I suppose so,' Cara said bleakly.

'What about you? How's it going?'

'As you said, one comes to terms, or tries to. I suppose I might in time.'

'Not might,' Ralph said. 'Will. I know you will.'

He offered her another glass of sherry, which she refused, and poured one for himself.

'There's something I have to say to you. I've wanted . . .'

He was interrupted by his housekeeper coming into the room.

'I'm just about to serve,' she said briskly. 'Don't keep it waiting!'

Whatever it was he had wanted to say, there was no chance of it while Mrs Robson trotted in and out of the kitchen, bearing dishes of delicious food, hovering with concern.

'It was all quite wonderful,' Cara told her as they finished the final course.

'Thank you. I like to cook when company comes,' Mrs Robson said. 'I tell Mr Benson he doesn't have visitors half often enough.'

'We'll have coffee in the sitting room,' Ralph said. 'I know Mrs Robson wants to clear away. She goes home at three.'

'I warned you I had something to say,' Ralph began when they were alone again. 'I'm not much good at flowery speeches, so I'll come right out with it! Cara, will you marry me?'

'Oh Ralph! I don't . . .'

He held up a hand to stop her.

'Hear me out, Cara. I'm not asking you to marry me this minute. I know you'll need time. But once before I didn't speak when I had a mind to, and I lost you to Marsden.'

'You still want to marry me, in spite of the fact that I was with him three years, what they call in the dale living in sin?'

'Don't be so damned daft!' he said sharply. '*He* sinned, you never did, and nobody in their right mind will think any different. My biggest regret is three wasted years.'

Were they wasted for me? Cara asked herself. She still didn't know.

'If I were to give you a quick answer, if you want one now,' Cara said, 'then it would have to be no. You're a dear friend and I think highly of you. You'd be a wonderful husband. But I'm not yet ready to decide anything like that.'

'I wouldn't rush you,' he promised.

'And it's not just you and me,' Cara said. 'There's Beckwith. I have to think about Beckwith.'

'I know,' Ralph said. 'I just wanted you to know how I felt. I didn't want to lose you a second time for want of asking. I love you, Cara. I've only ever said that to one other woman.'

'I *will* think about it,' Cara said. 'Give me a little time. But don't build up your hopes because I can't make any promises.'

'Very well then,' Ralph agreed. 'And now, though God knows I don't want you to go, I'm going to send you packing. It'll be pitch black in an hour or so. I know you're used to country roads in the dark, but you don't know this one as well as your own dale.'

It was not quite dark when Cara drove back through Arendale. There was light enough to see the majestic contours of the fells, almost black against the evening sky. Ralph had said 'your own dale', and he had been right, she thought. Every fell, every rise and fall, every twist and turn of the road, all were familiar to her. When Beckwith Farm came in sight, with the lights shining from the windows, she thought, I'm home!

A week after Cara's visit to Ralph Benson, the first snow of the winter was seen in Arendale, not deep, but covering the fells and the tops of the walls. Those sheep, the rams and the ewes not in lamb which had not gone for overwintering, were the only animals now left outside, and they had been brought close in, near to the house, so that it was easier to give them their winter rations when the ground was too hard and frosty for grazing.

The fells and the high rocky crags were left to themselves, as if in a long sleep under their blanket of snow. It would be many weeks before anyone climbed up there to disturb them. On the very highest slopes the snow would most likely remain, added to throughout the winter, until the spring sun came to melt it.

'Since there's not a lot to do at the moment,' Mrs Hendry said to Cara, 'why don't you and me redecorate the best bedroom? Something nice and cheerful; new paint, some new curtains and bedcovers. Can we run to it?'

'I think so,' Cara said.

'Well, it would be sensible,' Mrs Hendry said. 'We shall need all the rooms when your ma and pa, and Laura, come for Christmas.'

Privately, she thought it high time Cara faced sleeping again in her own room. It would be a positive sign of facing forward. In so many

370

ways now she seemed better, a little each day, which over the weeks added up to a lot. These days the expression on her face, caught unawares, was not so sad.

Mrs Hendry had expected that when Cara came back from her visit to Nidderdale she would be unsettled. Nothing at all had been said about what had happened there, but she was sure she knew – and she certainly feared – what was in Ralph Benson's mind. To her surprise, since then Cara had seemed not less, but more settled. Less restless.

'We'll leave Emily with Johann, and we'll both go into Shepton and choose some wall paint and curtain material,' Cara decided. 'We'll go on Friday when we collect David.'

She knew herself that she must make the effort. She couldn't go walking past the bedroom door, without entering, for the rest of her life.

'If there's any choice,' she said, 'I'd like something quite bold and bright, something lively.'

On Friday the snow still lay on the fields but the roads had been cleared, and in Shepton there was no snow at all.

'I wonder if we'll have a white Christmas,' Mrs Hendry mused.

'I rather hope not,' Cara said, 'as we're off to Bristol so soon afterwards.'

'I don't suppose they get snow there,' Mrs Hendry said. As far as she was concerned it could have been the South Seas.

'Are you sure you don't want to come, Mother Hendry?' Cara asked the question for the twentieth time. 'You know my mother would have Emily.'

'I think not, love. It's too far for me.' But it was nice to be asked.

Cara had written to Susan, sending her the money to book three good seats in the stalls, and asking her to find them accommodation, preferably where she herself was lodging, but failing that, in a guest house. 'Nothing fancy,' she wrote. 'Even though Dad's paying.'

They were lucky in Shepton. In the market they found material which was a riot of flowers on a cream ground, and in a small shop in one of the alleys, a deep cream paint for the walls.

'Are you sure it won't be *too* bright?' Mrs Hendry asked doubtfully.

'Quite sure,' Cara said.

'Have you heard from Susan?' David asked the moment they collected him from school.

'No,' Cara said. 'I expect she's very busy.'

'So where will we stay?' he asked anxiously.

'Don't worry, Susan will find somewhere,' Cara assured him. 'Your sister can be quite competent.'

The next ten days passed in a flurry of decorating and sewing.

371

Johann cheerfully undertook the work of the farm, while Cara painted the bedroom and Mrs Hendry sat at the old treadle sewing machine, furiously stitching curtains and covers. When they had moved all the bedroom furniture to different places, when the curtains were finally hung and the covers fitted, the two women stood back and gazed with pride at their handiwork.

'You were quite right in your choice, love,' Mrs Hendry acknowledged. 'It looks grand.'

Cara nodded.

'And so different. Almost a new room.' From tonight onwards, this was where she would sleep.

Because of Laura's afternoon concert it was late on Christmas Eve when the party from Akersfield arrived. Arnold Dunning had been reluctant to spend Christmas other than in his own home, but Beth had persuaded him otherwise.

'It's your duty,' she'd said. 'They can't all come here, and you wouldn't expect Cara to leave anyone behind. This Christmas she really needs us.'

Cara was glad of their company. Their presence helped to make the house a little less quiet, helped to fill the gaps which she, and Mrs Hendry too, felt so keenly at this time of the year. Even Johann, after the Christmas dinner, was persuaded to take his place in the parlour and join in the games they played for the sake of the children, though he sat silently through the carols which Laura accompanied on the piano.

When, finally, Emily and a reluctant David had gone to bed, he rose to leave.

'Don't go just yet, Johann,' Cara said. 'Laura's going to play something especially for you. A bit of Mozart, then some Schubert songs. You mustn't miss it.'

His face lit with pleasure.

'I should enjoy that very much.'

When it came to the songs he, very tentatively, with hesitations, joined in, singing the words softly in German. He had a pleasant tenor voice, and as he gained in confidence, the notes rang out.

In all the years I've known him, Cara thought, going to bed much later, I've never heard Johann sing. What a pleasure it had been! Indeed the whole day had gone well. Ralph Benson had telephoned her with Christmas wishes and, after church, Grant had called to bring presents.

'I'd like to spend the whole of the day with you, you know that,' he said to Cara. 'But I can't leave Aunt and Uncle to eat Christmas dinner on their own.'

'Of course you can't,' Cara agreed. 'But come tomorrow if you can.'

'You'll not keep me away tomorrow!' he said.

Boxing Day also proved enjoyable. It was fine and dry, and in the morning David went out on Bella while everyone else went for a walk. Grant arrived for tea, the main meal of this day, and in the evening they played more games and sang more songs, until it was time for him to leave.

'Walk with me a little of the way,' he invited Cara.

'Very well,' she agreed. 'It'll be good to breathe some fresh air. It's very hot in the house.'

Outside it was cold enough. She breathed deeply, filling her lungs with the clear air, then she turned up her coat collar against its icy temperature. The moon was rising, the sky was clear and high, star-filled. There would be a frost before morning. A barn owl, ghostly white against the darkness, flew low and slowly from the farmyard and across the lane in front of them.

As they walked, Grant drew Cara's arm through his and held her close to his side. She felt comfortable and content to be with him.

After a while she said: 'I must turn back, get to bed. We have a horribly early start for Bristol in the morning.'

'Then I'll walk with you,' Grant said.

As they turned, he took her in his arms and kissed her. With his lips on hers, his arms around her, she felt the passion in him – and with a small part of her felt it in her own body too, felt herself responding. Then gently she released herself from his embrace.

Grant pulled her towards him again.

'Cara, please! You know what I want, you know what I want to ask. Please give me an answer!'

'I can't, Grant. I'm truly sorry. I don't know the answer.' The feelings in her body had been so tentative, so fragile. She couldn't trust them.

'Then answer another question, Cara – and be honest with me. Is there someone else? I have to know!'

She hesitated. For several seconds, thinking of Ralph Benson, she was silent. Then she said: 'No, Grant. There's no-one else. There's no-one else at all.'

That much at least had become crystal clear in her mind. When she returned from Bristol she must see Ralph. He had a right to know.

Next morning all, except Emily who still slept on, were up very early. Arnold and Beth Dunning were to drive the Bristol party to Leeds to catch the early train, but before that Mrs Hendry insisted on nourishing breakfasts all round.

'I'm not the least bit hungry,' Cara protested. All she wanted was three cups of scalding hot tea; what she actually craved was another hour in bed.

'Get it down you,' Mrs Hendry ordered. 'You've a long way to go. Six hours on a train!'

'I'm really excited about the train,' David said through a mouthful – he had no difficulty in eating his breakfast. 'The farthest I've ever been on a train is to Akersfield.'

'Well, you'll get your fill of trains in the next day or two,' his grandmother pointed out.

'There's a restaurant car,' David said.

'You'll not need that,' Mrs Hendry told him. 'I've put you up some good ham sandwiches, and some spice cake and Wensleydale cheese. You'll not starve! *And* two flasks of coffee.'

For David, the high point of the visit to Bristol was the journey itself, plus the fact that they stayed overnight in a guest house. Every minute on the train was golden, even the long wait at Birmingham while they changed engines, which Cara found tedious. Because of the wait he was allowed to nip out to buy a comic from a barrow on the platform, and even that had its excitement. Supposing the train left suddenly, without him?

They arrived in Bristol in the afternoon, and since it was a Thursday and there was no matinée, Susan was at the station to meet them.

'How are you, Susan love?' Cara asked. 'How's everything going?' Her stepdaughter looked incredibly grown-up for one who had had her seventeenth birthday less than a month ago.

'Quite splendid, thank you!' Susan replied.

She took them at once to their lodgings.

'Laura can share my digs,' she said. 'But there isn't room for you and David. Anyway, my landlady's sister keeps a boarding house and I've booked you in there. It's at Clifton, a bit out from the city centre, but she says it's very nice.'

It *was* nice, and Mrs Trevor, the landlady, was a pleasant woman.

'What a long way for you to travel!' she said. 'You must be half dead. But you'll enjoy the pantomime. I've seen it. Miss Delamere is very good.'

Cara looked at her blankly, then caught Susan's warning look.

'Don't forget I'm *not* Susan Hendry, I'm Suzanne Delamere,' she said when Mrs Trevor had left them.

'I'll try to remember,' Cara said.

'I have to leave you soon,' Susan said. 'And I can't see you again until after the show. I have to be there ages beforehand.'

'Did you get the tickets?' Cara enquired.

'Oh yes. Front row of the stalls, right in the middle. And what do you think, the manager said *you* could have yours free because you'd come so far to see me!'

'How very kind!' Cara said.

'And he'd like to meet you all after the show. Now that really *is* something because he's a most important man.'

'I'm sure he is,' Cara replied gravely. 'I'll be honoured.'

'What did Mrs Trevor mean by saying you were very good?' Laura asked. 'Have you actually got a part?'

'Actually, I have.' Susan spoke with unusual diffidence.

'But that's fantastic!' Laura said. 'What is it?'

Susan blushed furiously.

'I'm a rabbit.'

'A *rabbit?*' David rolled on the floor with laughing. 'A rabbit!'

'It is *not* funny,' Susan said. 'Everyone has to start somewhere. When Red Riding Hood walks through the wood, all her furry friends come out to greet her. The rabbit is one of them.'

'Well, I suppose it could have been worse,' David conceded. 'You could have been a stoat or a weasel!'

'Do you have any lines?' Laura asked.

'Actually, no,' Susan confessed. 'But I make my presence felt.'

I'm sure you do, Cara thought. I'm sure you do that.

'Well, I'm really looking forward to it,' she said.

Susan and Laura left, the latter arranging to meet the others in the foyer later.

The company gave a good performance that evening, well applauded, very much enjoyed.

'You were a very good rabbit,' Cara told Susan after the show. 'You had a definite personality and it came through. Congratulations, love!'

'Suzanne will always come through,' the manager said. 'She's got real talent, that one. We'll have her back one day as the star. She's got star quality, that's what. Star quality!'

'What will you do when the pantomime ends?' Cara asked Susan later. 'What about returning to Magda Dale and finishing the year out – if Madame Simonetta will have you?'

'Definitely not!' Susan said. 'I've outgrown Magda Dale. Don't worry, I'm sure to get another job. There are lots of theatres.'

'When will you come to Beckwith?'

'Oh, when I'm resting. That's what we call it between jobs,' she explained kindly.

So, Cara thought, preparing for bed that night, Susan seems well set, and really happy. There appeared to be no cause for worry there.

Mrs Trevor had given them a bedtime drink when they arrived back from the theatre.

'I should warn you,' she said. 'If you're wakened in the middle of the night by a loud noise, don't worry, it's only the lions!'

'Lions?'

375

'We're very close to the zoo,' Mrs Trevor explained. 'Sometimes they get a bit restless, though actually they're as mild as milk.'

'Thank you for warning us,' Cara said.

They travelled back from Bristol next morning. Susan came to the station to see them off.

'I'm normally still in bed at this time,' she said, yawning. 'We theatricals sleep late. But it was lovely of you to come, all of you.'

'I always told you I'd try to come to your first performance,' Laura reminded her.

'And I shall do the same for you, when work permits, of course!'

On Saturday morning Cara telephoned Ralph Benson.

'Will you be in Shepton on Monday?' she asked.

'If you want me to be,' he said.

'It sounded urgent on the telephone,' Ralph Benson said when he met Cara in Shepton. 'Is it?'

'Yes and no,' Cara said. 'I had something to tell you and it seemed better not to wait.'

'Ah! Then I rather think I'm not going to like what you have to say. Is that so?'

'I'm afraid so,' Cara admitted. 'I have to tell you, Ralph, I can't marry you.'

'Am I to be told why?' Ralph asked quietly, after a pause. 'I'd appreciate it.'

'It's not to do with you, Ralph. It's me. I've never met a man better than you, I might never do so. But I don't love you enough. I can't give you the love you deserve.'

'It would grow,' Ralph said. 'And in the meantime I have enough love for both of us.'

'No, Ralph,' Cara said gently. 'You see, I asked myself, did I love you enough to follow you to the ends of the earth? That's how strong love has to be.'

'I'm not asking you to do that. Only as far as Nidderdale.'

'That's just it, Ralph! I realized I couldn't even do that. I can't leave Arendale. Almost without noticing, it's seeped into my bones, it's deep inside me. When I'm away I long to be back; when I'm there I never want to leave. I can't marry you, dear Ralph.'

'And is that final?' he asked.

'It is.'

'May I ask you a question?' Ralph said. 'Is there some man who also ties you to Arendale?'

'You may ask, but I don't entirely know the answer. I still have to work that out. Oh Ralph, I'm truly sorry! Can we still be friends? There'd be such a gap in my life if I lost you as a friend.'

'You're asking a lot,' he said gruffly. 'But I dare say we can.'

In January the winter really arrived in Arendale. The whole earth, it seemed, was hidden under deep snow, which remained, and was added to, throughout the month and well into February, piling in deep drifts against the walls. The air was icy, the wind cruel, so that even to walk from the house to the shippon was to feel the skin of one's face frozen and one's eyes stinging with tears.

Aside from taking David to and from school at the weekends – and twice the weather made even that impossible, so that he had to remain in Shepton – no-one at Beckwith went anywhere. They did what had to be done for the animals, fed, watered and milked, and the rest of the time stayed indoors. Mrs Hendry assiduously placed draught excluders against every door and window ledge, and piled the fire high, not allowing it to go completely out even overnight.

'If we can deal with the draughts, then we can keep the place cosy,' she said. 'These old walls were built to keep the cold out and the warmth in.'

Then gradually the days grew a little longer, a pale sun began to melt the snow, at least on the lower fells, and the new grass began to show, of a green bright enough to dazzle the eyes. And as soon as the snow had gone – even before the last of it went – the spring flowers came.

On the last day of February Grant Fawcett – whom even the worst weather of the winter had not kept away from Beckwith, he had visited almost daily – breezed into the kitchen.

'I found aconites and snowdrops today,' he announced. 'Spring has come!'

'And Marigold's calf is due two weeks from now,' Cara said. For her, that would be the highlight of this year's spring. 'I've never delivered a calf before.'

She had only once been present at such an event, several years ago during the war. Tom Hendry had delivered the calf then, and had allowed her, a new and raw land girl, to be present.

'Would you like Uncle Joseph to come over and take a look at Marigold?' Grant asked. 'I could do so, but he's far more experienced, and I'm sure he'd be glad to.'

'If he'd come in a week or so, a few days before she's due, I'd be really grateful,' Cara said. 'I've read the books. In theory I know what to look for, what to do, but I'm sure your uncle is better than all the books.'

'What about Mr Hartley?' Grant asked. Mr Hartley was the vet.

'I shan't call him unless it's absolutely necessary,' Cara said. 'I really do want to see it through on my own. But I'd be glad of your uncle's advice.'

377

Joseph Fawcett came, together with Grant, just over a week later. He examined Marigold carefully, with an expert eye.

'She seems in fine fettle,' he said. 'She's a good one, Marigold is. Happen I should never have let you have her back!'

'I'm thankful you did,' Cara replied. He was teasing, of course. There was a twinkle in his eye. 'How will I know when she's ready?'

'That's not difficult,' Joseph said. 'You just have to know what to look for. First off, her udders will start to fill out, then they'll get hard to the touch. The teats will get stiff – that's so the new calf will find it easier to suck. Then when you reckon her udders can't get any bigger without busting, press them with your fingers. If they leave a deep impression, slow to fill, then you can reckon she's within twelve hours or so of calving. There's a lot more from that point on,' he continued. 'Do you want to hear it now, or nearer the time?'

'Now, please.'

'Right! Well, make sure the shippon's warm. That's important. Then be ready to stay with her when it gets very near. I'll tell you all the signs. Of course she'll do most of the work herself, but you might well be needed, especially towards the end. And think on, she could be in labour up to two days. I've known it happen, though it's hardly likely.'

'Oh, I'll be there!' Cara promised. 'If need be Johann will help out, but most of the time I'll be there.'

'Or I will,' Grant offered.

Joseph then launched into what would happen, what Cara should look for and how act, until she felt there was nothing to do with the calving that she couldn't undertake. Even so, though she looked forward to the event, she was apprehensive.

'I feel more nervous than I did when I was having Emily,' she confessed. 'It's silly, really. Birth's an everyday event.'

Joseph shook his head.

'It's an everyday event in the world's calendar,' he said. 'But every birth is special to them that's concerned.'

Two weeks after Joseph Fawcett's visit – an anxious two weeks for Cara who, in spite of assurances all round that everything would be all right, had spent a great deal of her time visiting the shippon – Marigold gave birth to a bull calf.

With Marigold in labour, Cara had spent most of the night in the shippon, though not alone, for Johann refused to leave.

'I think it's going well,' Cara said.

'Certainly,' Johann agreed.

As morning came, Cara said: 'Why don't you go and have some breakfast, Johann?'

He shook his head.

'I would rather stay.'

'Very well.'

She had hardly said the words before it happened.

'It's coming!' she cried. 'Oh Johann, it's coming! I can see the first foot!'

'Let me help you,' he said.

'No! I want to do it on my own. Give me the rope.'

She fixed the calving rope around the fetlock of the first foot, then when the second foot appeared she attached the rope to that.

'Now, a downward pull,' Johann said. 'Can you manage?'

'Of course I can! Anyway, Marigold's doing most of it.'

In fact, it took all Cara's strength to hang on to the rope and pull the new calf out – the front legs, the head between the legs, then the body and, last of all, the back legs, quite straight. Though Johann stood near, not for anything would she have handed over to anyone else. Marigold was hers, and so was the calf.

When it was born – a perfect birth – she loosed Marigold's chain. She had been lightly tethered so that, in labour, she couldn't wander around the shippon. Now she needed the freedom to lick her calf clean, which she began to do with gentle thoroughness.

Cara and Johann stood watching. Tears of wonder and joy pricked at Cara's eyes. It was a miracle; she had taken part in a miracle. Every emotion which had been hers in the last few weeks came together, and overwhelmed her. She turned to Johann and saw the brightness in his eyes also.

'It is a miracle,' he said, echoing her thoughts. *'Gott sei dank!'*

A little later they left the shippon and went into the house.

'A bull calf,' Cara told Mrs Hendry. 'Quite perfect, and Marigold is fine. I shall let David choose his name.'

'At a guess, he weighs about seventy pounds,' Johann said.

'And now you should both snatch a bit of sleep,' Mrs Hendry advised.

'If I may, I should like to take my rest in the shippon,' Johann said. 'I can be comfortable there, and close by if I am needed.'

When he had left the house, Cara said: 'I think I'll walk up the fellside a little way, get some fresh air.'

She climbed quickly, then halfway up the hill she turned, and stood still, looking at the world below and around her, the dale decked out for spring. On this morning it was a beautiful world, bathed in pale sunshine, the air sharp and clean. There would be primroses in the shelter of the walls. It was a world in which it was good to be alive, good to be in this special place.

She was conscious, as she had not been for a long time, of happiness, of new beginnings, of the past – though never to be forgotten – being behind her.

She would never forget Edward, her memories of him were warm. She would learn to forgive herself for her foolishness over Kit. She was, suddenly, as she stood there, her own woman; positive and confident.

Who could say what the future held? She knew now that she would not marry Grant, dear friend though he was, and she must tell him so this very day. She was not yet ready to marry again. She wanted to be with her family and to get to know the dalesfolk. She needed her own space, and here, in the dale, she would find it.

Everything she wanted was here.